Neutral War

• • • • • •

Neutral War

A Novel of Soul-Chilling Barter,
Bioterror, and High-Stakes
International Poker

■ ■ ■ ■ ■ ■

Hal Gold

THE LYONS PRESS
Guilford, Connecticut
An imprint of The Globe Pequot Press

The Lyons Press is an imprint of The Globe Pequot Press.

10 9 8 7 6 5 4 3 2 1

Printed in the United States of America

Text designed by Kirsten Livingston

Library of Congress Cataloging-in-Publication Data

Gold, Hal.
  Neutral war : a novel of soul-chilling barter, bioterror, and
high-stakes international poker / Hal Gold.
      p. cm.
  ISBN 1-59228-059-5 (alk. paper)
  1. World War, 1939-1945—Prisoners and prisons, Japanese—Fiction. 2.
World War, 1939-1945—Japan—Fiction. 3. World War,
1939-1945—China—Fiction. 4. Biological warfare—Fiction. 5.
Prisoners of war—Fiction. I. Title.
  PS3607.O435N48 2003
  813'.54—dc22
                            2003017759

Introduction
by Robin Moore

My friend Hal Gold, a resident of Japan for the past thirty years, has brilliantly pieced together the enigma of the U.S. entry into World War II, from pre–Pearl Harbor days. To give the reader the experience of the war from the other side, Gold crafts his story in the form of the memoir of a neutral Swedish diplomat living in Japan for a decade, before and through the war. The Swedish protagonist is a friend and poker mate of the mastermind of the Pearl Harbor attack, Admiral Yamamoto. The two become friends at Harvard's special classes for foreigners in 1919—which Yamamoto in fact attended—and continue the friendship and correspondence until Yamamoto's death.

Thinking, like many serious writers, that the world is not yet ready for certain still-sensitive history in a nonfiction format, Hal balances thoroughly researched and documented facts with reasonably deduced fiction to fill in the gaps. Writers and researchers concerned with World War II, for example, know that Yamamoto was a skilled and feverish gambler. He firmly believed in the strategic lessons of Japanese board games and cards and incorporated these methods of critical thinking and planning into his military career. In *Neutral War,* Yamamoto does not die quite the way orthodox accounts tell it; rather he is influenced by omen numbers, which rise through the years and send messages to which the gambler and mariner in Yamamoto are susceptible. As his poker mate, the Swede takes us with him as he reads through official announcements and finds answers in so many unanswered questions.

At this point, I don't think anyone can state for certain how closely this story parallels history. I for one would surely like to know, but in making his case for the omen influence on Yamamoto's life and death, Gold supports his alternate history with numerical ill-omens that he uncannily discovered hidden in nomenclature and dates and pulled from little noticed and perhaps unimportant historical facts, many from untranslated Japanese sources—unimportant until we see them as Yamamoto would have seen them. As a military writer, I found this part of *Neutral War* mesmerizing . . . but the book has a far broader appeal. Gold's Japan-eye view of history creates the background for this account. He analyzed day-by-day calendars covering the war years, and wove these into the life of his protagonist.

This character is largely based on an actual Swedish consul who was asked by antimilitary Japanese to aid them as they attempted to negotiate an end to the conflict. Little is known about this real-life Swede, other than that he was a fifty-year-old bachelor, and I think it was this potential of filling in the spaces with the probable that attracted Gold to write the story. The Swede's lover in the story is a Japanese swimming enthusiast and schoolteacher who despises the military takeover of education and the required teaching of emperor worship. Their affair gives her momentary escape from Japan, and she is the reader's very human window into Japan's militarization of the national mind under the Japanese army's emperor cult.

As I am ever a fan of a good book title, I feel it important to give credit to Hal Gold for his choice. *Neutral War* is derived first from the protagonist's view that neutrality is but one way to wage war. It stems from Sweden's bartering her iron to Germany for the luxury of staying "neutral" at any cost. The protagonist also shows how neutral war will develop when he becomes an early discoverer of Japan's biological warfare program and the tenets of its founder. As the author of a nonfiction book on Japan's Unit 731, Hal drew from his extensive research into this ghastly aspect of medical science. In light of today's concerns, *Neutral War* could not have been more timely. It's a book I wish I'd written myself.

Hal has done a superb job of bringing the enigma of wartime Japan to the reader. Interweaving fact and fiction this way requires someone well versed in Japanese history, culture, and thinking. Not many people could have put together this kaleidoscope of fact and imaginative fiction. It is an entirely new World War II reading pleasure. I congratulate Hal Gold for giving us this vicarious experience of joining the protagonist as Japan and the world enter World War II, then head for the neutral wars to come.

Neutral War

• • • • • •

▪ 1 ▪
Pearl Harbor Attack Begins in Harvard

"Today I will speak about poker and military tactics."

Lieutenant Commander Yamamoto Isoroku carried no notes. The information was stored in him the way a gambler remembers his opponents' moves.

"Poker is structured on principle of international equality, because each suit hold same rank."

He was also gambling on grammatical errors lying like submerged rocks in the course of his message. The American instructor noted them.

"Poker is also based on equality of races, because colors have equal value."

It was 1919, shortly after the Versailles Peace Conference, where Britain, the United States, and Australia rejected Japan's proposal for racial equality for her nationals on a par with white nations. More than a decade earlier the "yellow peril" of those countries shifted from China to Japan, and white newspapers cranked out warning-siren editorials. Was Yamamoto trying to be heard in those capitals? The American instructor fidgeted.

"Within each suit, we go into monarchy. It is unavoidable when we remember that cards were born in society of kings and queens. But in poker we do not chop off their heads in European tradition, but rather try to play them to advantage."

This brought a few audible chuckles, except from his subordinates. Yamamoto was Japan's naval representative and language officer at special classes for foreigners, Harvard University. Even if some of the men under him understood his dry humor, none would commit the discourtesy of a smile while his commanding officer was speaking.

"Poker is *not* game of chance. It is game of psychology with *element* of chance. There are probabilities, but we assess them individually. This mean the value of each probability different according to who is assessing. And, in addition to assessing probabilities in cards," and here he pointed in succession to the hypothetical opponents in the space before him, "we must assess reaction of other players." He remained silent for a few moments but maintained emotional torque as he shifted his stare from one set of imaginary eyes to the next. "Thus, as level of total skill in game increases, role of chance become corresponding smaller. Luck become demoted. Skill take more command."

Yamamoto was thirty-five years old then, two years my senior. He was short even by Japanese standards, and at first appearance solidly built, but with a kind of gentleness under it. He always wore a single white glove on his left hand, and until I learned the reason for it, I assumed it was an affectation from the British model of the Imperial Japanese Navy. He wore the glove during his speech.

"Poker is combination of psychology and mathematics. In this, it is very close to military tactics." Yamamoto directed this last sentence toward his American instructor, almost carving the words into him. "The player must assess what cards other side is holding. In case of tactics, what armaments. Poker player must then assess likely reaction of opponent to various stimuli. Commander must do same in battle. In poker, in military tactics, assessment of opponent reaction cannot be taught by rule. Cannot be learned by rule. It is unique problem each time, and instead of learning rules, one must learn skill of assessment." Yamamoto took another pause, then went on. "I believe poker should be required training for all military officers." Americans and Europeans smiled; not one Japanese finger twitched or face thawed.

"Gambling sometime has bad name in society. This is not fault of gambling. It is because average player does not know basic strategy of 'only a fool does not know when to quit.' So fool lose all his money and cause harm to family and to gambling reputation. In military tactics, only fool commander does not know when to quit, and continue losing more men and equipment." American and European heads nodded in a signal that they were absorbing his logic. "In conclusion, I like to say, my instructors here at Harvard need not worry that I will not know when to quit playing cards in order to study. It is opposite situation. One of my problems at this university class, in addition to English grammar and pronunciation of course, is finding poker partners of sufficient skill."

Yamamoto finished his speech, part of his classroom practice in the "English E" course for foreigners. He bowed to the students in the auditorium, then to his instructor, and walked back to his seat. He was in charge of a contingent of navy men from Japan, and it was astounding how they snapped into complete, instant focus when they sat in front of a text, as if it were a religious tome transporting their minds with the Law of Grammar. They seemed driven by duty to capture idiomatic expressions like so many prisoners to take back to their emperor, and I am sure that if nude women paraded through their classroom, naked reality would not disturb a study of the subjunctive. When Yamamoto left the speaker's platform and the others in the room began applauding, his subordinates joined in, but in a mechanical cadence with arms that seemed controlled by a single command station. I applauded knowing that I had found a gaming partner, and the next evening when we were on free time, I approached him.

"The British call it a pack," I said, holding up an unopened one, "but here in America it's a deck. Any time you're ready. . . ." And that is how I met the future Admiral Yamamoto.

Two-hand poker was neither his game nor mine, but the tempo of the card table at Harvard increased, largely led by Yamamoto with me as his second in command, as we found other players to join us. On weekends, he often invited us to his residence in Brookline, at 157 Naples Road. We both preferred five-hand poker when there were three other players available with the skill we required and the willingness to neglect their studies. With less than five, the mental challenge lacks the complexity to whet the cunning. Going into six or seven players increases the role of chance and reduces that of psychology. With five, we played with little talk. When it was just Yamamoto and me, as many of our games were, it was for a chance to chat, even though conversation with Yamamoto often implied an economical meting out of words, until he rode the tide of a subject that interested him.

Our first game of poker was also the first time I saw Yamamoto remove his single glove. The index and middle fingers of his left hand were missing from the base. He sensed my reaction more than I did. "Russo-Japanese War," he said as he laid the glove to one side. Three sockets fell flat and limp. The other two were filled with dummies, and the glove maintained a two-fingered point in a random direction during our game.

As a Swede, I was a comparative rarity at the classes. In addition to English—the Swedish naval authorities thought some American influence might be good to balance our British English leanings—I took some engineering courses. But it was geography and history that produced a sense of common understanding between the Japanese and me. The huge landmass of the Soviet Union lies over the Asian continent like a two-headed bear, its western teeth gnawing at Scandinavia, its eastern jowls salivating over Manchuria and snarling across to Japan. The Japanese victory in the Russo-Japanese War, and especially the naval victory in the Battle of the Japan Sea, was part of our military history studies in the Swedish Naval Academy, and indeed studied by military men all over the world. It was awesome and inspiring how a country not four decades out of a secluded, samurai era defeated the land and sea forces of the Czar—the world's most powerful army, the world's second most powerful navy. Scandinavia's long history of trouble with the Russians generated a special admiration among us for Japan. Finland's location had made her Russian problems the greatest, and after the Japanese victory a Finnish beer came out under the label "*Amiraali*" with a picture of Admiral Togo on the label. Every bottle was a toast to the admiral from another tiny country that showed how the Muscovites could be smashed. I wondered whether *Amiraali* might help me get on board Yamamoto's ship in that battle.

"You probably know," I commented while I shuffled the cards, "that Finland put out a beer with a picture of Admiral Togo on it."

"Mm!"

I dealt. "Did you ever try it?"

We looked at our hands.

"I don't drink."

A week later I tried again. Yamamoto was puffing up a head of steam with the American cigarettes he had become fond of. I told him about our studies at the naval academy in Sweden, how the tactics of the battle were familiar to all of us. This led us to reminiscing about the days in our respective academies, our studies and parties and card games. That lasted for two cigarettes. On the third, he rode the smoke back fifteen years.

"After I got out of the academy, my first tour of duty was under an Admiral Kamimura, 1904. Three Russian armored cruisers out of Vladivostok were raising hell with our ships. They used to go out on the prowl like pirates, looking for Japanese targets. So we went on the prowl to find them. Our squadron had four ships, all better and faster. One was built at St. Nazaire, west coast of France; the other three were made in England. I was on the *Tokiwa*. Armored cruiser made in the Elswick yard of Armstrong-Whitworth. Nine thousand seven hundred tons. Launched 1898."

He paused to get his bearings on the Russian ships, and we played out the hand in silence. With the shuffle we were back on the *Tokiwa*.

"We sighted the Russians just northeast of Tsushima. Our squadron opened fire and made early hits on the *Rurik*. Knocked out her steering gear. That was good fortune—but our commander assessed it wrong."

Yamamoto took a long puff and played a card. "Someday I'll have to teach you how to play *shogi*. It's a little like chess, but there's more freedom in handling pieces. It's a little wilder—closer to a board battle than chess. You play chess?"

"I used to, but I haven't really played much these last few years."

"Both games have ancestral roots in India. We probably got *shogi* from China in the eighth century. Maybe that's why it's closer to a battle. The Chinese were good at those things. In either game, one move can win or lose a match. But you can't narrow your tactics by aiming just for one enemy piece. You have to see the board from above. When the Russian ship lost rudder control, Kamimura got so hungry for it he ignored the other two ships. He ordered us to concentrate all our fire on the *Rurik* until she went down. Four hundred men. But the other two ships escaped back to Vladivostok. If Kamimura had looked at the battle like a *shogi* board we could have put them out of commission, too. But he wanted that one enemy piece so bad, two got away. Stupid tactics. If a piece is neutralized, you can turn your attention to taking out another one. My first assignment out of the academy and I was given a commander with no total view. Bad power of assessment."

I could hear the guns of the *Tokiwa* in Yamamoto's memory. He looked at the cigarette in his hand. "Japan makes cigarettes, too," he said. I thought the cigarette had silenced the guns; it had not. "About the time the Russo-Japanese War broke out, Japan produced a brand called Cherry. It had a small anchor design on the side of the pack; we sailors liked that. Cherry took us through the Russo-Japanese War."

He stamped out his cigarette.

"You know from playing poker," Yamamoto went on, "that the value of any probability varies with the temperament of the player."

"If I did not know it before, I learned it from your speech."

He gave an internal chuckle that did not reach his lips. "Different players will play the same hand differently. Going into battle with a given number of ships, different commanders may handle them differently. Then after damage or losses—to one's own ships or the enemy—the options for assessing enemy reactions change. Options may increase or decrease, but it's not all a matter of armaments. Temperament can be more important to the battle than firepower. Kamimura would go broke as a gambler." He tightened the corners of his mouth and threw a look of disgust fifteen years into the past.

The Japanese have their own style of shuffling cards, not from the sides of the cards, but lengthwise from the ends. Yamamoto had to add an improvised grip because of the missing fingers on his left hand. He glanced at me while he shuffled the cards and commented with an almost-smile, "It's easier to play than shuffle."

We picked up our cards.

"It wasn't even the enemy," he continued. "The next year I was serving on board the *Nisshin*. She was launched in 1903 by Ansaldo of Genoa for the Argentine navy; Japan bought her the next year, just before the war broke out. I was a gunnery officer. We were fighting again in the Japan Sea. Firing heavy for a long time. Our guns became overheated. They also were being doused with water. You know how that weakens the metal so it can't hold the internal pressures. My gun exploded. Took my fingers."

Every naval cadet had studied the daring "crossing the T" maneuver of the Japanese fleet in that battle. As the Baltic Fleet steamed northerly into the Tsushima Straits, Togo's fleet made a surprise move that put the two columns temporarily at broadsides to each other. The Japanese were outnumbered in ships, but had speedier vessels. Naval ships in those days were weak in firepower at the bow and stern, and always attempted maneuvering their beams to face the target for maximum destructive power. Togo's faster fleet moved ahead of the Russians and crossed in front of their line of travel, putting the Japanese heavy guns against the bows of the Russians.

"The beam-to-bows position was part of it," Yamamoto said as we reviewed the battle. "Adjusting numbers was another part." He looked at me with a semi-smile and a touch of humor at the corners of his eyes. "Did you ever hear of Miyamoto Musashi?"

"Only over beer with some of the other Japanese men here. A famous swordsman who developed a two-sword style of fighting and spent his life accepting challenges. And winning."

"There's a famous story, when he and the headmaster of a school of swordsmanship had to meet in a duel. The headmaster was just a kid, a hereditary position. In a real duel with Musashi, the youngster would not last long enough to scream, so the swordsmen from his family's school decided to lay a trap and gang up on Musashi. But Musashi expected that; he knew the boy would not attempt a real duel. Musashi gave the challenge and set the time and place: dawn at a certain pine tree." He gave a decidedly visible chuckle. "Everybody knows this story. Some people might argue that one man can't fight off a whole bunch of swordsmen without the help of a story writer, but actually, it's not all fantasy. It's a little bit like what we did against the Russians in the Japan Sea."

I had to wait for the next cigarette to be pulled, like a sword from its scabbard.

"So! Musashi gets to the tree during the night and climbs up. And waits. The youngster comes surrounded by his whole school of swordsmen and they wait at the tree. Musashi stays quiet up there and keeps them waiting a bit to shake them up. Did you ever see pictures of Japanese rice paddies?"

"Yes, very picturesque."

"What makes them picturesque? It's the way they're surrounded by earth ridges that hold the water in. Now, the tree that Musashi chose for the duel stood at the edge of rice paddies. And it's the season when paddies are filled with water. So, when the men at the base of the tree are in the right position, Musashi jumps down, cuts down his opponent—that's simple enough—and takes off along a ridge. The men chase him, but a ridge is only wide enough for one person. Musashi turns and fights them off one at a time, runs ahead, turns to fight off another one. Some of the men at the back jump into the paddies and try to overtake him, but it's knee-deep water and soft ground underneath. So numbers lose face value. If the Russians knew the Musashi story maybe we wouldn't have had such an easy time of it."

"Since you put it that way, I see what you mean."

"Actually, it's an old British naval maneuver. But Togo's tactician added a few changes of his own. When our fleet crossed the T, our beam guns were looking into the bows of the leading Russian ships. We took them out, and as they went down the next ships became the head of the Russian column. We were fighting only a few Russian ships at any time. The rest of them were splashing around back there in the rice paddies."

After studying the Russo-Japanese War in books and on charts, I was on the opposite side of the card table from someone who was part of it. But Yamamoto was doing more than looking back at history. He was looking ahead—and upward. As we were settling in at Harvard, newspapers were reporting on an American brigadier general by the name of Billy Mitchell who was trying to convince his superiors that the future of naval warfare is in the air. The topic joined our poker games.

"Of course it is," Yamamoto remarked through the smoke. "The First World War should have demonstrated that. But the human mind is chained to its education."

"I think the mental limits are only half the problem," I offered.

"And the other half?" Yamamoto asked.

"Business, in a manner of speaking. Every bureaucracy spends a great share of its energies fighting for its own importance. And people in those bureaucracies are microcosms of their host body. In 1914, a British admiral said that a submarine blockade of England was like some fantastic story. You remember what happened right after that."

"The Germans put a submarine blockade on England."

"Then a British cavalry officer saw a demonstration of military tanks and said they would never replace cavalry. We know what happened to that prediction. It's not all lack of appreciation for mechanics. Military officers have invested years in their specialties, and it becomes their product, in a sense. Their own importance depends on the importance of their specialty, and if something threatens to lower that value they resent and oppose it—self-protective offensive."

"And now American naval officers educated in big ships and big guns are laughing at some brigadier general who says planes can sink battleships. I wish we had him in the Japanese navy."

The last remark was punctuated with the slam of a card, a paper-sized thunder snap followed by an extra thick cloud of smoke.

"I want to see a strong naval air wing," Yamamoto continued, "but I know I will have the same trouble convincing Japanese authorities as this Mitchell fellow is having here in America. He's too far ahead of his superiors."

While the instructors at Harvard were teaching us English, Billy Mitchell, inadvertently, was teaching Yamamoto the doctrine that aircraft can be mightier than battleships.

My father was an officer in the Swedish navy and a dedicated scholar of naval history and anything to do with ocean trade. He passed the interest on to me. I once read a Dutch captain's journal from 1530. As the captain rounded the Malay Peninsula eastward, he and the crew expected to encounter Chinese ships and possibly pirates. But he penned his amazement at finding the seas dominated more by Japanese ships than any others.

Japan's warrior classes wore body armor made of small pieces of lacquered metal tied together with strips of deerskin. In seventeenth-century Siam, Japanese merchants bought up so much deerskin to ship home for armor manufacture, they cornered the market and set off trade wars. And in Manila, the Japanese trading colony became a formidable community, while Japanese ships pushed her trade routes as far as Goa on the west coast of India. A Portuguese captain once wrote that he found it impossible to understand how a heathen race, with no help from the God of the Christians, could possibly attain sufficient energy to buy and sell over so much of the Lord's earth. Perhaps his prayers brought him the answer, but Japan's mercantile vitality was a continuing source of unanswered questions for me.

When I found myself in the midst of those Japanese at Harvard, I decided to use the chance to start learning the language. The normally reticent nature of the people made it difficult to approach any of them with a request to teach me Japanese. The one person I did have communication success with, a young ensign by the name of Mizuno, responded with a surge of back-pressure at the idea that someone would actually want to learn the Japanese language. The ambition to do so was inconceivable. I tried to justify his view by convincing myself that any non-Swede not living in the country and trying to learn our language might also be looked at in a similar light. I approached from the sea, reminding him of the victory at Tsushima, and from there I steered a course into an interest in learning more about Japan. My desire to learn the writing was a doubly confounding mystery to him.

"It is a very difficult system," he tried to dissuade me.

"I believe it is," I responded. "I should have started earlier. I'll just have to work faster to catch up."

We made several passes around the point and Mizuno finally agreed to take the challenge, with the understanding that he would not accept pay. His justification: "I am not a teacher." I countered by offering to make a social event out of our classes, and I would pay for the drinks. My future instructor, unlike Yamamoto, was moderately fond of drink, but he would never mix alcohol with instruction. Once he accepted the task, it became his mission.

We sat down to our first attempt at class. I felt the heat of his determination, but he could not find a starting point. Even though the Japanese were there to learn how to speak English, when most of them attempted putting a thought into words, they first fought a defensive battle and built mental ramparts of grammar rules that would ward off a mistake. They became like the centipede who was asked which leg he moves first to start walking and stood frozen to the spot. My Japanese teacher was paralyzed by not knowing where to start. I took over as navigator, and used my experience in learning European languages to set a simple program.

I started by asking him to say certain common verbs. I listed these, then I made simple sentences in English with them and asked him to put each sentence into Japanese. Then I asked him to say the concept in the negative. Next, I asked him for some tense-establishing vocabulary such as *yesterday, tomorrow, next winter, before high tide,* and made a list of these. Then I went back to the sample sentences and asked him to add the time-concept words and adjust the sentences accordingly.

After several classes, I asked him to turn the statements into questions. My destination was a question-and-answer exchange, and I tried returning the same questions for him to answer. At first he did not understand that I expected a real answer. One of the first verbs we used was, naturally, *study,* and I made the sentence, "I study four hours every night." With a time-concept word it became, "I studied four hours last night." Then the question, "Do you study four hours every night?" I learned it, took a pause, looked at my teacher, and tried to give the question back to him. "Do you study four hours every night?"

"Good!"

I tried again. "Do you study four hours every night?"

Again, "*Good!*"

Teacher-student exchange, I was finding out as part of my linguistic training, is not expected in Japanese education.

Then I tried injecting some humor into our meetings. My first attempt was, "The earth is flat." At first he merely smiled and corrected flat with "round." His education did not let him treat falsehoods lightly. I had to get him to accept fantasy as a part of serious study to develop lines of argument. Once he did, I asked him to convince me that the world is round. His argument—"because if we go in a straight line we come back to our starting point"—became new vocabulary for me and loosened up the exchange between us with a bit of humor. Our classes also became the talk of the other Japanese men at Harvard, and many of them exchanged friendly words in Japanese when we met. One evening over beer, one of them suggested that I learn their names in ideographs. I thought it a capital idea—I ordered a round of drinks as a salute—and they taught me the characters for their names and the correct stroke order to write them: "Nakamura, Suzuki, Mizuno . . . And the name of our commanding officer, Lieutenant Commander Yamamoto."

"And how do you write his given name?" I asked.

They all smiled. "It is very unusual. Perhaps he is the only person to have such a name."

"The only person?"

"I am sure," was repeated several times, until one of the men started writing it for me. "His name is written with three characters. First, the number five, then ten—this means fifty—then the number six, like this. Five-Ten-Six, meaning fifty-six, is our commander's given name."

"His name is 'Fifty-Six'?" I checked.

"Yes. Very unusual name."

"And how did he come to be named that?"

"Because when he was born, his father was fifty-six years old."

"In the Japanese system," one of the men added, "it is different from the West. In Japan, children are counted one year old their first year. So our ages are one year more than by the Western system."

"Yes," joked one, "we all became one year younger when we came to America."

This carried us into a conversation of the different ages of the men—Japanese are very conscious of ages—and birthdays.

"And when is your commanding officer's birthday?" I asked. I thought we might prepare some kind of celebration and wondered at the same time how to do it without beer or champagne. It seemed to throw a cool shower on the party. Then Mizuno, taking up his role as my teacher, filled in the embarrassing quiet. "Lieutenant Commander Yamamoto was born in April."

"On what date?" I asked.

Mizuno continued in a reluctant tone. "On April fourth. In Japan, number four is considered unlucky, so we do not like to think of it."

"And why is it an unlucky number?"

Mizuno answered again. The others stopped drinking while he did. "Because it is pronounced the same as the word for death."

I tried to bring the beer suds back to life. "Well, with us, four is just another number. . . ." I drank up to encourage the others to do the same.

A few days later when Yamamoto and I were at cards again, I told him of my progress in Japanese, and that I was learning to write the names of the men at the classes. "And, I can even write your name."

"And pronounce it. Most Japanese would not know how to on first seeing it because it is an unusual reading."

"I was told that. So I'm one step ahead of the Japanese."

"There's something else about my name. When my father gave it to me, he didn't realize it was a sign of things to come," he smiled—slightly, of course. "If you add the numbers—read them like dice—it's eleven. That was my number in the graduating class at the Naval Academy."

"So eleven is your lucky number," I said.

"I hope so," he answered, and played his hand.

Yamamoto's comment in his classroom speech, "colors have equal value," still interested me, and when I thought that we were friendly enough to touch on it, I did.

"That *was* in reference to Versailles, I take it."

"Something we've been trying to do since we dropped feudalism fifty years ago—gain equality with the white races. We thought our victory over Russia would do that, but Versailles set us back again."

A few cards later, he picked up Versailles again. "You know how the proposal was defeated, I take it?"

"Yes. President Wilson was chairman of the conference and suddenly changed the rules from majority vote to unanimity."

"There are complications I still haven't learned," Yamamoto continued, "but Japan's proposal got tied in with immigration problems. The British dominions were pushing Britain to turn it down—'White Australia' was leading that fight. Wilson needed Britain to create his League of Nations, so he didn't push Britain from the other side. And we know Wilson was being pushed to reject the proposal by political forces in America. Actually a strong majority at the conference backed Japan—eleven out of seventeen votes."

"At least your lucky number rose in the votes in your favor."

"Fleeting luck—another form of bad luck. Wilson pulled the unanimous-decision requirement out of his sleeve and put the onus on Britain to choose between her dominions and Japan. The Anglo-Japanese Alliance was in effect then, but that didn't mean as much to Britain as keeping her family together. Wilson got the proposal rejected without playing a hand himself."

Yamamoto went silent for a few moments, then added, "The peace talks are causing a lot of trouble in Japan now."

Toward the end of our study tour at Harvard, I picked up a copy of the *Boston Herald* and saw an article headlined, MITCHELL REQUESTS USE OF CAPTURED GERMAN BATTLESHIP TO DEMONSTRATE AERIAL BOMBING TEST. I showed it to Yamamoto. He studied it and grunted. A few lines down, it quoted the American secretary of the navy calling Mitchell crazy. Secretary of War Newton D. Baker was more dramatic and told reporters, "I'd be willing to stand on the deck of the ship while that nitwit Mitchell tries to hit us from the air." Yamamoto and I were stumped by the word *nitwit,* and he had just discovered that his English-Japanese dictionary offered no hint when a Harvard instructor came along and helped us out. I was grateful to the secretary of war for expanding my vocabulary. Yamamoto returned the paper to me with a silent nod of thanks.

"What do you think about this?" I asked him.

"The 'nitwit,'" he said, exercising his newly acquired vocabulary, "is the secretary of war. I hope he does stand on the deck. Then I'll go to a Shinto shrine and ask the *kami* for the success of Mitchell's pilots. He's thinking of the future of aircraft; if he can prove what they can do it might help me change some thinking in Japan about air power."

A short time later, as we all made preparations for sailing back to our respective countries, I thanked Mizuno for his time and efforts, and he thanked me for teaching him to be a teacher.

I was en route home when Mitchell's pilots sank the ship on which the secretary of war had offered to stand, the captured and "unsinkable" German battleship *Ostfreisland.* It was over almost in seconds. Yamamoto disembarked in Japan about the time the ship went down.

Yamamoto went to the Harvard classes to learn English, but I saw Billy Mitchell exert a greater influence on him than his English instructors. I did not realize how Phase One of an attack plan against the United States started back then at Harvard when I was sitting opposite "56" and his three-fingered grip on the cards. Even farther from my awareness was that at the same time Yamamoto was looking skyward, a newly commissioned army medical officer in Japan was peering down through his microscope at his own plans for military weapons. . . .

· 2 ·
Yamamoto's Letters

After leaving the United States and Harvard, I kept up my study of Japanese language and history, and Yamamoto and I stayed in touch with an occasional letter. I was sure that his mind would appreciate one of my own favorite English authors, Arthur Conan Doyle, and his perceptive sleuth. Sherlock Holmes's adventures started in the British press in 1892, when I was six years old. His popularity extended beyond the British Empire, and when I was learning English in public school in Sweden, my teacher had us solving crimes together with the problems of vocabulary and grammar. I kept a collection of the stories at home and occasionally I sent one to Yamamoto. And, according to Japanese custom, Yamamoto always sent me a card at the new year, with some news of the old year. His card for 1924 told me:

> I enjoyed the adventure stories of Sherlock Holmes you have been sending me, and I dare say that at times I ended up with a different criminal than he did. But I think I have the author's thinking pattern worked out now, and I am sure it will not happen again.
>
> Last year I toured the United States and Europe. My impressions of American industry are beyond any vocabulary I learned at Harvard. Japan, by comparison, produces from backyard workshops. As you know, we have to import almost every cupful of oil. The Texas oil fields make one realize how ill distributed are the resources of the earth.

And in 1925:

I think my gunnery career is over, at least for big guns. I have been second in command of a naval aviation corps, and the only guns I am interested in now are those that can be mounted on wings. I am doing what I can to add more air power to the navy, and encourage Japan to train more pilots, and engineers to design planes suited to our needs. You know how we Japanese love baths. I would like to find one that will wash away the Japanese custom of always running to borrow ideas from other countries. One idea I hope does not affect our leaders is Billy Mitchell's book that came out last year. I imagine that by now you have read his *Winged Defense*. In spite of his pioneering work in aircraft, he wrote that he has little regard for airplane carriers in the future of armaments. Of course, he is an army man, and in spite of his vision in air power, he can still think of an air base only as something stuck on land. I will allow him that one shortcoming; he has done more than his share of getting us to look aloft. Some day he, too, will see the advantage of a seagoing, navigable airfield.

That same year of 1925, a Japan-related book stirred the world's military. A British journalist, Hector C. Bywater, published *The Great Pacific War*, a fictional account of a war between Japan and the United States that breaks out six years into the future. His battles made extraordinary use of air power, even though the orthodox military mind of his day had not yet considered the flying machine effective war equipment. Mitchell's sinking a battleship with airplanes did not swing the thinking of the authorities of the U.S. armed forces, and in one of Bywater's fictional sea battles he himself stated, "How different now were the circumstances from those which aviation enthusiasts, deceived by artificial peace tests against helpless targets, had pictured!" Yet Bywater's war saw the greatest use of air power to date, as if pointing the way for America and Japan to do it when the time came. I wondered what Yamamoto might say about the book in his new year's card for 1926.

I am headed back to America. Somebody apparently thinks I would be of use as naval attaché at the Japanese embassy in Washington. I wonder if somebody is not just trying to save me from becoming seasick. As it is, I will be sailing through *The Great Pacific War*, but there will be no shells to avoid on the way. It is not scheduled to start for a few years yet, and right now the roar of battle does not violate the boundaries of boardrooms and bar-rooms. Nonetheless, it will be interesting to discuss it with American naval officers. I only hope a few of them are as good at the gaming table as some of our Harvard classmates. Have you thought about learning *shogi?*

From accounts I heard through Swedish naval channels and newspaper stories, military authorities of the world were animated in discussions over Bywater's war and the way it started with an initial Japanese sweep of the Philippines, Hawaii, and other American-held islands in a swift series of attacks that gained strong footholds in the Pacific. After America suffers initial setbacks, her industrial base gears up for the emergency and eventually defeats Japan. Most intriguing was the way Bywater had Americans fight with stepping-stone tactics across the Pacific, taking an island, then using it as a jumping-off place for the next one in succession across the ocean.

Yamamoto's assignment to America in 1926 looked like gambler's prescience. In May the following year, Charles Lindbergh made his flight across the Atlantic, followed the next month by Richard E. Byrd. Yamamoto was once again in America when it was making aviation history; I expected to read of it in his card for the next new year.

By the time you receive this, we should be well into 1927 and I will be pushing my first year here in Washington. Another American has advanced the cause of aviation, but in spite of his deed I feel there are still experts—a nice-sounding title for people of limited vision—who see this only as a feat of daring removed from practicality, like a circus stunt over the water. I regret that Byrd had to ditch at the end of his flight, but that is a minor point. Both men showed that the present British system of aviation is outdated. This is not just Britain's problem but ours: Japan has been practicing the British method of flying by intuition. The Americans showed that instrument flight is the way for aviation to develop, but neither the British nor the Japanese are ready to learn. I look forward to the day our own pilots gain the international spotlight, and I feel it will happen only when our planes navigate by science and intuition is left to the gaming table and battles.

And in 1928:

These American officers are astounding bridge players. If you are interested in strengthening your game, this is, as Americans say, the land of opportunity. But other things disturb me. As you probably know, back in December 1926 the United States Navy issued huge contracts to dredge the coral from that quiet navy yard in Hawaii and turn it into a first-class naval station. That will give American warships a berth which will cause discomfort in the Pacific. I hope it causes no more than that. There is a lot of talk about it in Tokyo and I will return there soon and join in. Then I will be assigned to some yet unknown duty. I would like to be appointed officer in charge of bridge, poker, and *shogi* for the Imperial Japanese Navy, but I do not think the people in charge have yet created so valuable a billet.

Yamamoto's new assignment was back on the ocean, and his card for 1929 filled me in:

I returned to Tokyo last March and it was decided that I should go back to sea. Apparently, the naval authorities were afraid of the effects of a sudden overdose of saltwater and gave me command of a light cruiser, *Isuzu*, which serves mainly as a training ship. I was hoping it was in preparation for command of a real ship, and just before the year ended I was overjoyed when I was given command of the carrier *Akagi*. As of this writing I have been on board less than a month, enough time to realize that this is my kind of ship.

The *Akagi* had already made it into the news, thanks to Hector Bywater. Writing as naval correspondent to several newspapers, he reported in June of 1925, shortly after the ship was launched, "The latest Japanese carrier is more powerful in all ways than the largest British carrier, and superior in fighting efficiency even to the giant American carrier *Saratoga.*" But his new assignment was shorter than I—and I am sure, he—expected. His card for 1930 told me,

> The new year is supposed to be a time for writing of the good news of the previous year. Unfortunately, it was not all good, so just consider this a letter. I was in command of the *Akagi* last year and ordered a routine flight. The weather was good when the planes took off, but a heavy fog rolled in and we lost every plane and pilot that was aloft. It was a disaster. I do not know if that influenced the decision to take me off sea duty, but toward the end of the year I found myself back at a desk at the Naval Affairs Bureau of the Navy Ministry. Even though I seem headed for some assignment of importance, no desk can compare with the deck of a carrier, and I would like to get last year's disaster behind me and put out to sea again.

I could not help reading the last two numbers of the Western year designation like dice, and coming up with the same eleven that I had said was Yamamoto's lucky number. In 1929, it proved otherwise.

Then came his card for 1931:

> Last year, the Imperial Japanese Navy saw fit to promote me to rear admiral. If they wish to raise the face value of this card, so be it. Also during the year, Fate chose a strange way to deal me an advantageous hand by sending me to participate in the London Naval Disarmament Conference. It is a strange time for us to be talking disarmament, or perhaps an appropriate one. This is the year we are supposed to enter The Great Pacific War between Japan and America, and one way to keep the fiction from becoming reality is to reduce the volatility of the seas.

I am sure you know that this disarmament talk dates back to 1921, after you and I put away the cards at Harvard. By the terms agreed to last year, Japan must extend the limits—60 percent of Great Britain, 60 percent of America—to both capital ships and auxiliary ships. Military circles here see this as an insult to Japanese integrity, and they are ablaze in the head, or as we say in Japanese, their "bellies are standing." I say let their bellies stand, because also last year I became head of the Technical Division of the Aeronautics Department of the Imperial Japanese Navy, something that means more to me than promotion in rank. I cannot say things like this here but I am delighted that we must reduce ship construction. London forced my government to free more funds for air power. If we do build large ships, carriers are more sensible than battleships. I only hope the influential people in Japan can read the game.

Speaking of games, I did some shopping in London and stocked up on some fine British playing cards. I am keeping one pack—they are British, so they are a "pack"—for our next hand, wherever we might meet. I look forward to the day we can break the seal.

The naval limitations that Japan agreed to in 1930 caused more than "standing bellies" in Japan. The Chief of Staff of the Navy resigned, an ultra-nationalist shot the prime minister, and demonstrations broke out against white arrogance. But my eyes kept returning to one line in Yamamoto's letter that seemed to flash like a channel buoy trying to lead me to something hidden in the dark: *Fate chose a strange way to deal me an advantageous hand. . . .*

Japan went to the 1921 Washington Conference to demand a fleet, made up of 70 percent of each of the fleets of the U.S. and Great Britain. Japanese delegates left Tokyo with this in mind. Then Tokyo decided that as a last bargaining point, Japan would let herself be pushed down to 60 percent. Coded messages went from Tokyo to the Japanese delegates. American cryptanalyst Herbert O. Yardley received the messages, broke the code, and gave America a peek at Japan's cards. Japan's navy was

squeezed at the gaming table of negotiations to accept her supposedly secret lowest bid. On the surface, it seemed that Yardley performed a service
for the white races, but I believe he was played by Yamamoto like a distant
piece on a global *shogi* board.

Yamamoto was promoted while in America and returned to Japan with
the rank of commander. This would not give him a position in the naval and
political hierarchy to officially influence the conference negotiations, but
he instilled his enthusiasm for naval aviation in others. Japan had some idea
of America's code-breaking craft, and I am certain that Yamamoto—with
Billy Mitchell at his side—did some spadework among his superiors and
sought out those who saw air power in the same light. He then convinced
his superiors to show Japan's hand by sending messages in a code that they
knew would probably be broken, forcing a course change of a greater portion of naval finances from ships to aircraft.

By 1930 Rear Admiral Yamamoto was a central figure at London, and
I could now see the "advantageous hand" he wrote about. Yamamoto knew
that the equality in the poker deck that entertained his Harvard instructors
was not at the conference table, that the racial inequalities of Versailles
were silent participants in the naval ratio negotiations. He let the others
play the white-race card, went along with the game, and accepted a continuation of the same 5-5-3 ratio expanded to cover a greater range of vessels.
White racism helped Yamamoto loosen funds for Japanese air power.

The one letter I received from Yamamoto that weighs heaviest in understanding what happened to him during the war era is the one he wrote
after 1934 ended. Subsequent world events must have made him regret
writing it:

Here I am again, where I was sent to navigate the famous "pea
soupers" of London. I hope you are in clearer skies and I hope like-
wise that the preliminary talks to the London Naval Conference
opening this year will also have greater clarity of purpose and
thought.

Last year I became attached to the Navy General Staff and the
Navy Ministry. As if those duties were not enough to shoulder, I
was appointed chief delegate to these preliminary talks that now

bring me to London again. Our party left Yokohama last September, then went to Seattle where we stocked up on cards and boarded the transcontinental train. A train is not for strolling, and this gave us time to wear out the cards before we got to New York, where we stocked up on a new supply and worked them well on the ship for Southampton.

It has been almost three months now and my work here in London is nearing its end. I will soon be back in Japan, after a journey on the inefficient Trans-Siberian Railway and another ration of poor Russian service and bad manners, well balanced with horrible food.

The conference brought me a valuable dividend: the rare chance to meet master journalist Hector Bywater again. We had met in 1930 at the London Naval Disarmament conference, and this time he called for an interview. We spent an entire evening talking in my suite at Grosvenor House. He is a most astounding naval authority, and I feel that he knows the location of every flake of rust on the naval ships of the world. Naturally his book and his war took up a good share of the evening's discussion. I am sure that he wrote the book not as fiction but as an outline of what would happen "If." As with all people ahead of their times, Bywater could not write what he did as a serious hypothesis without being called a "nitwit"—you remember our English lesson, I assume. I hope you have the chance to meet him one day.

Oh yes, I picked up a little treasure in a bookshop here: the complete short stories of Sherlock Holmes. I always wondered whether Mr. Doyle played poker, and what kind of game he would play.

Take care of your health and gamble with skilled opponents. I want you to be in battle condition when we meet again.

I believe that the major course of the Pacific War—and the first chapter in Yamamoto's death—was set that night in London.

▪ 3 ▪
The Olympic Alliance

I decided to attempt jumping ship from my naval career; I applied to take the examination for the Swedish Foreign Ministry and passed. I was assigned to several of our European offices. Then, one day in 1936, our foreign minister approached me.

"You have a reputation for being well versed in Japanese," he addressed me.

"As you know, I started studying more than fifteen years ago."

"And you have been keeping up with it, we understand."

"I found some sympathetic friends among the Japanese consular people here; I even play their board game, *shogi,* with them."

"There is a Swedish business community in Tokyo, and you would be a good person to have in the legation. We have to appoint a new minister there next year. Would you care to go?"

Naturally I accepted, and I wondered if my bachelorhood was not as great a deciding factor for the assignment as my knowledge of Japanese. The world was not preparing itself for moving about with families. Three years earlier, the League of Nations determined Japan to be an aggressor in Manchuria, and the Japanese delegation walked out of the meeting and withdrew its membership. In Europe, Sweden was joining other nations in reinforcing defenses and strengthening her armed forces as the minds of the German population congealed behind a strange, recently risen leader. The Soviets were jittery with fears of a two-front war against Germany and Japan and were trying to buy insurance by making comrades among capitalist nations. The coming Eleventh Olympiad that was energizing Berlin was one of the moves on the global board. A meeting of the International

Olympic Committee the day before the opening ceremony would decide the city to host the next Olympic Games. London, Helsinki, and Tokyo were in the race. One day, I had a visit from a Finnish acquaintance who was part of his country's amateur athletic movement.

"There are strange happenings among the IOC members," he told me.

"When you have a group of people from so many countries, strange things will happen. What is it?"

"First, as you know, England recently dropped out of the running for the 1940 games. That was suspicious."

"We know that the Japanese had been begging Britain to do that."

"Right," he answered. "So it came down to us and Tokyo, and now Hitler is trying to edge us out. Your expertise in Japanese is legendary, and we were wondering if you might have any advice on what is happening, and how we might counter Hitler's influence."

"How to counter Hitler's influence," I responded, "is the question all Europe would like answered. We know that Germany wants an ally in Asia to keep pressure on the Soviets. And of course, with Scandinavia's history of Russian problems, and Germany making the Russians sweat, it's a question of whether we're headed for a mixed blessing or mixed curse. But about your Olympic bid—do you have any idea how the International Olympic Committee delegates stand?"

"To some degree. We know that Avery Brundage is a strong supporter of whatever Hitler wants. He's president of the American Amateur Athletic Union and has a lot of influence. He and his associate, William Garland, are the prime movers in trying to give the next Olympics to Tokyo."

"Brundage was a strong supporter for selecting Berlin this time," I reminded him.

"Of course. The construction firm he owns got a nice piece of the business in building facilities there. He's a big part of our problem. He is obviously close with the Hitler government and will also bring a block of North and South American countries with him. Finland just does not know how to cope with the pressure that Germany is mounting."

Nor did I. On the afternoon of July 31, the International Olympic Committee met in Berlin, and under a verbal banner that no Asian country has ever hosted the Olympics and that Olympic ideals should be spread throughout the world, a vote of 36 to 27 awarded the 1940 Olympiad to Tokyo. The next day, in accordance with the Olympic charter, the head of state of the host country declared the Olympiad open. Of all Hitler's speeches it was one of the most low key, but the twelve-hour program that followed was more a statement of Nazi grandeur than dedication to the ideals of athletics. As ranks of German men stood and marched with military intensity, people on the other side of the ocean were celebrating the fiftieth birthday of the Statue of Liberty. Berlin and New York were thinking in different directions.

Less than four months after the IOC awarded Tokyo the 1940 Olympics, Japan and Germany concluded the Anti-Comintern Pact. On the surface, it was an agreement to combat communism, but a secret protocol identified the Soviet Union as the common enemy. Scandinavia's traditional troublemaker was in the gun sights of Germany, which was closing ranks with Japan as I prepared to leave for my Tokyo assignment.

▪ 4 ▪
A Spy in Kimono

Five-ring flags were flying over the Ginza, and Japan was electric with the thought of holding the first Olympic Games in Asia. For my part, I prepared for the years ahead by training the handshake to coexist with the bow from the waist. Incompatibility between Eastern and Western greeting forms caused muscular spasms in Japanese officials whenever they tried to force the two into diplomatic marriage. I came to Tokyo in 1937, a fifty-one-year-old bachelor with a title of weighty vocabulary: *Envoye Extraordinaire et Ministre Plenipotentiaire of His Majesty the King of Sweden to His Imperial Majesty the Emperor of Japan and his Government.* The ponderous wordage did not impede my social movement, and I continued preparations for my future life by making acquaintances among the ladies of the city. Some Japanese women were as excited about a "real-life Viking" as Westerners are at the thought of a geisha. I was quickly cured of my geisha delusions when I was invited to a so-called "teahouse" for my first geisha encounter. A government car called for me and we drove to the Akasaka district and a large building in tasteful Japanese architecture. As I took off my shoes at the entrance I wondered what further encounters were waiting for my stockinged feet.

"Do all your visiting ministers and ambassadors receive the honor of these invitations?" I asked my host.

"To tell you the truth, Mister Minister, it would be difficult. Geisha are trained in the art of conversation, and few foreign representatives have your Japanese language ability. So it would be very uncomfortable for everyone."

We dined and drank and were entertained with song, with dance that seemed dedicated more to showing various poses of the kimono rather than the person inside, and of course, the art of conversation. I discovered that the greatest charm of the geisha is in rolling the word around on the tongue with the image I had before I actually met one. When I heard that we would be attended by women who were considered the ideal of Japanese femininity, I erred by interpreting this to include sensuality. As my hosts tried to convince me that these kimonoed ladies were of "fine breeding," my impression was that they were products of *selective* breeding, the yield of a managed reproduction process to develop creatures suited to sitting on *tatami* mats. They were charming that way, legs doubled underneath, feet in white, skin-tight cotton footwear with toes overlapping and buttocks pressing their heels down toward quarter-to-three. But when these ladies stand with their toes properly pigeoned, the charm evaporates. Also, they live a very restricted life mainly within a few city blocks of space, residing under the wing of a combination house-mother and manager. Their time is spent training in song and playing the *samisen*, all while sitting on *tatami* mats. The enormous time they spend in that posture leaves them loose of buttock tone. Then when they walk, kimono constriction and training collude to produce a kind of waddle which is supposed to evoke graciousness.

For me, the geisha evoked recollection of my discovery of the charm of the albatross. They were fascinating birds in flight, captivating as they glided alongside our ship—rising, falling, veering, their wing movements just teasingly subtle enough to hypnotize us on deck when trying to detect them. Magnificent in the air, they become ungainly on land. They are clumsy and yes, they waddle. The Americans called them "gooney birds"; the Japanese term *ah dori* says the same thing. Every creature has its milieu: the albatross in flight, the kimono-clad lady sitting on *tatami* mats.

Of course, I was expected to admire the kimono. I do. They make exquisite wall hangings, but they are hideous devices for wrapping the female body. The *obi*, or sash, is a heavy brocade some thirty centimeters in width that is wound in several layers about the torso into a nonyielding tube. The female shape is forced to obey the garment's demand for nonrecognition of breasts and hips. I could not remain neutral to the cylindrification of women, but as a diplomat I fulfilled my duty by admiring Japanese garments as beautiful works of textile art, avoiding mention that as apparel I consider them Chinese foot binding applied to the most sensual parts of the female body.

Tokyo was a mixture of Japanese and Western fashions, and one day a charming young lady by the name of Noriko, in kimono, was visiting me at my residence.

"Why does the kimono require that Japanese women ignore their breasts?" I asked her.

She laughed. "But we Japanese women have small breasts."

"That's all right," I countered, "But the kimono and *obi* reduce this to zero. I think it's a shame."

"That is because the body line must be straight. Some Japanese women have a body that is right for wearing kimono. But some of us have too narrow a waist, and we must first pad it out into a straight line. Otherwise the *obi* will not fit correctly."

"And do *you* have . . . 'too narrow a waist?'"

She laughed. "I think so."

"So you must destroy your shape for the benefit of the kimono?"

Another laugh.

"And that means that your real shape is better than what one sees when you are in kimono."

"But I must fill out my waistline if I want to wear kimono."

"And how do you do that?"

She gave me a combination smile and giggle, looked away, then came back. "I can show you. . . ."

We exchanged a few words, then she reached behind her and opened the large knot in her silk *obi*. As the end fell to the floor, she rotated her body to unwind it. Brocade leaves and flowers turned deciduous, shed from her waist and spiraled down and around her ankles. She stepped out of the coil and with another coy giggle removed her outer kimono. Her body was wrapped in a long, thin undergarment. "The padding," she said with the same warm shyness, "is under this."

And it was, from the lower waist up to where it covered and squeezed her breasts flat like unwanted body barnacles.

"You see," she smiled, "we must first become all straight."

"As I said, surely you have a nicer figure without that padding."

"I have small breasts, though . . ."

"I think I'll like them."

"I can show you how the padding is . . ."

She did. Trying to appreciate the esthetics of the kimono as a garment proved more difficult than advancing my level of competency in Japanese grammar and vocabulary. Some women who could converse in English or French were happy if I spoke no Japanese at all, and I refrained from using it if my partner were sufficiently captivating and promising to inspire me to suffer in good humor her attempts to use me for language practice. Then there were those with no foreign language ability who were glad that "the Viking" could entertain them in Japanese. In any language, there were those like Noriko and her kimono, who brought delightful encounters with perils from which my nation's official neutrality offered no protection.

Japan's war in China was being condemned in foreign countries, and the decay in international relations turned to rich compost that nourished the ambitions of Japan's military. Not all Japanese citizens were partners to the dream of the nation's military goals, and the secret police and their agents were looking for dissidents. People were baited with suggestions that perhaps Japan should seek peace, and a careless hint of agreement could be dangerous. I was certain that Noriko and her kimono were on assignment to sound me out; that soon became as clear as her waistline without padding. In a moment of relaxation an hour or so after her kimono demonstration, she ran her fingertips through my chest hair and took a purring shift in conversation. "You think the war in China is bad?"

Noriko would make a terrible poker player.

"Some people," she went on, "how do you say . . . criticize Japan, for fighting in China. I don't know. What do you think?"

"I've never been to China. I like it right here." Noriko's skin had a tint of that chestnut coloring that is especially attractive to us fair-skinned Nordics. And her eyes had that Oriental quality that disturbs the male mind with excitement. But Noriko, like many of her sister agents, was not skilled in subtle tact. Most of these ladies steered themselves into their assignments like an incongruous course change in midocean. I attribute this to the basic honesty of the Japanese. The young naval officer who taught me Japanese back at Harvard had trouble discussing my comment that the earth is flat because he could not even handle falsehoods already understood as such. And on those occasions when Japanese prisoners of war were taken, they almost never lied under questioning, admitting troop placements and answering questions truthfully with whatever knowledge they had. Information was not a trade for life; after they told what they knew, they invariably requested to be shot. The Japanese have been educated to respect and obey authority, and it carries over to answering even enemy authority honestly before fulfilling the other duty of choosing death over the disgrace of capture.

The same education in humorless honesty made it difficult for women to gain the friendship of men in order to elicit information without revealing themselves when they came to the mission part of the rendezvous. Long years at the gaming table made me sensitive to the clues: a slight speech hesitancy; a sudden shift in voice tone or a change in locus of voice projection; accelerated eye-blinking; sudden tension in the forehead; an unnatural body movement, which could be a single finger twitch or a shift of body position—my favorite was the way some ladies curled their toes as they headed into their spy script. Japanese female feet are quite charming, and among all the ways Japanese ladies turned their bodies into lie detectors, I found the toe-curl especially delightful.

I owed a debt of gratitude to the Japanese secret police for the colorful encounters they arranged for me behind their drab desks. They provided me with the concomitant pleasures that accompanied amateurish attempts to probe my mind. At times, though, I resented the suspicion I had to assign those who might have been sincerely interested only in a rendezvous with the Viking. With the bureaucrat's daughter, my suspicion proved the most painful—the most painfully lasting.

▪ 5 ▪
Mariko

I met Miss Hiraoka at an informal buffet arranged by the Japanese Foreign Ministry. She was not quite what one could call stocky, but almost so. My impression was that she had been trained in ballet. Her thighs were strong and obviously well toned, and when she walked they attacked the inside of her dress as if trying to burst to freedom. She had a nicely sculpted neck rising from a well-postured back and an unusually high threshold of vibrancy for a Japanese. Her father held a moderate rank in the Foreign Ministry, and after the bowing introductions were completed, Miss Hiraoka came over and, with a less formal bow, introduced herself.

"I studied European history in college," she said, and that launched us into the Visigoths, the War of the Roses, and other quick tours of history.

"I was often puzzled," she commented, "by how a region with so many common cultural foundations could have had so many wars throughout history."

"Common culture. . . ?"

"Yes. For one thing, Europeans are almost all of the white race."

"Enough of us are so that you might consider Europe white; yes, you could say that."

"And it is almost all Christian."

"Almost."

"And yet the history of Europe is a history of war."

"The aggressive nature in Man. Which includes women, of course."

She laughed. It was a slight laugh, but real, not the uneasy smile of Japanese introductions and pattern talk. She called one of the waiters that wander about buffet parties and asked him to get me another drink. "But it is usually the women who are the sufferers," she continued. "War was invented by men. A few women simply learned to fight."

"Not the Valkyries. They were leaders, and superior to men in strength and fighting ability."

"Did you ever see one?" she asked.

"Of course. In paintings. Magnificent—flying to and from battle on their horses."

"People can do anything if it's mythology."

"But they were so strong it compensated for their mythical existence. However, there were some very real violent women in history. Pirates."

"Women pirates?"

"Ann Bonny and Mary Read of England were the most famous, in the early seventeen-hundreds. As cruel as any male of the trade."

"So not all women are the weaker sex," she laughed.

"Neither weak nor dependent. After the Great War, there was a movement for female independence, but it was already old as far as history is concerned. You yourself seem quite independent."

"That's the problem; everyone thinks that a woman my age should have been married long ago."

"There's no rush. You seem to enjoy independence."

"I enjoy it, and it's almost guaranteed." She punctuated it with another laugh. "I'm well into my thirties, and that makes me undesirable in Japan for a bride. So my independence will continue."

"Well, there haven't been any woman pirates for a while that we know of. You might always take up that tradition. Japan is surrounded by ocean."

"I don't know about women, but we did have some pirates in the old days," she reminded me.

"You did. And if you check the records you'll find that Japanese pirates and England—which is now the model for the Japanese navy—were once in a sea battle."

"When was that?"

"1604, and I'll bet on the date. It was the year after the Tokugawa shogunate was formed."

"And where was this?"

"Off Singapore. A great explorer and navigator, John Davys, was killed in the encounter. Japanese pirates were tough, to say the least."

"You seem to know a lot about pirates," she smiled.

"Because they deal with two concerns of mine, the sea and politics. And the two sometimes overlapped."

"Politics? Pirates and politics?"

"In a sense. For example, in the sixteenth century Spain and Portugal were the strongest trading powers in Europe. England, Holland, and France tried to get more of the trade for themselves and either sponsored pirates outright or unofficially encouraged them to rob Spanish and Portuguese merchant ships."

"So they were not really at war, but they were fighting."

"They were neutral on the surface, but warring for mercantile profits."

"So governments were also doing bad things," she joked.

"Governments are run by people—and you know how bad we can be. As piracy became lucrative, more sailors and navigators joined in and went robbing and killing just for their own . . . business and pleasure, you might say. But *you* seem to be getting pleasure out of these pirate tales."

"I'm a schoolteacher," she answered more seriously, "and I always look for things to make my classes interesting for the children."

"Here's my card. If you would care to discuss piracy in further detail, let me know."

A "discreet" number of days later a telephone call came to my legation: Miss Hiraoka Mariko was looking for another vicarious encounter on the high seas of yesteryear. When she arrived, a member of my staff, Mrs. Saito, showed her to my office. Mrs. Saito's husband was killed in China in the early years of fighting, and she had been employed at the legation since well before my arrival. Outwardly, she bore her loss with stoicism and resignation, the "swallowing of tears" that Japanese consider noble. Yet once, on the anniversary of her husband's death, she commented that while he was supposed to have died for the emperor, an honorable death, she would rather have her husband still with the family. The sanctuary of my legation brought out a bitterness that was forbidden in Japanese society. "The emperor cannot help me raise my two sons," she told me, "and someday I'm afraid the army may call for them, too."

Mrs. Saito asked Mariko if she would prefer tea or coffee. It was tea, which she brought with coffee for me, then left with a bow.

"Your pirate stories were very interesting," Mariko began. "I want to use them to add excitement to my classes."

"You might also tell the children that some pirates were well educated. It may encourage them to study."

"Really? Educated pirates?"

"The first one that comes to mind was an Englishman, Henry Mainwaring. Graduated Oxford, then gathered a following and built a small fleet. He robbed the Spanish ships at sea and brought in so much money he became a hero to the English, but also a political problem."

"Why was that?"

"England wanted peace with Spain. So Mainwaring was knighted and given a high position in the British navy to keep his pirate fleet off the seas. Politics can take strange turns."

She had beautiful teeth, something not very common with Japanese. And, unlike many Japanese women, she did not cover her laughs with the hand. "And you went from the navy to the foreign service. Did Sweden want to keep you off the seas also?" she joked.

"That," I smiled back, "was my own middle-of-the-road change. My ability in Japanese brought me this assignment in Tokyo, but my father was an officer in the Swedish navy, and I started out following the same career. Quite early in life, as a matter of fact."

"Early?"

"In a sense. I was reading constellations before I was old enough to read words. And I was taking star sights before I started school."

"You were going to sea so young?"

"Oh, no. From the beach near our house. I needed help in holding up the sextant in those days."

"I've seen pictures of sextants, but what do they do?"

I liked her straightforward questioning. She was not bashful about asking; I found it hard to control my inner curiosity as to how unbashful she might be in other respects. "They measure the elevation of a star or planet from the horizon. Then you look into tables and you can calculate a line of position."

"Line of position?"

"Yes. If your observation is accurate, you're somewhere on that line. Then you can cross that line with another—another star sight, or a radio direction signal if you can get one—and where they intersect is where your sightings say you are. There is always room for error, so we usually try for at least three lines."

"And from there, you became interested in pirates?"

"And, ladies who enjoy hearing pirate tales." That brought on a wholesome laugh. "Tell me about yourself," I said.

"I was interested in water also, but not oceans."

"Lakes? Rivers?"

"Smaller. Much smaller," she smiled. "Swimming pools. I became interested in swimming when I was a child. Every summer the Sumida River is roped off for swimming. One instructor said that I had promise, so my father sent me to a private pool for training in competition."

"And you competed?"

"My hope was to make Japan's Olympic team. I was taking part in national meets but I developed bronchial trouble, and that set me back too far. So . . . goodbye, Olympics." She added another smile with a humorous fingertip wave.

"And your bronchial trouble?"

"It's all right now, but it slowed me down too much for top competition. I still swim at my old university when the pools are filled and help out with training the students on the team. I learned a lot about coaching from my teacher, so I can use it now. And of course I take charge of the children's swimming classes at school and in the Sumida River during summer vacation. Maybe some of them will be Olympic swimmers one day. Do you swim?"

"Yes, of course. But I never thought of competition. In my younger days I liked boxing and fencing . . . and poker."

"Oh? You're a gambler?"

"A social gambler. That also came from my father. When it wasn't navigation and ships, he taught me how to gamble. You don't play poker by any chance?"

"No . . . not yet, anyway." I tried to read an optimistic meaning into her response.

"You might want to learn some day. Gambling, if handled right, can help you in other aspects of life."

"And was that also part of your father's lessons?"

"Very definitely. He always told me that there will be any number of options in life from which you will have to choose. And the choices are usually made in a maze: you can see only so far ahead."

"So that means that life is a maze?"

"Maybe not life itself, but to a large degree it is lived in one. Nobody has a bird's-eye view of things. That's why history is a record of options made with the intention of heading somewhere and ending up somewhere else."

"That is what happened to me, I guess. I was trying to find the road to the Olympic team but made a wrong turn."

"Of course, not all the choices are ours. But once we get shunted into a certain direction, there are still options that are open to us."

"Yes, I could have given up swimming altogether. But I preferred to keep at it and teach children. Perhaps more options will come my way. I hope I make the right choices."

"It is all a matter of playing for the average. In gambling, it is the average that counts. That is why gaming casinos always win."

"And the gamblers always lose?"

"Enough of them lose to maintain the casino's winning average."

"But I've heard that sometimes people hit a winning streak."

"Oh, yes. It happens. And the houses like to see it happen."

"But doesn't that mean the casino loses money?"

"Only for a moment. The house knows that a winning streak turns people reckless—on the average. It may be at a later date, but a winning streak—again, on the average—will eventually produce a deterioration in judgment. And, add to the house's winnings."

"And this gambling knowledge can help a person make decisions in life?"

"Some of us like to think so." As I said that, I remembered my father's teaching, that one can always learn something of a person's character through gambling. "It will help you read people all through life," my father said, and I reflected on the women spies who were as easy to read as novice poker players. But what about the bureaucrat's daughter before me? Was she here for social reasons only, or could she also be part of the secret police's eyes and ears?

She walked over to a cabinet where there was a photo of me on the deck of a naval ship. She was wearing mid-high heels, and her dress came to just below the knees, in the fashion of the day. When she strode across the room her thighs activated again—the vastus externus, the largest muscles in the human body, collided against the inside of her dress. Years of kicking the water had made them more erotic than fashionable by orthodox standards.

"You look very nice in your uniform," she said.

"I was much younger then."

"And maybe not such a good gambler yet?"

"Actually, I was. I started early, you know, and earned my drinking money in college that way. Which is why I usually have some good wine on hand, if you would care for a sip."

"Not now," she answered, almost with a wine glow. "Perhaps another day. I'd love to join you."

We spoke for a while and parted. At the door to the street, Mrs. Saito came to bow, where Miss Hiraoka also became momentarily reserved and also bowed properly, her hands on her dress giving her thighs another chance to press into prominence. As she walked away, I followed the flexing of her calf muscles to where they disappeared under the hemline.

Back in my office, I reviewed the options in my life that I told her about. I was never attracted to diplomatic-type people. I saw them as a poor socio-architectural design: too high in position for the thin foundation of talent that supported them, like tall, shallow-rooted trees that topple in a wind. At first I resisted becoming one, but when I looked at the maze from aloft I saw the appeal of moving among different nationalities, of "reading" people as my father had talked about. "In gambling, it's the final average that counts," and I decided to drop a few points, follow the required diplomatic routine, and win on the other hands it might let me play on foreign soil. Romantic possibilities, in all meanings, were part of my decision. As a dedicated bachelor and an admirer of women, each new encounter has an exhilaration similar to drawing a new card at the gaming table: each is turned face up—so to speak—with new excitement.

▪ 6 ▪
Japan's Giant Battleships

When Yamamoto and I renewed our friendship in Tokyo, he was navy vice-minister and my legation was housed in a building badly in need of undeserved repairs. It was an architectural monster built for one of Japan's nouveau riche, who all yearned for large, pseudo-European homes. I suggested to my government that rather than restore the ugly, we search for another place. In the meantime, it served for Yamamoto and me to break the seal on our first pack of cards in some seventeen years and for Yamamoto to loft his Cherry clouds.

"They went back into production in 1926," he said through the smoke. "American tobacco." He showed me the pack marked PURE VIRGINIA. "Control measures will cut off imports from America and it'll soon be domestic leaf, maybe some from other parts of Asia. But I'll stick with Cherry. They got us through the war with the Russians."

I offered Yamamoto his choice of soft drinks. "And how is navy life for you these days?" I asked him.

"Closer to politics than the ocean."

"You sound like you want to go back to sea."

"I do. But I'd like a little better luck on board with me next time."

"You mean, losing those planes on maneuvers?"

He pulled the corners of his mouth down to indicate a negative. "Another mishap. About two years ago. I was in the Fourth Fleet then." The number stood out: four, the bad-luck omen that was in the month and date of his birthday. "It was the year after I was promoted to vice-admiral. We were on maneuvers with two special-type destroyers. *Yugiri* and *Hatsuyuki.*"

I could not help commenting that they were poetic names: "Evening Mist" and "First Snowfall."

"We name destroyers after natural phenomenon. They do get poetic. Evening mist, the type of fog that moves in at the end of the day, is poetic if you're not navigating close to shore—or if you don't have planes in the air like I did in 1929."

He disappeared momentarily behind a cloud. "We ran into a storm. A really bad one. Both destroyers lost their bows. The *Yugiri*'s bow went down. The bow of the *Hatsuyuki* remained afloat—and the Imperial Navy's codes were in that bow. There were probably men in it also. We made attempts to take it in tow, but the weather was too fierce. High waves, high wind. We had no chance of retrieving the bow, so the fleet commander ordered it shelled. It had my number on it."

"Your number. . .?"

"Eleven! There on the broken bow. My name added like dice. My number in the graduating class at the Naval Academy. I had to watch our own shells pummel it—rip into that eleven and send it to the bottom." He paused for another grimace. "Afterwards, I was a member of the investigation committee for the incident. And I saw it again and again through the testimony, my number shelled by our own guns. . . ."

My staff finally located a building in the Azabu district in Nishimachi that was an ideal combination legation-residence. It was a successful blend of Japanese and Western styles, a three-story construction built in 1921 by an American missionary who was also an architect, William M. Vories. It had a basement, something rare in Japan, and something even more unusual. The owners disliked the Japanese education system and had planned on educating their children at home. The architect was told to include several small classrooms in the design. And, he employed solid stucco construction, for which I was thankful. Thin walls and close proximity of houses are architectural curses for most Japanese wives, demanding skill in biting the pillow. This is a sad burden to place on them in one of their few moments of release from the complicated demands of their society. The American—in his role as architect, not missionary—provided liberation for the highly personal moments of my lady friends.

The entrance to what became the legation part of the building was from the rather wide front street, and I had an indoor access to the residential portion remodeled with double doors. The residence looked out on an inner, spacious, semi-Western garden, and the residence could also be reached from the quiet side street where an unobtrusive entrance through a high wall opened into this garden. Japanese gardens are more for looking at than living in. Even those with walking areas do not allow for *participating* in the space. I appreciated the non-Japanese aspects of the garden and made two additions to help keep me in shape: punching bags—a heavy bag suspended on chains and an overhead bag, set up under a roof.

The garden entrance from the side street was convenient for private guests, not all of whom were lady friends. Yamamoto also liked the unobtrusiveness, the avoidance of courtesies that accompanied his arrival at the legation entrance. Part of his pleasure in visiting me was the escape from bows and salutes.

In July of that year of 1937, a skirmish broke out at the Marco Polo Bridge near Peking. A Japanese army unit—according to Japan's claim—was fired upon by Chinese troops, and the Japanese returned fire. The world did not believe the story, but the skirmish opened the way for Japan's army to expand the war to all of China while the debate on who fired first continued far from the front lines. Yamamoto was succinct in his opinion. "My first thought was that those army fellows are at it again. They're a tricky bunch, and they think that China is property of the Kwantung Army. But they're making trouble for Japan."

The Japanese army's adventures in China pushed her troops close enough to the Russian bear to smell the vodka and gunpowder on its breath. With Japan's leaders threatening to fight China with one hand and Russia with the other, the scheduled 1940 Tokyo Olympics started taking body blows. Tokyo questioned whether the country could play Olympic host during an expanding war in China, while overseas governments were sending messages that they could not send athletes to the games in the face of Japan's military exploits.

In the winter of 1937, Hector Bywater gained a scoop in the British press that rocked world governments. He reported that Japan was building giant battleships of forty-three thousand tons. The West cooked with concern.

Japan and other signatories to the Washington Treaty were limited to warships of thirty-five thousand tons until 1936. Western nations agreed to hold to the limitations after the treaty expired in hopes of reducing the volatility of the seas, and Japan gave a verbal promise to do the same. Now Bywater was writing that Japan immediately and secretly threw off the reins.

My naval background would not let go of me, and I did some research of my own. I contacted a naval architect acquaintance in Sweden, gathered some data on the Panama Canal, and had the facts ready for Yamamoto's next visit.

"Fuel?" I asked

"Seltzer will be fine," he answered. "You know this Cox fellow?"

"The Reuters correspondent? Yes."

"He came to see me the other day, right after that Bywater article broke. I think he's the one who searched out the story for Bywater in the first place, but he came asking for confirmation."

"And. . .?"

"I told him what I could. Not much."

The "not much" made international headlines. Yamamoto replied that Japan was a country with a small navy and therefore required special armaments and had a greater need for secrecy than larger nations; that by not revealing information important to Japan's security, the Western powers assume Japan is going beyond the limitations of the verbal agreement, and that this is an unreasonable and unfair attitude. It was as if he were fighting for logic, and this, in turn, made me suspicious in another direction. Was his public statement another play to sabotage Japan's top naval brass? Yamamoto knew how to fake a bet without making people jump—unless he wanted them to jump. His plans for the naval till differed from those who had control of it, and I wondered if he hadn't caused an intentional shock to bring on international pressure that would in turn choke off funds for the battleships and free them for carriers and aircraft.

"There's verbal shellburst over the oceans," Yamamoto said.

"Well, it's understandable that England and the United States are concerned about an armaments race."

"Understandable, yes. And I would like to see some intelligent discussions on all sides and have the battleship plan thrown overboard. I have other uses for naval funds. If Bywater helps that along, I'll make the Englishman a hero of the Japanese naval air wing."

"Bywater was perceptive and deductive," I told him, "but as you say in Japanese, 'even monkeys fall from trees.' I think he slipped a little on the size of the battleships."

"Hmm?"

"I see him short of the mark."

". . ."

"If you'll allow me to play a little naval Sherlock Holmes, ever since a sea lane was cut between the Atlantic and Pacific, the United States started thinking about moving fleets from one ocean to the other. That is general knowledge, I believe."

Yamamoto gave an affirmative grunt.

"Now, the width of the canal is one hundred and ten feet. So deduct the thickness of a sheet of paper on each side and I cannot see America building ships of greater beam. The beam is the deciding factor."

"Elementary," Yamamoto answered with his minimum smile.

"Cox and Bywater have the ships at around forty-three thousand tons. The Italian press jumped in and called it at forty-six thousand. I don't know where they got the figure; neither American nor British naval authorities seem to have their own intelligence information and are relying on what Bywater writes. I think they're all wrong."

"Swedish intelligence?"

"No, just one poker player's assessment—of the probability of a person's hand from the cards played. I did get a little help from Stockholm, but no secrets, just universal knowledge. Such as, right now the biggest American warships that can go through Panama are thirty-five thousand tons—equipped with antitorpedo double hulls. That gives them a leeway in the canal of two feet. The biggest battleship afloat that can make it through is the British Navy's *Hood,* forty-two thousand tons but a bit slender in the beam; she'd have a leeway of five feet in the canal. Now, from what I can gather of naval architecture, the upper limit for a warship that could fit through the canal—if built with that in mind—would be about sixty thousand tons.

"Your figures are right."

"In poker, we have to assess unseen cards by what we know of the player. I say America would probably not build anything larger than sixty thousand tons, but could be expected to go to that limit."

"They might."

"So I see Japan's new battleships somewhere in that class. Able to duplicate the size and firepower of the biggest possible warship that could squeeze through the Panama locks with soapy sides. Or ... even a little bigger, to take advantage of Japan's one-ocean concern."

Yamamoto lit a Cherry, puffed the smoke overhead, and watched it sail away.

"I'm also thinking of the temperament of the participants in the game," I chided him. "That's important. I heard something like that in a speech at Harvard once."

"That's a huge ship, sixty thousand tons. Do you think this little country of Japan could do that?"

"Of course."

He shook his head in agreement. "That's the problem. We have deadhead leaders who think that because a ship is possible it should be built." He took a swig of seltzer, then pointed the glass toward me. "You're close, and it will probably be out soon and you'll read it in Bywater's column. But you missed one assessment."

"Oh?"

"You underestimated the idiocy of our navy planners."

I waited for one Cherry puff.

"They calculated that America could go to about sixty thousand. Correct. So they decided to do better than just match that."

The cards were lying at the edge of the table. Yamamoto picked them up, fanned them out, drew two from the face side and threw them face down on the table. "I'm not supposed to say anything about it, so I won't." He glanced at his watch, stood, and we went through the garden to the door. As he walked down the side street I went back inside and turned over the cards he had thrown: a two and a seven. Seventy-two thousand tons? There had never been that large a battleship in the world. Was Japan really going to do this?

I went to my file of personal papers and pulled out Yamamoto's letter of 1934—I kept many of his letters and notes, especially those that pertained to navies and the seas. I also had a clipping of Bywater's article with his interview of Yamamoto. One passage stood out: "On the subject of Pacific naval bases the admiral expressed himself frankly. 'I and many other Japanese naval officers do not regard Singapore as a menace. It is too far away from our country to cause us worry. We should, however, be seriously perturbed if the United States were to create a powerful base in the Philippines.'"

The Monroe Doctrine of 1823 gave the United States domination over the Western Hemisphere. She tried to prevent outside interference when South American countries were fighting for freedom from Spain, and she did not replace Spain as the ruling power in her colonies with only one exception: the Philippines. And this brought American military power into Japan's sphere of concern. If Japan attempted a Monroe Doctrine–type of dominance in the Pacific, the Philippines would fall into an area of confrontation, and the United States would be in a weak position to influence Tokyo that it was unwise. Yet if Bywater—and Cox, presumably—were right, Japan's giant-battleship plans meant that she was reinforcing her naval strength for a Monroe Doctrine–type power grip in the Pacific.

▪ 7 ▪
A Trip to the Rear of Japan

Yamamoto's favorite venue in my legation was one of the classrooms that overlooked the garden. One day I asked him to put up with me in a game of *shogi*.

"So you learned it," he said with a relatively generous smile.

"Back in Stockholm I went to the Japanese ambassador with this strange request, and he got me started. Later on he handed me over to one of his staff who had a better reputation."

Chess and checker pieces are slid or moved quietly. In *shogi*, pieces are placed on the board with a large hand movement and a sharp snap, an audible commitment like a shot that announces a tactic is born. We played to my defeat. Yamamoto reached for his Cherry pack and said, "One day, you should see the rear of Japan."

"The rear of Japan?"

"That's what they call the region I'm from. Niigata. It's a rural area. Lots of farms, ocean . . . and it's cold."

"Cold weather to a Swede is like water to a fish," I said, and one day a locomotive pulled us to Yamamoto's hometown. He was an adopted child and came from a family of poor samurai background. With the end of feudalism in the nineteenth century, many of the samurai class entered the military of the new Imperial Japanese Army, and some of them were known as "country samurai," a derisive term for an inflexible mind of questionable intelligence. Yamamoto spent his naval career hating the Japanese army.

"The army did great things after the Meiji Restoration," he said. "The Russo-Japanese War was the peak of their moral fiber and chivalry. But then they went downhill. There's one army man I admire, a retired medical officer from those days. He was with my family in the local regiment, then he served in the Russo-Japanese War. He's one of the last of the good army men, and you should meet him while you have the chance. The officers in Tokyo are not made of the same material."

Colonel Sasaki fought the latter part of the Russo-Japanese War with a bullet lodged in his gut. He was wounded in the battle of Kinshu and ordered his medics only to stop his bleeding and prevent infection. Then he was at the front again, not the place most armies of the world would expect or tolerate a medical officer. Yamamoto and I visited the colonel at his home.

"The code of the samurai," Sasaki said, "teaches us to become one with the enemy. Then you know how he is thinking. That is what we learn in *kendo,* and it works on the battlefield."

"It apparently worked in the war," I commented. "I know only from studying about it. I think 'highly sacrificial' would be correct."

"There were sacrifices on all sides. But the Japanese army's view of sacrifice was different. Sometimes we had to cease fighting to bury the dead. We buried the enemy dead also. And many times we treated their wounded and sent them back to their lines."

"I don't imagine the Russians did the same for the Japanese."

"The Russians didn't even treat their own wounded. They left them behind to slow our advances. We could not abandon them, so we treated them."

The retired colonel was fairly tall for a Japanese, and in spite of advanced age and health problems, he walked erect and still reflected his military training and a proud background.

"Remember, Japan had the most advanced military medicine in the world during that war. Even some of our field hospitals had portable X-ray machines. An American army doctor came to our unit as an observer and he was astounded at our level of military hygiene."

"So Japan was ahead of Europe and America in medicine?"

"In the intelligent application of it, yes. Japan's medical education came from Europe, of course. But we realized that in all the wars of the world, 'the silent enemy' was killing more soldiers than bombs and bullets. In the Russo-Turkish War, twenty thousand soldiers died from wounds;

eighty thousand died from disease. That means one hundred thousand deaths were largely preventable. In America's war against Mexico, and in her Civil War, the death rate was about three from disease or infection to one killed in action. Japan's ratio of casualties was almost the same when we fought China in 1894, and that changed our thinking. We decided to fight the silent enemy first. We studied every medical system of the world, then formulated our own. It was not just a change in medical thinking but in military attitude."

My studies of the Russo-Japanese War had involved tactics. This was a new aspect for me. "And how was this done?"

"Western countries," the colonel continued, "kept the doctors in the background until a soldier was wounded or sick. In the Japanese army, we played a role in determining troop movements. We devised portable water-testing equipment and sent hygiene scouts ahead into the field to sample the water and determine safe food sources for the troops. It was not just local bacteria that could weaken the army. When the Russians retreated, they infected the water supplies with typhoid, dysentery, cholera. Sometimes they threw poison into the wells and spread disease germs on the ground and in the local food sources. They were using bacteria against us in their retreats. We medical men discussed these threats with field officers and then the battle plan was drawn up. From what we learned of the American system, the doctors had nothing to say while the soldier was healthy, no business near the front lines. Our first job was to prevent disease from reducing our fighting strength. Our next job was to prevent wounds from becoming infectious. In our war in Manchuria, the microscope and the Murata rifle held equal rank as weapons. The American doctor tried to get the same advances in America."

"And what was his result?"

"First he caused the American president, Theodore Roosevelt, to dispatch two more army doctors to Manchuria. Those American observers of our medical corps argued to get an act passed in the U.S. in 1908 that reorganized the army medical department closer to our system. Then, when the U.S. went into the Great War, they had a better medical department, thanks to the Japanese model."

"So, could you say that Japan saved American lives in that war?"

"Of course! But I doubt if any except the medical officers are really aware of the connection."

"And what," I inquired, "was the major difference?"

"In America, military doctors were only repairmen; line officers did not even consider them soldiers."

"You know," Yamamoto commented, "what the Western world called us? 'Scientific fanatics!' It's true. Japan almost made a religion out of Western science in those days. But it did good things for us. The Japanese navy was hit with beriberi, and it was traced to diet. We were the first country to make that advance."

"After the battle of Mukden," the colonel continued, "the Japanese army took sixty thousand Russian prisoners, many of them sick and wounded. When Port Arthur fell, we took seventeen thousand. Scurvy was extremely high among them, because we invested the port and they had very meager food supplies. We dressed wounds and restored health. Japan was relieving the burden on the enemy hospitals. Later, the Russians bragged about the low death rate among their wounded, but they never announced that a large percentage of them recovered under Japanese care."

The colonel reached for his Golden Bat cigarettes. "Japan still is at the top in military medicine," Sasaki continued, "and I wanted my son to follow me. But he was not destined to be a doctor. And much less suited to becoming a soldier. He went into business, then one of his sons started medical school, but he dropped out to follow art."

The colonel walked to a cabinet and took out a photo album. "I think you'll recognize Paris. My grandson, Akira, with some friends."

He turned a page and there was Akira standing next to a life-size wooden sculpture.

"This is one of his works," the colonel commented. "He left medical school and his father supported him to study in France. I was disappointed that he did not follow medicine, but Akira is not just a spendthrift of family money. He is now in Manchuria working as a civilian for the army there. And, at a very good salary. He sends money home regularly to pay back his father for his study in France. He's got a touch of the old discipline in him."

What, I wondered, *was an art student doing working for the Japanese army?* I paged through the album, and turned up photos of the grandson in a glassblowing workshop.

"He studied this, also?" I asked the colonel.

"Glass sculpture is one of his passions. That's what got him the job with the Japanese army. Perhaps you can meet him one day."

Glass sculpture seemed even more remote from military requirements. I could not realize at the time how grotesque the answer to the riddle would be.

1938: The Olympic Crash

Tokyo's Olympic fever rose on plans for a 110,000-seat main stadium in Setagaya that would require eight million yen, equal to 3 percent of the national budget. "That is the cost of one destroyer," voices in government cried, clouding the autumn and winter of 1937 with growing calls for cancellation of the games.

In December of 1937 the capital, Nanking, fell to Japanese troops after Chiang Kai-shek and his generals abandoned the city and their own soldiers and moved the capital up the Yangtze River to Hankow. Japanese military victories could not conceal the reality that even as Japanese boots advanced, they were bogging down in the muck of a venture that strained their army's strategic management. At home, Japanese athletes greeted 1938 by training for an Olympiad with doubts that it would be held.

"An Olympic is worth more than a destroyer," was Miss Hiraoka's comment on it. By spring of 1938 she was not a stranger at my legation, where we always met in my office. "If Japan has one less destroyer, what difference will it make? If we cancel the Olympics, it will be world news. The government people are thinking wrong." She made me uneasy, continuing her journey into uncharted grounds of frankness.

"They think strangely about other things also. The police gave orders that beauty shops may not install any new equipment for permanent waves."

"You wouldn't know it by all the permanent waves in Tokyo. Even you have one."

"I get one sometimes, though once the pools open I don't bother. But worse things are happening. Do you remember when the government closed a family planning center?"

"Yes, it was in the news early this year."

"This is already an overpopulated country, and the cost of living doubled from last year. *Doubled!* How can people keep having babies if they can't afford to feed them?"

I thought it ironic that while Japan was trying to increase population at home, it was reverting to the tactics of the Great War to eliminate lives faster in the war in China. The League of Nations shocked the world when it revealed and denounced Japan's use of poison gas against the Chinese in Shantung province. And another reflex juxtaposition I made was when the Japanese government decreed that wooden matches must be made shorter to conserve materials, then two weeks later launched an oil tanker of 10,500 tons—the world's largest class.

Miss Hiraoka always brought up some current event in her conversation, but just as we can sympathize with the pain of others, when we feel pain ourselves it becomes a new experience. One development struck her more personally than any other: government interference with students.

"The Ministry of Education is about to send out an order for students to work as trainees in factories. That is *not* what a Ministry of Education should be doing."

"I hope it will not interfere with their studies."

"It will be unavoidable. This is terrible!"

Something bothered me also: a youth group departed Japan and sailed for Germany "to cement cultural ties." Then Japan's Olympic skies darkened on June 23, when the cabinet of Prime Minister Prince Konoe announced that Japan was unable to spare resources for the proposed Olympic stadium. One week later, massive landslides and seventy thousand flooded homes under torrential rains seemed to be Nature's way of sluicing away any remaining hopes for a Tokyo Olympiad.

▪ ▪ ▪

In July of 1938 Japan and Russia were at war again. Fighting broke out after the Russian army occupied a disputed area at Changkufeng, bordering on Japan's puppet state of Manchukuo.

"The emperor was angry," Yamamoto said when we talked about it afterwards. "He practically swore at the army officers. We all know that the Japanese army fired first."

"I didn't think the emperor becomes angry."

"It's happened before. With each army promise to end the war his disgust for their incompetence increases. He has said as much. After this outbreak, he said that no man on the Manchurian border is to move unless he orders or approves it."

"And do you think that will keep things under control?"

"Bet that way if you want to. I wouldn't."

But Manchuria was far away for most Japanese. Tokyo, and the scheduled Olympics, were closer—until July 15 when the government officially cancelled them and they were awarded to Helsinki by default.

"The army again," was Yamamoto's comment on this.

"I did not think that one destroyer would make a difference with the formidable fleet that Japan has," I commented. "Of course, the stadium is not the only expense, but it seemed to be the deciding one."

"Money is not the only reason," he countered. "Domestic strategy is a greater one."

"Meaning. . .?"

"The army men don't want to dilute the country's concentration on war."

"I'm surprised they didn't think the same as the Germans."

"That shows how different the thinking is," Yamamoto said. "Hitler used the Olympics to unite the people into a military frame of mind; Japan cancelled them for the same objective. Yet, army officers are trying to push Japan into closer relationships with the Nazi government. They're both a dangerous bunch."

It did not require an Olympiad for Japan to make a showing in competition swimming. In August of 1938, Miss Hiraoka called. "If you will permit drinking a toast in your office," she said. "I'll bring the wine."

"A celebration?" I asked.

"It will be on the news today, and in the papers tomorrow."

It was. And she had the wine. "A friend's father had this stowed away for a long time and he doesn't drink anymore. Imported from France. Today, it's to Japan's new record in the pool."

"All right. A Japanese swimmer took the fifteen-hundred-meter free-style record from a Swede."

"He held that record for eleven years," she almost shouted.

"Arne Borg held a record for holding records," I reminded her, but the Japanese had all the statistics.

"Thirty-two world records," she filled in, "all set by 1929. We lost the chance to hold the Olympics, but we gained a world record."

I read the wine-bottle label. "This is to your liking, I assume."

"More or less, I think. It's white and slightly sweet, which I like. But whatever it is, it will taste fine today."

I turned the corkscrew. "And you know this Amano fellow who set the record?"

"Yes, I've watched him practice. He's twenty years old and would have been a strong contender in 1940. But here's to his record in 1938."

In the name of good sportsmanship, I toasted the victory of the Japanese over a Swede, then asked what other news there was.

"The other day I had my first ride on a charcoal-fuel bus."

"I see they've been growing in number."

"I have to admit that Japan sometimes comes up with unusual solutions, but it would be more clever if problems were avoided. If the government would get out of China we wouldn't need charcoal buses."

I remembered other women talking to me about the war, on obvious assignments to ferret out opinions. I stayed with the buses. "Yes, I would say they're clever. Once the charcoal burns, the carbon monoxide becomes fuel. But it takes an hour to get the fire going. I'll still take our legation car, even though it does have a few years behind it."

The summer of 1938 saw the first visit of the Hitler Jugend to Japan. About thirty uniformed seventeen- and eighteen-year-olds paraded for the cameras at shrines as honored guests. And it may be that the glory of their uniforms was still twinkling in the eyes of Japan's leaders that autumn when the League of Nations offered to discuss an end to the war in China—and Japan refused.

A month later, the depressing trends in politics were darkened further when Mount Asama, 150 kilometers distant, belched clouds of prehistoric glass particles that rode the northwest wind and darkened Tokyo, as a portent to two further dismal events. Within one week a Japanese author's book was banned for criticizing fascism and the Japanese army strengthened its handshake with the Nazis by appointing Lieutenant General Oshima Hiroshi ambassador to Berlin. Even with Tokyo's Olympiad cancelled, Hitler's IOC maneuver was still operational.

▪ 9 ▪
The First Atrocity Leak

Yamamoto called to ask if I would join him in Colonel Sasaki's Buddhist sendoff to the next world. The funeral provided the chance to fulfill the colonel's wish that I meet his grandson, Akira.

It was early spring of 1939. The Japanese army in Manchuria was tensed for another border outbreak with the Soviets, but Colonel Sasaki's background brought some high-ranking officers in from the continent by military planes. Akira was given the courtesy of transportation to attend. He knew of me from his grandfather's correspondence, and when we met at the funeral I invited him to visit me at the legation.

A Japanese funeral is occasion for eating and drinking with the spirit of the departed, and this also provided my first meeting with General Umezu Yoshijiro, commander of the First Army in China.

"I thank you for your friendship with Colonel Sasaki during his lifetime," Umezu said.

"I really met the man only once," I answered. "I am glad I had the chance."

"The length of time is not always important. Friendship and understanding can flower with just one seed."

"You knew the colonel well, I take it."

"He was my instructor in army college. He taught us field hygiene, how to protect the health of soldiers, how to prevent the wounded from dying from infection. He took a liking to me and said that he had faith in me to be a future leader in Japan's army."

"It seems that he was correct."

"I owe much to Colonel Sasaki and the inspiration he gave me. When the Russo-Japanese War broke out he requested to be activated to go to the front. He took some bad wounds, but the Russians didn't have enough to stop him."

"I see where you had a border skirmish with the Russians just last year."

"We did, last July, at Changkufeng. The two armies spent twenty days staring at each other and then the cannon took over. There might be another at any time. A plane is waiting to take me back right after the funeral."

When Akira accepted my invitation and came to my legation, he carried a rather large box.

"I brought you a little present." He placed the box down, removed another box from it, and handed it to me. I opened it and took out a hand-crafted glass bird, exquisitely turned and shaded with color.

"One of my works," he said. "I hope you like it."

I thanked him and placed the bird on a table, where the sun struck it and sent rays of light glancing onto the wall. I could not know at that moment how the bird was hatched from the same egg as Japan's advance into ugly, scientific warfare.

Sasaki's French was quite fluent, and he became more open when speaking it; the language apparently put him in a French frame of mind, less hesitant and freer with expression, an emotional slipping of the anchor from the restrictions of Japanese formalities. We sipped coffee.

"I saw photos of you studying glassmaking in France," I told him. "I am honored to have one of your works. Apparently, you are now busy with some type of glass work for the army."

"That also started in France. A Japanese army doctor came through. He was doing research in Europe."

"A Japanese army doctor?"

"He was attached to the Disease Prevention and Water Supply Division. It was formed in 1936 under imperial edict. Lieutenant Colonel Ishii was the head. He spent two years studying all over Europe, then he sent other officers for further research and information gathering. Many of the army medical officers knew my grandfather—some were his students— and when my grandfather told them what I was studying in France, they asked if they could look me up. So one day a bacteriologist from Ishii's out-fit called on me. He said that the army needed someone to make glass scientific instruments in Manchuria."

"In Manchuria? Not in Japan proper?"

"That was the interesting part. Manchuria is Japan's great frontier. The land of opportunity. Japan's new world. I was doing glassblowing in France and I became involved in other aspects of glassmaking. The officer asked if I could make laboratory instruments. And specimen jars. He said that if I accepted the job, the army would pay for any additional courses I had to take first. He was very clear that I would have to produce large specimen jars, up to about two meters high."

"That sounds like a craft far removed from sculpting glass birds."

"But it sounded interesting. I would be in charge of setting up a glass shop that could keep up with demand from the army. I could have all the assistants I needed and there was no limit to space or facilities. And, I could keep up my work in sculpture if I wanted."

"So that is how an artist went to Manchuria."

"That is how it started."

"Is there that much laboratory research going on there? And why in Manchuria? I would think that with all the medical schools in Japan, the need would be greater here."

Sasaki fidgeted with his coffee cup. "I have to tell you something in confidence. Strange things are happening over there. Army doctors and civilian doctors—huge numbers of them. Some come for a while, conduct their experiments, then go back to their universities. But they all come for one reason. To experiment."

"Is there some reason they run to Manchuria to work? Can't they do the same research here?"

"No! The material is different."

I thought I understood, but I fought my conclusion.

"You mean certain animals. . .?"

A moment of silence, then—"*Humans!*"

I glanced at the glass bird tinted a rich orange from the lowering sun and brought the conversation back with a feigned look of surprise.

"I'm attached to Unit 731," Akira continued. "It's on a rail line south of Harbin—a village called Ping Fan. The people were chased out to build a monster complex. Three kilometers long. Thick, high walls. When it's finished it will have more than sixty buildings, but it's already in operation. All for human experimentation with disease . . . bacteria and viruses . . . Any way people might be infected is being reproduced in human subjects. Then they are examined and scientific details noted—and the organs and body parts are preserved for study."

I merely acknowledged his words with a nod.

"The rest of the bodies are cremated. . . . no, that is too polite a word. The remains are incinerated. Like garbage. They burn quickly."

"Quickly?"

"They are empty. There are no organs in the bodies. The organs are in my specimen jars."

"And you are sure that this is what is happening?"

"I am part of it. I see the cadavers when they are cut open. This is a secret operation, but those of us working over there . . . nothing is hidden from us. The leaders look to us to carry on this work in the future. Sometimes I hear the screams. One day . . ." Akira paused, then with his elbows on his knees and his head sunk between his arms, he ran his fingers through his hair in a gesture of anguished recollection. "One day I was in a laboratory where three doctors were working on a Chinese woman. She was strapped to the operating table—the vivisection table."

"Vivisection?"

"The doctors said that this was an interesting experiment. They invited me to put on anticontamination clothes, the same kind they wear: long white gown, rubber boots, hood with glass eyepieces. The woman had been infected with venereal disease. She was under ether, but her arms were strapped to the table because sometimes people come out of the anesthesia. She did. Maybe it was the pain when the scalpel opened her up, I don't know. She woke up and pulled at the straps on her arms. I'm sure she could see and feel enough to know that she was cut open, that the men in strange clothes had their hands inside her, pulling and cutting at her organs. She screamed. 'It's all right to kill me. But please spare my baby.'"

"Her baby. . .?"

"She had been captured with a baby sucking at her breast. The baby was taken away and the woman was imprisoned by herself until the experiment."

"And, can you tell me something else about this experiment?"

"Venereal disease was a big problem in the Japanese army. It was weakening their fighting strength. So medical researchers wanted to learn more about it. To do so they had to cause it. At first they injected people, but in actual conditions, venereal disease is transmitted through contact, not injection. So now they infect one captive—sometimes male, sometimes female—and force that person into sex with another captive. Researchers stand there in their white anticontamination suits with a pistol, and force the people into sex."

"And vivisection was part of this . . . *experiment?*"

"Medical science never knew how the disease progressed in the body. The only clues were external observation of the sex organs. Now, a succession of people are cut open at different stages after contact—to study how the disease develops with time."

"And how many people are being used like this?" I asked.

"It is impossible to say. But I know how many specimen jars are being consumed, for these and other experiments. Unbelievable. There are other research units through China. One set up in Nanking after it fell. Another in Peking, and in Canton. I supply them also. Sometimes the jars come back with preserved bodies and organs in them. That's for further research at Unit 731—more papers for the doctors to write up."

"And the baby that the mother begged for . . ."

"I'm not sure what experiment it was used in. There are so many babies at Unit 731. Some were captured with the mothers, some were born in prison—some of them to syphilitic mothers, so those babies were part of studying how venereal disease is transmitted at birth."

This was obviously very sensitive information, but he soon made it clear why he was telling me this.

"As you know," Akira continued, "I went to this position in Manchuria through acquaintances of my grandfather. In Japan, this means that he bears part of the responsibility for my actions. I cannot dirty his name. Army doctors are taking advantage of Japan's control in China to use prisoners in medical experiments. You will hear of this sooner or later—the world will hear of it—and I want you to know that this is not the same army as his. My grandfather spent his medical career preventing disease and infection from killing our own soldiers. He even treated the enemy wounded. None of the men of his day would ever think of the things army doctors are doing now."

"I can understand that," I assured him.

"There is nobody else I can talk to about this—now. I would like to leave this information with you, in confidence. You may some day be able to explain that this is not what the Japanese army was when my grandfather was part of it. And I want you to know that the shock of what the army is doing now was a cause of his death."

"He learned about this?"

"I have no proof, but I am certain. He found out sometime after you met him. Before that, all he knew was that I made glass laboratory equipment. But he had so many acquaintances in the medical community, and the tone of his letters toward the end of his life . . . He found out. My grandfather did not die just from age and old battle wounds. Shock, depression, perhaps you could say a broken heart, were all part of it. He became a victim of the very army he held pride in."

"You have to go back to your job now. Will you be all right?"

"I promised to pay back my family for my study in France. The pay scale in Manchuria is high; my salary is very good."

Akira left. I stared at the glass bird. The Japanese army was taking horrendous measures to protect its soldiers from disease. I did not know yet that those atrocities were part of a greater plan, one that would affect the world and continue well beyond my lifetime.

▪ 10 ▪
Child Spies

A round of golf gave me an unexpected introduction to Japan's move to control the minds of its youth. I don't enjoy golf. As a collegiate boxer and fencer, I find no interest in hitting an immovable, unthinking object. Diplomatic life forced me to learn the game well enough to avoid embarrassing my government.

I was playing with two other foreign representatives and a retired Japanese naval officer, former Captain Nagashima. As we enjoyed a sip after coming off the links, I saw a group of Japanese finishing up their game, all clad in proper golf caps and rather expensive, ill-suited, knickerbockers. The short-leggedness of the Japanese takes place mainly in the femurs, and knickerbockers were designed for men with proportions that can tolerate the femur-shrinking effects of the garment. Nagashima pointed out one of the men in the group.

"The minister of education," he advised in a glum tone. "The game of golf is a step in the direction of the collapse of Japan's education."

"Collapse of education?"

"Those two men with him are officers in the Army General Staff Headquarters. They are getting ready to stage a domestic invasion, a takeover of the education system to train every Japanese like a soldier, to follow army leaders. I was in the Imperial Japanese Navy almost all my adult life, and I believe the military should serve the country, not run it. Army men think opposite."

The retired naval officer's comments on the golf course kept rising in my memory, and I decided to call Miss Hiraoka for a look inside Japan's schools. I wanted to see her again even if there were nothing to talk about, and I could not sort out which motive was stronger at that moment. We decided on a Sunday afternoon. "Nobody will be in the legation," I told her. "Walk up the narrow side street along the high wall until you come to a door. My name is on it. Press the button."

We sat by a window in a combination living room-guest room, where we found ourselves in European history again.

"Of course," I told her, "history is something that can vary with interpretation. The Spanish and the English would have different views of the historical relations between them. That is natural."

"But history is something that really happened. And it happened only one way. So where can we learn that true history?"

"That, Miss Hiraoka, requires search and effort. And perhaps some intelligent guesses."

"In our schools, we have to teach the accepted versions of history, and many times I cannot . . . I cannot agree. And I find it hard to teach."

I could never forget that every person I met was a potential informer for the secret police. Anything I said might be carried back and analyzed in some inner room at police headquarters under the eyes of the emperor and empress looking down from their imperial photo on the wall. I did not want to believe that the bureaucrat's daughter was also cooperating with the police, but I could not assume she was not, or never would be, voluntarily or by other means. History, the emperor, the war—it was not wise to challenge orthodoxy.

"The only Japanese history I know is what I've read on my own over the years."

Her eyes wandered about for a while—an escape, I felt, from my unwelcome non-opinion. "This is a beautiful house. So secluded from everything, and so foreign. I almost feel like I'm away from Japan."

"In a sense, you are. This was designed by an American architect. And since you are a teacher, take a look into that room over there. What does it look like to you?"

"It's unusual . . . like a small classroom."

"Exactly. And there's another over there, and one there. . . ."

"But why? Was this a school?"

"Not really, but in a sense, yes. The family who owns this house had spent a long time overseas, and they developed an international taste for education. They had six children and decided to educate them at home under private tutors. They seemed especially concerned about the daughters, I might add. So they had the house built with these classrooms for the children's private education."

"All right, then," she smiled. "You come into the classroom and sit in the student's seat and I'll tell you something about Japan in ancient times." We walked over and I took my place. "Did you know that the earliest records in the world of swimming as a sport were in Japan?"

"I did not. I fail."

"In 36 B.C. And did you know that at the beginning of the seventeenth century, soon after the shogunate was formed, a decree established compulsory swimming throughout Japan?"

"Maybe that's when you should have been born. You might have been a special swimming advisor to the shogun."

"Sometimes, I think so . . . really."

"Oh?"

She was not smiling anymore. "I love teaching. I love working with children. But there were always things in education that I . . . that I am afraid of."

"Such as. . .?"

"You know how Europe had its religious wars. Maybe something like that is happening to Japan."

"Surely not a 'Buddhist Crusade,'" I chided.

"Perhaps not so different. But not Buddhist. Our own religion."

I sensed hidden shoals ahead. I let her continue.

"You know how the emperor has been made into a god. Actually, this is only in the last seventy years or so, but it is being reinforced now. And there is a whole mythology that is part of it. We must teach history in school—but it is not history. It is all created, like a fairy story. 'Japan is a divine nation. The emperor is descended from ancient deities. All Japanese are racially superior with native ancestral spirit.' It is, as you say, the beginning of a crusade of sorts. The war in China is being supported by such religion. 'We are pure, other people are not.'"

The war in China made Japan a thorn in the international sphere and put foreigners in Japan under suspicion. Was Miss Hiraoka really depressed by changes in Japanese education, or simply a better actress than the others? I headed for neutral ground.

"As I just said, every country teaches history from a different viewpoint. That is only natural."

"But schools in Japan," she continued, "are becoming more frightening all the time. I watch every morning as the children are turned into soldiers. They come to school and the first thing they must do is go to the shrine with the pictures of the emperor and empress. The boys remove their caps, and every child must bow deeply. When there is a ceremony or a special day at school, the principal reads the Imperial Rescript on Education to the class . . . do you know about that?"

I did. I struggled through it as part of my studies in Japanese. It was written by the Meiji government in 1890 as a catechism in the religion of emperorism. Minds were forged into shape with weighty syntax, and while some of its tenets were morally agreeable—harmony among siblings, filial piety—the unwieldy vocabulary led to the final objective of a unified nation believing in a fantasy-inspired imperial history and obedience to the emperor. The rescript was just a historical document to me until Mariko told me more.

"The scroll with the Imperial Rescript on Education is enclosed in a paulownia-wood box and kept at the little shrine with the imperial photos. The principal puts on a pair of clean, white gloves—white is part of Shintoism; it symbolizes purity—and then he goes to the shrine and lifts the wooden box toward the photos of the emperor and empress in respect while bowing his head. The box must be raised higher than his head; this is important. Then he carries the box to the assembly hall, opens it, and takes out the scroll. Every movement has to be very careful, very gentle. He holds the scroll at arm's length and unrolls it. Then he reads it to the class. I have seen him, time and again, shaking from nervousness during this reading."

"Shaking? You mean, he is not yet accustomed to speaking in front of his own students?"

"This is not speaking," she came back with increased voltage. "This is a ritual. If the principal makes a mistake in the reading, or if he should drop that scroll, it would be an insult to the emperor. A teacher or student might tell the *kempei* police, and they would come and scream at him, maybe punish him.

He might even lose his job. Japan is living under a strange religion, and the image of the emperor has become the most important thing in our lives. This is how the military leaders can direct people as they like. That is why the principle shakes."

She looked down for a minute, and I recalled the words from my Japanese studies: *"Our Imperial ancestors founded our empire on a broad and everlasting base. . . . should any emergency arise, offer yourselves to the nation with courage, and protect and uphold the prosperity of the Imperial throne. . . ."*

"Then he puts the scroll back into the box and takes the box back to the little shrine, walking like he is carrying the spirit of some god. He raises the box toward the photographs of the emperor and empress again — again, it must be raised higher than his head — and puts the box back in the shrine. Then he can take off his white gloves and he can go back to being a normal person again."

"Many countries have some kind of patriotic oath or such," I commented from my neutral ground.

"No, this is more than just an oath," she went on. "This is mysticism. If people acted like that years ago in Europe, they would have been burned for a witch. The principal shakes and the children stand at rigid attention. I pray that no child coughs or sneezes or moves during the reading because that child will get slapped and punished. That piece of paper is fearful. And the children are losing all the beauty of childhood. They go directly from babyhood to soldiers."

"I see Japanese children in the streets every day," I answered, thinking about officers in a secret-police room sifting through my responses like prospectors looking for specks of gold. "They look pretty much like children everywhere. Perhaps better behaved, but healthy and active. But since you like wine, I have a fairly good stock here."

We went back into the combination living room-guest room that looked out over the garden. "I think I know your preference — white with a touch of sweetness?"

While it was my own curiosity about conditions in Japan that prompted me to call her over, I was looking only for a one-way input. And, as I found out later, she offered it because she was hoping for more recognition of her suffering than the neutral evasions I offered. Even after I popped the cork that Sunday afternoon and we tipped our glasses, she headed back voluntarily for another stretch on the torture rack of recollection.

"There are even worse things," she went on. "Recently we've been ordered to give more composition assignments to the children. Then we have to read them to look for signs of dissent in the parents."

"And then. . .?" I asked

She looked down. "Then we must . . . we must report any indication of deviation from national goals to the principal."

"And the principal calls in the child, I suppose."

"No. The principal reports to the Ministry of Education and then the police go to the home and question the parents."

"Do children really reveal that much in their writing?" I asked.

"Sometimes, yes. Children are innocent, and the government makes use of this. We are being told to give more and more assignments on themes like 'Mother' and 'Father' and 'My Family.' Then the teachers must study them, and . . . Last week, one boy wrote 'My daddy prays for peace.' The police took the father into custody and questioned him on suspicion of being a communist, or antigovernment, or . . ."

"And what happened to him?"

"I do not know, and I am afraid to ask. I am afraid to ask the principal, and I am afraid to ask the boy, because he may already feel guilty if he realized that his composition made the police come to the house. Children's innocence can be disastrous."

I thought it ironical that the minds of children were being formed into obedient Japanese purity by men in ill-suited knickerbockers playing the game of white foreigners.

"I love teaching children," she went on. "I studied to become an educator and I love being a teacher. But I cannot be a spy." The word stuck in my ears. "And I cannot . . ." She looked down again and bit her lip to cover a catch in breath. She took out a handkerchief and touched it to the corners of her eyes. "I cannot use my children like spies. But this is what I am being forced to do. That is why I am relieved when I can go into the swimming pool after school. It's physical and refreshing."

A touch of sadness adds an erotic depth to a woman. And normal compassion makes a man think of offering an embrace to heal the sorrow.

"If the conditions at school are causing you difficulties, I'm sorry that there's nothing I can do. But if another sip of wine would help...."

There was a moment of required reticence and a relapse into a Japanese script. "I should not bother you with talk like this. And I am sorry to take so much of your time." She folded her hands on her lap, tightening her dress over those vastus externus muscles that still screamed a cry for freedom to me.

"As a devotee of the grape," I told her, "I invite but never force. If you really don't want another, fine. But if you would care to join me...."

She made a slight effort and smiled, a minimal one, with moist eyes and the tiniest sniffle that, like a whispered version of a *shogi*-piece report, signaled a resolve: hers was to change moods. She gave a subtle nod, picked up the wine bottle, and poured into our glasses.

I had no doubt that the things she was telling me were true. My only problem was what level of security my words to her would have in the future. Under certain circumstances, she could possibly perform the same function as her child spies. There was one play that was safe. I proposed a toast to her happiness, and as we touched glasses I took her other hand in mine. The secret police would not object to intimacy; they had been sending me guests for that very purpose.

"I like this house," she said again. "It is so different. Refreshing."

"Like a swimming pool?"

"In a sense. When I am working with the children in the water, we are all clean. We are washed of the mind twisting and indoctrination. There is no emperor in the water. And after the children are finished, I practice until I am exhausted. It burns away my anger."

We were still holding hands "I have no swimming pool, but if you feel comfortable here, there is no need to leave yet...."

She did not.

With my first discovery of her body, I found myself massaging and stroking those firm muscles that gave even her yielding moments an assertive tone. I kissed her throat, her shoulders, and that inviting corner of the back just below the shoulder where swimming does wonders.

The short femurs of the Japanese female can have their own erotic thrill if they are developed through exercise. Men are educated into appreciation of the long, lithe leg, and as a fashion accoutrement it is an advantage. But in the clinch of passion, in the drive to satiate the lust for flesh, well-muscled, Japanese thighs offer the pleasure of a different level of dynamics.

"This is such a big bed. I like it," she said a while later.

"Because you're action oriented." She sat up and laughed. I massaged her shoulders. "What strokes do you swim?" I asked her.

"All of them. I'm not in competition anymore, so I don't have to concentrate."

"I'll bet you practice the butterfly stroke."

"How did you know?"

"I just guessed."

"But the butterfly is not so famous. It only started in the early 1930s because an American swimmer used it in breaststroke competition. He said that bringing the arms out of the water and pulling them all the way to the thighs was within the rules."

"I know. The son of a colleague of mine was on the Swedish swimming team at Berlin, and because of him I was following the controversy. The American swimmer at Berlin used it only at the beginning and end of the race in the men's two-hundred-meter breaststroke. Most swimmers, even sportswriters, said that it gave him no advantage."

"I agree. Remember, a Japanese swimmer took the gold medal in the women's two-hundred-meter breaststroke, and she didn't use the butterfly."

"Well, I tried it a few times," I told her, "and found it more exhausting than hard labor. What's happening with the butterfly now?"

"Swimming officials of the world are still trying to decide whether to allow it in competition or consider it a violation of the rules. Most breaststroke swimmers don't pay much attention to it, but some people like to use it just for practice. I always swim butterfly when . . ."

Her speech blocked. "When. . .?"

"When I'm angry."

"Angry?"

She *looked* angry. "When I do the butterfly I feel like I'm pounding the heads of those hateful army officers that are taking over our schools. I give it all the energy I have, and I beat-beat-beat the water until I'm exhausted.

Then I feel a little better." She thought for a moment, then came back. "But why did you think I do the butterfly?"

"Because it places tremendous demand on the abdomen—here—and the back—here."

"And that's how you knew?" she laughed, and pulled her hair back with two hands, making her armpits smile.

"I just guessed."

She laughed again. "I thought maybe you've been spying on our swimming pool."

▪ 11 ▪
Neutral War: The Barter Phase

Neutrality covers varying degrees of involvement in war; it is one type of war. Sweden's neutral war was based on barter. Our mines at Kiruna hold the world's largest deposits of the iron known as magnetite, Fe_3O_4, an ore with important differences from the more common hematite, Fe_2O_3. Around the fifth century, the Chinese discovered that magnetite aligned itself with terrestrial directions. They placed the ore in a wooden fish carving and floated it on water, and the fish always lined up north and south. It took them several centuries before they applied the principle to navigation, but the wooden fish of the Chinese developed into the world's first nautical compass.

In China, south was the favored direction—emperors sat facing south, the term for an instructor or master was literally "one who points south," and Chinese compasses pointed south. When the compass reached the Europeans, they added their own cultural interpretation and considered it pointing north, but they added more: historical deception. Europeans rearranged the game into a tie and claimed that the compass was invented simultaneously and independently in China and Europe. Westerners could not accept Orientals beating them in scientific accomplishment. Racism sometimes fictionalizes history—and also creates it. The great explorations by Europeans were fueled by a missionary zeal to adjust the thinking and "point the way" for lesser races.

I found another cache of magnetite in my high school English classes when I embarked with Gulliver to the land of Laputa, a floating island navigated by the power of a giant lodestone—another name for magnetite. Dean Swift's choice of name obviously was inspired by *La puta*, Spanish for "slut"—his evaluation of scientists who supported such blasphemy as belief in lines of magnetic force on the earth. His floating island was inhabited by the scientists he considered the whores of society.

Magnetite forges superior weapons—guns with higher resistance to rust. Sweden adjusted magnetite's political polarity to make it our barter for neutrality.

We had been exporting iron ore for centuries, and with Europe's march to war we wanted to cut it off from Germany, but we agreed to continue in a swap for neutrality.

When Germany started taking over Europe in 1939, a German-Russian pact was in effect. Things became more complex when Russia attacked Finland, putting Scandinavia in a German-Soviet horseshoe—a tighter version of the Allied horseshoe in the Pacific that was soon to activate the Japanese military. Sweden was playing a double game, hoping for Germany to fall but knowing that she would not, at least for some time to come. We gave Finland material and economic aid; Swedish volunteers crossed over to Finnish soil to join in the fight, then Finland formally requested Swedish troops. If Sweden had no iron we would have been free to accept, but answering Finland's request would put our mines under control of the Allies. That, in turn, would incite Germany to use force. While Swedes prayed for the Allies to crush Germany, the Allies requested permission to cross through Sweden to do just that. Neutrality took precedence over prayer, and our government refused. Germany's victims received sympathy and assistance from Sweden and shells from guns made from our iron ore.

In March of 1940, Sweden negotiated a peace between Finland and Russia. Then we had to face the other direction, the victims of Germany's military action who were angry at us for supplying the Nazis with materials for weapons. But those countries could only curse us as they took the blows of armaments descended from Kiruna. Sweden held a magnetite card and played it by switching polarity according to the ambient political lines of force. Sweden stayed out of the fight by floating like Laputa toward or away from one country or the other. We navigated with our lodestone mines through involvement and noninvolvement and maintained a polarity similar enough to Germany's to set up a field of resistance that repelled the war from our borders.

The Germans occupied Norway to grab the fjords for naval bases. They occupied Denmark for its food. They did not have to occupy Sweden. We opened our magnetite womb and became whore to the Nazis for the price of a license to conduct neutral war.

· 12 ·
Buddhist Studies
and a Length of Cowhide

Tokyo was rebuilt in the seventeenth century as a maze to confuse invading armies in their search for the shogun's palace. Small streets shoot off at illogical angles and end nowhere, or take one to an unexpected destination. It can be frustrating to someone with a destination, but a quixotic delight to strollers.

Sometimes I came upon "paper-drama" street performers who entertained children with fairy stories illustrated by large picture cards on an easel. The narrator changes the pictures in succession as his dramatic voice inflections tell the tale. Adults gathered also, and it became part of my Japanese language education. But the storytellers were among those integrated into the national education program, and the government ordered them to apply their talents to wartime heroics. Socially active and conversant animals and birds yielded the paper stage to fighting planes and tanks, and childhood fantasies were evicted by tales of battlefield bravery and the glory of serving the emperor. As Japanese patriotism became defined in terms of standing up to white intruders into Asian spaces, I sometimes walked Japan's streets to background mumblings of *spy-spy* and glances charged with the mood of *I wonder what he's looking for*. My genealogy sometimes turned children charming as they viewed me with a *maybe-we-found-one* smile. But in time, the childlike joy lost to indoctrination, and the discoveries started coming without the smiles.

My arrival in Tokyo coincided with a peaking of religious activity in the country, furthered by the talents of different types of street performers:

advocates of one prophet or other who heated the city with speeches of fire. One small Buddhist temple had opened its hall to a lecture by a certain Kawaguchi Eikai, a visually astounding man. He had traveled through Tibet gathering the wisdom of its Buddhism and its clothing. Photos showed him dressed in Tibetan robes that presented as strange a sight to the Japanese as it would to Europeans. In one of my city wanderings, Tokyo's labyrinth fooled me into walking to the temple where he was speaking. I scanned the field of shoes at the entrance to estimate the size of his audience and what percentage of the total my Western face would represent, then added my shoes to the assortment and took my place on the *tatami* mats.

There was a wooden desk at the front of the room, and on top of it Kawaguchi was sitting cross-legged in his Tibetan robes. His voice shot up from the solar plexus; it sounded like it was honed by shouting from one mountaintop to another as he lectured on a sutra he had translated from the Tibetan, known in Japanese as the *Nyôbosatsu-kyo*:

"If the entire earth were covered with cowhide, we could go anywhere barefoot, could we not?" He gazed over the audience, as if challenging anyone to defy him. "Of course it is impossible to do that. But! We can wrap a length of cowhide to each foot, and then go where we want."

Japanese do not usually gesticulate. Kawaguchi did, as if he were invoking lightning from his mountaintop. Each gesture came with an audible flow and ripple of the robes, like fabric thunderclouds that gave buoyancy to his words. "It is the eternal ideal, our wish from ancient times, to have a world of no sickness! No dispute! No war! However . . . this is impossible for us to achieve! It is impossible! As impossible as covering the earth with cowhide!"

He paused, like a thunderbolt suspended in midair waiting to strike. The thunderbolt softened, and he looked into and through his listeners, from one side of the room to the other, the faintest smile shining from his Tibetan tanned face. He spoke in a whisper that rolled through to the back of the room. "But the moment we arouse the Bodhi mind—the moment we become enlightened, and begin living our lives for humanity . . ." The smile grew deeper. ". . . it will be the same as achieving the goals we envision for the world." His gaze shifted back and forth through a roomful of awe. Then his eyes turned into two Tibetan suns, he summoned the thunderbolt, and roared from his mountain, "You cannot cover the earth with cowhide! So stop trying! Arouse the Bodhi mind! Wrap a length of cowhide to each foot! And live your lives according to the goals you envision for the world!" And in a final wave of the hand, flourish of the robes, and a bellow, he drove the thunderbolt into us and welded his message to our bones: "*A length of cowhide to each foot!!!*"

I was not yet ready to wrap my feet in cowhide, but that chance encounter gave me the idea of searching for a Buddhist priest to help me advance further in Japanese studies.

The Japanese language has an extensive scale of polite and formal speech; one advantage of this is that it lends itself easily to avoiding substance while increasing the intensity of courtesy. This is a nightmare for diplomatic translators who must often find a meaningful term to explain a meaningless one. Another characteristic of the language is that the speech of men and women are clearly different, in verb endings, in the use of particles. I avoided offers from women who suggested an exchange of Japanese for English or French—a few tried flattering me by pretending to want to learn Swedish—and avoided mixing females with language education.

The Buddhist priest who became my teacher instructed me in a cross-weave of grammar and tenets. His temple was open two days a week for citizens to come and sit in meditation, and I became the lone non-Japanese in the hall. Before each session, the head monk lectured to us:

"Live each moment only in that moment! Pour all your energy into the present, and do not let the mind wander into the past, into the future! Become one with the moment and live in the present! Forget the self! Pour all your energy into each moment, one moment at a time!"

The head monk lectured us after the session also, when we were still sitting, and the only tenet that might sound reasonable would be to straighten my legs. He admonished from the gut in words that came like daggers of compassion: "Become one with the moment. Live in the present! When working, work only! When eating, eat only! When in the bath, the bath only! When sitting in meditation, meditation only!"

During meditation, the monk walks in front of the line of us with a long, flat stick. When he senses a wandering mind, he stops in front of the person and strikes the top of one shoulder, then the other, the muscle just next to the neck. Actually, if done well it is a welcome massage to tensed muscles. But neither striking nor effort can keep the mind from wandering ... to leg cramps ... back pains ... shoulder tissues turned to wood ...

"When you sit in meditation, you must think nothing. Ah, you think that is simple, that nothing is just nothing! But nothing is *not* just nothing."

Legs and feet go numb; erotic images dance on the mind's stage. Noriko's brocade leaves fell over me again and again. Female spies bared their buttocks and curled their lie-detector toes into the agony of my back muscles. The swimmer's thighs assaulted me. Physical tension and mental wanderings are by-products of untrained meditation sitters—of the untrained in living life.

My Buddhist priest instructor taught me the prophecy of "The End of the Law." According to Buddhism, from about a thousand years ago the world entered a period of moral decay that marked the beginning of total disintegration of human life on Earth, the result of growing away from the teachings of Buddha. When I first heard of the prophecy, I still felt that intelligence had the power to neutralize the evil of its own creations. Things have happened since then that have changed my mind and that make me thankful for the wisdom of the Buddhists that I learned in Japan. And for the maze called Tokyo that zigzagged me to Kawaguchi in his Tibetan robes. His message came from over the ocean and has kept me alive to write these last words.

· 13 ·
A Puzzle in Kyoto

I was planning a trip to the ancient capital of Kyoto, and as I looked over the map of Japan, my eye wandered down to Hiroshima, where one of the world's better-known naval shipyards in the neighboring city of Kure snuggled into the eastern side of Hiroshima Bay. Kure was also a gateway to the naval academy at Etajima. The map I had was rather old, and I decided to obtain a newer one. When I did, I saw that a section of the bay that contained several islands was completely blanked out. Checking it against the old map, I noted the names of some of the islands that had disappeared, wondering why they had. That puzzle remained until I first solved another one in Kyoto.

I boarded the first-class car of the westbound express, the *Tsubame*—the "Swallow." The seats were lounge chairs that were not fixed to the floor, so one could slide them about at will. Kyoto was slightly more than five hundred kilometers distant. We departed Tokyo at 0900 under tow of an electric locomotive powered from overhead cables through a pantograph. One hundred twenty-six kilometers later, we emerged from the Tanna tunnel, almost eight kilometers in length, where a fast, well-rehearsed change gave us a steam locomotive up front, a handsome, three-cylinder friendly monster with six driving wheels.

One of the passengers I struck up a conversation with was a bank executive who was headed for Osaka. I mentioned the efficiency of the Japanese railway system.

"A railway system was one of the goals of the new government after the Meiji Restoration," he told me. "It was a visible, traveling symbol of the new government, something to stimulate both commerce and faith in the new nation—loyalty, if you wish. So Japan was eager to develop railways."

"Most countries without the technology have their railways built by outsiders. I understand Japan did it differently."

"Oh, Japan had offers," he responded. "The United States and England both offered to develop our railways for us. But the leaders back then were wary. Remember, Japan modernized to protect us against the colonizing nations—the white nations, if you will excuse me."

"No offense—history is history."

"Our leaders looked at India and Africa and saw how railways were instruments to further colonialism. So Japan wanted to go it alone, but we had no finances and no experience. Then our leaders fell victim to their naiveté. An Englishman came and offered to lend Japan the money personally, with no government or business involvement, no fear of colonization. Even in secret if Japan wished. At twelve percent interest!"

"A formidable rate. And how did Japan respond?"

"At first the leaders accepted. Then an article in the London newspapers opened the scheme; it reported that this same man had borrowed the money in England at nine percent interest."

"So he was making three percent just in the transfer. That explains the high interest rate he demanded, at a time when Japan was under a struggling, new government."

"I have to admire his cunning. After all, that is what banking is about—lending depositors' money at a greater profit then one must pay the depositor. I also realize that our leaders did not have experience in this kind of financial deception and were easy targets. After they recovered from the shock, they paid off the loan and applied to a foreign bank for a legitimate loan. They still needed technology, so they used the money to hire Western engineers—as employees only! And, Japan controlled her own railway destiny."

In silence, I recalled how India's railways were developed in a north-south direction to haul cotton out for the British textile industry, and how Japan herself used the South Manchuria Railway to colonize northeastern China. Yet I had to admire the insight that Japan exhibited in her modern-nation infancy.

▪ ▪ ▪

When the train approached a tunnel, the veteran riders knew it and closed the windows while the attendant in the car also went into action. Of course, smoke always found an entranceway. And, as we wound around curves, the smoke swirled back at us like a snake biting its own tail. The first-class car had screens on the windows that kept cinders out, but one arrives with soot as souvenirs of the trip. We pulled into the station at Kyoto exactly on schedule, at 1625. Washstands on the platform, where locomotive coal dust that had risen up through the stack continued its journey down through Kyoto's sewers, were well populated. Women rushed to the ladies' room in the station to change clothes before going into the city.

Relaxing in a bath at the Kyoto Inn was a welcome end to the journey, and I looked forward to several days of exploring the city and its environs.

I admired Japanese ceramic crafts, and in discussing this with the owner of the inn, he told me that his wife's brother was a potter. Mathematically, this was understandable. Ceramics and textiles formed the major part of Kyoto's traditional crafts for centuries, dating back to when these trades served the city's imperial court and nobility. Pointing to a Kyoto resident at random, like drawing a card from a deck, yields a high probability of choosing someone who is somehow related to one of those trades. I said that I would appreciate a chance to see ceramics being made, and the next day I watched the innkeeper's brother-in-law working at his potter's wheel. That evening I was standing next to the walled-in inferno known as a climbing kiln. These are a succession of long, walk-in chambers with rounded tops, each several meters long and joined along their length, each chamber rising in progressive elevations above the next like a series of earthen waves. Each chamber is entered at the ends for stocking the un-fired pieces, then sealed with bricks. Small openings allow for viewing the fire and feeding in wood fuel. This climbing construction causes the fire to circulate from each chamber into the next higher one and achieves ex-tremely high internal temperatures. The entire kiln has a roof above it, in essence a long umbrella. The innkeeper's brother-in-law was my guide.

"Those men throwing in the wood," he explained, "are fire tenders. Once a kiln is filled, they fire it and they live here."

"They live here?"

"Alongside the kiln. They watch the fire continuously and feed in the fuel at the right time to keep the temperature up."

"And how long does the kiln stay fired?"

"About four or five days."

"So they eat and sleep here, too?"

"That's right. These people are specialists in firing kilns. When they finish here they go on to the next, and the next, according to schedule. Then back here again for the next firing at this kiln."

The foot of the mountain range at the eastern edge of Kyoto has an ideal slope for climbing kilns, and over the centuries they flourished like a growing family of headless dragons clinging to the foothills, each breathing smoke for a few days, then relapsing into hibernation.

I looked through the viewing hole into the swirl of fire. Flames of twelve to thirteen hundred degrees Celsius whipped around inside. "This is my chamber," the potter shouted over the atonal drone. "I have about one half of it." We walked to a quieter place. "Each potter must fill the space he contracts for. If not, the fire does not circulate well, and this could affect pieces in adjoining chambers. So we are all responsible for having our part of the kiln stacked by firing time."

"And when will this firing end?" I asked.

"Tomorrow is the last day. Then it will take about a day to cool down enough to go inside and handle the pieces. If you want, you can come by to watch the kiln emptying."

I spent the next two days visiting Kyoto's gardens with a side trip to the village of Sakurai. I noticed something on Kyoto homes that I never saw in Tokyo: a figure of an ancient Chinese warrior, usually about twenty centimeters or so, fastened to the front of homes. I asked the innkeeper about it.

"That is Shôki," he advised. It comes from a Chinese legend and found its way into Japan around the ninth century. Kyoto was then the capital and absorbed much of its culture from China. Shôki became a protector of homes, especially in this part of Japan."

"I'd like to buy one to bring back to Tokyo with me."

"They're made by the same people who make roof tiles. I'll show you where you can find them."

When I went back to the kiln for the emptying, the end walls of the chambers were dismantled and potters were retrieving their works. At one corner of the site other potters were smashing pieces they had just retrieved.

"We always expect a certain amount of rejects," my companion explained, "because of defects that occur in firing. A glaze may run or become discolored. A piece may deform. If air bubbles remained in the clay before firing, they will expand and the piece will crack or break."

"And you could not sell some as seconds?"

"Our seal is impressed into the clay before firing and we do not want substandard works with our name circulating in the market."

The "smashing corner" was a pile of broken shards. Exquisite, hand-painted flowers on tiny flakes of porcelain blossomed into jagged edges, calculated loss averages suffered by heat, which can nurture clay into art or destroy its value.

I also saw industrial products coming out of the kiln, porcelain insulators for overhead electric wires and guides for yarn winding. There were ring guides, through which yarn passes in its journey from skein to spindle, and travel guides that reciprocate along the spindle to build up the yarn evenly.

"So Kyoto ceramics are not all art," I commented to the potter.

"That's correct. Look here. Can you imagine what these are?"

"Cores for resistors. I used to fool with radio sets."

"Kyoto has many cottage industries. These will go to families who wind them with the number of turns to reach the proper resistance. Then they send them to the manufacturer."

The size of the chambers permits firing large pieces, and as we talked three men were taking a strange-looking object from the kiln. It was a vertically standing cylinder almost two meters in height and one meter in diameter. Apertures about ten centimeters in diameter covered the surface, and a series of stubby arms, apparently mounts to hold other parts, jutted from the face of the piece.

"And what might that be?" I asked the potter. He gave me a slight nod of the head with a somewhat bashful smile, a bit uneasy over not being able to answer. He strolled over to ask.

"We were just given the design," I heard one answer. "We don't know either."

Another, who had given the potter a warmer nod of recognition, added, "Japanese army officers don't say much; only 'make this.'"

The men crated the piece to load and ship out. One marked the destination on the crate: "Okunoshima." It was a four-character name, not common in locality names. It was in my memory somewhere, and after I took leave of the potter and walked back through the street, I remembered: Okunoshima was one of the islands in Hiroshima Bay that disappeared from the map. But what was that strange ceramic piece? And why was it headed for an island that disappeared? When the boxes were delivered, would they fall into the bay where the island had been? Where was the island now? Navigating through the air like Laputa? I took those questions into the bath that night.

I returned to Tokyo with some splendid vases and fine pieces for warming and drinking *sake*, and a slate-gray figure of the protector, Shôki. I also carried the puzzle of that strange industrial ceramic of unfathomable purpose headed for an island that had disappeared.

· 14 ·
The American President Was Trying

The mood in America was bad for Europe. When Germany started taking over neighboring countries, I realized that nothing on the continent could match the Nazi war machine, and I looked for military assistance by the United States. Americans, though, were demonstrating against getting into another overseas conflict, and KEEP U.S. OUT OF WAR buttons were popular accessories. Congress was the real barrier, with only 10 percent of its members willing to go to war in Europe—"*Unless attacked!*" That was the phrase that closed all discussions about whether or not America should take up arms. And war declarations, according to their Constitution, are in principle made by Congress. If America were to come to our assistance, I saw hope outside of that principle, in a breakdown in American constitutional government. And, I saw optimistic signs it was happening.

I studied Franklin D. Roosevelt's rise in politics—the cards in his career—that would help me read his plays on the public table. Back when he was governor of New York, Roosevelt said that if he were to start life over in a new career he would choose advertising. Advertising and drama have something in common: both seek to convince that the unreal is real. Advertising tries to make one product among similar products appear superior, or convince its audience that a purchase will bring benefits beyond reality. Drama seeks to evoke real emotions for fictional situations. As radio and the movie camera developed, drama was given a chance for a bigger role in politics. I was glad to see a union of advertising and drama in the White House, because Europe's hope for American military help rested on the president's skill in making America believe the script over reality—in faking a bet.

President Roosevelt drew up plans for U.S. forces to occupy Greenland and Iceland and was aiming for an American occupation of the Azores and Martinique. This ignited congressmen and newsmen into protests that he was taking America to war and pushed America's war fears to a higher pitch. The president knew he could not counteract them by trying to scream louder. America's families wanted to be soothed, and he did it with his "Fireside Chats," radio monologues of skill and intimacy that bathed fearful Americans in the balm of what they wanted to believe.

Roosevelt's understanding of political drama led him to choose a playwright for a scriptwriter, someone with skills honed on a different grindstone from that of speechwriters. The president came into homes on radio waves in the role of family protector, the human counterpart of the ceramic Shôki that stands guard over Kyoto homes. Amidst the growing war fears in America, this was the only bid that could accomplish his first goal of breaking the two-term tradition to stay in office. Europe needed him in the game until he could throw out the card I knew he was holding. My fear was that if he could not play it soon, there would be no Europe left.

Optimistic signs emerged around the time I arrived in Japan. In October 1937, the president sounded warnings against America's trying to escape world events through isolation or neutrality—*conventional* neutrality, I am sure he meant. He said that "peace-loving nations" had to work together to quarantine and stop aggression. With Germany sending fear through Europe it seemed a welcome message, but the speech shocked Congress into raising its guard higher against another military move toward Europe. The president's direction was clearer, however, and this was encouraging.

In 1939 the president gave another reassuring sign when he tried to press a repeal of America's Arms Embargo Act. The firepower of the arms was of no consequence: America's weapons then were obsolete, but I would have been equally grateful for shipments of wooden rifles. Moves had to be made in steps, and the value of American arms would serve as the tip of a wedge that could open the way to meaningful involvement. The stay-out-of-war mood of the House defeated the repeal attempt, but again, the American president's hand bore hope.

Ambassadors are usually dead cards in political games, but occasionally they are played. The American president tried it with his ambassador to

France. In diplomatic terms of lace that leave interpretations of space and substance open to argument, William Bullitt uttered something between possibility and promise that if France entered the war, the United States would join her, and he urged the French to take a firm stand against Hitler. This was a strange reversal in the roles played before World War I, when Europe's leading families were pressing America to come and fight. America obliged then, and those memories were an obstacle to bringing us their forces again.

In September 1938, the term *appeasement* was given a new connotation. It shed the positive sense of a peacemaking process and method of coexisting that it held for five centuries when Britain and France split up Czechoslovakia and threw the Czech Sudetenland to Hitler. Neville Chamberlain, at the Munich Conference, attempted to satiate Nazi hunger by letting Germany swallow Poland and belch a promise to eat no more: an attempt to "live in the present" by trying to draw a line for someone else's ambition. Complications set in when British business declared neutrality: The Federation of British Industries—with cabinet men among its members—made a secret trade agreement with the Nazi government. Was British industry aiding in the destruction of Britain? And would British industry aid the Nazis in someday fighting Scandinavia? There was a limit to how many moves ahead I could see in this *shogi* match. Japanese leaders were reading it their own way. Yamamoto brought me the story.

"We have some anti-British elements in government, you know that," Yamamoto said. "And they're not all army, either. Now they have new fuel for their hatred."

"The appeasement at Munich?"

"Hmmm. They see it as a sneaky British diplomatic trick to push Hitler's armies eastward into Poland and away from France."

I had to admit to a certain logic in the reasoning. Then, encouragement came in messages from London. Harry Hopkins, a close associate of the American president, was becoming clearer in his promises that America would come to England's aid. But days of watching his attempts only convinced me again that diplomats are rarely of use in effecting changes, except in rescheduling cocktail parties.

The Danish underground intelligence network had grown into a formidable information organization. With the outbreak of war, the network's

Erling Foss and his wife moved to Stockholm and, since Sweden was not occupied by Germany, Foss made it a focal point for information from agents worldwide. In addition, I had personal ties with Danish underground members. I received a coded message from one.

"Disgust is growing in British government circles because the American president is not coming through with his promise. Things are looking up for us. Roosevelt asks for understanding and places all blame on Congress for his inability to act. The president reported to Churchill that he first has to win the war with Congress before he can get American soldiers overseas into the real war."

After Congress, the State Department was Roosevelt's next obstacle. It was our fortune that the president despised the State Department, and he handled it by appointing a secretary of state who was too innocent to realize that he was there to neutralize the post. Cordell Hull was the crybaby of Washington, repeatedly vowing to quit for being overlooked by the president. Roosevelt could read him, and kept him in the post with a carrot-on-a-stick promise of a chance at the presidency; Hull eventually set a record of twelve years in the position. He would have made a terrible poker player, perhaps on a par with Noriko. She could not fake a bet; Hull could not read a faked bet.

My studies in Japanese culture included brief lessons in the tea ceremony. I enjoy the tea—tart, piquant, stimulating—but I cannot say the same for the rote bowing, memorized motion drills, and the group silence it demands. My interest in the ceremonial part is in its use to prevent insurrection. In the sixteenth century, when leaders were constantly alert to betrayal by their subordinates, Toyotomi Hideyoshi ordered his commanders to study the tea ceremony. Launching a coup requires collusion and planning, while the tea ceremony is a lengthy formality heavily influenced by the Catholic mass that came into Japan with Portuguese merchant-missionaries. Both rites require a similar silence. Punctilious, time-consuming tea rituals imprisoned commanders in a communication vacuum; plans for insurrection were quarantined, one might say, in the confines of the tearoom. As Europe and Asia grew into the hot zones of the world, Roosevelt locked his secretary of state into a tea ceremony with an assignment to handle affairs concerning South America, where little of global importance was happening. The tail of the great snake of State twisted and whipped in the volatile regions of the world while the president had its head clamped in the White House desk drawer. Newspapers played repeatedly with Hull's glaring absence at one important international meeting after the other. Secretary of the Treasury Henry Morgenthau Jr. and Hull's subordinates played bigger roles than Hull in what was really Hull's territory. His energies were spent trying to grasp the illusion of his title, but like the dagger before Lady Macbeth, his authority was not palpable.

In March 1939, when Hitler seized the rest of Czechoslovakia, the president snubbed Hull and sent the undersecretary, Sumner Welles, to meet with State's European specialists and decide America's response. Welles came up with the predictable diplomatic stand that America would neither break relations with Germany nor recognize her annexation. Hull scrambled to gain credit for the move and told the press that he drafted the statement. When the truth broke, it was another embarrassment for Hull, another assurance to me that the president was eroding the obstacle of the State Department. It was frustrating, though, that Washington was moving with reaction times left over from the days of muzzle-loaders and sailing ships. They were out of pace with Europe's needs, out of pace with the ambitions of the American president. But, he was trying.

▪ 15 ▪

Japan's Army Versus Navy

" **W**hen I was appointed navy vice-minister back in 1936," Yamamoto said as he shuffled the cards one day in the spring of 1939, "I had to swap the ocean for an office-boy position."

"An office boy of considerable power, I'd say."

"I was trained as a gunnery officer, and now," he added with his brand of humor that often came without a smile, "my caliber has been reduced to the diameter of an official seal, stamping my approval on papers. There's no roar of gunpowder; just 'stamp-stamp-stamp.'"

"An official seal can have greater firepower than a warship's battery," I reminded him. "It can start a war. Or stop one."

"That's what I'm afraid of," he half mumbled into his cards.

"Oh?"

"You remember in 1936, our military attaché in Berlin, Major-General Oshima, pushed through the Anti-Comintern Pact between Japan and Germany?"

"Yes, soon after Hitler swung Tokyo into hosting the 1940 Olympics. They were both moves against the Soviet Union."

A long drag on his Cherry cigarette. "The pact was a faked bet! Sure, Japan would like to keep another Russo-Japanese War from breaking out. But the army officers had something else in mind. I didn't find out about it for a while, but Oshima and Ribbentrop were dancing together from early last year."

"Joachim von Ribbentrop, the German foreign minister."

"Hmmm. Hitler's top diplomacy artist. Oshima and Ribbentrop were trying to pull the two countries together into some kind of pact. As you know, we in the navy have been fighting any political moves that would put us against Britain or America. Britain is our naval model. It's also the model for the Japanese imperial family. And Ribbentrop is the worst man Japan could have in there as the contact between Japan and Germany. He hates the British for a personal reason."

"Personal?"

"A stupid personal reason. Ribbentrop was once ambassador to Great Britain. He was also in the champagne business. The British didn't like that—you know how the British can be; they have a great navy but they sometimes suffer from personality problems."

"Most people call it snobbishness, but it does have its charm, the way the British handle it."

"Well, they didn't handle it too well with their resentment for this German dealer in French champagne. When Ribbentrop's son tried to get into Harrow and Eton, he was turned down out of spite. And papa became very angry. And very anti-British."

"But you say that the military attaché was working all this in Berlin. That's not usually the office that directs national policy."

"Not usually, no. I was naval attaché in Washington from 1926, but I did not steer Japan's relations with the country. It should be the government acting through its ambassador. But the ambassador to Germany was Togo Shigenori, and he was against forming alliances. He was smart in that sense. So in 1938 the officers in Tokyo arranged some transfers and they got rid of Togo by making him ambassador to Moscow. That let them move Oshima into the ambassador's position. He was also promoted to lieutenant-general that year, because he's as stupid as the army idiots here in Tokyo." Cherry ashes fluttered to the table. "Oh, sorry," he said, brushing them into the ashtray.

"Out-of-season cherry blossoms," I chided.

"Of course," Yamamoto continued, "Hitler's Tokyo Olympic move was to gain a two-front military ally against the Soviets, but there is no need for Japan to take the bait."

I went to a filing cabinet and took out a folder of newspaper clippings. "I thought you might be interested in these. Hector Bywater has been throwing acid comments against the British government for some time; he sends warnings about Germany's motives and he writes that the Chamberlain government is not smart enough to recognize them."

Yamamoto looked over the articles and grunted. "I wish some of our own journalists could write things like that. But with the army in control they know better."

"The news often points up how the Japanese army and navy have different ways of looking at things."

"Just about one hundred eighty degrees different. Literally. The army's hypothetical enemy is Russia. That's no problem. The navy's hypothetical enemy has been America since 1909. The background for that was in preparation for an assumed American opposition to Japanese policy in China. But the purpose of a hypothetical enemy is for maneuvers, not directing national policy. The trouble with the army is that they keep advocating northward expansion in the nonhypothetical world. The war in China was supposed to be over in a matter of months and it's been eight years now. They've controlled China thus far because Japan has better weapons, but they keep looking at Russia and pushing for northward expansion. They think this country of eighty million people can take on China and Russia together. Those army men see dreams of heroes and think like children."

"And the navy has other ideas, of course."

"If Japan is looking to expand, we should take Great Britain as an example. And the British navy as a model."

"It always was, wasn't it?"

"In naval tactics, yes. But I mean national strategy. England is an island nation with few natural resources, like us. But she gained possessions far out of proportion to her size through naval power. The Japanese navy wants a southward-advance policy because it will take us to the resources we need. So now we're in civil war, army versus navy. You know my immediate superior, Admiral Yonai?"

"I've only met him briefly, never really spoken at length."

"Yonai and I were in gunnery school together. I know his thinking from way back. He spent time in Europe and he knows the German government. He's been telling the cabinet that the Nazis are a dangerous, strong-arm bunch, with strange ideas. He and I are the cabinet members working hardest to keep Japan away from forming an alliance. And the army officers hate us for it. They may look impressive in their uniforms, but those army fellows are like little kids looking for a big brother to latch onto." He punctuated his remark with a negative shake of the head, a look of disgust, and a sip of seltzer.

In April of that year of 1939, Yamamoto made a three-day trip to his hometown in Niigata. When he returned, the cabinet, under Premier Kiichiro Hiranuma, had already held seventy meetings on whether or not to sign a pact with Nazi Germany.

"Seventy meetings going in circles and hitting walls," Yamamoto said wryly as he opened a new pack of Cherry cigarettes." And the Imperial Japanese Navy is being blamed with stronger words every day."

"Oh? For the cabinet's circles?"

"For the walls. We are the walls, and we refuse to go along with the army's push to ally with Germany, so there's been no conclusion. Fortunately." Yamamoto took a puff and continued. "This Hiranuma is a prize prime minister. He's an aristocrat, ready to slaughter any Chinese standing in the way of Japan's occupation. You remember he took over the government in January from that other aristocrat, Konoe. So far, Hiranuma's magnificent accomplishment has been getting the emperor interested in composing *waka.*"

I did not quite follow the meaning. "Has poetry anything to do with the present situation?"

He laughed internally without changing expression. "You've studied enough Japanese to know how *waka* is considered the true mode of expression of the Japanese people."

"'The Way of Ancient Japan,' is what it's sometimes called, if I'm not mistaken."

"That was the problem. This emperor never composed *waka,* and Hiranuma thought this was a serious deficiency. So he set up a *waka* composition gathering in the imperial palace in order to catch the emperor's attention—nobody could approach him directly on this. When the emperor asked what these gatherings were, Hiranuma told him, then asked if his majesty would not care to join in. And that's how the emperor started composing *waka*. But during all this concern over the emperor's poetry, the prime minister and the army kept pushing us deeper into war in China, and closer to an alliance with Germany. The emperor and court circles all detest Germany, and they let it be known."

About a month after that talk, in May 1939, the clash that Umezu had expected broke out between Japanese and Russian troops at a place called Nomonhan on the Mongolian border with the Japanese state of Manchukuo. It was a full-scale battle with tanks, artillery, and aircraft over useless territory that was claimed by both countries. Japan could have called on Germany for help under the terms of the Anti-Comintern Pact, and as Japanese losses mounted, there was growing reason to make the call. But on August 21 in Berlin, the idol of the Japanese army slapped Japan in the face with one hand and shook hands with Stalin with the other: German radio announced that the Nazis would sign a nonaggression treaty with the Soviets. The pact stunned Tokyo's Nazi admirers. The Hiranuma cabinet went into accelerated confusion, during which time Yamamoto called and asked if he could drop in for a "break from the madness."

The world situation was becoming cloudier for both of us. A union between Germany and the Soviets meant that Europe could be trampled by the world's two most powerful military forces, with Scandinavia in the jaws of a pincers between them. Europe, passively, exchanged a German-Japanese alliance for a German-Soviet pact, and the Japanese army's efforts to unite with their heroes hit a stumbling block. I waited in the garden, hitting the overhead punching bag until Yamamoto came up the side street.

"Nice rhythm," he said as he came through the door. "I could hear it from the street. It's a shame you can't practice on some army heads like that. It might raise their intelligence."

We went inside and I opened a bottle of seltzer for us, with a touch of aquavit on the side for me.

"We've been trying to educate the Japanese that the Nazis are a tricky bunch—not to be trusted," he said as he lit a Cherry.

"The fighting in Nomonhan is turning into a disaster for the Japanese army," I ventured. "With the Germans and Soviets in a pact of nonaggression,

Japan lost the chance to call in the German army for help. It would have been a blessing for both Japan and Europe if Germany and the Soviets exhausted each other. The Russo-German pact changed that. What do you see as the outcome?"

"Disaster—unless a truce can be worked out. There's talk of it, in which case it will be disaster with a truce. The emperor told the army to avoid a clash with the Soviets, but army officers don't listen to anyone except each other. I just hope Germany's move woke up some army sleepyheads, but don't underestimate their stupidity." He exhaled in smoky exasperation. "What do you think is behind it? What's in those Nazi minds?"

"If it means anything, this pact came just after the Interparliamentary Union Conference at Oslo. I was in touch with events there. An American congressman, Hamilton Fish, was elected president of the American delegation because of his antiwar reputation. He believed that Danzig was the thorn in the issue. The city's ninety percent German, and years ago the people voted to be returned to Germany. But the Treaty of Versailles gave it to Poland. Germany wanted it returned to the Reich with a Polish access corridor. Before the conference, this Mr. Fish spoke with the leaders of England and France, then went to Germany to meet von Ribbentrop. Actually, von Ribbentrop provided a plane to get Fish to Oslo on time. Fish proposed a thirty-day moratorium on war to settle the Danzig issue."

"It didn't seem to get very far."

"Great Britain and Norway were against it. Talk among the delegates was that Roosevelt squeezed the British to refuse it, and our neighbors the Norwegians were aligned with British interests."

"Do you think it might have accomplished anything?" Yamamoto asked, with doubt in his voice and face.

"I really can't say. Honestly speaking, Germany had supportable claims to Danzig. Remember that the last day in March this year, Britain reversed five years of foreign policy when she announced a guarantee of Polish independence, and Poland included Danzig. Then about five months later, on the seventeenth of this month at Oslo, Britain refused the proposed moratorium, and four days after that Germany announced its decision to sign a pact with the Soviets."

"Hitler changed enemies," Yamamoto said half under his breath.

"Communism was Hitler's avowed enemy," I continued. "An unlikely partner for Germany. The question is, if Danzig had been settled, would Hitler then have carried out his plans to fight Russia? With Japan already fighting at Nomonhan, it seems like something that he would take advantage of. It's the beginning of the two-front war that Hitler was engineering when he pushed Tokyo for the 1940 Olympics."

Yamamoto picked up the cards and began shuffling. "As Yonai said over and over, they're a dangerous bunch with strange ideas."

Hitler and Stalin signed their pact that August 23, and Hitler followed up with an order to mobilize the German army. Britain reversed position and urged negotiated settlement of the Danzig problem. The prime minister of France, the king of Belgium, the pope, and even Mussolini protested the mobilization and negotiation, but Poland clung to its paper promise by the British and refused open negotiations. Nervous messages crisscrossed Europe.

On August 29 in Tokyo the madness from which Yamamoto escaped fell apart: the entire cabinet resigned over the "complex and bizarre aspect" of the situation and a new cabinet was formed. In the reshuffling, Yamamoto was relieved of his official stamp and given a sea position as commander-in-chief of the Combined Fleet. His immediate superior, Admiral Yonai, also lost his post and was assigned a nongovernmental position. The navy's two strongest opponents to joining the Nazis were removed from political power.

I received a call from Yamamoto on the evening of August 30. "I had my investment ceremony at the imperial palace this afternoon and I'm back at the Navy Ministry now, straightening things up."

"Trimming ship for your successor?"

"Yes, he can install his own confusion. I'll leave him the paperwork to do that and I'll take my copy of the *Manyoshu* to read on board. I'll be leaving Tokyo by train tomorrow—to Osaka. I'll stay there overnight, then a short train ride to Wakanoura Bay to join the fleet. So I just want to wish you goodbye."

"I'll be waiting for the next chance we have to meet again."

"It shouldn't be too long; Yokosuka is our home port, and I'll have to come to Tokyo and the Navy Ministry now and then. Keep the cards warm. And the seltzer cool."

Talk circulated in Japan that Yamamoto was the one who could stop Japan from joining the Axis; his transfer to sea was a victory for the pro-Nazis. In his "office boy" role in the cabinet, he could influence foreign policy, and Yamamoto himself often stated that naval officers not in a cabinet position, or chief of the Naval General Staff, should stay out of politics. Yamamoto's command of eighty ships of the world's third-largest navy seemed impressive, but he was evicted from a role of political influence to that of a naval tactician with the duty of obeying Tokyo.

Two days after Yamamoto's phone call, the first of September 1939 hit the calendar like an earthquake. Germany stormed into Poland; two days later, England and France declared war on Germany and looked to America to come through with her promise, while Japanese army officers admired their conquering heroes. But casualties in the Nomonhan border dispute had reached half a million, more than five to one against Soviet losses. Tokyo announced that it would not enter the European war, and America declared its neutrality with an announcement that it would not export arms to warring nations. As a punitive measure for the Nomonhan debacle, the Imperial Japanese Army replaced some of its top commanders in China, and in the shuffle Umezu was elevated to commander of the Kwantung Army, with a dual title of ambassador plenipotentiary to the puppet state of Manchukuo. All this in the first week of the month. On the fifteenth, in Moscow, a truce between Japan and the Soviets officially ended the fighting at Nomonhan. It yielded an education for Japan, showing her leaders that if the two countries were to come together in a conflict again, Japan did not yet have the military power to handle it, and her armies needed greater military science and physical endurance.

Yamamoto's subordinates had an ongoing guessing contest: Where did their commander spend his time ashore? When his flagship pulled into Yokosuka, he usually advised his staff that he was staying at an inn, and from there the question of where he really was became a shipboard game. Some of that time he spent with his wife; other times he was with one of his lady friends at a teahouse. And I am sure that on many occasions while we were at cards he was rumored to be with this or that lady somewhere hidden from view.

One afternoon toward the end of 1939, when Yamamoto was again navigating on seltzer water, I asked him about his move into command of the Combined Fleet.

"Once I got to the ships it was fine. But the trip down was marred by cockroaches."

"Cockroaches? On the train?"

"Secret police. They're marked cards."

"You mean the secret police are even watching the commander-in-chief of the Combined Fleet of the Imperial Japanese Navy?"

"They watch everyone. Probably you, too. Let them watch; there are more important things happening. You remember how my former navy minister and I had led the opposition to the army's push into the German lap?"

"Impossible to forget."

"Well, it looks like Yonai will be able to carry on the fight again."

"As navy minister again?"

He shook his head in the negative. "Prime minister."

"Admiral Yonai? How did that happen?"

Another swig of seltzer water. "He's supported by pro-British and pro-American statesmen, but they're not strong enough to counter the army's muscle."

"I would imagine not."

"That's why the emperor is putting him up for prime minister."

"The emperor!"

I must have dropped my poker guard. The emperor rarely pushes governmental changes or actions. This was a rare departure from normal practice, just as it was also rare for a Japanese to speak this freely about the emperor. But Harvard had bonded Yamamoto and me into a close friendship, and my residence was a psychological extraterritorial enclave for the admiral, as it was for the swimming schoolteacher. He continued.

"The emperor is worried about Japan's fate being in the hands of the army. And he is strongly against an alliance with Germany."

"Do you think that even as prime minister Yonai can gain enough influence over the generals?"

"The emperor hopes so. If someone doesn't put a course change on Japan, we'll be at war with Britain and America, and the emperor feels that Yonai is one man who can save us from that."

Europe's assistance from America was down to a question of global timing. If war broke out between Japan and the United States, it would force both countries to concentrate in the Pacific. The Japanese army would likely shift away from a German alliance, and America might turn away from Europe. If the American president could bring about a confrontation with Germany first, it would also tend to dissuade Japan from pressing an alliance that would involve her armies in Europe. The U.S. president's term would end the following year, and a change in presidency would interrupt the momentum toward the one-man rule in America that we needed. He took another step toward Europe in November of 1939 when he won a long fight and finally pushed through the repeal of America's Arms Embargo Act. This sent her Neutrality Act overboard and put the country closer to combat, at least on paper.

As 1939 wore on, Europe's fate was being decided by a game of shifting alliances being played against the clock; and the last chance to prevent Japan's alliance with Germany was falling into the hands of a Japanese admiral being readied for the prime minister's seat in a den of army wolves.

· 16 ·
America and I Were Curious

A Colonel John Hansen of the United States Army Medical Corps made an appointment to call on me. When he arrived, he was quick to inform me that he was of Swedish background. Apparently the Americans thought it might give us some camaraderie. He soon got to the point.

"You know about that battle in Nomonhan," he said.

"A real war, and one that the world paid little attention to."

"It seemed senseless as wars go," he continued. "A sort of 'war of the maps' you could call it. That stretch of land has no real value, but on Soviet maps it was theirs, and on Japanese maps it was Japan's."

"Value," I countered, "is not always intrinsic. The value of gold in a coin may be just a tiny fraction of the coin's buying power. It's the surrounding social organizations that change meaning and value. In the thirty-plus years since the Russo-Japanese War, the fighting continued in the guts of the Soviets and the Japanese. The territory had greater meaning as a trigger mechanism than any use it might be put to. But I agree with you that there was also a senseless element involved. Not one soldier who fought on either side for that land would want to live there. Or even visit the place again."

"There is one thing that we are looking at surrounding that battle, and perhaps your experience in Japan might help."

"Well, I've been here only three years or so."

"But we notice that you communicate easily in Japanese circles."

"Oh? You've been watching me?"

"Not in that sense. But we are interested in anyone with . . . *insight*, let us say. And we admire your ability with the language. Also, the 'war,' such as it was, involved Scandinavia's thorn, so we were wondering if you would lend us any opinions. Actually, it concerns my branch of the service, the medical corps."

"I don't know if I can help, but please go on."

"We understand that a medical officer in the Japanese army by the name of Ishii received exceptional awards and commendations for his service at Nomonhan."

"Yes, I know of it."

"Frankly, we are puzzled why an army *doctor* should rate this attention. A military commander, perhaps, but medical people do not conduct wars. We—Washington included—are interested."

"From what I understand," I told him, "Ishii developed a portable water filter machine that cut down on cholera among the troops. I'm sure you know that much. There was a saying going around then that the Japanese army was hit so hard with diarrhea, most of the soldiers were fighting without pants. Ishii's system was given credit for 'getting the soldiers back in uniform,' I guess you might say."

"And you think that's all there was to it?" he asked.

I did *not*, but I was not ready to tell the American that. I was putting together some very disturbing pieces of information, and the fact that even Washington was curious about the unbalanced praise and honor thrown upon Ishii for what seemed no more than a successful carrying out of his duty gave me another piece to add to the puzzle. Colonel Hansen continued.

"There have been some leaks from imperial . . . *sources*, let me say, that when the Nomonhan dispute first started festering, the emperor warned his army leaders against letting it grow into a military conflict. He did not want to start another Russo-Japanese War."

"Apparently he did not have much success."

"Certainly not. From what we learned, after Nomonhan erupted the emperor was furious. He opposed the war when he saw it brewing and went through the ceiling afterwards. Then what happened to Ishii? First his unit was given special commendation from the commander of the Kwantung Army, and then Ishii was singled out for personal honors."

"You have much information on a person who is rarely seen."

"There are cooperative persons who would like to see Japan's army held in check. Most of the aristocrats close to the imperial family resent the army leaders—that is no secret, but it does give us eyes, so to speak, into the throne room."

"And this Ishii fellow has caught the attention of the American military?"

"Exactly. His water filtering devices were clever. The Japanese army loaded them onto trucks, drove into the battlefield, and put the pants back on the soldiers. But why are he and his unit being built up so? Medical intelligence is asking questions."

I went to a file cabinet, drew out a folder and from it and took out a clipping from a Japanese newspaper. Ishii's picture looked out from a lengthy article. "Is this what you mean?" I asked Colonel Hansen.

"That's the man," he said. "I see you're interested in him also."

"I'm interested in anything that happens. And, I'm a newspaper clipper."

"We had the article translated."

"I imagine it gave your translators a job—and maybe a few smiles, also. It sounds like the poor reporter wrote it with an army committee standing over him. Wordy and gushing, I would describe it."

"The translation came out that way. But again, look at the medals he received."

"'The Third Order of the Golden Kite,'" I read from the article, "'and the Middle Cord of the Rising Sun' is what it says here . . . 'For rendering extraordinary services.'"

"And all this for service in a conflict that the emperor ordered his army to avoid, and one that made him angry when it happened."

"On the surface," I agreed, "it does seem that it was an affront to the throne. But surely, the American army is not concerned with protecting the inviolability of the Japanese emperor."

"No, but when the Japanese army ruptures that inviolability, then pours undue honors on a medical man who was involved in it . . . But actually, that was only the first stage of America's concern. There is more we're looking at."

"Not more *awards*?" I joked.

"Not that," he responded, "but perhaps more *than* awards. Ishii apparently always had a large budget to operate with. Ever since that incident—or perhaps we are only now finding out things we did not know—he has been granted enormous funds for his use in Manchuria, and for his Army Medical

College in Tokyo. *Tremendous* sums! It's completely out of balance with any military medical unit, no matter how glorious a history it might have. It is even more puzzling to us than the awards, because medals and accolades do not strain the national budget. Ishii's expenses appear to be doing just that. And, at a time when Japan is spending huge sums on the actual fighting in China."

"On one hand," I told the American, "Japan has a history of valuing its medical department. You should know of that from the reorganization of your own medical system three decades ago."

"Yes, we did make major changes back then; my instructors in the army told us about that."

"But it does seem illogical," I had to agree. "And it's logical that you would notice it."

"We know that you are in touch with much that is happening here, and in view of the friendly relations between our two countries, we would be grateful for any information you might offer. Here is my card. Or if you wish, you can inform your ministry in Stockholm and they will contact Herschel Johnson, the American representative there."

We shook hands, and I added what he told me to the pieces of information that I was fitting together. Others came later.

One day, an article in the Japanese press once again caught my attention: ANOTHER VICTORY SHOUT FOR MILITARY MEDICINE IN MANCHURIA. Under this, the subtitle announced, "Pathogen for strange hemorrhagic fever is discovered." Then came the dramatics: "The invincible Imperial Japanese Army scores another glorious triumph!"

The leader of the army medical team, Kitano Masaji, presented his research at a convention for parasitology at Tokyo Imperial University. After that, his findings were carried in Japan's highly prestigious *Japan Journal of Pathology*. According to custom in Japan at the time, the report was titled in German; the research paper itself was in Japanese. I armed myself with a medical dictionary and drew the story from the journal.

The Manchurian disease was a local affliction that had been centered mainly in the northern region of Manchuria near the Soviet border. The disease had been called by a variety of names, usually taken from the locality where it broke out, and produced a high fever and internal bleeding. The army doctors discovered that the carrier of the disease was a virus that was carried by ticks. According to the report, the army team's methodology was intentional infection of numerous monkeys in succession in order to isolate the pathogen. With the success of the research project, the Japanese doctors standardized the name of the disease in Japanese, which translates to "epidemic hemorrhagic fever."

Something struck me in the poker-player's region of skepticism, and I wanted to get a medical man's view of this. I knew a Danish doctor in Tokyo and decided to ask his opinion. The doctor did not know much Japanese, and I started explaining the project to him, reading and paraphrasing from the Japanese medical journal.

"'The researchers went into areas where the disease was found, captured rats, and removed ticks from the rats' bodies. Two hundred ticks were ground and mixed into a saline solution. This was used to infect a monkey through injection. When the symptoms appeared . . .'"

"What kind of monkey is specified?" he asked.

"Kind of monkey? It is not stated; only 'monkey.'"

"That is strange," he said.

"Why?"

"A research report always identifies the subspecies when using monkeys in experiments. Different monkeys react differently, and identifying the subject only as 'a monkey' is not professional. It reduces the value of the report. My first impression is that the man who wrote that is an amateur."

"No," I advised the Danish doctor, "the team leader is an officer in the Japanese Army Medical Corps, with a strong background in bacteriology and virology. The German in the title is a bit broken; they need remedial work there, but the scientific credentials are all in order."

"How did the experiment proceed?" the doctor asked me.

I continued: "'After the symptoms of the disease manifested, blood was drawn and injected into the second monkey.'"

"Still no identification of subspecies?"

"Just 'monkey,' as before. 'Then, when the symptoms in that monkey were observed, the organs were removed and a portion of organ material was ground fine and mixed with a saline solution. This was then injected into another monkey, and the process was continued until the pathogen was isolated.'"

"And nowhere," the doctor asked again, "is the subspecies of monkey identified?"

I assured him not.

"Sloppy researchers," the Dane said.

I read further, where the disease generated in the monkeys caused temperature rises: "39.8 degrees Celsius, 40.2 degrees Celsius . . ."

"That's impossible," the doctor said.

"Oh?"

"No monkey can sustain body temperatures that high. It must be an error."

"I cannot guarantee that it is not. It might happen; perhaps even a misprint. But you can see the figures here, several readings from different monkeys, all centering around forty degrees."

The doctor looked at the report and asked again, "And these temperatures were observed in monkeys?"

"That is correct."

"As you surely know," he continued, "those are extremely high fevers for a human being, and they do occur. But they are impossible for a monkey. Any type of monkey. I have studied numerous reports involving animal experimentation, and I can assure you that there is error somewhere in here."

To the doctor, these were research data that did not fit. It did not take long for him to see it from another angle.

"If these men are the scientists they appear to be," he said, "the omission of clear identification of monkey subspecies is . . . *suspicious,* shall we say, when held against the obviously human characteristics in body temperature readings." The specter of his own conclusions shocked him. "My God! What kind of research *are* they doing? . . ."

"Do you mean," I asked, "that if these were humans, the report would make sense?"

"It would make *scientific* sense, yes. Horrible sense. And in a way that goes beyond the experiments themselves."

"Meaning. . .?"

"If this is a highly regarded medical journal, it means that these experiments are read by the entire medical community. What I interpreted to be sloppy research may be an open code—an admission—that humans are being sacrificed in laboratory experiments." The Dane reflected for a moment, then continued. "You have to remember that Japanese doctors are not accustomed to experimenting with monkeys; they are prohibitively expensive here. So researchers would not be familiar with a monkey's body-temperature characteristics. But in the country's most prestigious medical journal . . ."

The doctor asked me to read further. After he had heard enough, he said something as shocking as the "monkey" revelation.

"It sounds to me like they are not trying just to isolate the pathogen, but are working to increase its virulence."

"And the purpose of that would be. . . ?"

"For one thing, it would be the reverse of the normal goals of medical science. We attempt to *combat* infectious viruses and bacteria. Increasing the ability of a pathogen to *create* disease is working in the reverse direction. For any other purpose to their experiments, you will have to ask your Japanese friends. But since these are army doctors and researchers—which is to say *medical soldiers*—I would not rule out that they are developing this as a weapon."

· 17 ·
An Intimidating Fleet Move

The new year of 1940 brought the emperor his wish: Admiral Yonai became prime minister, and in mid-January he formed his cabinet. The following month his foreign minister announced, "Japan has no territorial designs in Southeast Asia, only economic. We will conclude nonaggression pacts with any other nation that has interests in the region." Army officers fumed, and the army–navy confrontation elevated. Yonai and his supporters insisted that joining with America's most hated country could steer Japan into war with the United States. Ultra-nationalists plotted Yonai's assassination; police discovered the plan and arrested more than thirty men.

Yonai's appointment to premier came by providential timing. After the blitzkrieg of Poland, Germany's conquering drive lapsed. That lowered the threshold of hero worship among Japanese army officers, and just when their enthusiasm for a German alliance was dampened with sulks of disappointment, Yonai took his post.

The Yonai cabinet was in its fourth month when the swimming pools opened in the spring of 1940, and Miss Hiraoka was looking forward to flinging her arms again in the controversial butterfly. The Western mind is baffled at how the family name is used in some cultures even among those who have become—close, in one way or another. She was still "Hiraoka-san," Miss Hiraoka, and after the German army animated itself out of the "phony war" and moved in to occupy Denmark and Norway, she brought news of one of the results.

"Helsinki cancelled the Olympiad," she said with a frown.

"I think it was expected, even before Europe was really at war."

"After the Tokyo games were cancelled my friends on the swimming team thought they might compete in Finland. Now nobody is sure if there will even be an Olympiad anymore."

"You're that pessimistic?"

"Europe is falling apart," she said with a teacher's directness, tempered with a touch of pathos. "And Japan is moving toward uniting with Germany. If it happens, the whole world will be divided into two groups: the military on one side and victims on the other."

She walked to the window, gazed out for a few moments, then turned and asked me a question almost as if I were her pupil in school. "You are always talking about probability and chances and odds. What do you think are the odds that the alliance will go through?"

The first thing I did was to look at the probabilities behind the question. She might have been looking—hoping—for assurance from me that there was a gambler's chance against it. Or, could it have been a question on her assignment?

"This," I answered, like a pupil trying to fool the teacher with a question he can't answer, "is one game that I really have trouble reading. I wish I knew. But I think that all we can do is watch and wait."

I could not tell her that I was wishing for any change in the world that would put American forces in Europe, and that I was looking at the looming German-Japanese alliance in that meaning. Once again, our day ended with an embrace that warded off the realities of the world outside.

The next day I received a call from Grand Chamberlain Admiral Suzuki Kantaro. His title identified him as an official close to the emperor, a contemporary version of the court nobles of past centuries. We had struck up an acquaintance lubricated by my naval background and my history as Yamamoto's classmate. Suzuki was in his mid-seventies, a veteran of the Russo-Japanese War and a victim of the 2-26 army revolt the year before my arrival. When army assassination squads killed ministers and officials who stood in the way of their takeover, Suzuki was shot and came very close to death, but he survived to take a post close to the emperor, and to cut the deck with me on numerous occasions. Something happened during May of 1940 that made him want to unload his mind, and he needed a listening ear. I received another invitation to join him in a game of cards.

The Japanese house has a scroll hanging in the *tokonoma* alcove in the main room, usually a painting. The scroll is changed with the seasons to represent the mood of that time of year, but its function goes beyond mere adornment. Japanese often have difficulty speaking on a one-to-one basis, and the mute, immobile scroll becomes a social matchmaker with the power to flex conversation paralysis. The visitor admires the scroll; initial talk then centers on the artist, the theme of the painting, and reading the characters of the accompanying calligraphy. Scrolls contribute to the social graces with calligraphy that is often illegible, with stylish brushstrokes taking precedence. This opens the way for discussion of what the characters are and interpreting their meaning. The scroll becomes a conversation catalyst that opens the gates of verbal exchange. Suzuki was using cards for a scroll. I dealt.

"The army leaders are fuming," he said.

"Again, or a continuation?"

He hid a conversation block behind a play and threw out a wrong card. "We received word that the American fleet commander had a big argument with the president. . . ."

"Oh?"

"Because he objected to the president's order."

"Well, the American president is known as a single-handed decision maker," I offered, reminding myself silently that it was Europe's hope and a card that I could not show here.

"But this decision . . . looks bad."

He both wanted and didn't want to say what was on his mind. The cards played their role of making the pauses easier. "What was the argument about?" I asked.

"The Americans . . . the American president ordered the ships that berth on the West Coast moved permanently to Hawaii."

"Hawaii. . . ?"

"The army leaders feel intimidated. We get our rubber, oil, tin, and bauxite from the Dutch East Indies and Malaya. America is holding a gun to our head. They're saying that Britain can be in there. And Holland. But the white men want to keep the yellow people out. Those battleships are there to intimidate Japan. I hate those Japanese army stoneheads, drunk on the victories of their German heroes. They're not much different from the turncoats who tried to kill me in 1936. But this is one time I can agree with them."

Once Suzuki got his message to me, he lost his desire to play cards; the scroll could be put away. We chatted a while and parted.

Japan had grievances that should have received understanding in even a moderately objective international hearing. There were convincing arguments that racism was dominating international affairs, and even in the American Congress voices were raised against the racial basis on which the major world powers decided which nations can and cannot occupy or possess other regions. "Why," some congressmen asked, "must America defend European countries' rights to raw materials in other countries and exclude Japan? Why should we pull the chestnuts out of the fire for Britain?" Western countries were mute about the correlation between race and the right to the natural resources of other regions; Japanese leaders were screaming it.

About the time Yamamoto and I reached Harvard, Washington looked at the Japanese navy and realized that the world's sea power was out of balance, with America on the weak end. Japan's lead made Congress move fast and sign the Naval Appropriations Act; it became the starting gun in an armaments race with Japan that was in momentum when Yamamoto was deep in prepositional clauses. He was in America as both guest and rival.

When Japan's request for racial equality was refused at Versailles, it became a background ingredient for Yamamoto's speech at Harvard. Japanese leaders knew that ethnic symbiosis was impossible, and options for existence excluded racial equality: Japan had to accept a position below the white man, or find one above. When Versailles convened, Tojo Hideki was military attaché to Germany. When Japan's proposal was refused, it stoked the fires of racial superiority theories among Japanese, and it burned especially hot in Tojo in Berlin. The Germans showed great interest in his doctrine. Two decades later, when Japan's leaders saw the American navy in Hawaii as a threat to expansion and colonization by non-whites, the self-proclaimed superior race of Asia reached across the ocean to its European counterpart.

· 18 ·
Changes in Fashion and Power

Summer seeps into Japan with a burden of hot, waterlogged air. The summer of 1940 carried the added weight of an occupied Denmark and Norway, a Europe without France, Belgium, or Holland. The charm of the Low Countries, the art and engaging antisocial brusqueness of the French—could all these be pulled away like the Japanese islands that disappeared, leaving just a blank space on the map?

In the same month of June that France fell, Italy joined Germany in the war, while German warships moved into the Norwegian fjords. The submarines nestled in like predators looking out to the North Sea, ready to launch wolf-pack tactics against British and French ships. But there was another welcome move in America: The president pulled a hidden card on Congress and slipped through a secret sale to Britain of nine hundred field guns and eighty thousand machine guns. I pitied anyone who would have to fight with such obsolete weapons, but their real value was not a transfer of firepower but the transfer of authority from Congress to the president. He was still trying.

In America, young girls in bobby sox were screaming over the songs of a thin crooner while Japan's army leaders were equally giddy over the conquering performances of their Nazi idols. "There is no way now that Great Britain can stand up to Germany," the dour-faced, male bobby-soxers screamed. They picked up rhythm to oust anti-alliance obstacles from government, and the Yonai cabinet became an increasingly hateful roadblock to Berlin.

July 7 is a romantic holiday in Japan, a night when two star lovers who meet only once a year across the Milky Way have their tryst. This year the holiday came in on a promulgation that prohibited wearing, making, or selling fashion accessories. Signs and billboards in the streets announced EXTRAVAGANCE IS THE ENEMY.

I was meeting my swimming schoolteacher friend for dinner and I agreed to pick her up by car at Tokyo Station. I parked by the curb, and when she saw me she strode over with her back straight as always, her thigh muscles still fighting to break free from her dress, and a pout on her face. She got into the car.

"People are going crazy," she said.

"What happened?"

"They're hunting extravagant women."

"And are you one?"

"I was. All these neighborhood-association women—they walk around in work clothes and point to women on the street wearing jewelry or rings and scream 'Extravagant woman!' I felt like a monkey in a zoo. So I took off my rings and necklace. See! No accessories."

"They got your smile, too."

"Idiots. My father brought that ring back from France years ago. How will it change the war one way or the other?"

"You look fine without jewelry, but this car won't go without a smile. Not even charcoal will help. Are you hungry?"

"Hungry."

"So am I. If you smile, we eat."

She did her best. But the anti-extravagance movement stayed with her. "You know how some kimono cloth has silver- and gold-colored threads woven in?" she said as we were eating.

"I think I've seen something like that."

"What do you think the government is making the merchants do? They have to pull out all the gold and silver threads."

"After the cloth has been woven?"

"Right. The merchants hire school girls to pull out the threads with tweezers. Or else the cloth can't be sold."

"Well, it gives the girls a chance to earn a little money."

"Our government is being taken over by soldiers, and they want every-one to *look* like soldiers."

"Maybe you're not an extravagant woman, but believe me, you don't look like a soldier either. And if you don't talk about something else you'll get an upset stomach."

Extravagance was also erased from the restaurants: rice disappeared and Japanese were forced to eat wheat, sweet potatoes, and other substitutes. Lack of rice was no particular burden for us Westerners, but to the Japanese it was a staple next to air. Diplomatic position and finances to buy on the black market brought me a supply when I wanted it, and I distributed some to my staff. Japanese families took household treasures to the country as barter for some of the rice harvest, which farmers kept hidden from government authorities. Secret police watched train stations, inspected baggage, and confiscated any rice they found. As life became more stringent, Japan's farmers came into possession of fine kimono, ceramics, and swords.

With the outbreak of war in Europe, many of Tokyo's foreign residents bought or rented houses in the town of Karuizawa, about one hundred kilometers to the north. In 1888 a British missionary discovered the town to be an ideal summer escape from Tokyo, and it grew. The Swedish legation thought it wise to establish a base outside of Tokyo and obtained a house there, where I first met the architect of my legation building in Tokyo, William M. Vories.

"I'm up here visiting some missionary friends," he told me, "but many people are thinking of moving here if the war situation gets worse."

"Allow me to thank you for your exquisite design," I told him.

"I understand that you are a bachelor. I don't suppose the classrooms are serving you very much," he commented.

"To the contrary. They are well used."

"You are teaching in them?"

"No, I'm a dedicated social gambler; they make fine gaming rooms. Oh, and thank you for the sturdy construction."

"With the growing war fears these days, I only hope it never has to be tested under those conditions."

"I hope not."

A political plot against Yonai brought Yamamoto to Tokyo again in the summer of 1940.

"The assassination plot didn't work," he said, "and now the boys are planning political surgery."

"Army officers again?"

"Them and their lackeys. Konoe, that sly aristocrat, is announcing a 'new political structure' in Japan."

"Another political party?"

"No, he avoids the word party, but it amounts to that. In fact, he and his army clique are forcing political parties to disband. He's pushing a 'domestic reconstruction.' He's screaming 'Japan cannot miss the bus to world victory; we should join with Germany.' And he's gathering power into his own hands to bring Japan under a one-party rule."

"One party—like Germany."

"The army people are calling it a 'domestic revolution.' They want to remake Japan into a mirror image of Nazi Germany. Great minds they have."

"Will Yonai as prime minister be able to check this?"

Yamamoto grunted pessimism. "You know that Oshima came back from Berlin. That means his scheming there is finished and he's going to work with Tojo here to push the alliance."

"There is no ambassador in Berlin?"

"Kurusu Saburo went in his place."

"Kurusu? He doesn't seem the type to advance a German alliance, but apparently Oshima finished his mission."

A few days later, Konoe's "New Political Structure" started taking shape. The police box in each neighborhood was the center of that neighborhood group, and residents had to report any hint of deviant thought to the police box. All neighbors were potential spies on each other. Then the vice-chief of the army general staff, General Sawada, set up a squeeze maneuver to overthrow the prime minister. He ordered his minister of the army, General Hata, to resign from the cabinet.

"I resign due to illness," Hata repeated, and the army general staff refused to name a successor. A cabinet could not legally exist without an army minister, and Yonai had no option other than to resign with his entire cabinet. The emperor's—and Japan's—last barrier to a German alliance fell.

Several days passed before the next premier was announced, during which time Yamamoto called: "I'd like to invite you to lunch one day soon, before the next prime minister is announced. I also want to introduce you to a newspaper man I know—someone I think you should meet."

We gathered in a private room of an upscale restaurant on the Ginza. The other person was a Suzuki Bunshiro, a journalist with the *Asahi Shimbun*.

"There are so many Suzukis in Japan," he greeted me, "I hope it does not cause you confusion."

"Your namesakes do seem to be quite numerous," I agreed.

"According to statistics, 'Suzuki' and 'Sato' contend with each other for first place."

"Suzuki, here, has been named a director on his newspaper," Yamamoto commented, "so this is also a sort of celebration."

"I heard all about your poker skills from Admiral Yamamoto," Suzuki said.

"It's too bad you couldn't have joined us back at Harvard," I replied.

"The admiral is far above my ability; even back when he was a lieutenant commander. Actually, at the time I was still busy writing commentary on Versailles."

"Versailles?"

"I was there; I covered the conference for my newspaper, and the repercussions in Japan went on for a long time. Actually, the effect has never ended."

"He graduated from Tokyo College of Foreign Languages a few years before then," Yamamoto advised. "His English was far above those of us at Harvard. Besides, it was better to have him at Versailles. Someone else who was there was Prince Konoe, as private secretary to the delegate head, Prince Saionji."

"But the most active Japanese there," Suzuki said, "was Baron Makino, the de facto chief."

"We had an assortment of aristocrats," Yamamoto chided, "but it didn't help with the racial equality proposal."

"The whole matter was misunderstood from the beginning," Suzuki commented. "One problem was that Tokyo leaders were jealous of their authority, and Makino had to report everything back to them, then wait for instructions on what to do."

"So even with the conference in the hands of Japan's aristocrats," I asked, "they were not really in control?"

"The political mind," Yamamoto grunted. "It wouldn't yield."

"It was a good chance for Japan to change its thinking on that," Suzuki continued. "They could have blamed it on technology. Versailles was the world's first big international conference that made use of the typewriter, so it produced huge volumes of documents in English and French. And this information had to be translated into Japanese and cabled back to Tokyo. Then Makino had to wait for instructions on what to say next. The system paralyzed him—that's why Japan was called 'the silent partner.' Makino represented the only non-white power at the conference, and he wanted to do something for his country on his own, independent from Tokyo. That's when he came up with a proposal for racial equality for Japan."

"That should have showed," I ventured, "that he was capable of doing more than relaying Tokyo's moves."

"He was capable," the journalist agreed. "But, as the admiral said, the political minds in Tokyo wouldn't yield their own territory."

"I read how the colored races made Japan a hero after that," I recalled.

"After Makino made the proposal, a man from Liberia came to his hotel to thank him for working for racial equality, and begged him to continue. And an Irish woman came to say how her people suffered under British domination. All this astounded Makino, because his only purpose was to give Japan equal standing with the white nations—he was not out to change the world."

"Colored people in America," Yamamoto added, "wrote articles making Japan their hero. After the big earthquake in 1923 in Tokyo and Yokohama, the colored people in America—the poor classes—pooled money to send to us."

"Apparently," I commented, "the proposal was squashed because it became entangled with immigration. With Australia the biggest opponent of equality of immigration."

"Another problem that Makino never expected," Suzuki replied.

"Australia," Yamamoto said, "was a Dominion of Great Britain. They could have been represented by the British delegation. But Australia fought a good piece of the war, so they asked for their own delegation to the conference and got it. And their prime minister pushed the British delegates hard to keep their white Australia policy. He was up for reelection, too, and he wanted to use the fact that he kept Australia white for his campaign."

"Wilson had opposition from his Congress," Suzuki said. "He couldn't do anything that would be interpreted as equalizing white and colored in America, and Lord Robert Cecil of Great Britain argued that racial equality was against British economic interests. After all, their source of wealth included colonization of nonwhite regions like India and Africa."

"Even so," I added, "Lord Cecil was awarded the Nobel Peace Prize. They apparently have their own understanding of peace."

"We must remember," Suzuki said, "Wilson's big ambition was to create his League of Nations, and he needed Britain for that. So he couldn't confront them over the racial issue."

Yamamoto almost smiled. "I don't know if this Wilson fellow was a gambler, but he defeated Japan's proposal without throwing a card. If you recall, the vote was eleven to six in favor of the proposal." He grunted an unhappy chuckle. "At first it looked like my number was lucky. But it turned sour. Wilson used his position as chairman to change the rules and said that with the racial equality proposal majority vote was not enough. He changed the rules and required unanimous decision. So even when it looked like my number won for us, it lost." Yamamoto took a pause to turn sullen. "I remember the date it happened: the eleventh of April."

"What he did," Suzuki added, "was put the onus on Britain to cast the 'against' vote. America was clean and Australia stayed white. As the admiral said, Wilson defeated the proposal with a non-card. He opposed without opposing."

"I arrived here when the furor was still smoldering," I replied. "The rejection became a platform for building an alternative world order—and an 'Asia for Asians' campaign."

"But in all honesty," Suzuki said, "Japanese leaders were not ready to grant Asian countries equality with Japan. 'Asia for Asians' meant under Japanese plan. But the rejection of the proposal was a big shock in this country. To the Japanese, it was a heavy anti-Japanese move."

"Konoe came back from the conference filled with resentment," Yamamoto remarked. "That's understandable. But now that fancy aristocrat is going to be our next prime minister."

"Again?" I responded.

"Again," Yamamoto frowned. "He's lining up his future cabinet now. The minister of the army will be Tojo Hideki. He once headed the *kempeitai* in Manchuria. Then at the time of the two twenty-six revolt in 1936 he used that organization to prevent the revolt from spreading to Manchuria. That got him promoted to lieutenant general and moved up to chief of the Kwantung Army. He was vice army minister in Konoe's first cabinet in 1938, and now he's inspector general of the army air force—though he doesn't know what makes an airplane fly. He's in Manchuria touring air bases, and once the decision is final, he'll be called back to take his post."

"And the other members?"

"The foreign minister is another problem. Matsuoka Yosuke."

"The famous walkout from the League of Nations," I reflected. Shortly after we had settled into the room, the attendant started bringing in our lunch.

In Japan, chopsticks for ladies are shorter, to suit their hand size, and bowls are made in male and female sizes, so that the thumb and middle finger of the average hand encircles one half the circumference. Yamamoto had to improvise; he picked up his bowl of miso soup in his three-fingered grip, stirred with his chopsticks, and took a sip. "Matsuoka was president of the South Manchuria Railway Company. Realistically, it was a branch of the Japanese army—the lifeline for materials and troop movements. That brought Matsuoka close to the army people. When Tojo was running things in Manchuria, Matsuoka was a big help to him."

I recalled my talk on the train to Kyoto, when the banker told me how Japan developed her own railways to prevent their use as a colonizing tool. "He didn't help Japan when he led the walkout from the League in 1933," I ventured.

"Hmmm," Yamamoto grunted. "The League of Nations judged Japan an aggressor and refused to recognize Manchukuo as a country. They termed it 'Japan's puppet state'—more correctly, it was the army's puppet state. Matsuoka got up and made a great little speech in English: 'It is a matter of common knowledge that Japan's policy is fundamentally inspired by a genuine desire to guarantee peace in the Far East, and to contribute to the maintenance of peace throughout the world.' If it was such common knowledge, why was the vote forty-two to one judging Japan an aggressor? The 'one' was Japan's vote."

"Matsuoka," Suzuki explained, "went to America in the 1890s, when he was about thirteen years old. He worked on railroads, farms, washed dishes … always on the receiving end of prejudice. But he struggled and graduated from university in Oregon with a Bachelor of Laws degree. Japanese immigration caused big problems in America. The California government and labor groups protested. An immigration law was passed to limit certain races; Japan was on the low end of the quota. Japanese children were segregated in California schools. People put up sign on their homes: 'Japs keep moving! This is a white man's land!' But the strangest thing was the photograph incident."

"Not industrial spying I take it?"

"That would have been more understandable," Suzuki added. "But it was about all the single men who immigrated and were lonely, especially isolated farm workers. So friends in Japan sent photos of prospective brides. These photo-introduction marriages were running about one thousand a year in California when Americans protested. 'It was a barbaric practice, not in keeping with Christian tradition, etcetera, etcetera.' And it was prohibited. Another blow at immigration. Then came Versailles, and next the League of Nations. To Matsuoka, the League was just one more way for the white nations to control the non-whites. So when the League decided against Japan's takeover of Manchuria, all he could do was make a dramatic speech and walk out. It would have been good if he had used his American education to change the thinking of the member nations, but he drew some similarities to Japan being like Christ on the cross and walked out. Then, when Germany rose in power, he advocated making them our ally."

"It's understandable," Yamamoto said, "But it's an unfortunate memory to carry into government in the present." He took a moment for historical reflection.

"The League awarded Japan mandate over Germany's holdings in the Pacific, so they treated us well in that respect. But that walkout isolated Japan from the world. And now Matsuoka is lined up for foreign minister. Twenty-four centuries ago Sun Tsu wrote, 'Do not enter into alliances with neighboring princes until you understand their designs.' He'd never make a pact with the Nazis. Konoe's new cabinet will be dedicated to it."

▪ 19 ▪
Assassination by Police

Yamamoto read foreign magazines like a gambler looking for the pulse of his opponents. "News is somebody else's poker bet," he once told me. "The reader has to decide if it backs up the cards or if someone is faking. Believe every bet and you lose."

Roosevelt had been telling America, "We will not participate in foreign wars," but I was not discouraged; I saw him throwing different cards. In 1940, though, his second four-year term moved toward its end, the limit by precedent. I knew that a change of president would probably mean greater intrusion by an antiwar Congress.

Then, fresh hope whirled in from Washington. Stories circulated that Roosevelt was aiming for a third term. Trying to break the unwritten two-term limit would put him at a disadvantage, and when his own party was outraged at the attempt, it looked like the end of his bid. But that summer of 1940 the president's party *did* put him up to run again, and with a touch of disbelief, I "voted" for him.

In July 1940 Tokyo demanded that all routes to China through Indo-China and Burma be closed. Three Japanese divisions poised on the Kowloon border while the British evacuated Hong Kong with eyes cast over their shoulders, trying to get out before the rising-sun flag came in. In Tokyo, several Britons were arrested for questioning on suspicion of being spies, which brought me a call from Melville Cox of Reuters. We had met on several occasions, but when he came to my legation he was not the same penetrating journalist that had probed Japan's giant battleship construction. He was worried and tense.

"The Japanese are in a new phase of spy phobia," he said. "Human rights are being violated, and foreigners are worried."

"The problem started building up last year, did it not?"

"It peaked then, when the Japanese blockaded the international concessions at Tientsin. They also targeted Britons in Japan and some fifteen were taken in by police for interrogation. But remember, the military is leading the people in a war of the divinely descended against those who are mere barbarians, or whatever the rest of the world is supposed to be. So it will not be only the British from now on."

"Japan is naturally concerned about security," I started off in my role as political maitre d', "and I see the Japanese move as expected."

"We see this as an infringement on our rights," Cox went on. "If the world's diplomatic circles made an issue out of it, things might improve. Any influence you can exert through your ministry would be beneficial for human rights in Japan."

I told him I would discuss it with Stockholm and wished for the best in the tightening international situation. Two days later, Cox's wife received a call from the police to retrieve his body. Melville had been arrested and the police record listed the cause of death as a suicide leap from the third-floor window of the detention center. It was obviously an official ceremony to close the books. A European doctor examined the body and found more than thirty needle marks on him.

"He passed out from the questioning," the police officer explained, "and we tried to revive him with injections."

Japan had no laws against torture to gain confessions, so accusations of its use would simply document accepted procedure. Bywater lost his information contact in Japan but he would not miss him long. Bywater himself died in Richmond less than twenty days later during the London air raids, not from bombs but from too intensive a pub schedule.

I knew that in spite of the official courtesies given me in Tokyo, only a fool would bet that I was not being watched. Yet I also knew that Japanese army doctors were cultivating a new type of warfare in China. Would the war come to an end before the micro-organisms could be mobilized for duty?

· 20 ·
The Emperor Weeps

In July 1940 I received a coded message that originated in the Swedish embassy in Washington: "Herbert Yardley, American cryptographer in Chungking breaking Japanese code for Chiang Kai-shek's intelligence suddenly called back to Washington because war between U.S. and Japan expected at any moment."

After the Burma Road was completed at the end of 1938 to supply the Nationalist capital at Chungking, the Japanese began routine air raids on the city. They increased to four waves daily, widely spaced, to force people underground for up to ten hours a day. Yardley's recall to America was a bad forecast for Europe: another Bywater war would drain American military power to the Pacific.

On August 5 I received a coded message from an associate in the Swedish embassy in London: "Two American army officers on military mission under direct orders from U.S. president arrived London to make recommendations back to president for setting up U.S. military bases in Britain. Mission secret in U.S. and Britain. Seen as American preparation for entry in war." Roosevelt had taken another step toward Europe.

At the time I suspected it was an intentional drop of the card. Britain wanted to halt Swedish ore to Germany, and leak of an American step toward entering the war would press Sweden to cut it off. But Sweden remained calm; our mines at Kiruna continued supplying Germany and preparations for setting up U.S. military bases moved ahead. My fear was the American elections coming in November, in about three months. If knowledge of the plan for bases reached voters first, Europe might lose the American president we needed. Could he keep the information blanket over Americans until then?

■ ■ ■

I had another meeting with the other Suzuki, the admiral, shortly after our last game of cards. "I have never seen the emperor in such an emotional state," he told me. "He cannot show this in front of others, but my age and our long relationship allow him to be more open with me. He is not the same person as when he is in the imperial meetings."

"And what is the cause?" I asked.

"The army leaders, as usual. First, the army toppled the cabinet of the man the emperor himself wanted for prime minister. Then, when Tojo became minister of the army, it raised the military's fever. They have been reviewing history with a bitter taste in their mouths."

"History is more distasteful than not," I commented.

"Their perception of white racism in Asia and the Pacific is especially bitter to them, and it ignites their resentment."

"Yes, the past century or so from an Asiatic viewpoint would throw light on their feelings," I agreed. "The white nations annexed, forced leases on, or occupied Punjab, Singapore, Burma, Cambodia, Ceylon, India, Vietnam, Batavia, Nanking, Peking, and Hawaii."

"And America purchased Alaska," Suzuki added. "China tried to prohibit opium in the country and the British forced them to buy it. That brought on the so-called Opium Wars."

"That," I continued for him, "led to the British forcing China to trade, and pressing China to lease them Hong Kong in 1842."

"Against that historical background," the admiral asked, "how do you think the Japanese felt when British ships entered Japanese ports in 1849 without permission and took depth soundings?"

"Not very comfortable, to be sure."

"Then in 1853 Commodore Perry came to Japan with his black ships and cannon. He demanded a coaling station for American whalers and that forced the country into internal conflict."

"And the end result was your Meiji Restoration."

"You know enough history," Suzuki continued, "to realize that the Meiji Restoration was not merely a domestic incident. Now, some seventy years later, Japan is without equal in the Asian and Pacific regions. No other country has parried the thrusts of the white intruder into Asia like

Japan. We have the highest level of literacy in this part of the world—higher than many white nations. Also, Japan has the highest level of industry in Asia. All these are now dangerous in the hands of army men. Pride in their ancestors—their victory in keeping the white colonialists from our shores—is making them reckless."

I felt a dual role in discussing these things with the Japanese. I am obviously white, yet I am also from a small, noncolonizing country, and one with a bond with Japan through the common problem of Russia. I was a guiltless white, an empathetic neutral.

"But all of Japan knows," I reminded Suzuki, "that the Restoration was followed by a rush to Westernization. People took up the dress, the customs, the music. The government ordered men to cut their topknots and adopt Western hairstyles. Literature was patterned after Western writers. Loan words poured into the language. Japan wanted to become the West of the East."

"Yes," he agreed, "we wanted to join the Europeans and Americans on an equal basis, but they did not want us. And the only way the military men know to meet this frustration is by showing military strength. That is why they want to push through a pact with Germany. They say it is to present a deterrent to America, but that is only rationalization. They have dreams of conquering the world with Germany. The emperor is extremely worried and sick over this."

"I can understand that. But everyone knows that as a constitutional monarch, the emperor's control is limited."

"I wish it were not so," Suzuki said. "The Constitution gives the emperor imperial prerogative of diplomacy, but Ambassadors Oshima in Berlin and Shiratori in Italy have been maneuvering Japan into an alliance. The emperor literally scolded Tojo, and told him that the army should stop usurping legitimate authority."

"That sounds unusually severe for the emperor."

"He feels strongly that with Europe in this condition, it is the ultimate national foolishness to join with Germany and Italy. The emperor said that seeking support from Germany now will build entanglements in the future. For one thing, we would align with the enemy of the United States and Britain. The imperial family itself is patterned on British royalty. We would, in effect, betray the imperial tradition that started with his grandfather, Emperor Meiji."

Emperor Meiji is best known by his photographic portrait in a naval uniform—painted by an Italian. The emperor's photographs were disastrous. As a youth he was slouched and slovenly, an appearance that did not impart an image of divine origin and would not help government leaders build a strong imperial military. Only an artist could give him an impressive posture, and since Japan had no history of lifelike painting, a European brush gave him a military bearing that existed only on canvas. The painting was photographed and reproduced in mass, looking quite like a photograph and displayed and revered in schools, offices, and homes, just as the photos of the current imperial couple were when I came to Tokyo.

"The emperor," Admiral Suzuki continued, "tells me that the tense situation with America is mainly because of oil. If we sign a pact with the Nazis, America will surely cut off oil to us for fear that we will re-export it to Germany."

"That is sensible reasoning," I had to agree.

"The emperor told me—he was very sad about this—that we Japanese underestimate ourselves, and therefore we seek an alliance. He said that he wished Japanese leaders had more self-confidence. He was close to tears." Suzuki himself started trembling in sympathetic vibrations. "His Majesty was almost weeping, or perhaps weeping, that we have become a country under leaders who suffer from an inferiority complex. 'The army leaders are destroying the magnificent heritage of Emperor Meiji. I have become . . .'" Suzuki was torturing himself to go on; he would have been tortured more to have nobody to share it with. "The emperor told me, 'I have become a . . . a third-generation son!'"

An old proverb states, "The third-generation son writes a house-for-sale sign in feminine script." The reasoning is that a man builds a family business through hard work. The second-generation son will not be up to the quality of his father, but the business foundation is strong enough to continue in spite of the son's management. By the third generation, the family vitality is thinned, the son is interested more in pleasures then diligence, and he finally has to write a sign, in a feminine hand that reveals his degeneration, selling the assets he inherited.

"The emperor is exerting maximum efforts," Suzuki said. "But the audacity of the army officers is overwhelming."

I saw similarities with centuries past when the military tilted the throne as they liked, when ruling warlords forced dethronements and placed their own choice of puppet-emperor on the throne. It could not be done as blatantly in the 1900s, but it was not necessary. The emperor could be ignored, except for ritual meetings and for his role as a symbol to unite the country behind military aims, like a movie star in a testimonial for some product or other.

Suzuki continued. "Army Minister Tojo is screaming at cabinet meetings that America aims for world domination. He keeps repeating, 'The Philippines have been turned into an absolute American military base! The islanders are again resigned to being sacrificed!'"

I recalled the interview in London in 1934 when Yamamoto told Bywater that Japanese naval officers "would be seriously perturbed if the United States were to create a powerful base in the Philippines." This was said after an act between the Philippines and the United States set up a ten-year Philippine commonwealth with American jurisdiction over defense and foreign affairs. In the years following, the war in China pushed more than 20 percent of Japan's national budget into military purposes. Douglas MacArthur was retired as army chief of staff in Washington and began strengthening America's Philippine base.

Suzuki continued. "Then two days ago at an imperial meeting, Tojo began laying the groundwork for what I believe is a very dangerous confrontation. I made notes of his speech. If you are interested . . ." And he pulled out a memo pad filled with extremely fine characters.

"'The history of the world shows that the trend since the nineteenth century has been a record of the eastward movement of Occidental influences, with the peoples of Asia compelled to lie inactive before the onrush of economic forces and military power. Many Asiatic countries are losing their territories and independence. Even our own country was bound by unequal treaties and deprived of autonomy. Then, with the Spanish-American War in 1898, a small but powerful group of big navy advocates in America dragged the American masses to abandon the country's tradition and annex the Philippines. With that, America joined the European powers in the encroachment upon East Asia.'"

Suzuki stopped to wipe his eyeglasses. The lenses were not dirty; he needed an emotional break. He picked up his notes and began reading again.

"'America and Britain supported Japan in the Russo-Japanese War because they perceived Russia as a potential threat to themselves. But when Japan became the victor and took a leading position in East Asia, the "yellow peril" arguments of the white nations changed target from China to Japan. America turned traitor and the president tried to bring his railroad baron friend in to neutralize the South Manchuria Railway and build his own line to control the region. The fruits of that victory belong to us, but America tried to steal them.'"

Tojo did not seem to mention that the war left Japan on the verge of bankruptcy and it was an appeal from Japan to the American president that brought a negotiated end to it. Tojo's father was a hero of that war, and the resentment of his father and his father's contemporaries through the years was part of the general's education. In the generations of both Tojos, a President Roosevelt was the hate symbol. In 1940 the fuel of history fed the heat of a Tojo family vendetta.

I had met Tojo at different functions in Tokyo after he took his cabinet post. We exchanged words, sometimes even complete sentences, without really conversing. With Sweden in a state of neutral subjugation by a Germany that he admired, I know that he considered me something of a cockroach, but he was too humorless to be impolite. Suzuki continued with Tojo's speech.

"'The American presence in Hawaii is another effrontery to push the non-white races out of British and Dutch colonies, and we cannot forget that Holland is the ancestral home of the American president. France already occupies more land in Asia and the Pacific than Japan, including Manchukuo. The British holdings are more than ten times greater. The so-called ABCD countries are forming an economic horseshoe supported by military bases from the Aleutians to Chungking to step on Japan like an insect on their trail of world domination. Germany and Italy perceived this trend of encroachment and asserted their right to establish a new order in Europe. They now recognize as legitimate the establishment of a new order in East Asia by Japan.'"

"That *is* direct," I said.

"Japan's army leaders want a strong anti-American, anti-British, white ally. The emperor weeps over the direction of the government."

Suzuki ended his visit with the very Japanese custom of considering the entire nation one family: "I deeply apologize for the Japanese nation's association with Germany."

The "association" had a series of vectors pressing it forward toward an alliance. The American fleet in Hawaii that intimidated Japan by protecting white interests in the Pacific; Tojo, Matsuoka, and others of the same mind who claimed that an alliance with Germany would deter America from military action against Japan; Prince Konoe preaching that "Japan cannot miss the bus to world victory" and should unite with Germany now to be on board. And, if the emperor's diagnosis was correct, lack of self-confidence among the Japanese who were in command of the government.

The alliance was aided by a rare example of a foreign diplomat actually doing something in steering a course for his country, although in this case the action amounted to collusion in an army takeover of the government. Lieutenant General Oshima Hiroshi, Japan's ambassador in Berlin, controlled all incoming and outgoing messages between Japan and Germany, filtering out any that did not further the aims of an alliance. Foreign Minister Matsuoka went to Germany and Italy to lay the groundwork and on September 7, 1940, Heinrich Stahmer arrived in Tokyo as special envoy from Berlin. Instead of the usual splash for foreign dignitaries, it was as if he had parachuted in at night. There was a round of secluded meetings and on September 20, a celebration party was held at the German embassy in Tokyo. Newspapers carried a photo of the participants raising their long-stemmed glasses in a toast to the alliance—except Tojo: When the picture was taken, he alone was already drinking, as if to signal his will to leave off with ceremony, drink up, and get into battle formation.

The Japanese principals then headed for Germany—the disciple goes to the master for the major act—and on the twenty-seventh in Berlin, Kurusu Saburo signed the Japanese alliance with the Axis. Flags of the three countries flew at Brandenburg Gate, and German beer halls shook through the night. A monster cake stood like a monument in a high-class restaurant in Rome. On Tokyo's Ginza, radios blared the news and extra editions of newspapers carried details. At the prime minister's residence, the German and Italian ambassadors joined in *banzai* shouts, and Mrs. Tojo organized a celebration party for women only at the House of Peers. Among those present were the wife of ambassador Oshima and the wives of the German and Italian ambassadors. When I read that a Japanese soprano sang folk songs of the three Axis countries, I took comfort that gender and neutrality made me doubly ineligible for joining the party. I was an official guest in a country allied with Sweden's rapist, but I felt relieved: The Japanese-German alliance came before Washington's expected war with Japan.

More encouraging news from America came that same September of 1940, when President Roosevelt outsmarted Congress again and ordered fifty destroyers transferred to Britain in an exchange for British naval bases. With those bases arguably representing American territory, a strike on one could satisfy the "unless attacked" condition and bring us America's military assistance. Against this, on October 30, shortly before the presidential election, Roosevelt made a reelection speech that was stirring and convincing enough to discourage: "And while I am talking to you, fathers and mothers, I give you one more assurance. I have said this before, but I shall say it again and again and again. Your boys are not going to be sent into any foreign wars." As Americans bathed in the comfort of that speech, the swimming schoolteacher brought another story.

"Do you know what they are doing in the schools?" she asked, then answered. "The army officers are teaching girl college students how to handle guns and how to march."

"And this is part of their education?"

"Only two hours a week, but it's ridiculous. Those girls are about twenty years old, and they have to learn field drill, target practice   "

"So the army is getting more involved in education?"

"Most of the trouble started back with the Konoe cabinet in 1938. You know who he chose for the so-called minister of education?"

"Yes, we diplomats have to learn those things. Araki Sadao."

"*General* Araki. He's a war-crazy monster. He was part of the Manchurian Incident in 1931 that put Japan and China at war with each other. After that he was army minister, then education minister. Emperor worship and militarism are all he knows. His policy was to suppress all antiwar thought in Japan. He said that Japanese should 'purify their thoughts' and pushed for newspaper censorship. He set a pattern, and now anyone who opposes the army officers is in trouble. That's why the army influence is so strong in our schools today."

"I remember reading about him as a strong supporter of the Boy Scouts. That doesn't sound pure Japanese."

"Because the Boy Scouts became a military youth movement in Japan—a mirror image of the German Youth Corps. It made Japanese boys soldiers early in life."

"Well, if you can't change things now, perhaps a sip of wine will help you forget."

"There's too much happening to be able to forget. Did you see the paper? The Hitler Jugend are visiting again." She showed me a picture of a group of them at a private demonstration of *bunraku* puppets.

"At least they're appreciating Japanese culture," I said.

"I think they're interested because the Nazis want to make everyone their puppets. Maybe they're looking for a hint. Whenever I see those uniforms I remember the photos and newsreels of the Berlin Olympics. That's a frightening country for Japan to be associated with."

"As a teacher and as a swimmer, there's not much you can do to affect things. All you can do is get an upset stomach."

"But look at what's happening in Europe. Including Scandinavia. Doesn't anything make you angry?"

"If anger is the only thing anger will accomplish, I try to avoid it."

"Well, I can't. And now the country is losing its mind over this twenty-six-hundredth anniversary. What nonsense! Japan didn't come into being twenty-six hundred years ago when some deity dipped his sword in the water. . . ."

"It's the Japanese version of history; why not just have a sip of wine . . ."

"It's not history. It's fabrication."

"White, slightly sweet?" I took out a bottle and poured. I held out the glass for her. She did not move.

"Don't these things bother you?" she asked with a teacher's terseness, her arms at her sides.

"It would bother me if you didn't join me."

She held her pose for a moment, then took the glass. But the Hitler Jugend marched in her head and the twenty-six-hundredth anniversary burned in her like an inflamed ulcer. I clinked glasses. Nothing changed. I followed the Roosevelt script and clinked "again and again and again. . . ."

We drank.

▪ 21 ▪
Imperial Cult Creation

The United States moved closer to the one-man rule that could answer Europe's prayers: In November 1940 Franklin D. Roosevelt broke precedent and won the election for his third term. Meanwhile, the Japanese government moved closer to war in its own strange way with a national purge of the English language. Words like trumpet and clarinet were replaced by heavy-sounding terms that strung ideographs together like models of heavy chemical compounds. Baseball continued, but under its Japanese name, with terms such as strike, ball, and home run also replaced by Japanese equivalents. The government swept foreign names from products, and Cherry cigarettes became the Japanese equivalent, *Sakura*.

This purification of the Japanese language was joined with an enhancement of emperor awe and the fortification of accompanying myths. Ancient emperors lived in sanctioned sexual permissiveness that surpasses bachelorhood and invites envy. An emperor was allowed a main wife, three consorts, nine wives of high court rank, twenty-seven wives of lower court rank, and eighty-one concubines. At times, the throne was taken by sons born of one of those wives, concubines, or consorts, but only faith in odds no gambler would take could assume that all the children of those secondary companions were fathered by imperial seed. Some emperors produced no heirs and maintained succession by adopting the son of a prince from aristocracy, not of the imperial blood. The Japanese imperial line is one of the most broken in world history.

In 1868, a coup from the top brought about the Meiji Restoration. The shogunate fell, and the former members of the new government wanted a visual symbol to make it clear that Japan was under imperial rule. The new emperor was perfect for the role: a pliable teenager with no particular personality and easily handled by the new leaders. It so happens that he was born of a common court lady—not even of imperial concubine status—but that is a foreigner's argumentative distinction.

The boy's name was Mutsuhito, and after the leaders of the new government drew up a generally commendable constitution, they renovated "ancient" imperial history and Shinto: The new emperor was descended from ancient deities who had descended in body from heaven in a stone boat and created the nation of Japan. Schools taught the official history of an unbroken imperial line—unbroken in unspoken fact only, in the sense that one emperor succeeded another—and displayed the imperial photos, but reality had to stay hidden: The nation's new leaders knew the dangers of information exchange, and their constitution prohibited citizens from *discussing* the emperor.

I advanced my knowledge of colloquial American English with stories about gambling, and I discovered the humorist Damon Runyon. In one story, a toughie proposes a one-roll, high-point-wins throw of the dice. The toughie's opponent rolls first. The toughie has to better the point and throws the dice into his own cap, where only he can see them, and declares himself the winner. Japan's new theocracy started with a roll of the historical dice in a cap, but the power of emperorism produced armies that defeated the Chinese in 1894 and the Russians a decade later. After the Russo-Japanese War, General Kuropatkin wrote that Japan defeated Russia mainly because "we underestimated her moral tone." This was emperorism. The secrecy that brought success to the plan robbed it of the honor of joining works like Plato's *Republic* and Sun Tsu's *The Art of War* as doctrines for managing mass thought. Even Western scholars on Japanese history were fooled, and repeated the myth of unbroken dynastic lineage as fact.

Mutsuhito, posthumously known as Emperor Meiji, fathered thirteen children by various women while the empress went childless; cynics wonder if by neglect. One of those sons became emperor in 1912. Then in 1926, about a decade before my arrival in Tokyo, his son, Hirohito, took the throne. By Western standards, both his mother and father were illegitimate, but there was no peeking allowed in Japan, and in the 1930s the emperor image was reenergized with military polarity to head the state religion.

The imperial line started in what we call 660 B.C. Authorities somehow have knowledge of this fact, despite the lack of written records. This is when Emperor Jimmu—his name translates as "Sacred Warrior"—ascended to the throne. Twenty-six centuries later, the event was being kept alive in military nomenclature. The Type 94 reconnaissance plane was officially commissioned in the Japanese year 2594—1934 to us. The Type 97 attack plane was commissioned three years later, in 2597. In 1940, a fighter plane came into operational use, and in commemoration of the twenty-six-hundredth anniversary of Japan, it was designated the "Zero." Each reference to a military plane evokes the divinity of purpose that accompanies takeoff.

The identical final digits in the foundation dates and the Western calendar are a coincidence which some Japanese found unfortunate. At one reception, an officer well into his drink commented with equal parts of joking and resentment, "It is unfortunate for Japan that our foundation year and the Western calendar year end in the same digit. I wish your God would have either rushed or delayed the birth of Christ."

"Sweden," I answered, "had no jurisdiction in that matter." Diplomatic humor should be trite, to keep relations smooth.

Japan's leaders looked for an inspiring example to etch emperor-obedience into its citizens, and history was called upon again.

In medieval Japan, ruling military clans furthered their political goals by pressuring the imperial court in Kyoto into dethronements and enthronements. In the fourteenth century, a hard-headed Emperor Godaigo took the throne and set off a series of skirmishes. The imperial court in Kyoto was about to come under attack from a force advancing east from Kyushu. A warrior clan-leader, Kusunoki Masashige, had fought for the imperial cause before and was called again to defend the emperor. Kusunoki's tactical skill was legend, and he proposed letting the attackers enter Kyoto where street fighting would reduce the enemy's overwhelming advantage of numbers. Court nobles refused to have their city turned into a battle site and ordered Kusunoki to intercept the forces at Minatogawa, some ninety kilometers distant. Kusunoki knew that the terrain was advantageous to the enemy and it was a poor tactical decision, but these were his orders and, according to orthodox history, Kusunoki displayed his deep loyalty by setting out to defend his emperor knowing that he would not survive the battle.

Kusunoki mounted his horse and led his army out of Kyoto with his young son at his side. Also with the commander was his own younger brother. A day's march outside the capital, camp was made in the small settlement of Sakurai. Kusunoki told his son to return to Kyoto and spend his days being a loyal servant to the emperor, and from there the commander continued with his forces to the encounter site.

The battle was the disaster that Kusunoki had predicted. He and his brother, both wounded, made their way to a farm shack at the edge of the battleground. The commander uttered the oath, "Man is reborn seven times; I will vanquish this traitor," and the brothers ended their lives with simultaneous sword thrusts to each other.

That was 1336. With the defeat of Kusunoki's forces, the emperor fled Kyoto to a range of mountains south of the capital and set up what came to be known as the Southern Court. The victorious leader, Ashikaga Takauji, marched into Kyoto and enthroned a young puppet emperor from another branch of the imperial line, establishing the Northern Court. The new emperor granted Ashikaga imperial sanction and the commander set up a shogunate which ruled for the next two and a half centuries. The legitimate Southern Court of Godaigo lasted some sixty years, during which time his descendants tried to restore themselves to their rightful rule. The Ashikaga clan tricked them with promises; the Southern Court eventually relinquished the symbols of imperial rule and—ostensibly—faded from history.

The defeat of Kusunoki caused a break in the imperial rule which made Hirohito a descendant of the false line. The government's choice of a servant-of-the-emperor figure had self-contained defects if one thinks logically. But school texts take no such side roads, and Kusunoki became a model of loyalty to the emperor for all Japanese.

In Tokyo, my punching bags and long walks helped keep me in shape. Sometimes I had my driver take me to distant neighborhoods where I spent an hour or two in foot exploration. I became curious about schools, and when I spotted children in the morning I followed them to their destination. Some schools had the shrine with the imperial photographs just inside the entrance, where I could watch the children come onto the grounds and perform their rites. Boys removed their caps, and all stood at attention, then performed the bowing ritual. Postures and movements were identical. Zero tolerance! There was a complete absence of those personality differences which are natural in children. As my schoolteacher friend said, they were already soldiers.

I saw something else at several of the schools: action on the part of the children themselves, in the form of handwritten signs announcing NO DOGS OR OKINAWANS ALLOWED! The former Ryukyu Kingdom was incorporated into Japan only in the late 1800s, and its people have had to shoulder racial disdain. As I looked on those signs—in exceptionally fine calligraphy for children—I did not yet know how this racial attitude would later enter Japan's biological warfare plans.

On my trip to Kyoto—back when Cherry cigarettes still went by that name—after my first visit to the kiln, I took a few hours to visit the site of Sakurai, retracing by hired motorcar the route taken by Kusunoki six centuries earlier. The scene of the famous parting was a small park, and a sign advised that it was officially designated a "Famous National Natural Historical Monument" in 1921—two years after Japan was refused racial equality at Versailles. The loyal fourteenth-century warrior was resurrected into one of his promised rebirths in the heat of Japanese indignation over white arrogance. School textbooks carried the picture story of the parting at Sakurai, and songwriters were hired by the government to create patriotic melodies with inspiring lyrics: "Kusunoki, holding back tears at the Sakurai parting, told his son to return to serve the emperor, then went to meet his death . . ." Toy makers marketed dolls of father and son facing each other in their final talk. I passed a shop one day and bought one for my office as a reminder of the role symbolism plays in this society.

As I strolled around the small park at Sakurai, groups of people were being led in by guides or instructors who retold the story. I saw students, factory workers, a tightly knit miscellaneous neighborhood group, and other citizens whose common factor evaded me. Inside the park there is a piece of a tree carefully protected in a wooden enclosure, and each group's guide explained, "This is part of the tree under which father and son sat in their final talk, when Kusunoki told his boy to go back and serve the emperor." This always raised the threshold of reverence among the listeners.

I strolled over to a small tobacco stand at the edge of the park.

"A pack of Cherry, please."

"Ah, you know Cherry cigarettes?" the man in the stand beamed.

"I heard about them a long time ago from a friend of mine. He's in the Imperial Japanese Navy, and he said that they came out just a few months before he fought in the battle of Tsushima—the pack with an anchor design on the side."

"Eh!? You have a friend who fought at Tsushima?" The bow that followed was no mere formality; it was extra deep in body angle and sentiment. "Yes," he said upon recovery, "the first packs had an anchor on the side. Navy men liked that. *So your friend fought at Tsushima. . . ."*

Some people from the tour groups came over to make a purchase.

"This park seems quite lively," I commented.

"Yes. Every day people come and go, come and go."

"It seems that way. From where?"

"Some from companies, some from factories. Students also. The government wants people to learn about the parting at Sakurai."

"Well, that should be good for business."

"Ah, very good. Every day sales go up. This last year I sold more than double the previous year."

The tobacco-shop barometer showed that Kusunoki was gaining rank in the government, and being recruited to lead Japan against the enemies of the emperor. And now, in the twenty-six-hundredth anniversary year of the founding of Japan, special Shinto ceremonies were held in shrines throughout the country for the commander who gave his life for his emperor and brought rising sales to the tobacco shop owner. Newspapers carried photos of dignitaries and military officers in shrine visits to prepare the Japanese to follow the fourteenth-century warrior in the nation's twentieth-century ventures.

· 22 ·
The Twenty-Six-Hundredth Anniversary

"It's about to start," the schoolteacher said as she came through the door in the wall. "I just had to get away from all this Foundation Day talk." It was a brisk, sunny day the first week of November 1940 and we sat in the garden. "As soon as summer vacation ended we were ordered to get the children excited about it. Ridiculous!"

"Actually," I jested, "I think the Ginza looks quite colorful."

"But I must teach this as history. I hate destroying young minds."

"In school I was taught that God made the earth in seven days, but later I accepted this as a poetic way of stating that the earth was formed, by whatever means, in seven periods of some kind of time."

"Well, there's no poetry in what we have to teach about the deity coming from heaven in a stone boat and the magic creation of Japan. If I could teach those things as myth, it wouldn't bother me. It would be like teaching the Greek myths."

"Ah! But to the Greeks, those were not myths."

"That's true," she said with an almost-smile. "But that's another story. We have to teach a combination myth and religion as if it were historical truth. Any teacher caught doing otherwise would be punished by the principal and probably receive a call from the police."

"And everything else at school is all right?"

"No. Army officers come to train the children in military drill. And talk about loving the emperor." She walked over to my heavy bag and started punching it. "Army officers!" *Punch!* "Secret Police!" *Punch!*

"You'll hurt your wrists."

"If this were swimming season I could forget this twenty-six-hundred-year propaganda by working out in the pool until I'm exhausted."

"Butterfly, of course?" I asked with a sense of carnal appetite.

"I started using the dolphin kick last season. At first the butterfly used the same frog kick as the breaststroke. Then swimmers started experimenting with a dolphin leg action."

"And that's faster?"

"It's faster, and it takes more energy. It puts even more action in the back muscles and abdomen."

"Then I like it," I said.

She gave the heavy bag a series of one-twos. "Officers!"

"Forget the heavy bag," I told her. "You'll damage your wrists."

"I'm just exercising. All swimmers exercise in the off season."

"Then use the overhead bag. I'll set it for your height." I gave her my punching-bag gloves. "These are a bit large for you, but they'll protect your skin from abrasion till I can get a pair closer to your size."

She slipped on the gloves and gave the bag a roundhouse.

"That's not how to punch a punching bag. Don't try to smash it. Think rhythm, not power. Roll the wrist, like this. Then the other hand. Think rhythm. Now an easy one-two, one-two . . ."

She had the usual failures as she tried to get the bag into a rhythm cycle; then when it started to work right for a few seconds, she added more power.

"Don't try to kill it," I told her. "Rhythm, not power."

Eventually she managed to get a few repetitions. "I like this when it goes right," she said, without taking her eyes off the bag. I sat down and gave her a few pointers.

"Not bad for a beginner," I complimented her when she came over to take a rest. "That's just the basic punch; there are other rhythms in there when you're ready. Are you tired?"

"Not really tired, but it's a different kind of exercise for me."

"Then perhaps you need a Swedish massage."

We went inside and I started massaging her shoulders, her arms—then her whole body. I held her in a tight grip so I could feel her muscles come alive and press into me. She wanted shelter from the doctrines out there that depressed her, and part of her love drive came from escaping that Japan, a desire for internal explosions to transport her away from the distress of common awareness.

I embraced her; I passed my arms around her back, slid my fingers into her armpits, and clamped her tightly to feel her pectoral muscles tense and press their energy into me. I gripped her latissimus dorsi muscles. They were magnificent from pulling back the water, and they seemed to return the grip. It was an embrace that would cause discomfort to less trained women. "These are your butterfly wings," I told her. "While I've got you like this, you can't fly away." She gave a murmur of comfort.

I worshiped her long back muscles as they ran from below her neck to where they formed a spinal valley as they approached the waist, then to the solid blossom of buttock that drove her through the water and powered her erotic attacks. Sometimes when I massaged her, she would fall into the Japanese mood of reticence and tell me not to trouble myself. But massaging her was my aphrodisiac.

The seat of energy, according to Oriental principles, is located about two fingers' breadth below the navel, around what we would call the solar plexus. During Zen meditation, my instructors taught me to concentrate on this point. If this is indeed a person's energy center, it would be reasonable to attribute it with the power of erotic assertion. Mariko's belly would support the hypothesis. It had an aggressive expression that invited sensual confrontation. I placed the palm of my hand over her center of energy and pressed, slowly increasing pressure until I reached the fine edge of the threshold of discomfort. It required considerable effort.

"You're using your butterfly muscles more," I said.

She responded with a small laugh.

"I'd like you to be my own butterfly," I told her.

"But butterflies fly away."

"Not all of them. Madame Butterfly didn't. She waited for her man to return."

"And when he did, he came back with his real, American wife and found Butterfly with their baby. And Butterfly killed herself."

"But we have no baby and I have no wife. And Madame Butterfly probably couldn't even swim, even though she lived near the ocean."

"How do you say butterfly in Swedish?" she asked.

"*Sommerfogel.*"

"That sounds like summer."

"It is. Literally, it means *summer bird*. Like you. When summer comes near, Miss Hiraoka starts flying in the water."

She let out a girlish laugh. "Why do you still call me by my family name?"

"It's a Japanese custom. You know that."

"Yes, but when people are close, we often use given names. Why don't you call me 'Mariko'?"

"All right. But I'd also like to think of you as 'Butterfly.' May I call you that?"

She laughed again

And so she became "Butterfly." My residence was an extraterritorial escape for her, and each time I gave thanks for the real-wall construction. Sometimes we went out for dinner or to Japanese style drinkeries, where we could sip *sake*, and chat through the evening. As rationing came into Japan, *sake* became scarce, replaced by illegal, risky substitutes. Diplomatic position kept me stocked with alcoholic pleasure, and some kind of white wine with a touch of sweetness. Sometimes we drank mead in the garden, while other times I tried without success to exhaust her in passionate encounters.

But I always fell into neutrality when she mentioned matters of government, the army, the war in China, the German alliance, the educational system, the emperor—I felt as if I were obeying the constitutional provision that prohibited discussing the latter. I had long been convinced that she had no direct connection with the police. I believed her and her anguish and anxieties. But belief exists in religions also; it does not eliminate the role of prudence. The strongest believer looks before crossing a street. I could not close my mind to the complexities and interweavings of Japanese society. Her father was a civilian bureaucrat with ideas that conflicted with the army leaders. The *kempeitai*, for example, could use threats against him to pull out information. I knew the methods of Japan's information-seeking organizations. When I embraced her, realized that she was seeking 'balm in Gilead' for her distress, a change in consciousness that obliterated the irritants in her life. Sex was her opium. I knew that she wanted more—an exchange, verbal compassion, a sign that I understood. While I seriously believed that 'it would be better for her' if she had no stories to carry about me, I also accuse my diplomatic training which processed me—as the Japanese were processed into becoming children of the emperor—to keep my thoughts hidden like a hand of cards where it concerned "delicate" matters. Even as I enjoyed Butterfly's splendid nakedness, I kept this one veil of neutrality between us.

The Japanese characters for 2600 were flying from buildings all over the city. Tokyo trams were covered with flowers and illuminated at night and moved through the streets like massive floral bouquets on steel rails. The actual festivities consisted of five days of celebrations during which the emperor appeared on his white horse. *Nobody* except the emperor ever mounted that horse. And not one of the mounted military leaders or imperial family members accompanying the emperor rode a white horse.

On November 10 a massive public ceremony filled the grounds of the imperial palace, and the next day newspapers carried photos of thousands of tightly packed citizens waving their hands overhead in a greeting to the emperor. TWO THOUSAND SIX HUNDRED YEARS AFTER THE ORIGIN OF OUR NATION, the headline intoned, THE GRAND CEREMONY ILLUMINATES ALL.

The following day another ceremony was held with the emperor and Japan's top-ranking political and military leaders in attendance. I was invited to observe as a diplomatic representative, and I also received a call from a Japanese army officer advising me that Umezu would be at the ceremony, and would like to meet me after his obligations were completed. We agreed on a date, and Umezu called for me in an army car with his flag displayed on the front fender. He took me to lunch at a club filled with officers, where the first course was a huge succession of salutes, until he ordered us left alone.

Umezu had just been promoted to full general, and since he also held the title of Ambassador Plenipotentiary to Manchukuo we had a political relationship as well. But it was not an easy time for a Swede and a Japanese to meet: The cards on the world's politico-military table overlapped at awkward angles. The previous year, 1939, Hitler had proposed a nonaggression pact with Sweden and we had refused. Then, earlier in 1940, in addition to our obligation to send iron to the German war machine, the Nazis forced

Sweden to let German troops cross on her railroads into Norway and Finland. And one month before Umezu and I sat down to lunch, Japan entered into the alliance with Germany, putting Japan in brotherhood with Sweden's enemy in neutrality.

Japan also had her own self-contained complexities. The ten-year mutual nonaggression pact between Germany and the Soviet Union signed in the summer of 1939 meant that the Japanese army's hypothetical enemy was allied with Japan's Axis partner.

"Congratulations on your promotion," I offered. "I trust that life in Manchuria has been easier for you this past year since the Nomonhan battle ended."

"It is an end that contains its own promise of a beginning," he commented. "You know the Russians."

"Yes, we have had . . . relations, shall we say. I must admit that I was a bit surprised when fighting broke out against them in 1938. Then last year it happened again."

"The emperor was not happy about it. He wanted to avoid trouble there, and it seemed easy enough to do. It was a remote area of no use and terrible weather, but the borders are not well defined and either army could be seen by the other side as an intruder. The emperor gave one of his strongest orders since he took the throne to avoid a clash, but the Kwantung Army went its own way and intruded on the territory."

"At least the post-Nomonhan shakeup made you commander of the Kwantung Army. It seems as though somebody expects you to be able to avoid a repetition."

"It was deplorable that the fighting broke out in spite of the emperor's wish, but Nomonhan did serve a couple of purposes."

"Oh? And what might they be?"

"We found out that the Russians are tough, but we also learned some of their tactics. We know what the Japanese army has to do to train for the big one."

"And the other reasons?" I asked, not merely for curiosity. Sweden had tried to form a Nordic defense union, and the Soviets had interfered to prevent a unified Scandinavia. Any fighting the Russians had to do at Japan's end of the globe would hopefully weaken them at *our* end.

"There are other things I am not yet free to speak about," Umezu said. "But we will be better able to smash them if they start again."

"Are you really expecting something?"

"It has been thirty-five years since the end of our big war. The revolution that came in between did not change the mood in that country. Somebody up there wants to fight again—or continue, whichever way you wish to look at it."

"Yes, but for now the bear is hibernating."

"With one eye open." He left the Russians and moved the conversation southerly. "You know that trouble that just happened between Thailand and French Indochina?"

"Yes. Thailand tried to annex parts of the French-held territory and moved her armies in to do it. Japan intervened and made a settlement." I did not have to bring up the point that Japan's intervention was more forced than requested.

"And Japan settled the matter with a decision very favorable to the Thais."

"That definitely seems to be the way things turned out."

"Perhaps you also know," Umezu went on, "that the Thai army was equipped with Swedish Bofors seventy-five-millimeter anti-aircraft guns."

"The news reports mentioned that. There were even photos in Japanese and foreign magazines."

"Swedish weapons are superb. Your ore is superior, and also the Swedish foundry methods. Together they produce extremely fine weapons, with exceptional resistance to rust. And Japan—and the lands we are moving into—are all regions of heavy rainfall and high humidity."

"Well, I am not in the arms business, but I do know that Swedish ore and metallurgy are exceptional."

"Japan has to import everything," the general went on. "It actually fooled people into misinterpreting our moves. In 1904 we had almost no reserves of coal or iron. Our big ships and big guns were foreign imports, and we had no industrial capacity to replace losses. The world thought that Japan would never go to war against a material-wealthy country like Russia. But we made the Russians cry."

"I would be interested in your own view of how Japan did it."

"One big reason was that every Japanese was behind it. We had fought in Manchuria ten years earlier. Then, after the Triple Intervention in 1895, Russia obtained a lease on a strategic port on the Korean peninsula, just opposite the island of Tsushima and staring Japan in the face. All Japan was in shock. We knew that Russia made that southward advance to establish a naval base there and bring Japan under the Russian boot. The Japanese were of one mind: We beat the Russians or vanish as a country."

I recalled again Yamamoto's speech: *The value of any probability varies with the temperament of the player.*

"The world was calling the Japanese superhuman," I commented, "and looking at some of the odds they were up against, it would seem that there was something more than muscle power. Frontal attacks against well-fortified mountain positions that marked so much of that war astounded the world. And of course, the Battle of Tsushima that became part of every naval officer's education."

"The navy did a great thing," Umezu said. "I cannot reduce the scale of that victory. But remember that the Baltic Fleet was just that: *Baltic.* That's in *your* neighborhood. The Russians had to send more than forty ships halfway around the world—eighteen thousand nautical miles—then fight with tired crews. The fleet left the Gulf of Finland in October, and it was more than seven months before they went into battle. France was against us and aided the Russians by letting them use Madagascar and French Indochina for coaling stations. The Baltic Fleet commanders were planning on making the trip to Russia after they beat us, so they steamed into battle heavily laden and deep in the water. That lowered their speed and hindered their maneuverability."

"I remember Britain's anger at France," I commented, "for giving the Russians coaling privileges. I was eighteen years old then, but with the excitement the war created in Scandinavia—and with a naval-officer father— I kept up on the details."

"The Japanese navy," Umezu continued, "was in its home ground. People in Kyushu could hear the guns. The Japanese fleet could go into battle lightly fueled for more speed. With our army in Manchuria, it was just the opposite. The Russians were closer to home and had rail communication for troops and equipment. Japan had to bring in everything. The twenty-eight-centimeter guns that smashed Port Arthur were made in Germany by Krupp."

The land war was, one had to agree, a logistic advantage on the Russian side. But Umezu was not inviting me to discuss history. He continued. "Right now, Japan is the only country outside of Europe and the United States that has annexed or colonized other lands. A big reason for Japan's moving into Manchuria was the resources there. But we have the Russians breathing down our necks, and we always will. I want Japan to secure sources of materials in diverse locations."

He paused while a waiter cleared away empty plates.

"Some day," Umezu continued, "I hope that Japan can become a customer for Swedish raw materials. And weapons. Japan and Sweden live at opposite ends of a devil. We subdued that devil once and we may have to do it again. Japan must diversify our sources of iron and weapons. I am looking to Sweden." He allowed a few moments for me to absorb his comment, then continued. "Of course, I am an army man, and you are a representative of your country's foreign office. Decisions like this are not made at our levels. I say this in the Japanese sense of 'digging around the roots,' an unofficial preparation to help something come about later."

Umezu's name was circulating as a possible future prime minister. This was surely in his mind when he was "digging around the roots" of our iron mines.

"There is no question," I answered, "that Scandinavians would like to see Japan able to stand up to Russia again if necessary."

"Also," Umezu went on, "there is a possible mutual advantage in materials exchange that might be worked out."

What, I wondered, would Japan be able to offer in raw materials? Her economy depended almost entirely on imports.

"Oil is always a source of trouble," Umezu went on. "The Soviets are trying to get free access to the oil in the Middle East, the Balkans, Finland, the Turkish Straits. They are making demands on Germany, and wanted to seize the Romanian oil fields also."

"And," I added, "the Soviets began taking over territory in the Balkans and eastern Europe without informing their so-called partners in Berlin."

"Territorial expansion and oil are behind it all, and Japan is a small island country that has to import almost all its oil. We cannot continue this way. And we may not have to."

"Meaning. . . ?"

"Japan expects to come into rich oil fields. We will be able to export a portion of it, but I will press for controlling such exports only to those nations with which we enjoy mutual benefit. I want Japan to have Swedish iron. We will soon be able to offer oil in exchange."

"And the source of this oil?"

Umezu reached for his briefcase and withdrew an envelope. He removed the contents and handed it to me.

"This looks like money," I said examining it. "And it is issued by the Japanese government. . . ."

"That is only a design test sample. It will be money soon. Two months ago, the Konoe government ordered bank notes printed for our occupied territories in Southeast Asia. The oil fields there will be part of Japan's colonial empire. As someone who has seen your guns perform, when the time comes I will press for an exchange of oil for iron and arms. I am even thinking of working it on a barter system, eliminating the transfer of funds. Something similar to what Hitler is doing."

"Yes," I said, "Germany's barter system is a headache to the financial centers in America and Europe because it circumvents the use of gold. They would like to squash it, but it does have sound principles that can work in international trade. I am sure there would be endless toasts of Admiral Togo beer to the strengthening of Japan's ability to stand up to the Soviets again."

"While I look to the future when Japan can reinforce her conventional arms with Swedish ore and guns, we are not thinking merely . . . *conventional* arms."

I wanted to hear more, but I could not press. I let him continue.

"The advantages we had in 1904 are not with us today. The Soviet Union has enormous resources: a large population, mines, industry . . . Most important, technology has changed. In a war of purely conventional weapons, Japan would be at a tremendous disadvantage. We need something more."

"And you are developing these now?"

"I'm sorry, I am not free to say too much at present. But I think Japan can destroy a good part of the Soviet fighting potential in the near future, not by killing one Russian at a time. We will always need iron and guns, though. And one day I hope Sweden and Japan will enter into an agreement similar to what I have just outlined. But Japan also has to do something different—with unconventional arms—to offset the imbalance against us. I cannot say more."

· 23 ·
Another Glimpse into Unit 731

The twenty-six-hundredth anniversary celebrations gave Akira a chance to request leave from work to come to Tokyo. When he came to my legation this time, he did not have the "French verve" I saw in him before. At moments he was agitated, then he fell into an uncomfortable nervousness. He was like a wind that picks up, dies out, then gusts in a different direction. His fingers were in constant battle with themselves and with space, searching for an emotional harbor.

"The Japanese army is embarked on a strange path," he said.

"From what you told me last time, I can understand."

"What I told you last time—what I *knew* last time—is only part of it. The truth is . . ." He lost focus, then brought himself back. "Last time, I told you about Japanese doctors using captives for experiments, to learn more about disease in order to protect Japanese troops. It is worse." He looked around without really looking. "Japanese doctors are preparing to make war with disease. Bacteria . . . viruses . . . biological warfare."

"So disease is not being combated; it is being cultivated."

"Oh, of course disease prevention is part of it, but preventing disease in our own troops while they attack other people with it. Disease is the coming weapon of the Japanese army. This is why they test. Japanese planes have attacked entire Chinese villages. *Plague!* Hundreds of people falling, turning black, rotting in the streets."

"You were not there when it happened, I take it."

"No. The researchers tell us the details. And there are photos and movie films. They went into the villages in anticontamination suits to do research. Sometimes they work with sibling units, but the specimen jars are from my shop. They come back to the unit with body parts."

"And how," I asked him, "do they deliver these pathogens?"

"That is also part of the tests. At first they filled bombs with infected fleas. The bombs exploded on contact and killed the fleas. So then they tried non-exploding glass bombs. I made them. And ceramic bombs. There was a metal bomb, with compartments inside for infected rats and fleas. The fleas attach themselves to the rats and suck their blood. The body temperature of the rats keeps the fleas alive. The bomb opens on landing and within three days people are dying. The Japanese researchers like the plague because it acts fast."

"And these are villages, you say?"

"Sometimes villages. Sometimes they test in an open field, a place called Anda. Twenty . . . thirty . . . forty men and women are tied to stakes in the ground. The bombs are dropped near them, then the researchers check the results. Some of the areas that were tested, some of the villages, will be uninhabitable for years. Not all the tests are air drops. Some are attack by infiltration."

"You mean, disease-spreading spies?"

"One of the researchers told me about a cholera test. The team captured a bunch of dogs in a village. Chinese villages always have dogs running around. They brought the dogs back to the unit, infected them with cholera, then drove back to the village and released them. You can imagine what happened."

"Yes, and it sounds gruesome."

"The dogs get sick and vomit. Other dogs come along and eat the vomit. The cholera spreads from dog to dog, and to people. After the disease takes hold, the researchers put on their protective clothing and go back. The village was piled with sick and dead. It was summer, and the dying were covered with flies and groaning. Those who could walk or run, left the village—and spread the disease. The Japanese researchers walked in and took over a temple for a laboratory. They announced that anyone who was sick could go to the temple for treatment."

"And, were they treated?"

"If it served the research, perhaps. To test a medicine under development, for example. But most of the people were cut open to study the progress of the disease. One day a man came looking for his wife. When he ran into the temple, his wife was being opened up. He saw her feet still wiggling, and started screaming and crying. Her parts are in my specimen jars."

"And you say this is in preparation for waging war?"

"Ishii's thinking is that conventional arms are too costly for a country like Japan. Weapons of bacteria and viruses can be produced at a fraction of the price and kill more efficiently."

I told Akira about the research paper I had read, and the monkey experiments.

"I never heard of monkeys used in research," he said.

"And yet," I questioned, "this report was in a highly prestigious Japanese medical journal."

"There is practically no medical university or research facility in Japan that is not involved, so writing monkey for human would be understood. Experiment data are sent to the Army Medical Research Laboratory in Tokyo, and from there distributed to different researchers at universities and hospitals all over Japan. If a project needs further experimentation, word goes through the Army Laboratory back to the researchers. They choose other human subjects and continue."

"What you say is shocking—that medical schools all over Japan are involved. . . ."

"They are. Two postgraduates just came to the unit. They didn't want to, but they were sent by their instructor at the university."

"And they had to obey?"

"The organization in Japanese academia is very tight. One fellow told me that he tried to refuse. He was working on his own research project and wanted to continue. His instructor screamed at him, told him that if he did not do as ordered, his medical career was finished; the professor would blacklist him."

"And why was the professor so insistent that his student go to Manchuria?"

"Because professors use the data gained there for their own reports, to elevate themselves in the medical community."

Medical communities in any country have an element of exclusivity, but I could see the feudal remnants in this power of an elder over his disciples.

"And, they are teaching a different profession," Akira went on. "The other graduate said that his university instructors told them, 'In the past, medical science was used to eliminate disease. That era is over. Now, medical science is the new source of military weapons. It is being used to kill the enemy more effectively. This is going to be your study.'"

"And you say there are many sibling units to Unit 731?"

"Many. Back in 1936, a center for prevention of horse diseases was set up in Changchun. But 'prevention' was only a cover. They are developing weapons from animals."

"Such as?"

"Do you know about anthrax?"

"Yes, of course. There was a massive outbreak in Europe in the seventeenth and eighteenth centuries. It was called 'woolsorters' disease' because it was found among people who handled sheep's wool."

"You may know that it's also one of the oldest diseases known to humans. It's in the Old Testament, in Exodus. Hippocrates and Homer wrote about it. And Pliny."

"You seem quite informed on this, for one with an artist's heart."

"The unit has a very well-equipped library, with specialists to help us. The officers encourage us to study. The limited medical school education I had helps me understand some of the reports. With anthrax, inhalation is the deadliest form of infection; that is how woolsorters' disease occurred. It can infect by ingestion. The spores dry and retain virulence, so it can be used in sabotage. Ishii was experimenting with spreading it on paper money. The rumor is that he wants to try killing off an entire area as a test project. And if anthrax is spread on land, it will stay contaminated for years—a semipermanent source of death. And, it's a hideous death."

It was clear that his comment was not based on secondary sources. "You have . . . witnessed the victims?" I tried to ask softly.

"Yes. The disease produces ugly, black pustules. Like coal. Anthrax. Anthracite. The same roots. That's what it does to people." He cupped his two hands together. "Just this much of the bacillus will kill half a small city."

"And how much are they preparing?"

"It is impossible to say. It may be that seed pathogens isolated at the Changchun unit are sent to other units for cultivation. Since these men are all dedicated scientists, I assume they are also experimenting to produce the most virulent strains, maybe much greater than those which caused outbreaks of the disease until now. Perhaps only Ishii and his top aides know the real story."

"These men are all doctors, then?"

"Doctors, bacteriologists, microbiologists. It is a precise, scientific study. Ishii makes regular flights to Tokyo with the plane loaded with specimens. Then he lectures on them at the Army Medical College."

"Specimens?"

"The results of the experiments. Organs, body parts, whole bodies. In preservation jars that I made. Ishii is also a pilot and likes to fly himself, with his strange passengers."

"So the specimens come here to Tokyo? And what happens with them later?"

"I heard that they are just buried around the laboratory once they have served their purpose, because the planes are filled with other cargo on the flights back to Manchuria."

"Other cargo?"

"Rats."

"And where do these come from?"

"The army pays Japanese farmers to raise them. Army trucks gather them from the rural areas and bring them into Tokyo, to the Army Medical College. Then they are flown to China for cultivating plague germs. But not only bacteria and viruses are being used. Poison gases also."

"They are producing poison gas in China?"

"In China, and here in Japan to be shipped over."

"Do you have any idea where?"

"Some small island. Near Hiroshima."

Island and *Hiroshima* connected with an island that disappeared. And a strange piece of industrial ceramic headed there.

"Okunoshima?" I asked him.

"How did you know?"

I told him of my experience with the map, and of the discovery at the Kyoto kiln. And how the question marks had all been resolved now with his information. "That was a piece of equipment for the poison-gas manufacturing process," I said half to him, half to myself. "Ceramics are used because they do not react chemically."

"That sounds like a cooler," he said from my description. "The stubby arms are for holding a coil; the gas circulates through it, around the ceramic core, to lower the temperature. They teach us about that, too, in the unit's education program."

"And," I asked again, "they are also testing this poison gas in China?"

"They've used it against Chinese troops. For tests, sometimes they use chambers. They put people in and use different concentrations to determine lethal doses. It is all very scientific; the chambers have glass walls and the researchers take movies and still photos. They make very careful notes. Sometimes they tie several people to a dolly and wheel it into the chamber. And some tests are done outdoors with people tied to posts. Then the researchers remove organs from the corpses for examination—and preservation. Some of the victims are preserved whole to show the skin symptoms—blistering, and so forth. The orders come to my shop for specimen jars."

"These researchers—do any of them have moral problems with this human testing?"

He swallowed hard. "A few do," he said looking away. "I've seen doctors run out of the lab vomiting. These are experienced professionals. They have operated on people before. But this is different. A while ago, a . . . one researcher could not stand it anymore. He took poison."

I sensed that Akira had known the man personally, but I did not want to ask.

"The moral problem," he continued, "is eliminated by the scientists' desire to experiment. By the military's desire to produce new weapons. By this strange religion that Japan is under."

"Religion?"

"Or whatever you might call it. Japanese are trained to believe that we come from a sacred country, that we are sacred people and children of an emperor descended from heaven. So we can use Chinese and Koreans like animals. There's a special railroad siding that comes through big iron doors in the wall that surrounds the unit. The terminal is very close to my workshop. Sometimes I see them coming in on freight cars, tied up, then unloaded onto flat trucks head to foot, like pigs going to slaughter. After all, these people are not 'sacred.' Only we Japanese are children of the emperor."

"I see you do not fit in too well with the teachings."

"Maybe I spent too much time in Europe. I just can't take this combination—emperor, military, superior race, medical research—it is a dangerous union. In my grandfather's day, emperorism was a basis for morality. Today, it is just the opposite. A reason for treating other people like laboratory specimens. And my works are part of it."

He stood and walked over to the window, looking out on the garden for a few moments. "In my grandfather's day," he went on, "the medical men served. Now they are leading. They used to work to eliminate disease. They even treated sick enemy soldiers. Now they use disease to kill."

He came back to his seat and the cup of coffee in front of him. He stirred it, then just put the spoon down. "I had to take a rest for a while," Akira continued. "The twenty-six-hundredth anniversary gave me a reason to come to Tokyo again. As a civilian, I have latitude in that respect. But seeing these celebrations . . . In reality, there is not even a Japan to return to. Everything is military and nationalistic. There is no art anymore. No art in life."

"Surely," I tried to tell him gently, "the times will stabilize one day, and art and music will return."

"It does not seem like such will ever happen. I studied art because it is uplifting. But there is no room for that in Japan now. Art is being made the slave of the state."

"How so?"

"There is a Japanese painter," Akira went on. "His name is Fujita. He was living in Paris when I was there—took the name Leonard Foujita. We used to drink wine together. He was one of the freest souls anywhere. He wore his hair in bangs—what they call *frange*. And he used to joke, *'Vive la frange!'* He was a fine painter. Not anymore."

"Where is he now?"

"He is back in Japan. His *frange* is gone, and he is painting for the government. War scenes! Naval battles! Heroics! His art is being used to help military goals." Akira's fingers speeded up their aimless journey. "Mine too! Only worse!"

"I realize," Akira continued in a weaker voice, "that you will be glad to see the Russian threat reduced, but I am afraid of the growing influence of Japan's army people. If they are successful in defeating the Russians again, their power will grow—like the very infections they are playing with. What they are doing is ugly even by war standards."

He got up again and went to the window. He walked over to the glass bird he had given me. "The indoctrination that the Japanese are getting. That we are a sacred race. A superior race. In the end it will have the opposite effect."

"Meaning . . . ?"

"Things happening in China will make us the object of disgust throughout the world. When people find out about this—the Chinese already know that strange things happen inside those walls—Japan will be considered a land of ogres. Army officers talk about the coming glory of Japan, but they are making us a nation of ugliness. We will be remembered as the ugly race." He stroked the glass bird. "I just want you to know that this is not Japan anymore. Our entire nation will become a victim of Unit 731. The men that call themselves doctors will make us despised by the world. Until their weapons run wild and there are none of us left to be hated. And nobody left to hate us."

· 24 ·

Deducing Captain Aiko's Invention

Captain Aiko's enthusiasm for Viking naval architecture suggested that he was some sort of dilettante—until I put the story together. At first I was merely amused that his knowledge of my ancestors' ships seemed eccentrically out of balance for a Japanese naval officer in the twentieth century.

"The English never thought that an attack from sea was possible," Aiko said, recalling the history I had learned in boyhood, "yet at the end of the eighth century, the Vikings made a quick, open-sea crossing—their invention of the keel helped them do that—then ran their ships through the surf and onto the beach. Those are distinct design requirements. That meant the landing was not only fast, but the men could jump into action without expending energy on swimming or wading ashore."

"Yes, the English were caught by surprise," I commented.

"They never expected an attack from the sea because the English knew nothing about Viking naval architecture," he continued.

As we talked, he sketched a head-on diagram of a Viking ship to illustrate, more for his self-musings than for me. "They were shallow draft, but slender and stable. And they could maneuver in waters where most European ships could not. They were flexible! And slender! Lapstrake construction for resistance against rolling!"

The Japanese have an expression borrowed from Confucius that teaches, "Study ancient wisdom for new intelligence." It influences the Japanese approach to a problem. They tend to study how it was handled in the past as a basis for solving something now. Aiko was holding hands with Confucius, but at the time I had no idea what "new intelligence" he was building.

"The hull design let them row upriver. The Thames, Shannon, Elbe, Seine . . . The reason the Viking age came to Western Europe was Viking ship design."

Aiko had introduced himself as "an inventor of sorts," and I later found out that he was a specialist in sea mines. Any time I inquired more into his specialty, the conversation was brushed away with a smile and polite vagueness. He also mentioned that his home was in Kagoshima, at the extreme southern tip of the island of Kyushu, and he took opportunities to visit there whenever he could. I first met the captain in 1940, and from January of 1941 visits to "his home province" seemed to be taking an irrational amount of his time. The Japanese typically desire to return to their native village when they reach advanced years, but Aiko was a naval officer just turned forty and a reputed inventor with his country at war in China and on the road to world conflict—not a combination to send a man on repeated visits to his native village.

Aiko's time in the Tokyo region seemed to be spent mainly at the naval bases in Yokohama and Yokosuka, and he often contacted me for a game of cards and a chat. This invariably meant discussing naval design—and Vikings. One day I was in front of the Office of Naval Affairs speaking with another officer acquaintance when Aiko came by.

"Ah, Mister Minister. Admiral Yamamoto sends his regards."

Yamamoto? Whatever Aiko was doing, he was in direct contact with the commander-in-chief of the Combined Fleet. Surely he was not Yamamoto's consultant on Viking ships!

I was in my office alone one day wondering about this Aiko fellow when my naval habits made me search out some navigational charts, a bit dated but sufficient for tabletop navigating. I opened them and fueled up on the best coffee available—Japanese coffee fans had to roast soy beans as a substitute, and one privilege of diplomatic status was genuine caffeine. With the first sip I steamed southerly through the Korean straits—where Japan in the sixteenth century made the double error of invading from the sea with land troops and a naval force commanded from land. It was fortunate for the Koreans. Right about . . . here, they ran into Admiral Yi-sun and the world's first armor-clad ship. A big, oar-driven iron turtle. Devastated the Japanese fleet.

I held course to take me down along the western coast of the island of Tsushima. Russo-Japanese War, Admiral Togo, and his fleet—right about here—lying in wait for word on the approach of the Russian fleet. Togo about to earn his place on the Finnish beer label; Yamamoto on the *Nisshin* about to lose two fingers. The Japanese navy set up a communications net on tiny islands—some of these—and enlisted local fishermen and their boats as lookouts. Probably some scattered through here. They spotted the Russians and the message went to Togo's flagship by battery-powered radio. Some of the first batteries made in Japan. The Baltic Fleet was smashed. . . . here!

Japan was at the bottom of her finances from the cost of the war. So they played a clever game. They had beat the Russians in Manchuria and on the sea, but no Japanese troops had advanced into Russia itself, and that would have been another kind of war. Japan saw Russia tied up in civil violence—"Bloody Sunday" in January 1905, at the height of the war, when soldiers killed workers in an orderly petition to the Czar; the rebellion on the battleship *Potemkin* five months later. The Japanese played against Russia's internal problems: Three days after the naval battle, Tokyo ordered its ambassador in Washington to request President Theodore Roosevelt's intervention to negotiate a peace. Russians and Japanese signed in Portsmouth, New Hampshire, and Japan pulled out ahead on the field and ocean but almost bankrupt. Protests erupted in Japan against the American-brokered treaty—offices of newspapers that supported it and the prime minister's residence were attacked, police boxes torched. The Japanese were not told the real story. Tojo Hideki graduated from military academy in the heat of the protests.

I continued steaming south. The disparity between the inventiveness of the Japanese and their role as the always-underrated stayed on board in my mind. The underrating infection spread to the Japanese themselves and probably blocked Japan from producing the world's first aircraft. I remembered the card game with Yamamoto when I learned of this.

"If it were not for the army," Yamamoto said, "the Wright brothers might have been second."

"The Japanese inventor was really that advanced in thinking?"

Yamamoto lit up and sent a puff aloft. I watched him watching the world's first airplane—made by a Japanese—fly through the cloud. "He was on the mark. That Japanese fellow, Ninomiya Chuhachi, was building kites since he was a child. Then he started watching crows for a hint on how man could fly. Of course, for centuries everybody who thought about flying watched birds. But what did they watch? Wing movement! People always thought that's where the secret to flight was. Not Ninomiya. He was interested in how crows fly when they *don't* move their wings. His objective was re-creating flight based on a crow's outstretched wings."

"We've seen the same thing with sea gulls," I commented. "And albatrosses." I smiled internally at the albatross recollection.

"We're oceangoing. We watched from ships under way when birds glide along with us for a long time. Ninomiya didn't have that advantage. He was in the army; he had fields and crows. He threw rice on the ground to bring the crows close to him, and he noticed that when crows glide, the leading edges of their wings were angled up slightly. He reasoned that this angle was the key to flight. In other words, he discovered the principles of angle-of-attack and running lift."

"Yes, that was ahead of his time."

"He started building models. He was a sick-berth steward in the army, and he cut an old stethoscope into fine strips to make rubber bands. And he carved a four-bladed propeller. It looked very close to our training-plane propellers today."

"And, his model flew?"

"Thirty meters from a taxiing takeoff. He used a tricycle landing gear. It was a beautiful plane, designed after a crow, fifty-five centimeters overall, a single wing with a span of forty-five centimeters."

"And when was this?"

"In 1891, twelve years before the Wrights flew. So he was applying the basics of modern flight by then. He made one flight after the other with his model, and he extended the distance. The elastic was anchored at the nose and the prop was over the fuselage at about midpoint, just over the wing. His plane looked very much like aircraft after they evolved from biplane to single wing."

"Did he ever try to make an actual plane?"

"He tried. He designed a one-man plane for mounting a twelve-horsepower motorcycle engine. Remember, this was in the 1890s. The only engines like that were imported from America and extremely expensive. He took the plan to his superior officers and requested permission and materials to build it for reconnaissance against an enemy. They turned him down. Called him stupid. 'If Western countries don't have such a machine, how could Japan build one?' That was their answer. Army officers! They're no smarter today!"

"So Japan came close to beating the Wrights in manned flight."

"He lost that chance but kept at it. After Ninomiya left the army, he worked for a pharmaceutical company. Made quite a bit of money developing new medicines, then bought a plot of ground to build and test his plane. He was in the middle of construction when news of the Wrights' success came. Ninomiya closed his workshop and kept quiet about it. But years later someone discovered his shop and the story."

Yamamoto dropped out of the conversation for a few moments while he dealt. He returned in a different place. "Do you know about the fight for 203-Meter Hill in the Russo-Japanese War?"

"Yes, of course. British war correspondents covered the battles in detail, and that one caused a lot of attention. A big turning point in the siege of Port Arthur."

"One of the more costly land battles of the war," Yamamoto continued. "Frontal attack against a well-fortified, well-dug-in enemy. You remember why we sacrificed so many men for that hill?"

"For an observation point. At two hundred three meters' elevation, it had a view of Port Arthur."

"Right. Only for eyes. Japan had twenty-eight-centimeter guns. The Japanese army could use those guns because Admiral Shimose invented a new type of gunpowder. The army didn't even have the brains to do that for itself. So they had big shells and range but they couldn't see their target. They needed that hill to put observers on top and direct the fire. The Russians knew it; they had plenty of time to set up defenses."

"The foreign war correspondents were astounded at the willingness of the Japanese soldiers to sacrifice themselves."

"It was so fierce, so many men falling on both sides, the army had to take time out to bury their own dead, and the enemy's. That's the way we were trained then. They took the hill, got a radio transmitter on the top, and started directing the fire. Then the shells began hitting the ships in the harbor and the fort."

The hand ended. Yamamoto poured himself a glass of water. He took a long sip, a combination of easing throat parch and a medium to help him travel back in time: the wine of the nondrinker.

"I studied Ninomiya's plans with aviation engineers," he went on. "By present knowledge of aeronautical design, the wing area was just right for twelve-horsepower. He calculated that; he was sharp in physics. All self taught."

Yamamoto put down the glass to light up another cigarette. "Imagine what would have happened if the army had the brains to see that a flying machine could be used for surveillance work. It could have been used instead of Two Hundred Three-Meter Hill to get a spotter aloft. One shot—long-short-left-right—and another shot after compensating. It would have saved a lot of fighting. And the Wrights would have been second."

"Of course, the Wrights' plane wouldn't have been any good," I reminded Yamamoto. "It didn't get high enough or stay aloft long enough. It only proved that a machine could fly."

"The Wrights did a great thing," came the reply from the cloud, "but they were bicycle mechanics. Look at their plane. Two large, slow-turning propellers driven by chains. Just like bicycle wheels. Why the chains? Speed reduction, to cut down propeller rpm. Ninomiya was thinking just the opposite: small, fast-turning propellers. The Wrights had great vision on one hand and stayed tied to bicycle-type energy transmission on the other. But Ninomiya aimed for increasing rotational speed and a propeller that makes sense by today's knowledge of engineering. He had propeller sense. And I bet you can guess why."

"If you put it that way, the answer is practically in the question." Yamamoto gave a minimal chuckle. "Hm! Bamboo dragonflies."

"I've seen children sending them aloft all over Tokyo," I said, "but I never thought they had anything to do with aircraft. . . . until now."

"Every Japanese child has made them. Even poor kids can get a knife and some scrap bamboo. They're simple, right? Just a propeller and a shaft. Spin the shaft between the hands and if the blades are carved right—*and if you spin it fast enough*—it takes flight."

"I've watched children playing with them in parks and school grounds. Some of them really go quite high."

"We kids gained a feel for propeller efficiency. How much pitch to carve to get a bite on the air. We all developed a feel for rotational mechanics, the relationship between propeller speed and thrust. We knew then that if the propeller is too long—like a Wright propeller—it loses rotational speed and lift. We wanted our dragonflies to go high and fly long, and we knew that it took a fast spin of the shaft, and that large, slow-turning blades would wobble, not fly. We kids all learned those things, but Ninomiya applied the knowledge to something besides making a better toy."

It was my turn to deal. I had nothing to say.

"In the Russo-Japanese War, I was fresh out of the Naval Academy," Yamamoto continued. "I never fought land battles. But through the years I fought at Two Hundred Three-Meter Hill over and over in my head with the world's first airplane. Or maybe the second or third; with a little support, the prototype could have been built and revised several times. A flight time of less than one minute per sortie would give the pilot a view of the target. Just a pilot and a radio transmitter or some method of signaling long-short-left-right. It would have been a magnificent first in aviation. If those army idiots only had more self-confidence in the Japanese race. 'If the Western countries don't have such a machine, how could Japan . . .'"

Now four decades later, the emperor blamed the army's same lack of self-confidence for pushing Japan into an alliance with Germany.

Back on course, I bore slightly east to pass between the Goto Islands to the west on the starboard side and Hirado to the east off to port. Hirado, where the Dutch and English set up trading posts in the early 1600s. The Japanese showed inventiveness here, too: market segmenting. When Lord Elgin came to Japan in the nineteenth century, his eye for quality was sharp enough to note that European traders who pulled into Japan were satisfied with pottery of a lower grade of craftsmanship, and the Japanese made it for them. The better wares were sold in the Japanese market.

Captain Aiko. What was he up to in his "home province"? I took a bearing on the Uji Islands, gave left rudder and bore southeast, bringing the island of Tanegashima dead ahead. Tanegashima—1540s. Where a Chinese ship sailing between Siam and Liampo ran aground. Three

Portuguese on board brought the first tobacco and firearms into Japan. Pretty soon the Japanese were making better rifles than the European originals. Matchlocks that worked in the rain. Nobody else did that. They fitted the guns with small, umbrella-looking accessories that protected the rope and the pan. They were charming little creations, like folk craft applied to military use. They even treated the ropes to make them more resistant to moisture. Years later the flintlock was invented, and in Europe they would not work in the rain either. During Napoleon's time, battles were called off because neither side could fire their guns. The French became great admirers of Japanese art, but they never thought of enlisting their military craftsmen. If they did, they would have had guns that could fire when the enemy's could not. When Japan was not underestimated, it was overlooked.

In the 1930s and '40s, with metal scarce and concerns over invasion, military leaders looked for metal-saving ways to make land mines. They went to the pottery villages and ordered earthenware mines. Circular, about ten centimeters high and twenty-two in diameter, they could almost be used for flower-arrangement vases. Only the pressure sensor on top was metal.

Tanegashima fell abeam as I rounded the southern tip of Kyushu and headed northeast into Kagoshima Bay, then wore around the point and steamed northwest. Farther north up the bay lay Sakurajima, a smoking volcano on a peninsular landmass that jutted out from the east side of the bay, dividing it into upper and lower harbors. A channel off the tip of the peninsula afforded passage between the two harbors.

I steamed around the lower harbor for a while, wondering where Captain Aiko might be. Up in those hills writing poetry? Whatever it was that brought him down here all the time, it might be something that this harbor offered that Yokohama and Yokosuka did not, probably relating to his specialty in mines. That would be more logical than a longing for his native village. I was in the coffee shallows; maybe an answer would float up on the next caffeine tide.

As I steamed around, I checked the depth markings on the chart—one always checks depth when navigating offshore and in harbors. Twenty meters. Twenty meters? A harbor with only twenty meters. . . ? Something connected: a different cup of coffee over another harbor chart—years earlier on a naval ship, moored, with a gathering on the bridge of the ship's officers, coffee and the harbor chart. Both above and below water, I recalled, that harbor was more suited to romantic cruise liners than naval vessels—the shallowest harbor I had ever been in: twenty meters, even less in some places. Pearl Harbor, where big naval ships, "fatties," Americans called them, had to crawl forward at just a few knots, or the combination of mass and acceleration would displace enough water under their hulls to turn their keels into plows and leave them stranded. Ships advanced with minimal movement that blended in with the lazy mood of their surroundings. One of the other officers and I hired a car for a tour of the island. "The best view of the harbor is from the residential heights of Aiea," the driver told us. It was. We had a wonderful view of "Battleship Row," while we were surrounded by Japanese tourists and their cameras. Ships moved like huge snails through the harbor as if they did not want to blur the images in their photos.

Standing out to sea from the harbor, ships have to pass through a channel that narrows to about four hundred meters. From an upper deck it feels like levitating out over the palm trees lining the shore. After the channel crawl, vessels eased into the open sea, threw back a parting bouquet of white brine from their screws, and finally moved out at a speed that looked right on a ship.

When the American president ordered the Pacific contingent of the fleet berthed permanently at Hawaii, it upset more than Japan's military leaders. I received reports later that Fleet Commander James O. Richardson objected for tactical reasons, that he argued with the president and called Pearl Harbor a "goddamn mousetrap" from which ships under attack could not escape. In January 1941 the president argued back: He fired Richardson as commander of the U.S. Fleet.

I refueled on coffee, thinking about the similarity in bottom characteristics between Pearl Harbor and Aiko's "home-province" harbor. Was he working on shallow-water mine laying? If so, it could mean practice for another shallow-water harbor.

Mentally, I reviewed the types of mines—sea mines, submarine mines—and drifted into their nomenclature. In Japanese, all end in *rai*, the character for thunder. I went through the list mentally, then recalled the term *gyorai*—literally, "fish mine"—the Japanese term for torpedo. Every time Aiko's specialty came up in conversation, he was some sort of mine expert, and the subject was brushed aside. Linguistically, a torpedo was one type of mine; was Aiko also into "fish mines"? If so, what would harbor depth mean? Twenty meters is deep enough for subs, especially the tiny, two-man Japanese subs. Depth under the keel? Torpedo nets?

Aiko was working under Yamamoto, and ever since our days together at Harvard, when Yamamoto was under the distant tutelage of Billy Mitchell, his name always had wings attached. The Japanese already had a formidable air fleet, built up by buying one plane of each type from foreign suppliers, analyzing them, remodeling them to their needs, then producing them. In 1939 Yamamoto became commander-in-chief of the Combined Fleet, and he pressed air power forward with the added force of his new authority. Was the navy thinking of mining Pearl Harbor? Dropping them from planes? "Fish mines?"

Pearl Harbor was no place for plane-launched fish mines. They plunged to a depth of about a hundred meters before they rise to striking depth. Pearl Harbor would be impossible, and Kagoshima was no place for aerial torpedo practice.

Or was it? Aiko's interest in Viking design — was it really the Confucian way of developing new weaponry? *Shallow draft, but slender and stable.* Was he thinking of a torpedo mounted on a hull that would give enough buoyancy to keep the missile from diving into the shallows? *Lapstrake design that resisted rolling.* Rolling destroyed the function of a torpedo's fins. *Flexibility that absorbed shock.* The shock of striking the water from an air drop? *Slender hull.* To reduce air resistance during the plane's flight? Viking ship design had the characteristics that an air-launched torpedo needed to operate in shallow water, if the characteristics could be applied.

Fish mines! If Japan was thinking of using them against the intimidating ships at Pearl Harbor, no torpedo in existence could be used. But if Aiko was developing torpedoes that *could* be used there, the chart showed that his "home province" was the place for testing them.

The only way planes could get within flight range of Hawaii would be carriers. And that would require a whole new type of naval thinking: a task force with the purpose of serving the carriers, which in turn serve the planes. No navy in the world had given carriers and aircraft such a central role. Yamamoto preached it, and his position of commander-in-chief of the

Combined Fleet convinced me that there was at least one Japanese naval officer who could contemplate a carrier-based air attack on a distant target.

The next sip of coffee brought recollection of November 1940, when the British achieved a milestone in naval history with a less-than-task-force surprise attack on the Italian fleet at its base in Taranto by carrier-based, lumbering Swordfish biplanes. They hit in two waves of ten planes each. In one hour the Italian navy lost more than half its battleships, and the balance of naval power in the Mediterranean shifted in favor of Britain. From what I could tell, Aiko was working on his project under Yamamoto when the British hit Taranto, and it would have been an inspiration, especially with Japan's faster planes. After that, Aiko began increasing his trips to his "home province."

The story took shape: Aiko was developing fish mines in the shallow-water harbor of his home province to go after the American warships in the goddamn mousetrap.

Anyone with a knowledge of Japanese history would expect an attack on a foreign naval base to be reenacted with the surprise and precision displayed against Russia four decades earlier. If Japan knocked out a good part of the United States Fleet, America would have to divert her naval forces from the Atlantic, where I would rather have them fighting against Germany, and that gave me reason to sabotage the plan. But every American attempt to pull Germany into battle on the high seas ended in failure. With Germany and Japan now in an alliance that did not exist in Bywater's time, I saw hope of America's coming in against Germany through a reenactment of *The Great Pacific War*. If it did break out, America's entry against Germany would not be guaranteed, but an intelligent bet. The chart in front of me and my deduction of Aiko's invention were telling me that the only condition which would move Congress, "unless attacked," was being created in Kagoshima. The question was, what should *I* do about it?

▪ 25 ▪
Moves on the Global *Shogi* Board

" **L** ook at this Cadillac advertisement," Yamamoto said. Overseas publications were his stethoscopes to foreign political and social bodies. "They build a wonderful car; I've ridden in them. And I learned some smooth English phrases from their advertising. But what are they saying now? 'In 1939 we began working on our first wartime job.' There's a sketch of an M-5 tank that carries their engines and they advertise how these will bring victory. America is not even at war."

"Maybe cars aren't selling in these economic times," I offered, reminding myself that the American depression was an advantage to Europe in giving the president a reason to enter the war.

In January 1941, with Roosevelt settled into his third term, I received a coded message through Scandinavian underground agents, who had pieced together information from their people in Washington and London: "Harry Hopkins to London again as presidential envoy with new promises to Churchill that America will join Britain in war." Then another message the same month: "Encouraging news. American president introduced resolution to give White House new freedom in handling funds, weapons. Will inform on progress."

The president showed his advertising bent by titling his new bill "1776." He aimed for an initial appropriation of seven billion dollars' worth of arms and military equipment that he could dispose of at his discretion. My first reaction was that the pot was too high, and it did generate protests in America over the virtual transfer of war-making powers to the president. If the bill were enacted, it would link the American economy directly with the war in Europe. That was to our advantage, but the problem was that others saw it the same way, and I feared a setback when I heard that the American Chamber of Commerce joined the opposition. KEEP U.S. OUT OF WAR pins were still fast sellers, and voices in Congress were saying that if Germany did win, America should concentrate on defense and stay out of Europe. The bill went up for a vote.

Another coded message arrived: "President fighting for 1776 as peace measure. Huge opposition, but president applying political pressure against dissidents. Seems to be moving in favorable direction for us but outcome difficult to predict."

The tug-of-war ended on March 11 in Washington with a win for 1776. Yet the promise of European salvation carried its own potential threat: financial and military aid could be sent to undefined countries, including the Soviets. Others feared the same, and when the bill was termed Lend Lease, one American opponent labeled it "Lenin Lease." Since Germany and Russia signed their pact in August 1939, the Soviets partitioned Poland with Germany's cooperation and supplied the Nazis with oil that fueled the German air force in the Battle of Britain. Now the United States was about to supply materials to the British to help them fight Germany. Would the United States also supply arms to the Soviets for use against Scandinavia? The patriotic ring of 1776 in America had double overtones for us.

Sommerfogel came into the garden through a light snow with an angry question. "Did you hear what's happening to the elementary schools in Japan?"

"I can't say that I keep up with everything."

"They won't be called elementary schools anymore. They're being changed to 'People's Schools.'"

"That's what the Germans call them: *volksschulen*."

"Our leaders do everything the Germans do. If they want to be leaders, why do they imitate the Germans so?"

I agreed with her silently, aware that if Japan moved too close to Germany it would mean that Japan could hide behind her big Nazi brother and demand, not negotiate for, our steel and weapons.

"But you know that the *volksschulen* is not a Nazi idea; they existed in Germany before the Nazis took power."

"I'm not arguing about the concept. Schools should be for the people—young people. But the Japanese military like the idea because it's good for training children to follow the imperial way. They interpret 'people' as subjects of the emperor. We'll be getting orders to give students so-called 'spiritual training.' And you know what that means."

"It means you will have to teach those things to the students."

"It means I'll be *ordered* to do it. It does not mean that I'll do it. Then there's that Field Service Code that Army Minister Tojo issued the beginning of this year. Did you see it?"

"Impossible to avoid. It was in the papers and he even made a record of himself reading it, that soldiers in Manchuria should not disgrace themselves by being captured alive."

"That's the type of mind we're supposed to form in children. And did you read about the plan for making more babies?"

"I saw that, too. The government told women to marry young. . . ."

"And bear five children each. I'm sure someone is willing to make ten children to compensate for me. Then the government can stop bullying those of us who don't want to raise soldiers for the republic."

"That sounds like Plato."

"I think he was a bully, too."

▪ 26 ▪
Operation Snow

Japanese Foreign Minister Matsuoka had a grand plan for defeating the United States and Britain: a four-nation alliance of Germany, Italy, Japan, and Russia. In March of 1941 he brought his idea to Japan's Axis partner in Berlin, where Hitler told him to stay away from Stalin. He did not: the following month, Matsuoka was in Moscow to enter into a Neutrality Pact with the Soviets. As he wiped his round "Harold Lloyd" eyeglasses—the Japanese called them that in all seriousness—to sign, Soviet intelligence agents of the NKVD in another corner of the Kremlin finalized a different plan for Japan. Japan's position with the United States and Britain was worsening against the memory of two border wars against the Soviets in the last three years; Japan's hope for the pact was to eliminate the Soviet threat from the north. The secret NKVD scheme was to eliminate the threat from Japanese forces south of the Soviet Union. I put the whole story together some years after the war, when the pivotal agent in the NKVD operation was then assigned to the Soviet embassy in Canada. I traveled there, and back in time, to reconstruct the story of America's last communication with Japan before Pearl Harbor.

Japan and the Soviet Union both considered their Neutrality Pact a smiling stall on the way to Russo-Japanese War II. While the ink on the signatures dried, Vitaly Pavlov, twenty-seven years old and a top man in American affairs in the NKVD, was preparing to leave Moscow. His target was Harry Dexter White, special assistant to the U.S. secretary of the treasury.

Pavlov's mission started back in January 1940 in a Moscow briefing with Ishak Akhmerov, one of his subordinate agents. Akhmerov was educated in

America and lived there, passing for an American under the name Bill. Previously he had been assigned to Peking to investigate Japan's China expansion and her potential to intervene in Siberia. The Soviet Union and Germany signed a ten-year Mutual Nonaggression Pact in August 1939, but both sides also felt that to be a toast of empty cups. When Akhmerov and Pavlov met that January, the smell of a coming war with Germany saturated Moscow's air, and the Soviets felt threatened by the Asian part of Russia's dreaded, potential two-front war: the growing Japanese Kwantung Army in China. Pavlov and Akhmerov worked on a plan to use America to reduce the Japanese threat—while frostbite experiments at Unit 731 were being carried out to prepare for war in Soviet winters.

"I have many collaborators in the United States," Akhmerov told Pavlov, "in Treasury and State Departments. They are not agents, just collaborators. But I also have my own subordinate agent in the Treasury Department. And under him is collaborator Harry Dexter White. He is the right man for helping us with our Japan problem."

"And you know this White personally?" Pavlov asked.

"Yes. First through an introduction by another collaborator. After that we spoke many times and often had lunch together. In the Capital Restaurant. Remember the name; it will come in handy for you."

"I know of him through the work he is doing for us," Pavlov recounted, "and by his code name, 'Snow.' He has been very helpful in sending us photos of documents from the U.S. government."

"Snow is extremely anti-Fascist. Extremely. If war comes with Germany, he will be even more inspired to help us."

"And you say he can help with our Japan problem in China?"

"White is not just very close with the secretary of the treasury, he is indispensable to him. How this happened is very interesting—and a gift to the Soviet Union. It seems that the secretary of the treasury, Henry Morgenthau Jr., knows very little of financial matters."

"Repeat that please."

"It is true. This has been learned from our collaborators in the American government, including White himself. The secretary of the treasury has been quoted saying as much."

"Then how did he get his position?"

"Mr. Morgenthau has a wealthy father who helped Roosevelt with financial deals. Both families are longtime friends from the same New York State. Once, Mr. Morgenthau the father convinced Mr. Roosevelt to buy some securities that later fell. Morgenthau comes to Roosevelt's rescue and arranges to protect him against loss. And with the favor, Morgenthau asked Roosevelt to find a place in government for his son." Akhmerov pulled an American dollar bill from his pocket. "And now the son's signature is on American money." He handed Pavlov the bill.

"A nice partner," Pavlov said, studying the signature, *Henry Morgenthau Jr.* above the words *Secretary of the Treasury*. Pavlov placed the dollar bill on the desk, making Morgenthau a member of the meeting. "And where does Mr. White come in?"

"White graduated Harvard with a doctorate in economics. He joined Treasury in 1934 and gained a reputation for his knowledge of international finance. And, since Morgenthau knows nothing of finance, White was promoted to be his special assistant. Mr. Morgenthau relies very heavily on White—he has to. So thanks to Morgenthau's lack of knowledge of economics, our collaborator is in a key position."

"But the secretary of the treasury does not formulate foreign policy."

"In reality, he has more power than the entire State Department. The American president is famous for hating State Department. Our collaborators there report that the president constantly ignores Secretary of State Hull. American newspapers ridicule Hull for being absent from important conferences while the president sends other people to do his job. Hull is the crybaby of Washington, always threatening to quit because the president never tells him anything. This is important to us, because on key matters the president confers not with Hull but with other cabinet members. And with one more than any other." Akhmerov picked up the dollar bill from the desk. "With him! And I do not mean Mr. Washington."

Pavlov nodded: "We will need Beria's approval."

Laurenty Pavlovich Beria, former director of the Soviet police, was a leader in purging Stalin's opponents, and his purges pushed him up the Soviet ladder. Pavlov submitted the plan and it still lay on Beria's desk in September 1940 when, hours after General Douglas MacArthur stated, "Japan will never join the Axis," Japan joined the Axis. The framework for a two-front war against the Soviets was in place. A few weeks later, Beria called Pavlov to his office and told him, "Let's go ahead with 'Operation Snow,' but it must remain top secret."

In May 1941, Pavlov flashed his diplomatic passport and entered Washington. His English ability was limited and he practiced his lines for weeks before his arrival. He ran through a final rehearsal in his Washington hotel room and, like an actor stepping into the footlights with stage fright for his first performance, picked up the telephone and called Treasury.

"I would like to speak with Mister Harry Dexter White please."

It was a long wait before White came on.

"I am friend of Bill," Pavlov started. "Maybe you know, Bill is now in China. He suggested that I call you when I am coming to Washington and give you his message for you."

"A friend of Bill? Yes, I would like to meet you."

"How about I inviting you for lunch tomorrow at Capital Restaurant."

"Thank you. Shall we meet there at noon?" suggested White.

"Lunchtime too many peoples. Why we don't meet little later."

"Two-thirty?"

"Very good, two-thirty. I having blond hair and will carrying *The New Yorker* magazine."

Pavlov hung up and stood in front of the telephone for a long time. The pressure was lifted; he was recovering from the bends.

He arrived at the Capital Restaurant well ahead of time. As he had hoped, there were only a few scattered customers. He saw there was no other blond male, then went to a table at the far end of the restaurant and placed the magazine on it. White had no trouble locating him. Pavlov's hair was not only a screaming blond, it was abundant and flowing. His jawbones looked like they were forged in a Soviet naval shipyard. Pavlov was visible long before *The New Yorker* was and contrasted with White's soft, roundish, intellectual face set off with eyeglass and a tiny mustache. The two ordered lunch, sipped water, moved their silverware around . . .

"Bill sends you his regards," Pavlov opened. "He also wanted me to tell you that he was worried about Japanese advances in Asia. He asked me to meet you and let you hear what he has to say about that. I think you will be interested in his message."

"Of course. Please go on."

"First I must apologize. Bill thought my English not enough reliable, so he is writing out his message for to give you." Pavlov handed the message to White, who smiled at this strapping Russian, his ruddy face that seemed like he was looking into a gale and not bothered by it, handing over someone else's homework. It had been banged out on a typewriter in need of maintenance, but the crooked and smudged letters and jumped spaces were clear in content. White read the paper and almost shouted, "These are precisely my thoughts."

"As you see," Pavlov went on, "Bill wants America to oppose Japan's expansion in China, with measures that Washington should take against Japan in handling the situation."

White—and the NKVD—expected the document to take the customary, direct route to the president through Morgenthau. Back in Treasury, White began drafting a document, applying his logic and rhetorical skills to the instructions with crooked and smudged letters and jumped spaces:

The Franco-British brand of diplomacy emulated by our own State Department appears to have failed miserably. Due to half-measures, miscalculations, timidity, machinations, or incompetence of the State Departments of the United States, England, and France, we are being isolated and we find ourselves rapidly moving toward a war that can be won by us under present circumstances only after a costly and bitter effort. . . .

Virtually surrounded by a world ablaze, and with the fire growing hotter, nearer and more dangerous, our diplomatic machinery concerns itself chiefly with maintaining a facade of important goings-on, an appearance of assured and effective functioning, whereas behind that front is largely hesitation, bewilderment, inaction, petty maneuvering, sterile conversations, and diverse objectives.

White also saw a chance to throw a broadside of ridicule at State while sailing around it, and further erode Hull's thin authority.

I am convinced that the proposal will not even get a serious hearing unless pushed by high officials outside the State Department.

Yet, if America does not strengthen her diplomatic arm, we will
have to face a victorious Germany, with Japan and Italy her allies
and all of Europe turning out arms for them. In the light of requirements of modern diplomacy, American foreign diplomatic
maneuverings are pathetic, nineteenth-century patterns of petty
bargaining, with their dependence upon subtle half-promises, irri-
tating pinpricks, excursions into double-dealing, and copious *pro-
nunciamentos* of good will alternating with vague threats—all
veiled in an atmosphere of high secrecy designed to hide the es-
sential barrenness of achievement.

In the postwar years, a former Soviet official who worked under Beria
and later antagonized him, realized he was on Beria's hit list and defected
to Finland. He knew Pavlov and the inner workings of the NKVD, and told
what he knew to save him and his family. He said that Pavlov was assigned
to a Soviet embassy in Canada. It would be an embarrassing revelation for
his government if it surfaced that a Soviet espionage agent was working in
the embassy and an advantageous card for me. But blackmail needed a
friendly balance.

From my hotel room, I called Pavlov at his embassy in a mirror image
of his call to White years ago.

"I was an acquaintance of Bill's."

"Bill. . . ?"

"Yes, who lived in the United States."

"And what you want?"

"I'd like to invite you to lunch or dinner."

We met. Pavlov was skeptical. "You knew Bill?"

"We were not close, but . . ."

"And you wanting talk to me?" His English had not improved.

"I'm interested in your meeting with Harry Dexter White."

His jawbones tightened. "I met such a man? Who he is?"

"Was! He died back in August 1948. You met in 1941. Washington."

"I meeting so many peoples. I don't remember all."

"Look, we can be honest about it. We both know that you met White
in Washington. That has no value to any nation anymore. I am interested in

it only for my own purposes and I am willing to pay for it." His jawbones softened. Then I played the blackmail card.

"I know you were a top man in the NKVD." His jawbones tightened again. "But I don't care about that. Maybe people here in Canada might, or even in the United States . . ." His concern showed. "But that's your business. Personally, I don't even think you are still in intelligence, but you know how governments are sensitive about things like that. I only want information from the past. And, as a researcher, I am willing to pay for it." I wrote a sum of money on a piece of paper. He faked nonchalance, then stepped lightly.

"This White person. He was. . . ?"

"He was named by a former diplomat from your government. Because of that, White was summoned before the House Un-American Activities Committee and died a few days later. I'm sure you know."

"Ah, I remember now. Was in newspapers. He have heart attack."

"Officially."

"You think something else?" Now Pavlov was questioning *me*.

"Only a guess, but you remember Alexander Gregory-Graff Barmine?"

"So many peoples in Soviet Union . . ."

"The former Soviet diplomat who told the FBI that White—and Alger Hiss and others—had worked for Soviet intelligence."

"Maybe he say; I don't know."

"After White died, a journalist wrote that it was from an intentional overdose of digitalis. But at any rate, he's no longer here. So how did you and he get involved?"

Pavlov thought for a moment, nodded his head slightly to signal resolve, and spoke slowly. "The Japanese army in China was independent government. We make pact with Tokyo, but Tokyo no could make pact with own army."

"There was no question about that," I responded. "When civilians did try to talk to army officers they were chased back to Tokyo, literally at sword point."

"We understand we no could evict Japan from Manchuria. Business, agriculture, raw materials. Was New Japan."

"Yes," I agreed, "Japanese in Manchuria referred to Japan as 'the mainland.' Manchuria was part of the empire."

"So, we settle for reducing military in China. If could force change to civilian rule, and get army away from Soviet borders, would be good for us. We all expecting war with Germany. And we already have two border wars with Japan."

"Of course, the Soviet Union was concerned about a two-front-war situation."

Pavlov nodded agreement. "Is why, in 1936 when Hitler push Tokyo for next Olympics, we know what he thinking—to use Japan to squeeze us in two-front war. But when Soviet have border wars with Japan—1938, 1939—Germany was too busy looking at Europe to join Japan against us. Then Japanese army near our borders keep getting stronger. Hold maneuvers. We see ghosts of Nomonhan and Russo-Japanese War. So in NKVD, we decide we use America to force Japanese army out. Here, Harry Dexter White is good for us. His direct line to White House."

"How much influence did he actually have in Washington?"

"'Snow' placed many members of American Communist Party in Treasury Department, in State Department, in Agriculture, War Department. . . . many places. You know some names from investigations in America. But in Moscow, he known as member of Silvermaster ring. Always sending information. They have photographic laboratory in Mr. Silvermaster's home." Pavlov broke into a slight smile; it looked like it might crack his jawbone. "Mr. Silvermaster, he have good name. He use silver bromide to make microfilms of documents for us."

"And how did you obtain these?"

"He . . . send them." Pavlov was reluctant to tread on Soviet compatriots.

"Not by mail?"

"He give them to someone, I don't know who. . . ."

"Not Ovakimian, was it?"

"Who?"

"Gaik Ovakimian. He was one of your agents and not a very well-kept secret. His name was on the intelligence list of a number of countries and undergrounds. So it's not possible that you never heard of him. Was he the contact man for the Silvermaster group?"

"Maybe was him. I don't know."

"He was arrested by United States authorities as an unregistered agent of the Soviet government."

"Maybe I hear something like that, I don't know."

"It's impossible that you did not. I'm interested in only one thing about him. As an unregistered agent, he should have been questioned by the FBI. That's their jurisdiction. But he simply returned to the Soviet Union. How?" That squeezed another slight smile from Pavlov.

"You ask how. That American government decision."

"How did you work it?"

"Me? I work nothing. But you know already. If FBI question him, maybe the story come out about Silvermaster, White, microfilms. And that connected with agents and cooperators in U.S. government. So White's associates in State Department work intervention. They give Ovakimian diplomatic courtesy to return his country."

"And did that lose the contact man for the Silvermaster ring?"

"Another take his place."

"Another?"

"Someone else."

"And that was. . . ?"

Pavlov had another stroke of reluctance. I slid the paper with the sum of money written on it toward him and finished the sentence with a question: ". . . Anatole Gromov?"

"Gromov?"

First secretary of the Soviet embassy in Washington."

"You have good memory."

"I've studied. But Gromov also became head of your organization— the NKVD—in North America."

"You know many things."

"And you say that he was receiving microfilmed documents from White and Silvermaster?"

Pavlov cocked his head to one side. "Maybe."

"So, you met White in the Capital Restaurant. What were your instructions to him?"

"We tell him, America to recognize Manchuria as possession of Japan. It's all right. To demand more would be impossible. Then maybe we have chance to push only army out. So White starts list of proposals. America recognize Manchuria as part of Japan Empire. But Japan must to give up all extraterritorial rights in rest of China. And withdraw military and police forces from China, Indochina, Thailand. If no, America should threaten embargo of materials to Japan. Also, Indochina to be placed under joint commission: British, French, Japanese, American."

"You felt safer with those countries included, of course."

"Naturally. Stalin already have Roosevelt in his hand. And with our agents and cooperators in America, we have eyes everywhere in Washington. Churchill? He do what Roosevelt say. And French already strong in Asia. No can kick out. But no need. Only must hold down Japan army. Then we use America to help fight Germany."

"And did the NKVD make plans for that also?"

"Of course. The note I give White—and White himself have same idea—it outline plan that if Japan withdraw military from China, the United States withdraw bulk of naval forces from Pacific. This mean can relocate to Atlantic to fight the Germans. This what we need."

"And White was willing to work for the NKVD that way?"

"White never know I belong to NKVD. I tell him only I was ordinary citizen concerned about world situation."

"When White was questioned by the House Un-American Activities Committee, he denied being a Soviet spy. Was he?"

"I don't know if could call spy. Cooperator, yes. He cooperate with our agents, so in that sense maybe could call spy. But he not agent. We never make him agent. Not necessary."

"Did you think that putting this pressure on Japan would push them and America into war in the Pacific?"

"We think about it, of course. But was not our main purpose. Main purpose was prevent two-front war. But if it happen war between Japan and America, is all right, too. If Japan busy fighting in Pacific, is more difficult to attack us. Is natural, yes?"

"... Yes."

▪ 27 ▪
Master-Spy Sorge's Labyrinth

An argument with a rickshaw man in Formosa launched Stalin's espionage eyes in Tokyo. The *jinrikisha*, "human-powered vehicle," was the invention of an American missionary in Japan soon after the Meiji Restoration; he made it for himself, to pull his disabled wife about. A Japanese businessman saw it as a convenient way of hauling goods and a potential taxi, and produced similar vehicles. With Japan's incursion into Asia, they were exported in the tens of thousands and did indeed become taxis. Formosa had been a Japanese possession since 1895, and one day a Japanese resident of Formosa by the name of Ozaki rode home in a rickshaw. He and the rickshaw man had an argument over the fare and Ozaki took his cane and beat the rickshaw man. Ozaki's small boy, Hotsumi, was waiting at the window for his father and saw the scene. As he grew, the shock stayed with him and made him conscious of Japanese mistreatment of colonials. When Hotsumi reached adulthood he was drawn to the communist doctrine of equality and became a Communist Party member and a journalist for the *Asahi* newspaper in Tokyo. In 1927 his newspaper sent him to Shanghai as a special correspondent.

Richard Sorge was born in Russia of a Russian mother and German father and was educated in Germany from childhood. He was wounded in the leg during The Great War, which turned his passions antiwar and made him receptive to the communist propaganda of peace and harmony. Sorge became a journalist for the German newspaper *Frankfurter Zeitung* and worked as a correspondent in Shanghai, where he secretly collected information for Moscow.

The Communist Party decided that Sorge and Ozaki should join forces. A coded personal ad in a newspaper set up the meeting at a restaurant. It started with the usual cat-and-mouse password, a reply, a counter-reply . . .

In 1931 Ozaki returned to the Tokyo head office and in 1933 Sorge was also transferred to Tokyo. He joined the Nazi Party to cover his role of espionage agent for the Soviets, and in Tokyo he was a master actor: his Nazi salute was the highest, his praise for Nazi aims the most exuberant. With the outbreak of war in Europe in 1939 he was invited to work within the German embassy in Tokyo, even though he had no official status. In this position he handled and edited official bulletins from Berlin and became partner to secret information.

Ozaki worked into an even stranger position to bring sensitive information into the spy ring. In 1936, friends of then–Prime Minister Konoe organized a research and advisory board as a brain to the prime minister. Ozaki became consultant to the group as a China expert and a confidant of high-ranking persons in inner government circles, who unwittingly provided him with intelligence for the ring and for Moscow.

When there was information for Moscow, the ring stretched a six-and-a-half-meter transmitting antenna in the upper floor of a house in Tokyo; the location was changed constantly in case police tried to home in on the radio waves. For code, the ring used a ponderous, obscure catalog of no relevance. A number identified a page, then the line on that page, a word in the line, and a letter in the word. It was a simple, unwieldy system with no logical repetition of characters that cryptographers look for in breaking codes. The Sorge ring and its antenna served Stalin well with information, but the Soviet leader *mis*read the most important message that Sorge ever sent him, which brought a telephone call to my office in May 1941 from Richard Sorge, German journalist, who would like to interview the Swedish minister "on his life in general in Tokyo."

I had met Sorge several times and we exchanged casual greetings. He was also a bachelor and had an active social life. He was a heavy drinker but I noticed he stayed very well in control of himself.

Early in 1941 Hitler drew up plans for violent termination of the Nonaggression Pact signed in 1939 between Germany and the Soviet

Union. Sorge, through his work at the German embassy, learned of a coming attack, and in April 1941 the antenna beamed a warning to Moscow. It was Europe's loss that Stalin read a bluff where there was none. He believed in error that Sorge had been duped with false information to break up the Berlin-Moscow agreement.

Sorge's dilemma brought me his call for an interview. He came with two bottles of fine Scotch, loot taken by German armies—an inordinately extravagant gift for a mere journalist on a meaningless assignment. "We can open one bottle now," he said, "and you can keep the other to entertain someone more enticing."

He played his role with stage presence. With polite, professional directness he asked about my life in Tokyo, my taste in foods, any shortages I felt. . . . and then worked around to the world situation.

"Do you foresee any radical changes in Europe?" he asked.

"As you know, I am from a neutral country, so Sweden is expected to be free of major changes." We spoke around things, and he noted down my words with the same empty courtesies as I gave them. I was still not sure about the real reason for this visit. Whenever we came to an impasse in our ritual, he complimented the quality of the Scotch—an overture to pour another. I realized later that it was to give him license for an indiscretion already written into his script.

The Argentine author, Jorge Luis Borges, was fascinated with labyrinths. In *El Jardín de Senderos que se Bifurcan*, a Chinese man spying for Germany during the First World War was in England with important information: the location of a British artillery battery. His problem was how to communicate this back to Berlin. The spy locates a British scholar who is known to possess an ancient Chinese labyrinth, and goes to the house. The approach to the house is itself a series of bifurcating paths, and after traversing them and reaching the front door, the Chinese presents himself as a researcher of labyrinths, and requests to see the one owned by the scholar. Both men go inside to the study, where the spy pulls out a pistol, kills the scholar, then surrenders to the police. Newspapers carried the story of the unexplained murder and the strange Chinese who did it for no apparent motive.

Borges's Chinese spy writes, "We live in a labyrinth with paths that continually bifurcate. In some choices we are allies; in others, enemies."

The scholar had the same family name as the village where the gun battery was located. When the press carried news of the murder with the names of victim and perpetrator, the Germans understood.

Sorge was in a labyrinth. In his secret life as a Soviet agent, we both shared the same desire for the fall of Germany, yet there was no way he could let me know. His path to Stalin was blocked, and now he sought a bifurcation that would reach the same destination from a convincing direction. He increased his compliments for the Scotch as his time between drinks grew shorter, while he played each word like a turn in a labyrinth, looking for the path that would lead him into the bluffed slip he was trying to reach.

"I know, Mister Minister, that you and your countrymen are not happy with the German arrangement."

"We have a cooperative agreement," I said; the words tasted like sugared sewage.

"And how do you see the Soviet situation?" he asked.

"As far as Sweden is concerned, the Soviets are not a problem."

"But Scandinavia is filled with Russian problems. After Sweden declared neutrality in 1939, the Soviets attacked Finland. You sent the Finns materials, and Swedish volunteers even went to help Finland."

"We've had our moments."

"Then when Sweden tried to form a Nordic defense union, or would even settle for an alliance with Finland, the Soviets barged in to prevent it. Sweden must have bitter feelings toward the Soviets."

"But the Soviets, as do other countries, respect our neutrality."

"They have been a problem for you in the past, and they may repeat their troublesome behavior at any time. Suppose, for example, the Soviets came in demanding your iron?"

"They would have to work that out with your government," I responded. "After all, Germany and Russia are allies."

That was it! I had opened the path in the maze that Sorge wanted. He finished his drink in one gulp, with a flourish. When he spoke again, his slur had gained weight.

"Don't count on that forever," he said with a wry smile that obviously invited me to press the point. I did: "Oh? Germany and Russia may split?"

"Well, I am only a journalist, but I respect Sweden's cooperation and her determination to remain neutral and not side with the Allies." The labyrinth was unbending into a straightaway. He poured again and took another sip. "And for that I will tell you something in confidence, something that I should not really say."

He waited for the lure of *something he should not say* to press me into the next move. I said "Oh?" with an extra touch of interest.

"Stay with us a bit longer and your country will be rewarded for the support it has given the Third Reich. Your iron will be more important in the months ahead."

"It already is important to you now."

"War ... politics ... things change as nations take different turns of the road. Germany is on the threshold of removing a lifelong threat to the Scandinavian countries. Stalin—his name, of course, means *steel*—will be melted down by the heat of guns you helped us build."

"You mean ... Germany is going to war against Russia?!"

"I am only a newspaperman. I cannot give you any official information because I am not supposed to have it. But any attempt to choke off your iron could be a setback to the honorable aims of the Third Reich. When June arrives," he added more wobble to his head, "you will see. And please, remember that I tell you this in the strictest confidence."

He left, and Richard Sorge, reputed drinker, did a commendable job of staggering.

We live in a labyrinth with paths that continually bifurcate. ...

I encoded a message to my minister in Stockholm, advised him of the imminent attack, and added, "A weakening of the German armies on Soviet soil would be welcomed." The answer came the following day: "The information appears interesting. Sweden takes no action. Let us not break the contact." Neutrality won.

The attack came on June 22. Within hours German planes destroyed sixty-six airfields and twelve hundred aircraft; German armies thrust fast and captured almost two thousand cannon and three thousand tanks. If Stalin had lived by his own rules, he would have been eliminated. If he had listened, he could have reduced Germany's power even more than eventually happened.

The Japanese, I later found out, were not out of the information circle. Tokyo received advance news of the attack from Ambassador Oshima in

Berlin. The question for Japan was how close to stay to their German allies. The Soviets tensed for the answer with eyes on the Manchurian border. I remember Yamamoto's comments on that knot in Japan's relations.

"Matsuoka was a problem as foreign minister. He opposed Japan's moves into French Indochina, but he was always against anything anyone else said. He's weird that way. And a good actor. He cried at a cabinet meeting when he heard that the emperor was worried about world affairs. A realistic performance, but an act. He's also a good poker player, and the Soviet pact was his faked bet."

"You mean he never meant to keep it?"

"He thought it would open the way for him to negotiate with America. But when he went to Berlin in spring of 1941, Oshima told him an attack was being planned. Matsuoka screamed that it was stupid to think it would happen, but that was one faked bet to open the way to the next one; he knew the attack was coming. He signed the pact with Moscow as another faked bet, then after Germany attacked he tried to push us to violate the pact, join Germany and strike north."

"The two-front war Russia was afraid of—and another Russo-Japanese War with Germany as an ally."

"Hmmm. If we had to fight, I'd rather Japan do it without the Nazis. It's easy to guess what they'd do later. But Matsuoka pushed and the emperor was worried, so he asked Konoe to get rid of him. Konoe had to resign with his cabinet to do it, then formed his third cabinet with only one change: Matsuoka was replaced. It's too bad we couldn't have kept him out of government and prevented the alliance with the Axis. But at least the emperor saved us from fighting Russia again."

The attack brought a meeting at Japan's General Staff Headquarters to decide whether to move north against Russia or south into Asia and the Pacific. Ozaki gleaned the information from his associates, and the Sorge ring's antenna and ponderous catalog advised Moscow that Japan was going to advance south, not north. This time Stalin believed. The Soviets would not have to fight Japan yet, but the growing Kwantung Army still caused sweat in Moscow. And as the sweat ran, Japan's advances into Asia were helping the NKVD bring America and Japan to the boiling point.

▪ 28 ▪

Undeclared War

"**I** find it difficult to believe that you've never been to Japan," Kurusu Saburo said when we first met in Chicago. I had occasion to pass through that city when a colleague was living there. He knew of my interest in the language and history of Japan, and introduced me to Kurusu, a member of Japan's Foreign Ministry, and his American wife, Alice. "Your knowledge of the Japanese language and our culture are admirable. We need people like you to help bridge the gap between East and West," he said. We kept in touch with an occasional letter, and after I took my post in Tokyo, Kurusu and I met from time to time. Soon after Germany's attack on Russia, we were discussing the turn of events.

"The Japanese government's military color has been deepening," Kurusu said. "Now that their German heroes have attacked Japan's traditional enemy, I fear the army leaders will become even more irrational."

"Can the civilian element retain any influence?"

"There has to be compromise. We civilians consider the best way to keep peace with the United States, Britain, and the Soviets is to let the army have Indochina. We're giving them free rein to go wild in that region to satisfy their hunger for conquest."

A gambler cannot give an opponent a partial victory to water down a craving for further gains. A win blossoms into greater lust with the constancy that a mustard seed produces a mustard plant and not a tulip. Chamberlain's fallacy was being replayed by Japan's civilian factions toward her own military when, in the summer of 1941, American Under-Secretary of State Welles sent Japan an ultimatum: "Japan's advance into Indochina is incompatible with the negotiations between Japan and the

U.S. now in progress. America knows of Japan's intentions to occupy the region." While Welles made incursions into the secretary of state's territory, Japan continued hers into Indochina. Aside from raising racist hatred—"the white man telling us again what we can and cannot do in Asia"—it was handled with the Japanese tactic of "kill with silence," ignoring something until it goes away. The ultimatum did not slow the Japanese advancement, but it taught Harry Dexter White that if Japan were to be forced into action with a document, it would have to be one that could not be ignored.

At the end of July, the United States, Britain, and Holland froze Japanese assets and imposed trade embargoes on her. Shortly afterward, I was speaking with the American ambassador, Joseph Grew.

"The embargo, to most observers, usually means oil," he told me. "But there is more."

"Such as. . . ?"

"Bauxite is almost as critical to the Japanese."

"For aircraft, of course."

"Exactly. There can be other sources for oil, but Malaya and the Indies are providing Japan with ninety percent of her bauxite for aluminum manufacture. Her stockpile is now around two hundred sixty thousand metric tons."

"And how long will that last her?"

"At present rate of use, nine months. But Japan is increasing plane construction, and that makes it seven months. I am going to communicate this to my government, and I hope they see how the bauxite squeeze could be disastrous to the present situation."

That summer of 1941, Mrs. Saito, my staff member, came to the legation with a booklet, *The People's Way*. "This is the latest in the government's plans to educate us citizens," she said. "You might care to read it."

"Are you permitted to show this to non-Japanese?" I half jested.

She smiled as much as she ever did. The loss of her husband and the burden of raising two sons had turned her somber, but she had a warmth under a thin veil of constant sadness that generated empathy. "Sweden was not a colonizer," she answered, "so I think you are not included here. It tells how the world crisis is a result of the West's aggression and colonization. I'm afraid they are preparing us for something. There are two questions that may interest you."

I looked at them: *How did America treat the American Indians? How did America treat African Negroes?*

The questions had to linger as that same summer the Japanese news screamed, "American ships carrying munitions to the Soviets." Ships steaming for Vladivostok flying the American flag stoked fever in Japan. Radios and newspapers announced, "Voices in Japan call for sinking the supply ships." There were Japanese leaders who would be glad for a chance to polish apples for their Nazi idols, and with a German-Japanese alliance in place, an attack on American munitions ships could be a stepping-stone to an American-German confrontation that the Nazis had avoided. It was apparent that Hitler first wanted to defeat England before getting involved in a war with America, and America had to come in sooner. But Japan remained calm and the ships went through, supplying Japan's — and Scandinavia's — nemesis.

Under this growing friction between Japan and the United States, Kurusu was scheduled to leave for America that same summer of 1941. Then I received word that he was hospitalized with an attack of conjunctivitis. I went to visit him, and found him with his eyes bandaged and Alice at his bedside.

"I've got as much vision now as our military leaders," he said when he heard my voice. "But I would be glad to go even with the bandages." There was not a trace of joking. "The American president cannot walk, so what does it matter if I cannot see? We can discuss."

He remained hospitalized for months, and I went to see him occasionally. "Do you remember Admiral Zacharias, of the United States Navy?" he asked me on one of my visits.

"Of course. I knew him when he was naval attaché in the American Embassy here. He was fluent in Japanese and perceptive in understanding Japan. We spoke together several times."

"We came to know each other quite well," Kurusu told me. "Zacharias is now in command of a heavy cruiser, *Salt Lake City*."

"Zacharias?" I was surprised at this news. "The last I heard he was an intelligence officer in San Diego."

"He was transferred to sea duty last November. He put in a request to the naval command to meet with me when I pass through Hawaii. I am looking forward to it."

Why was the man who probably knew more than anyone in the American military about Japan and Japanese thinking pulled from intelligence work just when America needed his expertise and perception? If America had known about Captain Aiko's work, would Zacharias have been sent to sea? It was fortunate for us, but I could not tell this to Kurusu.

"This past February," Kurusu said, "Admiral Nomura went to Washington to assume his post of ambassador to the United States. He made an appointment to meet Zacharias in San Francisco. Nomura told him that Japan regrets its partnership in the Axis and its adventures in China, and hopes for a peaceful solution with America."

"And were there any results?"

"I don't know. Nomura just wrote me that the two drank Scotch together and had a pleasant meeting. I want to meet Zacharias in Hawaii on my way to Washington, as soon as I can get out of here."

I lied when I wished Kurusu best of luck in his meeting with Zacharias. I did not want it to happen. The American admiral might cull just enough information about Tokyo to anticipate Japan's tactics. He was uncanny. I believed him capable of reading the probability of a Japanese attack plan to where it would seem he had previous knowledge, well enough to convince the Japanese that the attack was expected. And that posed the chance that Japan would cancel the attack.

America took a step toward mobilization by putting a Selective Service Law into effect to conscript men for the armed forces, and on the way to its enactment in September 1940 and following its passage, the American president's poker and advertising spirit elevated. In one of his most dramatic and impassioned speeches ever, he announced that he had obtained secret Nazi plans to divide all of South America and part of Central America into five German vassal states and abolish all religion. Soon afterwards, strange things began happening on the high seas of the Atlantic. American naval ships began firing on German submarines. The action seemed like open attempts to incite the Germans to return fire. There were several incidents, but German commanders were under orders to avoid conflict with America, and the greatest fire was in the American press itself, which screamed against the president's "undeclared war in the Atlantic." I admit an admiration for German discipline in resisting return fire, but it did not hold forever: On September 4, the American destroyer USS *Greer* spotted a German sub's position for three hours, radioing it to a British plane overhead to guide depth-charge drops. The plane flew off to refuel, the *Greer* continued the hunt alone, and the U-boat finally surfaced and fired on the American ship.

On October 12 the USS *Reuben James* tried to incite a German U-boat into battle off Iceland. There was an exchange of fire and the American destroyer was sunk with the loss of one hundred fifteen men. The presidential claim that the Germans fired first was not convincing enough to move America closer to entry into the war, and the American press poured more ink into criticism of the president.

On October 16 the USS *Kearny* was escorting convoys of war materials on the high seas. It dropped depth charges on a German sub, the sub surfaced and retaliated with fire, but the American Congress won again. None of these incidents unsheathed the pen to bring America's armed potential to European soil. Neutrality can be as tenacious as it is vague.

· 29 ·
Tojo Rises

"This is one time I wish I were still in the government and yet I'm glad I'm not," Yamamoto said on another visit to escape another madness.

"The problem with America, of course."

"Since America cut off oil shipments to Japan, the cabinet is doing what it does best: running in circles."

"It seems that Konoe and his cabinet are really up against a problem they can't handle," I offered.

"You're too kind. That vacillating aristocrat tries to be a friend to everybody and advisor to the emperor. The only thing that qualifies him— if you could call it that—is his bloodline. Aristocrats like him would serve us better if they just sat in their estates and drank tea."

"And what do you see as the cabinet's next step?"

"First, more quibbling. Konoe says that neither America nor Britain will go to war to save Indochina from France, but he wants to convince the world that our army will stop advancing into the region. Our emperor stopped believing the army leaders; why should foreign countries believe them? Meanwhile, America is pressing Japan to stop the war in China. So our cabinet is going in circles."

"And the options. . . ?"

"Compromise with America over Japan's withdrawal from China, or take a chance on war."

"With the war in China still pulling Japan in like quicksand, do you think Japan would risk war in the Pacific?"

"You think too logically. Some cabinet people see this as a continuation of a trade war that started two years ago. There were three moves that always came in July, a year apart. In 1939, just before war broke out in Europe, America denounced its commercial treaty with Tokyo. That freed them to take further economic steps against Japan."

"I remember that. Another hot spot in relations."

"Then, in July 1940, America put scrap iron and oil shipments to Japan under a licensing system to cut down their volume. More problems for Tokyo. Now this year in July, as soon as the Japanese army landed on Indochina, America froze Japanese assets. So we've been dealt three sevens."

"And July is the month of revolutions," I reminded him. "America, France . . . But this year's second big move missed July by one day."

"A bare miss: August first. The United States banned oil shipments to Japan, then Holland joined and stopped shipments from the Dutch East Indies."

"And there does not seem to be any chance of compromising on the China problem?"

"We've got a hard-headed army minister. They've all been hard-headed, but Tojo is especially tight in the brain. He screams that the army will never compromise on troops in China. He's afraid that if we give in to American demands, Japan will lose everything we achieved there and our control in Manchuria and Korea will be jeopardized."

"What about the prime minister?"

"Konoe is showing a scrap of common sense by saying that Japan would be foolish to jump into war against the United States and Britain when we still can't end the war in China. Maybe he's trying to compensate for pushing us into the alliance with Germany. Right now, he's the only hopeful influence for avoiding war with the West. Our foreign ministry people here are on the phone constantly with their staff in Washington over what we call 'Mariko.'"

"*Mariko?!*" Yamamoto caught the surprise in my voice.

"You've heard of Mariko?"

"I know someone by that name. . . ."

"No connection, I'm sure. That's our code for the situation between Japan and America. The embassy's phone in Washington is probably tapped, so Mariko's condition is discussed almost daily."

"And, how does 'Mariko' look now?"

"The only hope for her improvement is while Konoe is still prime minister."

"So the Konoe cabinet may fall?"

"Like always, when the problem gets too big for the government, the government changes."

"And who do you see taking his place?"

"The emperor wants to avoid a replay of the army's deviant behavior that put us in the mess in China, and he's looking for someone who can control the generals. I'm not sure I agree with his choice. And 'Mariko' will suffer for it."

The "problem too big" this time was indeed "Mariko," and intra-cabinet quibbling over how to handle America raised frictional temperatures in the government. On October 10, Konoe's third cabinet blew apart from internal pressure. The emperor's choice for a prime minister who could handle the Japanese army was General Tojo Hideki, the first person to hold the post while on active military service. On the eighteenth, he formed his cabinet, still retaining the position of minister of the army. He also took the post of minister of the interior, an aptly named organization if one interprets "interior" as the recesses of the mind; the ministry was a national propaganda and thought-management organization.

Three days after the Tojo cabinet formed, Mrs. Saito came to work dejected.

"The ministry of education has restricted the advancement of students to higher education."

"And that will affect your sons, of course."

"It will. The military wants to release students to the home front."

"The home front?"

"To work in war factories. My eldest son wanted to study engineering, but now he will be a laborer making bombs or some such."

On November 22 the American president took another initiative in sweeping aside the cumbersome Constitution and ordered U.S. troops to occupy Iceland. When Icelanders opposed it, I feared an incident that might force an American softening, but the president remained bold and took another step toward Europe: He braved shouts of protest in Washington and ordered American troops to Iran to protect British shipping, while the seed of the NKVD's plan germinated on Harry Dexter White's desk.

· 30 ·
The NKVD's "Hull Note"

I did not realize why it took Harry Dexter White six months to send his draft of the NKVD's outline on its way to the president—especially after Germany's attack on the Soviet Union gave it new urgency—until I fit the jigsaw puzzle of events together.

White was in a bind of events. He was the hidden originator of the plan for Lend Lease as a way to aid the countries fighting Germany, above all the Soviet Union. His draft took the Morgenthau route to the White House, and Roosevelt was enthusiastic: The bill stipulated that arms and funds could be distributed at the president's discretion. When Roosevelt introduced "Bill 1776" in January 1941, opposition in Congress was monumental. The president fought; he threatened dissenting Congressmen with loss of patronage and political opposition in reelection campaigns, and warned they would jeopardize appropriations for their districts. "You would be held responsible for running out on the party and on the president," he warned, and he finally pushed through the enactment on March 11. "But no aid to communist Russia!" was the next scream in Congress and throughout the constituencies. The mood in America against aid to Russia—White's main purpose in devising the plan—was strong when he and Pavlov met in May at the Capital Restaurant. In June Germany attacked, and White learned that the following day Secretary of the Interior Harold Ickes sent a memo to Roosevelt: "Embargo of oil to Japan would be a popular move. This would make it easy to get into the war indirectly and avoid criticism that we came in as an ally of Russia."

With this squeeze on Japan at work against a background of national opposition to extending Lend Lease to Russia, it was a clumsy time to initiate another squeeze; White's document stayed shelved.

In Tokyo on July 2 at an imperial conference, the cabinet informed the emperor that Japan would not join Germany in the war against Russia. Ozaki gleaned the information, the antenna sent the message to Moscow, then Ozaki went to Manchuria to verify that the Kwantung Army was not preparing for a northern move. The Soviet Union was safe from Japan—at least for the time being.

Morgenthau brought disheartening news to White. The president's close associates—especially and ironically two military men of the president's six-man war council, General George C. Marshall and Admiral Harold R. Stark—appealed to Roosevelt that America's major objective was the defeat of Germany. They asked that America do nothing to force a crisis with Japan and to send her no ultimatum for three or four months, until the Philippines and Singapore could be strengthened. White could not go upstream against this. His plan slept.

In mid-July when the Konoe cabinet reformed to get rid of Foreign Minister Matsuoka—Nazism's great fan—it looked like a softening in Tokyo and another setback for White, but the Japanese army continued laying the groundwork for his move. The new foreign minister notified the Vichy French government that Japan would march into French Indochina by force on July 24. At the last minute the French decided it wiser to agree to a peaceful occupation; Japanese troops marched in.

The Vichy government was officially recognized, if not admired, by America, but Roosevelt seized the chance and two days later he froze Japanese assets. Trade between the countries ceased and the flow of oil from America—Japan's major supplier—stopped. The *New York Times* called it "the most drastic blow short of war," but it still remained "short of," and the president continued his battle to extend Lend Lease to Russia. White wanted that before adding more straws.

In late October it happened: Roosevelt gained congressional approval to extend one billion dollars in Lend Lease to the Soviet Union. American finances and industry were now linked with Stalin.

I received a call from Ambassador Grew. "I am going to advise my government of the situation," he told me. "I respect your understanding of this country and the people. Would you give me your opinion and any comments?"

He gave me a copy of the draft of his message. When I read it, I wished I could have prevented him from sending it. I saw the chance of avoiding the war I knew was in the making:

> Japan is preparing a program of war to be carried out if her alternative program of peace fails. Resort may come with dramatic and dangerous suddenness, an attempt risking national hara-kiri to make Japan impervious to economic embargoes abroad rather than to yield to foreign pressure. I wish to ensure against the United States becoming involved in war because of possible misconception of Japan's capacity to rush headlong into a suicidal struggle with the United States. While national sanity dictates against such action, Japanese sanity cannot be measured by American standards of logic.

I could do no more than tell Grew that I could add nothing—which was a lie. I knew that an attack on Pearl Harbor was in some stage of planning and I did not want him to sabotage it. He thanked me and sent the message to the State Department in Washington.

Fortunately, State Department staff ignored it—except for White's associates who microfilmed it for Moscow. This was the direction White wanted: a military engagement in the Pacific to drain Japan's military strength in China. The message carried a hint that would guide White in revising his document when the time came.

On the battlefields, it became obvious that Germany launched her attack without planning for the fight to last into the Soviet winter, and with no plans for supply lines as her troops advanced into Russia. Each drop in temperature was a Soviet advantage, but there was a chance that Germany's setbacks might make her call on Japan for help in the war, and America was not yet in it.

In Washington, White watched like a boxer in extended slow motion for the opening to strike his blow, when he heard that Kurusu would depart Tokyo on November 5 for the United States. I spoke with Kurusu the day before he left.

"I am finally headed for America," he said. "I hope I can relieve the tense situation and restore peaceful relations between us." I rated his chances low: I knew of Captain Aiko's work. Kurusu departed for Hong Kong, where the flight of the *China Clipper* was delayed for two days on his behalf. What I could not know then was that the day Kurusu departed Tokyo, Prime Minister Tojo announced at an imperial conference that on the thirtieth of that month or shortly after, Japan would go to war against Britain and the United States. Yamamoto told me about it some time afterwards.

"I came into the conference with the attack plans in my briefcase," he said. "I had already designated the thirty-one ships that would make up the task force—they were berthed in different harbors to avoid a conspicuous grouping, and they were going into a state of readiness when the conference was in session."

"And how did the emperor react to Tojo's announcement?"

"With silence. He didn't like the idea, especially of Japan being run by the army. Remember, the emperor expected Tojo to control unruly officers. I felt resentment from the throne, but we heard only silence. After the conference I gave orders for the ships to proceed north to the rendezvous in Hitokappu Bay, on Etorofu Island. It's remote—good for a quiet departure."

"And how much did the crews know of the mission?"

Yamamoto chuckled. "They were puzzled. We issued both winter and tropical clothing. That northern route eastward is gloomy and cold. Little sun, but even fewer ships; that's why I chose it. Then there was a southerly leg into tropical regions to the takeoff point, about two hundred nautical miles north of Hawaii. Hmmmm. The crews were puzzled."

While the ships that would form the task force pulled out of their respective berths and headed for the Kuriles, November 10 arrived in Washington, where Kurusu and Roosevelt were in a special conference. The Japanese army advanced into Asia with no sign that they could be "satiated." This disturbed the dream of Japanese civilians in government and raised the level of impatience in America as Secretary of State Cordell Hull prepared for meetings with Kurusu and Nomura.

White knew that Hull's docility before the president was an advantage to the NKVD plan, and a week after the Kurusu-Roosevelt meeting, on November 18, White launched his document on its voyage to the White House. He handed it to Morgenthau accompanied by a draft of a short message for Morgenthau to send out under his own name: "Dear Mr. President, I am sending you herewith for your perusal a memorandum on the Japanese situation which was submitted to me by one of my assistants."

And, underlining his encroachment on the secretary of state's territory, Morgenthau wrote Hull, "Dear Cordell, I am enclosing a copy of a letter and memorandum which I am sending to the President." Following Washington procedure, both messages carried the initials of the person who originally drafted them: HDW. This humiliation for the secretary of state was a prelude to the greater one to follow.

About a half day earlier, the seventeenth in Japan, Admiral Yamamoto had given a farewell toast to the commander-in-chief of the task force, Vice-Admiral Nagumo, and his crew on the flight deck of the carrier *Akagi,* the flagship of the task force. He wished them success on their mission, the destination still known only to top ranking naval officers, though those I spoke with later all agreed that the admiral's sendoff was illogically somber for the occasion. Yamamoto returned to his own Combined Fleet flagship and the next day the *Akagi* headed toward the rendezvous.

On November 20 in Japan, ships of the task force were steaming into the harbor at Etorofu and dropping anchor in their assigned places while the carrier *Kaga* was still under way to the rendezvous with a load of Captain Aiko's shallow-water torpedoes. A half day later, the same twentieth in Washington, Kurusu and Nomura handed Hull an outline for a modus vivendi that included a twenty-day truce with a promise for Japan to pull out of south Indochina, and with an obligation for America to cease support for Chiang Kai-shek in Japan's war in China. Hull later began working on it, but protests from Great Britain and Chiang Kai-shek gave it a negative-looking future.

▪ ▪ ▪

The carrier *Akagi* eased into her anchoring position in Hitokappu Bay on November 22 in Japan, and the next day the last major ship of the task force, the carrier *Kaga,* entered the rendezvous with her load of "fish mines."

At noon in Washington on November 25, President Roosevelt met with the five others on his war council who were conducting foreign policy with cards hidden from Congress: the secretaries of State, War, and Navy, chief of naval operations, and chief of staff. Roosevelt set the agenda: "How to maneuver the Japanese into the position of firing the first shot without suffering too much danger to ourselves." When the meeting broke up, it was the dark pre-dawn of November 26 in Japan, where adrenalin fueled initial preparations for getting under way to a destination still unknown to most of the crews.

The task force departure was delayed about an hour to 0900, when the ships started weighing anchor in sequence according to their assigned positions in the formation. The flagship of the attack force, the carrier *Akagi* held a special place in Yamamoto's career, with much of his life in the Fourth Fleet spent on board and commanding it. Now, Yamamoto was sending the *Akagi* to lead Japan into a conflict that he did not want.

As the lead ships passed through the harbor mouth and the surface chop beat an overture to war on their hulls, people in Washington were sitting down to dinner on November 25. By dessert time, the lead ships were clear of land and the carriers were making ready to stand out to sea, crews dressed in winter clothes with summer issues wrapped in question marks.

The secretary of state had been working on the modus vivendi offered by the Japanese side and was expecting to hand it to them, with revisions, the following day. He worked on it late that night, as the last of the carriers were standing out of the harbor.

The secretary of state's revisions to the Japanese proposal never surfaced. Roosevelt thrust his finger into the wound in Hull's pride with an order to scrap the modus vivendi and proceed with the memorandum from Treasury.

On November 26 in Washington, Nomura and Kurusu called on the American secretary of state. Hull shielded the embarrassment of his puppet role with silence and handed the Japanese representatives the document that had evolved from the message with skipped spaces and smudged letters banged out in Moscow.

White's original draft of six months earlier stated that the United States would consider Manchuria a part of the Japanese Empire. As he revised the document, the Manchurian recognition continued, and the demand on Japan was to pull her military and police forces from China, "except Manchuria." Two days before the document was handed to the Japanese representatives, *except Manchuria* was removed from the terms. The question lingers: Who deleted those two words? Was it Hull, in a bid to claim his existence by doing something? Was it White, adding extra weight to the straw that would drive the Japanese into a corner with no chance to save face? Or was it the president himself?

Hull handed the document to Kurusu and Nomura. They read it and, with their shock, the memorandum "submitted to me by one of my assistants" became known as the "Hull Note." Meanwhile, the real crafters of America's last message to Japan—White in Treasury, Pavlov in Moscow— were as unobtrusive as the task force, which was then opening into a ring shape—an open-ocean formation developed by the U.S. Navy—that covered a patch of ocean one hundred nautical miles between lead ship and rear as it steamed into the cold, bleak northern Pacific.

▪ 31 ▪
Pearl Harbor Attack to an Old Poem

In Bywater's war, Pearl Harbor was a sleepy naval repair yard and depot with no warships stationed there; it was just one Bywater landing site for Japan's Pacific thrust. In 1929, four years after the book, a fifty-million-dollar dredging operation began converting it into a first-class naval base, and in 1940 President Roosevelt ordered the Pacific Fleet to make it home. This massive change would give Hawaii a different role if Japan opened a Bywater war in 1941. Added to this, in February 1932, seven years after *The Great Pacific War* was published and with Pearl Harbor now a full-fledged naval base, the United States Navy held drills under a hypothetical, surprise air attack to evaluate the base's vulnerability. The conclusion was that America's naval capacity could be greatly nullified in a similar attack. When I deduced Captain Aiko's torpedo project, I saw a weakness in the Japanese plan's requirement to maintain the surprise element against a target more than halfway across the Pacific. This was on my mind when I thought about sabotaging the attack. I could have informed the American ambassador, or warned the United States through her minister in Stockholm, though I doubted that either of these would have brought a warning from the president: the results that eluded him in the Atlantic were developing in the Pacific. But I could have arranged for the underground to send a message that appeared to come from an American source. Even with the fleet at sea, if the Japanese picked up an uncoded message of an impending attack it would pull the surprise element from the plan and probably bring cancellation, with a claim that the navy was merely on maneuvers. But in spring of 1941 I received information that showed that an attack on Pearl Harbor should be allowed to succeed.

Members of our underground had infiltrated the American Communist Party and received information from fellow members unwittingly planted in government agencies through people such as Harry Dexter White. Those in the War Department learned that in May, America was placed under a War Plan Rainbow Five, which stipulated that in the event of war Europe was to become the decisive theater, Germany the predominant enemy. America would devote its energy to Europe. "Main U.S. Navy task would be protect Atlantic shipping," the message informed me. "Bulk of aircraft and land to be shifted to Europe. Pacific would be defensive action." This, of course, was of interest to those concerned about the position of the Soviet Union, and my worry that a Pacific clash would drain American ships from the Atlantic seemed opposite to her war plans. I decided to watch it happen. It would be more effective than the president's pinpricks against German ships, but I had one apprehension: Unit 731. Would a raid on Pearl Harbor re-create Ishii's attacks on Chinese villages? Would Hawaii be transformed into islands of black corpses fanned by balmy winds, carrying the stench of the dead and the cries of the almost-dead out to sea?

On November 28 the *Mainichi* newspaper reported on the Hull Note. The paper carried the year 2601, reckoned from the ascension of the first emperor, a daily reminder to readers of Japan's divine origins. The Hull Note shared the same page with an advertisement for the movie *Kawanakajima*, the film version of a sixteenth-century battle.

In 1561, Takeda Shingen camped with his army on the bank of a river for an attack on his enemy, Uesugi Kenshin. During the night, Uesugi split his forces and led one contingent in a sweeping movement. Horses and men quietly forded the river to an unexpected quarter, and with the first light of day Shingen and his men were startled to see the enemy facing him in battle formation a short distance away.

Uesugi led the attack with drawn sword—a masterwork by Nagamitsu—and rode his mount through the defending troops to single out Takeda, then brought the blade down. Takeda blocked the cut with the thick, metal, fan-shaped symbol of authority carried by commanders of those days, and slipped away from the attack.

A four-line, Chinese-style poem written two centuries later helped make all Japanese familiar with the Kawanakajima battle.

The hushed whispers of riding crops
  cross the river
Dawn reveals a thousand soldiers
  standing by their battle flag
Damnation!
  after polishing this sword for ten years
The big snake escapes
  under a shooting star

Takeda—born in the year of the snake in the Oriental zodiac—evaded the "shooting star" of his enemy's blade, but the battle erupted with one of the heaviest uses of firearms in Japan to date. The episode became legend, part of history classes in schools, and in 1941 it became a movie with Japan's leading period-drama actor in the starring role of Uesugi Kenshin. The Japanese looked forward to the first week in December, when the movie was due to open, to ride with him again in the river crossing and surprise attack, while the task force crossed the Pacific in a magnified version of the "hushed and quiet" sixteenth-century maneuver. America waited to fill its corresponding role of being surprised at dawn.

Japanese newspapers carried the story of the Hull Note—the United States Congress had not heard of it—and Japan exploded emotionally. Compliance would mean a coup, or at least uncontrollable riots in the country, exactly as Harry Dexter White had planned. The task force was scheduled to reach the point of no return when it was December 1 in Tokyo, the opening date of the film *Kawanakajima*. The question clings: If the words *except Manchuria* had remained, would it have left enough negotiating room for Japan to reverse the course of her ships? Yamamoto was prepared to do so; others were not.

On December 1 in Tokyo, Premier Tojo and his cabinet were in an imperial conference. With the task force straddling the International Date Line on its sixth day at sea, Tojo made the formal decision to go to war against the United States, Great Britain, and Holland. As he spoke, it was midnight of November 30 in Washington, where the American president was still discussing with his war cabinet "how to maneuver the Japanese into the position of firing the first shot."

The Imperial Japanese Navy always used Japan time as the standard when navigating in different time zones. On December 2 Yamamoto beamed a radio message to the task force: "Climb Mount Niitaka 1208." The attack was to go ahead according to schedule, December 8, Tokyo time.

Four days later, December 6 in Tokyo, the task force sighted a Russian merchant ship. There was a stare-off through binoculars with Japanese radiomen listening and gun crews at the ready. One radio signal from the Soviet ship would send it to the bottom.

There was no signal. The task force continued with the mission, and *Kawanakajima* went on screen.

Two days before takeoff time the bleak ocean dropped astern of the task force and tropical weather rose up on the horizon. Crews broke out summer clothes, and the puzzle of their issue was solved. But the commanders sailed into an enigma of another kind: The sector north of Hawaii that the ships were sailing into had mysteriously been taken off the American patrol area—a few months earlier, it was later found out—leaving an unguarded gateway to Hawaii.

Sunday morning at Pearl Harbor started with two waves of planes, 353 in all, screaming out of the sky. Forty of them were torpedo planes armed with Aiko's invention; his breakthrough came just weeks before the task force's departure. In his search for a way to limit the depth that a torpedo submerges, Aiko realized that the answer had to be something smaller and simpler than a complete hull. He designed a fin that kept a plane-launched torpedo within twelve meters of the surface after launching, but it could function only if the torpedo entered the water at the proper angle, and they often did not.

When a torpedo is released from a plane, it describes a parabola in its descent. Ideally, the fore-and-aft axis should stay parallel to the line of the parabola, but plane-launched torpedoes misbehave in the air, pitching and rolling. Pitching—deviation in the fore-and-aft axis—affects the angle at which a torpedo meets the water: too steep, and the torpedo plunges to the depths; with the nose too high, it bounces off the surface. Rolling causes the fins to affect the torpedo travel differently from their intended purpose, turning the missile off course. With a ninety-degree roll, vertical and horizontal fins exchange positions.

Aiko's final breakthrough was a framework made of ten-millimeter plywood, not quite a meter in length, fitted to the tail section of the torpedo and enclosing his special fin. The framework acted aerodynamically and prevented both pitch and roll in flight. The torpedo hit the water at the proper angle. The impact smashed the framework and exposed the extra fin that kept the torpedo running shallow. American authorities later reported that plane-launched torpedoes caused the major damage to naval vessels at Pearl Harbor, yet as the ships of the Pacific Fleet listed, smoked, and settled, nobody noticed fragments of ten-millimeter plywood bobbing on the water, brittle molts that held the iron serpents to their invisible parabola and trained them out of their habits of pitching and rolling. But there was also an exceptional and obvious skill among the torpedo-plane pilots that America did not report, something I found out later, when I met Yamamoto again.

Five of the ships that were hit settled partially submerged on the bottom, their superstructures rising from the surface as if trying to lift themselves in an escape from the "goddamn mousetrap." They testified to the limited depth available for Aiko's fish mines, and to the validity of the American admiral's objection to Pearl Harbor as a naval base.

The attack came shortly after 0300 on Monday, December 8 in Tokyo. I was awakened by a call and went into the legation to receive messages. I remained there until the stunned legation staff started arriving; they had all heard the reports on Radio Tokyo. I went back into my residence and locked my thoughts in the sturdy Western architecture that insulated me from my official neutrality.

It had come! The Congressional obstacle could not stand up against this. At 1100, an Imperial Rescript announced the official declaration of war, and as added assurance that the president still maintained his original goal, he tried to convince Congress that swastika-bearing German planes were among the attackers. It would be a two-front war for America, but her armies were at the doorstep of Europe at last.

Mariko called; she wanted to come over. In late afternoon, when it was past midnight in Washington, I went into the garden and punched the heavy bag absentmindedly while I waited for her to come through the door in the high wall.

"I can't believe it," was the first thing she said. "Why did the Japanese military do such a stupid thing?"

"I can only repeat what Japanese leaders are saying. It was due to America's freezing assets and cutting off oil. And demands . . ."

"But how can they do something like that? They've been trying to fight China for ten years now and they couldn't finish that war. Then on top of it, they have now made an enemy of the Allies. They're crazy. It was stupid-stupid-*stupid*. And actually, it's a violation of the Hague Convention of 1907."

"You could say that," I agreed, "but countries don't always pay attention to pacts and such."

"But Japan ratified it four years later. What kind of country are we if we don't adhere to pacts and start idiotic wars like this?"

"A sip of wine won't change things, but it might calm you down a bit. Let's go inside."

"And it happened," she continued, "with nobody realizing it."

"Not completely," I said. She gave me a question-mark frown.

Sudden release from the pressure of uncertainty melded with my desire to share something with Mariko, even a turn into disaster.

"I knew it was going to come. I didn't know when, but I knew it was in the plans."

She looked at me, her face still tortured by the history Japan was writing around her. "I don't understand," she said. "Sweden is . . ."

"This has nothing to do with Sweden. I just put things together. I had read the cards, you might say."

Perhaps it was because she was still at the upper limits of shock that she could be shocked no further. She just looked at me and waited. "I had no secret information," I told her. "I just deduced."

"But *how*. . . ?"

"We'll talk about the details some other time. I just figured it out."

"If you knew Japan was going to do this, couldn't you have done something to stop it?"

"That would be interference in a government. Nobody has a right to do that." I was ashamed of myself for having to answer that way. In many of our moments together, I wondered if Mariko might not be the one to end my bachelorhood. No, I had no wide-eyed dreams of a family and ideal bliss. We made good companions. By this time I no longer believed that secret police were draining information from her, but I understood Borges when he wrote, *We live in a labyrinth with paths that continually bifurcate. In some choices we are allies, in others we are enemies.* In the Tokyo labyrinth, Mariko could have been interrogated and coerced into revealing information. Her parents could be threatened to bait her. Torture was as routine a police method as writing a prisoner's name on the record. There were possible bifurcations in the labyrinth that could lead to her saying something that could land me in Melville Cox's cell, to the same window. My diplomatic training kept me neutral in matters that made me cry internally for her. I could not tell Mariko the real reason I did not foil the Pearl Harbor attack, but my foreknowledge of it was one bit of information I could share while still keeping touch with reality. If she carried the news that I had deduced the attack but kept the secret, I would not appear contrary to Japan's national goals. No, I did not like using Mariko that way, and I was not using her; I was considering the Borgian labyrinth.

"What will happen now?" she asked. "What can anyone do to stop this from becoming a horrible war?"

"We cannot change anything," I told her. "We can only wait and see what happens when Monday dawns in America."

Unless attacked had been achieved. On Monday, December 8 in Washington, a radio broadcast from the House of Representatives carried the voice of Hamilton Fish, a leader in keeping America out of the European war: "I have consistently opposed our entrance into wars in Europe and Asia for the past three years, but the unwarranted, dastardly attack by the Japanese, while peace negotiations were pending at Washington, means that the time for debate and controversy within America has passed. The time for action has come."

Congress declared war against Japan. For four days Europe and I watched to see the response vis-à-vis Germany. Ironically, Germany did Europe a favor, dropped its avoidance policy, honored its pact with Japan as a member of the Axis, and declared war on the United States. The Nazis did not want to go to war with the Allies yet, and they were angry at Japan's act, but they still wanted to use her in the fight against Russia.

Japan made two moves that brought Europe the American muscle we needed: a partnership with the Nazis and an attack on America. *If Yamamoto had remained at his shore job—and avoided assassination—Japan might never have brought America into the war for us.*

"I had to threaten the navy to get the go-ahead to strike Pearl Harbor," Yamamoto told me over his first seltzer since the attack. "Everyone wanted to head right for the oil fields of the Dutch East Indies. I said first we neutralize the American ships in Hawaii. And if I don't get permission, I'll quit with my entire staff."

"And apparently they finally agreed."

"But that wasn't the last fight I had. I didn't want to go to war against America and Britain, but if it came to it, I wanted it to go according to my plan. And, I was still hoping the negotiations would succeed. I said I would cancel the attack at the last minute if we received word that there was success in Washington."

"And what was the reaction to that?"

"A bunch of excitement. The officers all protested. I told them that if the talks reached an agreement, I'd cancel even if the planes had left the carriers. And anyone who doesn't agree can resign now."

"That's almost a paradox, isn't it?"

"Not really," he said, turning to his second fight. "The duty of the military is to protect the peace of the nation. Any idiot can scream war, especially if there's some sort of profit in it. Our weapons have advanced since the caveman era; we should be smarter than cavemen in using them."

I went back to his first fight and asked, "And your tactical reasons for fighting to hit Pearl Harbor?"

He took a sip of seltzer and held onto the glass to gain extra seconds for himself. He pulled himself out of the silence: "We'll talk about that another time."

I did not press the question and switched to the success of the attack. "As you know, America is not releasing the full effect of the raid to its own citizens, and Japanese news sources are . . . well, Japanese news sources. But from what I can deduce, your pilots were extremely skilled."

"Hmmmm. They were training in Kagoshima Harbor. It's surrounded by mountains, like Pearl Harbor."

"And, it's shallow," I added. Yamamoto cocked an eyelid: "You've been there?"

"No, we sailors like to read charts."

"Planes had to practically ski down the mountains to get to the harbor. But our torpedo-plane men also had to learn something they never did before—we had to break our own rules to do it."

"I believe Captain Aiko invented a new device for you." There was just a hint of a smile, an expression that said, "So you figured it out, eh?"

"That was for normal altitude torpedo launching—we always trained releasing at fifty-meters elevation, one thousand meters from target. But at Kagoshima we trained the pilots to come in at five meters elevation. And release two hundred meters from target."

This was difficult to fathom. "Five meters? That's almost a landing."

"We kept the speed down to one hundred thirty nautical miles per hour. The navy prohibited low-level flying. We had to ignore our own rules for special training. Remember, there is no five-meter marking on our altimeters—they're calibrated in ten-meter increments. We have good pilots."

"And were their any mishaps at Kagoshima during this?"

"They overturned a few fishing boats in the harbor—but not one accident to our planes. Good pilots!"

"I've been saving this," I told him, "I could not help noticing this juxtaposition," and I took out a copy of the newspaper with the advertisement for the *Kawanakajima* film. "The tactics Uesugi used," I said, "were almost a miniature of the Pearl Harbor attack: 'The hushed whispers of riding crops cross the river . . .'"

My comment was like a sword coming down on him that he wanted to evade. After a few moments, he finally responded, "This time, *two* snakes escaped."

"The carriers?" I asked gently.

"Hmmm! You know how I feel about air power."

"I remember from our Harvard days."

"Planes are still underrated. No navy ever formed a carrier task force until my Pearl Harbor attack. America's Pacific Fleet had two carriers on active duty assigned to Pearl Harbor, and I wanted to knock them out of service. They always spent weekends in port, and they should have been there that Sunday morning. But by the evening of December 4 in Hawaii, they were both gone. Escaped—from under our shooting stars."

Just 380 years after the Kawanakajima battle, it was Yamamoto's turn to cry *Damnation!*

▪ 32 ▪

Japan Proves the Power of Aircraft

An army-navy football game program from America arrived in my diplomatic pouch. It was dated November 29 and carried a photo of the USS *Arizona* underway with the caption: "It is significant that despite the claims of air enthusiasts no battleship has yet been sunk by bombs." A colleague in the Swedish embassy in New York attended the game and thought the program would interest me. I calculated that when fans were cheering the kickoff, the task force was in its fifth day at sea. The *Arizona* was moored in Pearl Harbor. It still is: it survived the attack just nine minutes. But men with careers invested in big ships and big guns still refused to recognize aircraft potential. After Taranto and Pearl Harbor, they argued that planes could not sink a battleship *in action*. In a few days this argument ended.

Japan's attack on Hawaii was part of a grander strategy familiar to anyone who had read *The Great Pacific War*. The master plan started—not quite by plan—two hours before the strike on Pearl Harbor with a shelling from sea on Malaya. On December 10 Japanese troops began landing on Malaya, and the British 32,000-ton battle cruiser *Repulse* and the 35,000-ton battleship *Prince of Wales* closed in to hit the transports. Japanese planes sent the two ships to the bottom. It was naval history, and Radio Tokyo screamed the news. I was looking forward to Yamamoto's comments on this when he came through the garden in a billow of Sakura smoke.

"I think we convinced the naval experts of the world," he said.

"I've been getting the reports. I never realized those ships were in Singapore." I put out seltzer water for both of us.

"It surprised us also. It happened fast. The Pearl Harbor attack force was seven days at sea—Tojo had just announced the final decision for war that day, December second—when England announced she was forming a new Far Eastern Fleet. At the time it was only a cruiser squadron."

"A moderate force," I agreed.

"Then we heard that the new battleship *Prince of Wales* and the battle cruiser *Repulse* were added to the fleet. You knew the *Prince of Wales*—newest ship in the Royal Navy; thirty-five thousand tons with fifteen-inch guns. No Japanese ship in the area could match that. England wanted to hold her position in the region and block our southward movement." He took a sip of seltzer. "But Japan wasn't going to be blocked. We were scheduled to shell Malaya after the Pearl Harbor strike, but it happened first because the risk of carrier takeoffs in pitch black delayed the Hawaii operation. Our Malayan Expeditionary Force sailed southerly out of Hainan Island and rounded the southern tip of French Indochina."

"That's a route of high visibility," I mentioned.

"Hmm! We couldn't slide in unnoticed as we did at Hawaii. Our ships had to pass through the narrow South China Sea and into the lane between Singapore and Hong Kong. They were exposed to observation by merchant ships and land-based scout planes of the Royal Air Force, as well as their patrol plane, which sighted our ships off French Indochina. But they held course and speed and started midnight troop landings along the east coast of the Malay peninsula."

"And the landings went according to plan?"

"Pretty much. They hit us with some air raids at one location, but no big interference. Then one of our submarines radioed that British warships had pulled out of Singapore and were closing in to threaten our landings. Our ships called off the landings and steamed into Thailand Bay. We had set up three naval airfields in French Indochina the month before, and planes from those fields were ordered out to shadow the British ships. We didn't know yet about being able to hit them from the air. We planned on engaging them with our ships."

"The bigger guns on the British ships would put you at a disadvantage, wouldn't they?"

"In gun caliber, yes. So we planned a night attack by a cruiser division and destroyer squadron—we Japanese are good at night fighting, you know that. Then we planned for a fleet with two battleships and two heavy cruisers to arrive at dawn with all ships scheduled to join in a daylight attack."

"And you didn't plan on using carriers?"

"None available. Remember, we had six of them detached from other fleets tied up in the Pearl Harbor attack; they were still in the northern Pacific headed back to Japan. But land-based air power cancelled out the need for a surface engagement."

He looked at the Sakura in his hand. "I still like to call them 'Cherry'," he said. "This army government worries about things like English words. They should spend time improving their minds instead."

"You still use English nomenclature in the navy, though."

"Of course. Even if we're at war with the British, that's our naval heritage. You know, our auxiliary ships use quartermasters who work on army vessels also. They tell stories that if they use terms like *port* or *starboard* on an army vessel, the officers scream at them. They have to use Japanese terms only. *Stupid!* What the hell, the purpose is to know which way you're going."

After a moment, we were back off the coast of Malaya. "It was getting late in the day, but the naval air units sent out four reconnaissance planes to look for the British ships, and followed an hour later with bombers and torpedo planes. They searched through the night while other planes at the airfields were readied for dawn takeoff. The reconnaissance planes turned up nothing and flew back to their bases. Next morning scout planes were sent out, then bombers and torpedo planes. Nothing sighted. There was cloud cover, and visibility from the air was not good. The pilots started back to base, then luck came into the game. One plane found a break in the clouds and spotted the *Prince of Wales* with three escorts fifty miles off Kuantan. He radioed and all planes headed for the area. It was around noon, five and a half hours after takeoff. They were low on fuel, but eager for the fight. They started their bombing runs, and about an hour later torpedo planes joined the battle. Time was not on our side; fuel was running out."

"And there was still no air cover for the British ships?"

"We had the skies to ourselves. It looked like the British still did not believe in airplanes. This was a pure plane versus ship encounter."

"And how did the battleship handle the attack?"

"Heavy antiaircraft. No Japanese ship could put up a wall of fire like that. They hit eight planes of the first attack group at three thousand meters. The combination of their rapid fire and explosions from our bombs and torpedoes was so fierce, our torpedo-plane pilots couldn't see their buddies attacking from the other side of the ship. Eighty-four planes in the attack, three shot down, twenty-eight damaged. But our torpedo planes were too fast for them to hit."

"Your planes were too fast for the British?"

"British gunners had been practicing against their own torpedo planes. Naturally. And British planes launched at a maximum one hundred miles per hour. That's what they considered top launching speed."

"And your pilots. . . ?"

"At least one hundred fifty, sometimes up to one hundred ninety miles per hour. The British gunners just couldn't handle it. That's why torpedoes caused most of the damage; fifteen were launched against the *Prince of Wales* with seven hits. Only two bombs hit her."

"The reports said that the *Repulse* took even more hits than the *Prince of Wales.*"

"Fourteen torpedoes, one bomb. That's against a twenty-five-year-old ship. The British make them well."

"Radio Tokyo said that the battle lasted only an hour and a half."

"They were right. Good for them. Their news is usually fiction."

"After Vice Admiral Tom Phillips went down with the *Prince of Wales*, he was criticized posthumously for taking his ships into a zone where Japan had control of the air."

"He had no choice," Yamamoto answered briskly, coming to the British admiral's defense. "There were no planes available to him. England and America were still behind in thinking about the air age. Remember, Phillips was an authority on naval aviation. He and I thought pretty much alike. He just didn't have the British government on his side. You remember what the Chinese strategist Sun Tsu said: 'He will win who has military capacity and is not interfered with by the sovereign.' If his sovereign did not provide one of their finest naval officers and the pride of the Royal Navy with aircraft, that's interference through neglect. The British government was on *our* side."

"I heard that Churchill ordered the ships to Singapore with the remark that this meager show of sea power combined with the American presence in the Philippines would deter Japan's southward expansion. I thought of your Harvard speech: 'The value of any probability varies with the temperament of the player.' Quote-unquote."

"I hope you didn't learn my English."

"No, I've my own accent. But do you think that if Churchill had heard your speech, *Prince of Wales* and *Repulse* would still be afloat?"

Yamamoto gave one of his internal chuckles. "It's just as well that he didn't. It gave our navy pilots the chance to prove that planes can sink battleships in actual battle conditions." He pulled out a Sakura and held it like a divining rod focusing his thoughts. "You know, that's the only reservation I have about the operation. I just wish we had carriers available, and carrier-based planes had done it."

"Not to be pessimistic, but even Billy Mitchell didn't put much faith in carriers replacing land-based planes for sinking ships."

"Army and navy men are always at odds. If we disagree on the role of carriers, it's a minor difference. Mitchell believed in the potential of air power in naval battles, and I always believed he was right. He died in 1936. If he had stayed around longer I'm sure his thinking would have changed." Yamamoto broke a slight smile. "He might have even left the army and joined the navy."

The argument that planes could not sink a battleship in action was finally flushed from the throats of the skeptics with the waters that washed over the two British men-of-war. About ten days later, on December 21, 1941, the newly commissioned battleship *Yamato*—seventy-two thousand tons—pulled into its berth on the island of Hashirajima, offshore from the city of Hiroshima.

▪ 33 ▪
Bywater's Philippine Campaign Repeats

Deterrents played a large role in bringing on World War II. Japan joined the Axis to deter the Allies. Roosevelt claimed that shifting the Pacific fleet to Hawaii would deter Japan. Churchill's belief in deterrents cost the British the pride of the Royal Navy. America wanted to deter Japan with a military buildup in the Philippines, where Yamamoto told Bywater back in 1934 a powerful American base would make Japanese naval officers "seriously perturbed."

Japan's grand scheme included removal of American military power from the Philippines. Japanese naval officers formulated and revised plans over the years on the contingency of war with the United States, but by the fall of 1941 Yamamoto had maneuvered himself into an unusual position for a fleet admiral: total control of the assault plan. The attack was almost like reading *The Great Pacific War* again.

"The Philippine landing was so close to Bywater," I said to Yamamoto some time after the islands were taken, "yet from the reports I received— and interpreting a few things—it seems that the Lamon landing on the east coast of Luzon fooled MacArthur."

"Well, there was no opposition there, and we moved in with twenty-four troop transports. That was also strange . . ."

"The Philippine landing . . . ?" I asked.

"We had five hundred planes based on Formosa. Their job was to take control of the air over the Philippines and cover the landings. The Americans had their new B-17 bombers and fighters in the Philippines. We expected them to hit us on Formosa and put up defense against our landings. But you saw what happened."

"It seems that Japanese planes destroyed most of the American planes on the ground."

"That was no surprise attack," Yamamoto said half to himself. He looked at me and reviewed: "That was nine hours after we hit Pearl Harbor. *Nine hours!* It doesn't seem logical. General MacArthur should have been ready for us to hit the Philippines. They had to know that the islands were in our plans. Every Philippine native who heard about Hawaii must have expected our attack. Why didn't the Americans?"

"If that's a question," I responded, "I don't have an answer. All I know now is that MacArthur moved to Australia with his top officers and left others to fight a war with no replacements."

"That's the same thing Chiang Kai-shek and his commanders did in Nanking in 1937—deserted their troops and the city."

"But it was still a tough landing I see."

"The American and Philippine soldiers MacArthur left behind put up a tremendous fight. We allotted fifty days for taking over the Philippines. Even after we destroyed the major part of their planes it took us one hundred thirty-five days. Of course there were problems of geography. It was not a straight thrust; the ships had to weave between islands to reach the landing site."

"The Americans were surely expecting a landing by then."

"Part of the puzzle," Yamamoto answered.

"Stories circulated later," I said, "that the commander at Lamon sent repeated requests for defensive arms—one-hundred-fifty-five-millimeter and seventy-five-millimeter guns to prepare for a possible assault on the bay. But MacArthur refused and kept them instead on Luzon's west coast."

"Well, we landed there also."

"And so did Bywater. He had Japan coming ashore on Luzon, at Lingayen Gulf on the west and Lamon Bay on the east to put Manila in the center of a pincers movement. And a third landing on the southernmost island of Mindanao."

Yamamoto asked with a glint in the eye, "Bywater wrote that?"

"Unless he came back to edit it, it's still there. And that means the world's military men knew it also. MacArthur became a major general about the time the book was published, and he was appointed army chief of staff in 1930. . . ."

"You've got all the facts on him," Yamamoto chided.

"My naval-diplomatic backgrounds make me a fact gatherer. You must have expected that MacArthur had read and discussed Bywater the same as other military officers, yet your landing almost paralleled Bywater's, even though Lamon Bay was an illogical site in December."

"It did have drawbacks. Winter monsoons, heavy winds, rain."

"Then a rough hike through mountains and marshes to reach Manila. Yet you followed Bywater, landing at Lamon, *and* Mindanao."

"Why," Yamamoto asked with a wry smile, "do you think I would follow a book written fifteen years ago?"

"Did you ever read Edgar Allen Poe?" I asked him.

"I like him. Exquisite language. Strange stories."

"Do you remember *The Purloined Letter?*"

"Mmm! I had to look up the word 'purloin.'"

"A letter was left in an obvious place to prevent its theft. Deception by the apparent is itself a tactic."

Yamamoto chuckled internally. "I liked that story. Interesting word, *purloin.*"

▪ 34 ▪
Hitler's Maneuvers

George Orwell sat behind the BBC microphone for his broadcast to India: "The plan is for the Germans to break through by land to reach the Persian Gulf, while the Japanese gain mastery of the Indian Ocean. This tenuous thread of communication would remove the value of the Burma Road as a supply route to China, while the most practical supply route to the Soviet Union, through the Persian Gulf and Iran, would be cut off, probably forcing the Soviets to retreat behind the Ural mountains." It was February 14, 1942, and this was more than Orwell's sense of drama. A clasp of German and Japanese hands would isolate the Allied nations from each other. And, while Tokyo expressed its zeal for India's independence from the white man, the Japanese army would probably aim for dominance over India itself, and a naval vantage point from the northwest of the continent looking out on the Persian Gulf.

Soon after that broadcast was aired, Georges Bagulesco, the Romanian minister, came to my legation. "I received some devastating news yesterday," he said. "I was at a private reception when some members of the Imperial Household Ministry called me aside to advise me that on the twelfth of this month, Hitler proposed to Stalin that they mend fences and divide eastern Europe between them."

Bagulesco was a wealthy art collector. He produced Japanese art exhibitions in Romania, Romanian art exhibitions in Japan, and authored books on Japanese culture. These activities brought him into contact with the aristocratic members of the Imperial Household Ministry, a centuries-old organization that managed the affairs of the emperor and imperial family, people who sided with the emperor in detesting Japan's alliance with

Germany. This also made them sympathetic to the fate of countries like Romania, and friendly with a touch of apologetic guilt toward Bagulesco.

"The news that the aristocrats leaked to me," Bagulesco went on, "a revival of the German-Soviet alliance, would devastate Europe. And I don't have to tell you that Scandinavia would be like jackal's pluck torn between two lions."

"The whole outlook is dreadful," I had to agree. *Ally* and *adversary* were terms that could change value overnight. Two months after Pearl Harbor, Germany had plans for an Asian-European clasp on the world by meeting with Japan in the Persian Gulf zone and simultaneously splitting up the Soviet-American partnership by baiting Stalin with eastern Europe. Hitler might also have been trying to compensate for his bungled attack on Russia, when he sent his armies out with no plans for the Soviet winter. Fuel oil in German tanks froze stiff and engines had to be thawed into life with primitive bonfires. There was no thought for supply lines, and German tanks moved forward carrying drum cans of fuel on their exterior.

"And what," I asked Bagulesco, "would that mean for Romania?"

"We would be cut in two. Half our people would go to one monster, half to the other."

"What is happening in Romania about it?"

"That is part of the problem. Nobody there knows about it. The Japanese government received the news from their embassy in Berlin, and it reached the Imperial Household Ministry people who told me."

"Surely you are going to advise your government?"

"I did, but I am sure the Germans have access to our diplomatic code. There are German collaborators in Romania. And perhaps even here in our Tokyo."

"In Tokyo?"

"I suspect. As you know, the Nazis have only to burp and the Japanese army officers bow down to them, like obedient coolies. When Germany began marching into Romania in January 1941, I was one of the leaders in an opposition movement. My assignment to Japan came shortly after that, so it is completely expected that the Germans have me on their blacklist."

"But you sent the message anyway?" I asked.

"That was my duty to Romania. My only other option was leaving my government in the dark about the scheme. I may suffer consequences."

▪ 35 ▪
From Doolittle to Midway

The first planes to bomb Tokyo were named after the "nitwit." In April 1942 I watched them come over, sixteen North American B-25 Billy Mitchells, twin-engine bombers with widely spaced double rudders. Yamamoto must have had mixed feelings, to see his inspiration for air power promoted to hero and to hear the Bywater proclamation in the explosions. Jimmy Doolittle's raid on the city was not devastating—office workers ran out to watch as if it were a street performance, and the Japanese tried to joke their way out of it by calling it a "do-little" attack— but the psychological impact was clear: sacred Japan had been violated.

"Maybe we were playing too much *shogi*," Yamamoto said afterward.

"*Shogi*?"

"We were fooled by watching the board. Doolittle finished his move *off* the board. We thought Japan was safe from carrier-launched strikes because enemy ships were kept out of flight range. But we were thinking round-trip distance. Doolittle's planes took off from the carrier, made their runs over Japan, then flew on to China." He thought a moment, then added, "In *shogi*, a game starts off with the same pieces for each player. Whenever we thought about carriers, we thought carrier-based planes. But Billy Mitchells are army planes; they can manage to take off from a carrier deck, but they can't land on one. And they have greater range than carrier planes. So it was like throwing chess pieces into a *shogi* game. That was an army-navy cooperative operation, something this country could learn from."

"The physical damage was apparently slight," I said.

"Maybe Doolittle doesn't know that he killed more Chinese than Japanese."

"In what way?"

"The army realized that Chinese airfields could be used for raids against Japan—they were intelligent enough to figure that out. So after the raid the army pulled a major land offensive in China to keep the airfields from American hands. Indirectly, Doolittle killed maybe half a million Chinese. But he showed what planes can do."

About two months before the Doolittle raid, Yamamoto's command had moved to the seventy-two-thousand-ton *Yamato,* moored in Hiroshima Bay. The battleship had spent most of its time there since it pulled in at the end of December the previous year. The passenger ferry operating in the bay was ordered to close its shades when it passed the naval yard, but law was ignored for just a glimpse. "*Huge*," passengers gasped. But *Yamato's* guns sounded only for practice firing, while the real fleet fought the war.

"Every time I board that ship," Yamamoto said, "it reminds me of how paralyzed the human brain is. Just because there was no history of aircraft being effective in actual battle, the dull minds in the naval ministry and government were stingy in financing air development. Many people have a brain that operates on an odd law of inertia: the organ remains at rest until acted upon by a precedent. It has no motive power of it own. All they knew was, the bigger the projectile, the harder it hits. So with America limited by beam to ships that could carry a maximum of sixteen-inch guns, the intelligence of our leaders told them to go higher, to eighteen inches."

"Formidable," was all I could say.

"Primitive man thought the same about wooden clubs. Our naval brains wanted to out-club the Americans. Twenty-meter barrels. Shells almost two meters high—one and a half tons each." Another look of disgust and he continued. "I started off in the navy as a gunnery officer, so some navy leaders think I should be thrilled with bigger guns because they have greater range. But they don't realize that a carrier can take planes longer distances to do more damage. That's on my mind every time I head back to my command."

The Solomon Islands, lying southeasterly from Rabaul to Guadalcanal, appealed to the Japanese General Staff as valuable naval bases. They also calculated that moves to seize them could bait the United States into

Japan's naval specialty of decisive sea battle. Yamamoto disagreed. He reasoned that America would tolerate the loss of Wake and Guam, which lie on Japan's side of the 180th parallel, but not a move beyond it to Midway. He argued for an assault on the island to lure America into decisive battle.

In May 1942 the U.S. Navy sank its first Japanese carrier of the war, the eleven-thousand-ton *Shoho,* as it was escorting a transport convoy from Rabaul to Port Moresby. The next day, planes from two Japanese carriers, *Zuikaku* and *Shokaku,* attacked two American carriers, the *Lexington,* which had "escaped" from Pearl Harbor, and the *Yorktown,* which had come in from the Atlantic. The *Lexington* was sent to the bottom; the *Yorktown* and *Shokaku* sustained almost equal damage, putting them both out of service. This Battle of the Coral Sea—Yamamoto was on board his command in Hiroshima Bay when it happened—ushered in a new phase of naval warfare: two task forces engaging on the high seas. Other history was being made in strange juxtaposition, when during the same month, two professional baseball teams—one from Nagoya, one from Yokohama—met under clear skies in Tokyo and played nine innings to a 4–4 tie. The game went into extra innings and ended because of darkness, with the same score, at a world record twenty-eight innings.

Three days later, the *Yamato* finally moved out to taste deep waters. Yamamoto had won his argument for an assault on Midway, and from the end of May Japanese ships began pulling out of their bases to rendezvous for the operation. The attack force was led by Admiral Nagumo from the carrier *Akagi,* both man and ship Pearl Harbor veterans. Six aircraft carriers were supposed to take part in this operation, but the Coral Sea battle left one sunk and one out of commission, leaving four carriers for Midway.

The battle did not go as Yamamoto had planned. On June 14, the *Yamato* and the remainder of the defeated Midway strike force returned to Hiroshima Bay. Yamamoto was busy in Tokyo with post-battle reports, meetings, criticisms, and questions; he needed brief escapes from the navy and officialdom, and between his return from Midway and his next departure, we met several times.

The summer of 1942 was hotter than usual, with a rainy season of very little rain. The heat was lightened for the Japanese citizenry by news of a gallant stand at Midway, and announcements from Imperial Headquarters of two enemy carriers sunk, one Japanese carrier sunk, and one badly damaged. Reports I received from overseas told of a one-sided defeat for Japan: Tokyo created a fictional victory, and Yamamoto had to return to praise based on myth. Duty compelled him to bear it in silence. He would never cheat at cards and he did not like others to do so. My residence remained a temple of honesty for him, insulated from the propaganda alchemists who created history from emotions. Naturally, Yamamoto knew that I received news from outside sources.

"I don't like telling lies," he said. "If you lose a game you throw in your hand and that's it. If there's a chance to play another hand, fine. These government people like to write lies." He took a few seconds for a grimace, then went on. "Years ago, when I was joking around with some American officers back in Washington, one of them asked me a riddle: 'How far can a dog run into the forest?'"

"Is that the whole question?"

"Hm!"

"I'll give up quickly."

He frowned the answer: "Halfway. Because after that he's running out. I was counting on a victory at Midway to negotiate a peace. Midway should have been the end, but our losses there were so devastating, it was prophetically named. Up until then, Japan was going into the war. The leaders do not want to realize that we are now on the way to the other side. And it's quicksand there."

"You think it's that bad?"

"You must also, unless you believe Imperial Headquarters. After the Pearl Harbor attack, officers at Combined Fleet headquarters wanted Nagumo to hit the American base at Midway on the return. It lies just alongside their route. I objected to sending an order and left it up to Nagumo if the situation permitted. He decided against it—for reasons of weather, he said, but I knew that after Pearl Harbor he didn't want to be sent on an errand-boy's assignment by some far-off brass. So six months later we had to do something about the island."

"But it was a different kind of attack this time," I said. "If he attacked on the return from Pearl Harbor, there would have been no intention to land on the island. You had no troop transports."

"Right. This time Nagumo commanded a carrier strike force again, but the intention was an air attack prior to an assault landing. I'm sure you know what happened."

"The general results; there were no details."

"We decided that Japan's outer defense perimeter would include Port Moresby, at the southern tip of New Guinea. That would put Australia within easy bombing range, just across the Torres Strait. But we lost the *Shoho*, and the next dawn scout planes from both sides discovered each other's ships. Then we made history: the first naval battle in which no ship fired a shot. Everything was fought by aircraft. Losing the carrier the day before was rotten luck. The *Shoho* was part of a task force under Admiral Hara Chuichi. He was supposed to take some islands as stepping-stones to Port Moresby, but when the carrier was sunk, Hara became too cautious and withdrew. We suffered damage to another carrier, sank the *Lexington,* and damaged the *Yorktown.* If Hara had held on, he could have sunk that carrier, too. Numerically, Japan came out ahead at the Coral Sea, but the early withdrawal was a mistake, and it carried over to Midway."

Half a cigarette later he moved into the Midway operation.

"Nagumo sailed to two hundred thirty nautical miles of Midway. Just before sunrise one hundred eight planes took off—dive bombers, level bombers, fighters. They bombed the island but they didn't hit much. An enemy PBY flew over and spotted the fleet, and Nagumo expected American ships to close in. He ordered a second wave of planes readied on the decks armed to strike the ships. Also one hundred eight planes, including torpedo planes and dive bombers. After that . . . confusion! At about 0700, enemy planes came out from Midway to attack the carriers. There was no real damage, but it made Nagumo decide to launch another air attack on Midway. That was at 0715. He gave an order to replace the torpedoes and antiship bombs with land bombs. The changeover takes an hour plus, and it was just about finished when a flight of B-17s from Midway came in high on another bombing run on the carriers. Our captains were good at maneuvering; they avoided damage. That attack lasted fifteen minutes and the B-17s headed back to Midway. It was around 0830. Our planes from the Midway attack wave were still airborne and began coming back to their carriers. Then . . . real chaos!"

Yamamoto stood, walked to a window at the far end of the room, and stared out at the battle in my garden. "One of our scout planes reported ten enemy ships. There were one hundred eight planes on the decks of our carriers ready to raid Midway. Nagumo was sure there were no enemy carriers around, but an hour later the scout clarified his report and said that a carrier was among the ships. You know what it was."

"From what I heard, it was the *Yorktown*."

"We hit her hard at Coral Sea, and our officers estimated she would be out of action for three months. But she was back in three days. Three days! Our officers overestimated the repair period by thirty times. This is where the Americans began to show their engineering ability." And in that comment, I knew Yamamoto heard Bywater speaking. "Americans are good at those things," he added as a punctuation that contained an accent of admiration. The *Yorktown* was not finished with its surprise performance. "Our planes were on the carrier decks loaded with land bombs. When Nagumo heard there was an enemy carrier nearby, he ordered the planes re-armed a second time with torpedoes. It had to be done while the returning one hundred eight planes were landing. Local time was approaching 0900; the changeover was almost complete and the planes were almost all back on board. Nagumo radioed me: 'Proceeding to engage and destroy enemy force of one carrier, five cruisers, and five destroyers.' But it was too late. You heard the rest."

"Again, just the general results."

"The *Yorktown*'s planes came in on the attack. There were forty-one torpedo planes, and our interceptor pilots fought well. Only six of the forty-one got away. Now it was time to go after the enemy carrier. You know what our torpedo planes did to the British ships; we had the planes and skill to take care of the carrier and her escort. But . . ." He turned from the window and nodded his head in a negative movement.

"At 1020 Nagumo radioed me that he was about to launch for an attack on the enemy ships. Just as he turned his carriers into the wind, enemy dive bombers came in. Because of the double changeover the crews had no time to store bombs and torpedoes. And the decks were filled with fueled and loaded planes ready for takeoff. It was disaster. Direct hits on three carriers. Heavy explosions. Heavy loss of life. Two carriers knocked out of action. My *Akagi* was badly damaged and I sent word to scuttle her to keep her from falling into American hands." He walked back to where I was seated. "My subordinate officers protested that—scuttling the *Akagi*. That was my ship in the Fourth Fleet. It was Nagumo's flagship on the Pearl Harbor attack. But I had to order her sent down. So we were left with one carrier in operating condition. At 1100, six fighters and eighteen bombers took off from her and hit the *Yorktown*. The pilots were sure they had put the carrier out of action, but her damage control was amazing: she was back in five hours. She was repaired so fast, our pilots thought they attacked another ship. Then thirteen enemy dive bombers came in and hit our last carrier. She struggled through the night, then next morning the order was given to abandon ship; she sank later in the day."

He sat down, pulled out another Sakura and lit it. He exhaled with a tone of discouragement and resignation. "Things would have been a lot different if Admiral Hara had gone after the *Yorktown* when he had the chance. We finally sank her at Midway, but it was her planes that finished off my *Akagi*. I lost the chance to use a victory at Midway as a bargaining chip to negotiate a peace with the Allies. We've passed the halfway point in the forest. You know that Midway became big news in America. In Japan, the real story has not been told."

And it would not be told until after the war. Something the world's military authorities still did not know was the real size of the *Yamato*, and most of Japan's military authorities did not know its true uselessness.

On August 5, 1942, the *Yamato's* sister ship, the *Musashi*, was completed at the Mitsubishi yards in Nagasaki. A few days later Yamamoto sailed from Japan on the *Yamato* and headed for the new Combined Fleet command at Truk, in the Caroline Islands. That summer of 1942 would be the last time for me to see him.

▪ 36 ▪
Myth of a Misnomer

Even orthodox war gives some people a form of neutrality: repatriation. After hostilities began in the Pacific, fourteen hundred Japanese boarded a Swedish ship in New York and sailed for Portuguese Mozambique. In June 1942, two ships left Yokohama for Mozambique with foreign passengers headed for America, my acquaintance American Ambassador Joseph Grew among them. Berths were exchanged and the ships with Japanese passengers docked in Yokohama on August 20, 1942. Kurusu and Nomura were among the repatriates, and Sweden's cooperation in the transfer brought a call of appreciation from Kurusu. We met that autumn.

"At that final meeting with Hull on November twenty-sixth," he told me, "I had the impression that he was not really present. I know the feeling of distrust, of racial hatred . . . but this was different. He was distant, somehow struggling with an internal problem. The memorandum was a shock to us. When I had time to review things later, I thought it strange that Hull's attitude did not match the tone of his message. I would expect him to be as brusque and stern as the terms in the paper he handed us. But he was rather . . . childlike, one might say. He handed us the note and sulked, then turned his back."

At that time, I had not yet put the entire story together, including the role of the next fragment of information Kurusu told me: "There were Americans who were doing what they could to help avoid war."

"And you met with some of these people?"

"One especially, a Mr. Bernard Baruch. A confidant of President Roosevelt."

"He's famous for his wealth. In the Great War, he was chairman of the War Industries Board. Perhaps you also know that he financed Mr. Roosevelt's political career."

"Apparently he is very close with the president. Four days after Hull handed us that famous memorandum, I met with this Mr. Baruch about it. He said that after he read it, he felt that the heads of Japan and America should meet and discuss ways to avoid a war. But it was too late by then."

Very close with the president indeed. As I learned later, members of the United States Congress did not know about the message that Hull handed the Japanese, yet Baruch was discussing it with Kurusu days afterward. Baruch was also named as one of four men who were considered responsible for causing the stock market crash of 1929. But when I spoke with Kurusu at that time, I was more concerned—intrigued, I think—with this financier confidant who was involved with America's foreign policy.

"And your attempted meeting with Zacharias before that?" I asked.

"That was very disappointing. Almost suspicious. The Navy Department would not give him permission to leave his ship."

"Was he on maneuvers or on some important project?"

"With America and Japan in a worsening situation, what could have been more important than avoiding a clash? The Navy Department did not want us to meet."

Testimony later came out in the investigations in Washington that after Zacharias met with Nomura in San Francisco in February 1941, the American admiral sent a long, opinionated message to Chief of Naval Operations Harold Stark. A month later, Zacharias squeezed his cruiser, *Salt Lake City*, through the Pearl Harbor channel and met with Admiral Husband Kimmel, commander of the Pacific Fleet; Kimmel had replaced Admiral "goddamn-mousetrap" Richardson.

"If Japan attacks," Zacharias warned, "it will be from the vacant sea northwest of the islands. You know the area, where we used to hold maneuvers on the hypothesis of a Japanese attack from that quarter. It will happen on a weekend—probably a Sunday morning—and it will begin with an air attack. You don't have to worry too much about ships. Be ready for air attacks."

I began to realize how America's entry into the war had balanced on the permission for Zacharias to meet with Kurusu. If they had met, the Pearl Harbor attack may well have been cancelled, not through diplomacy but inadvertently. It would have depended on how much Zacharias told Kurusu, and the American admiral was known to be blunt. If he had given Kurusu just a suggestion of what he told Kimmel, and if Kurusu had relayed this to Tokyo, top brass in Japan could have mistaken insight for a leak. With the surprise element removed, the attack would probably have been cancelled.

"I feel guilty for not reaching America earlier," Kurusu said. "I'm haunted by the thought that my sickness prevented a peaceful solution."

"If I may offer an opinion . . ."

"Go ahead," Kurusu invited. There are times when one is bitten by Edgar Allen Poe's "imp of the perverse." I felt like a doctor not sure about how much to tell the patient. I told.

"Even if you had left as planned, I don't think things would have been different."

"Oh?"

"I have no special knowledge of what goes on in Tokyo's secret government circles, or how the Pearl Harbor attack came about," I said, not telling quite all I knew. "But as a former navy man, and from reports on the attack . . . Let me ask you—just how much preparation do you think was necessary for the operation?"

Kurusu paused. "I am not a tactician," he replied.

"Going by subsequent reports, there were about thirty ships, including six aircraft carriers with more than three hundred planes in the attack. This kind of force had to be in the planning stage long before your originally intended departure date."

Kurusu was silent for a moment, then nodded in understanding said quietly, "So Nomura and I were sent as decoys. To shake hands while they loaded the bombs."

"Again, I do not know what others in Tokyo were thinking."

The imp bit me because I felt empathy, even sympathy for the man. Kurusu, as a civilian, had enemies in government, and if his realization had erupted with anger in the wrong company, it could be dangerous for him.

Perhaps this caused him to take up the flag of Japanese innocence. On November 26, 1942, the first anniversary of the Hull Note, Kurusu spoke before the Imperial Rule Association.

"This day last year is particularly unforgettable for me, because it was then that the Japanese ambassador and I received from the American secretary of state a very important note which marked a crucial turning point in the final stage of the Japanese-American negotiations and which may well be said to have been decisive." He denounced the "impossible demands" of the note, and blamed it for what followed: "About ten days later, war broke out between Japan and America." His speech crystallized the national notion that the "Hull Note" triggered the war, a myth heaped upon a misnomer.

And, in the crossweaves of misunderstanding and error, I made my own misreading. From the beginning of German aggression in Europe, I was anxious for America to enter the war and disheartened by the obstacle of her unwieldy process of government. I erred at the international gaming table. Congress had been performing a deed for us: it prevented a unified German-Soviet assault on Europe by holding the president in check until after the German attack on the Soviet Union. If there had been no congressional structure steering America away from war, America could have been fighting Germany six months to a year earlier. That would have prevented the German attack on the Soviets and kept the German-Soviet pact in place, at least until both countries together could defeat Europe and America. Congressional backpressure gave Germany time to turn on its ally, and gave the Soviet Union the chance to destroy vast parts of the German army, its tanks, planes, artillery, equipment, and oil. Like Aiko's plywood creations that performed their function to the point of their own destruction, the antiwar framework of Congress kept America on the parabola of neutrality through the German-Japanese alliance and Germany's assault on the Soviet Union. Pearl Harbor ended the framework's job.

· 37 ·
Suicide in Bio-Hell

In May 1942 I received a message from the Kwantung Army Headquarters of General Umezu: "Dear Mr. Minister; I regret to inform you that Sasaki Akira, civilian employee of the Kwantung Army, died an accidental death from a mishap in his glass workshop. Since you knew Akira, and also his grandfather, my former instructor at the army college, I thought I should advise you of this unfortunate news. I thank you for your friendship in his lifetime."

Several months later an unstamped letter marked PERSONAL was placed in my letter box. Inside was a note that read simply, "Akira wanted this delivered to you." With it was Akira's suicide note:

The direction of the Japanese army is hideous. In September of last year, General Umezu ordered the Kwantung Army to prepare for biological warfare. The aim of the army's medical education as my grandfather knew it was saving lives in the field. Now medical knowledge is being used to create the most ugly of weapons. This will no longer be merely war. Wars eventually end. General Ishii is indoctrinating us in the benefits of biological warfare research. One of his tenets is, 'Disasters of human origin cannot be distinguished from those of natural origin.' This means that Japan can attack wearing an innocent face. The next step will be an endless war between humanity and microorganisms. In the end, Japan will become known as the ogre country that started it, and we will be despised for eternity. I cannot be part of that Japan.

I have seen how even our own soldiers who die from disease—some who become infected through their work in creating it as a weapon—become laboratory studies, and are separated, part by part, organ by organ, then put on permanent display in my preservation jars. I will not leave a single part of me to occupy my own crafts. Thank you for your friendship, and please forgive me.

So Akira's death was not accidental. I wondered how he had been able to take his life so that his body would never be found . . .

Later, I was informed that the army returned Akira's ashes to his family in Niigata. Whose ashes would they be? Some random assortment of remains from resistance fighters, farmers, and suspects whose diseased inner parts were preserved in Akira's specimen jars?

The import of the letter, the thing that made him want to "disappear," was that Japan was leading the world into an eternal battle against microscopic enemies. If that did start, it could fulfill the Buddhist prophesy of the End of the Law, and the earth would be covered not with Kawaguchi's Tibetan cowhide but with corpse rot. Would the crawling blankets of flies survive on the corpses? Or would they melt together with the decomposing world population and cover the globe in a putrescent lacquer?

I recalled the Christian teaching of the meek inheriting the earth. If *meek* can be understood as small in size, one more prophecy would come true as the microscopic soldiers multiplied across international borders. Then after humanity had decomposed, the final struggle in the days of the End of the Law would be a contest between rival microorganisms; there would be no pundits left to argue over the victor.

▪ 38 ▪
Playing with the Mind

"**A**re you doing your morning exercises?" Butterfly asked when she came through the door in the garden wall.

"Oh, those? No, but once in a while I listen to them. Sometimes I'm still in bed that early in the morning."

"With whom?" she asked, her professionally direct question twinkling with a smile and topped with a dollop of jealousy.

"If you're not here, with the radio. The government started a campaign to make everyone join in, I see."

"More of our government's plans to make us uniformly healthy. We are all supposed to raise our hands together, twist and bend together. It's happening in all the neighborhood shrines and playgrounds. Someone plugs in a radio and everyone follows the leader on the speaker. Very military. Did you see the crowds at Yasukuni Shrine?"

"Photos, yes. Thirty thousand people. Unbelievable."

"All bending left and right together."

"The punching bags and brisk walks are fine for me. No radio needed."

"Sometimes I think our government also needs more coordination," she said with a touch of sarcasm. "On August twenty-first they started promoting the radio exercise programs. Then on the twenty-second they cut the amount of soap we can buy. If you exercise more, you need more soap, right? That's logical."

"Logical," I agreed.

"But now, families of four or more can get only two cakes of soap a month. Others only one. They tell us to exercise more and bathe less. Not very good planning, I'd say."

"We diplomats have access to supplies. Maybe now you'll take more baths with me here. There's a good point to this rationing."

"I knew you'd say something like that. Or think it." She gave me a kiss on the cheek. "Maybe you told the government to do it."

"I didn't. And I didn't tell them to send an opera singer to the mines either."

"Did you read that, too?"

"It was difficult to miss her picture. That woman is quite generous in size, especially for a Japanese in these days of food shortages."

"Miura Tamaki, Japan's first international prima donna."

"Apparently she was quite active in Europe and America."

"She spent more than twenty years abroad. A friend of mine is a music teacher and she adores Miura. Do you remember her specialty?"

"Now that you mention it . . ."

"Ha ha! The song from *Madame Butterfly*. She performed it about two thousand times abroad, but it's banned in Japan."

"But Puccini is Japan's ally," I reminded her.

"Ah, but it's the story of an American naval officer who married a Japanese girl."

"True," I rebutted, "but he was a cad. He made her pregnant, then he left Japan and came back with his American wife. Madame Butterfly had given birth to his blue-eyed baby and she was so sad she killed herself. It's a perfect story for generating hatred for Americans."

"Don't look for logic in the way Japan does things these days. By the way, can a blue-eyed father give a Japanese girl a blue-eyed baby?"

"If he's a cad, perhaps it makes his genes more aggressive."

"Well, Miura couldn't sing her *Butterfly* piece, but she did perform for the copper miners—to get them to increase production."

"Do you think her singing will do that?" I asked, only partly in jest.

"If I gambled I would bet on it. You notice that they aren't called miners; they're 'pick soldiers.' More word games by our government leaders."

"Copper is needed for shell casings, so that seems accurate."

"It's also accurate to say that miners don't understand opera, but it was an emotional gesture and they'll respond with muscle."

That summer of 1942, as the "pick soldiers" redoubled their efforts and the population of Japan followed early morning radio commands to stretch and bend in unison, the Germans attacked Stalingrad. In the Pacific, Japan planned to cut the line of communications between the United States and Australia by taking New Guinea and the Solomon Islands. Japanese forces started building a secret airstrip on Guadalcanal. It was spotted by scout planes and America decided to thwart Japan's move by wresting Guadalcanal and nearby Tulagi from their hands. The tactic was to land marines under protection of American and Australian cruisers positioned around Savo Island, on the northern approach to the two islands.

On August seventh the Marines started landing. Soon after midnight of the ninth, a Japanese cruiser force under Admiral Mikawa Gun'ichi closed in undetected, and in a thirty-minute lightning strike cut down the Allied naval screen; one Australian and three American heavy cruisers were severely damaged and more than a thousand Allied lives were lost. I received reports from overseas that the blame for the Allied defeat fell on the pilot of an Australian scout plane, who spotted the Japanese cruiser force but failed to report it. I found out later from Admiral Suzuki about the real cause.

"The Allies should have taken Guadalcanal and Tulagi easily," Suzuki said, "but they ignored Mikawa and he took away the ships that were supposed to be covering the landing."

"I heard that an Australian scout plane spotted the cruiser force but failed to report it."

"We heard that also: a fabrication. Mikawa was spotted off Bougainville on the eighth and he knew it because his flagship picked up the message from the Australian plane. It was a stroke of bad luck and still fifteen hours to Savo, so Mikawa expected the Allies to be in formation ready to meet him. But he found them unprepared."

"Why was that, assuming they were expecting your strike force?"

"The message was ignored. Someone didn't take us seriously, still didn't believe that little Japan could bring off an offensive sea battle against their cruisers. Japan is always underestimated, and at Guadalcanal it made it easy for us to wipe out the naval screen—and it made the Allies pay heavily for the island. The plane didn't send the message? The same story came from Britain and America. That looks like a cover-up."

"Cover-up?"

"By the British for sure. Remember, the Australian cruiser was under a British captain. It would be a disgrace worthy of court-martial if the story surfaced. Look how many men they lost in that landing because they did not give Japan the respect of a real enemy. The only way to hide the error at the top was to make a scapegoat of the scout plane and say 'we didn't know.' Underestimation by an enemy is a valuable asset. Tacticians wrack their brains to achieve it. At Savo Island we got it without effort—thanks to our race."

With autumn and the end of swimming season, Butterfly began fluttering to me more often. I was not jealous of the workouts that took her away from me. They made her all the more toned and firm for our moments alone. I offered her a rare harbor where she could speak her mind and vent anger over the military invasions of education and society, but I could only give her guarded responses and physical comfort. I avoided—or worse, evaded—talking about the Japan that was tormenting her. I tried not to sound as if I was following some manual in diplomatic protocol, and I was often convinced that I failed. With the charmers that I knew were sent my way by Japan's information-gathering police forces, it was a game; Butterfly was more to me. As a teacher, her assigned role was to transmit government-generated thinking to Japan's youth, but she tried her best to be a protective filter. I knew her suffering and anger, but I never allowed her to deprive me of caution. That was my one reservation. I cherished it like a virgin determined to remain pure. When her invectives against government became too forceful to talk around without the evasion becoming too stark, I always had one escape: an embrace and a move to another room. Sometimes it was the bath, and I thanked the architect's wisdom of keeping it Japanese style. "I only wish it were big enough for you to swim in," I told her one day as we snuggled into the hot water.

"It's just the right size for us. Don't change it."

"But I'd like to watch you swim like this—no bathing suit."

She flicked water into my face. I grabbed her butterfly wings and massaged them. "If I ever get a swimming pool built here, promise you'll swim nude for me."

"I won't."

I think she would have, but there was never to be a pool. The world was moving into greater disaster.

In September, as the German army entered Stalingrad, Prime Minister Tojo and his medals held a big celebration in Tokyo's Hibiya Park for the tenth anniversary of Japan's contrived state of Manchukuo, then a region of forty-three million people. Only eleven countries including Germany and Italy recognized the puppet government, but this did not detract from the pomp and scale of the ceremony.

One day that autumn, Butterfly arrived carrying a single small, red flower. "This is ridiculous," she said. "I can't call it by its name."

"What is it?"

"A cosmos."

"You just called it by its name."

"Here, yes. But in school . . . The government ordered foreign names to be replaced by Japanese, and *cosmos* is foreign. Since I was a little girl I always looked forward to seeing them blossom alongside roads in autumn. In Japanese it's sometimes written 'autumn cherry blossom,' and that's what it has to be called."

She took a small glass from the kitchen, put water into it, and placed the single flower by the window. "In this house," she said to the flower, "I can call you 'cosmos,' as I did when I was a little girl."

"Actually, 'autumn cherry blossom' is sort of poetic," I said.

"Perhaps. But not when it's an order from army generals. Other words, too. Even 'kangaroo' has to change."

"Maybe the kangaroo *should* change," I answered. "I think it's an ugly animal. Long, flat feet, ungainly hop . . ."

"Do you know what else is happening? The police started arresting foreign missionaries and taking them to detention centers for interrogation."

That was news I had not yet heard. The Japanese government was having problems with Christians—if that is not putting it backwards—because their teachings contradicted the divinity of the emperor. This news showed that the government was getting more nervous. Unlike Melvin Cox, missionaries were not liable to have military secrets, only "wrong thoughts."

"Pretty soon," Butterfly continued, "textbooks for our elementary schools—*People's Schools*—will include the term 'war deity.' You know the word, right?"

"It was in the news about two months after the Pearl Harbor attack: nine 'war deities' were among the submarine crews."

"Japan lost five two-man submarines in the attack. That's ten men. America reported one man captured from a beached submarine—I heard that from my father—but our government does not want to admit it, so they reported nine 'war deities' at the attack. Ridiculous."

If Butterfly did not like evasion, I wondered what she thought when I did the same.

"But now," she continued, "they want to put the term into elementary school textbooks—to make children want to die in battle and become a war deity. That's horrible. Meanwhile, the government is collecting metal. Statues are being melted down. The iron stoves in schools are being melted down. I cried as I watched each stove tied to a long pole. Then several children lift the pole onto their shoulders and march the stoves out of the school grounds, in rows, like little soldiers. There will be no stoves in the schools in winter. They will become bullets or something like that. If the army didn't have enough metal to fight a war, why did they start one? The government takes our metal and tells us to use eggshells for laundry soap."

"I saw that in the newspapers also. Supplies of everything are becoming scarcer. Aside from that, is everything all right at home?"

"Yes and no. Since General Tojo became prime minister, government bureaus started getting shaken up, and anyone who was too friendly toward England or America in the past is not in favor. That includes my father. He's taking early retirement—that's a nice way of saying it. He's being forced out. People in government who are not army or pro-army find obstacles in their way."

"And what will he do now?"

"He'll move to his family's house in the country in Saitama. They have a vegetable garden, chickens . . ."

"To forget the world of politics, I imagine."

"I think so. Maybe a little like the Chinese poet Li Po. He resigned from government and spent his time in the mountains drinking with friends and writing poetry. That was twelve hundred years ago, but I think politics has always had something that made decent people want to go to the mountains. The problem is, my father doesn't want to leave mother and me in Roppongi. It's a family discussion now."

"I always wondered about your neighborhood. *Roppongi*. That means six trees. Are there really six trees there?"

"There used to be, but only one is left. The others were cut down. I hope they leave just that one."

Japanese authorities expanded their metal collection to include the bells of the nation's Buddhist temples, and in late November—it was just after the Soviets started their counteroffensive at Stalingrad—Butterfly came with a small bouquet of flowers carrying the name of Goto Florists in her neighborhood of Roppongi.

"We lost the last of our six trees," she said with a frown. "The government said it might be an air raid target, so they ordered it cut down. They're probably thinking about Teru-no-Miya."

"The imperial prince?"

"Yes. He has a large house some distance from our neighborhood and the government is worried about it. Not about us, about the prince. Since Doolittle's air raid the army leaders are expecting more, so they're taking precautions—and we lost the sixth tree." She put the bouquet in a vase, the smallest she could find. "There are not many flowers either these days, but here are a few." I placed them next to Akira's glass bird, and in the days following I nurtured them as long as I could, changing the water and snipping the stems. But they withered before the year ended when, on December 31, the Japanese Imperial Headquarters decided to withdraw from Guadalcanal.

1943 entered in gray shades. The new year is ordinarily a time of feasting in Japan, but food shortages left little more than patriotic slogans to fill up on. A meeting between Britain and the United States at Casablanca called for the unconditional surrender of Germany, Japan, and Italy, while in Japan, study time was divided with work in a labor draft to help the war effort— a draft that left only elementary school students exempt.

"Even girls are being called to the factories," Butterfly cried. "Schoolgirls from twelve years old and up are drafted to wind armatures and file down machine parts. And some of the work is being done in the schools themselves. This war is robbing the children. All for what? A war that was not necessary. The Japanese army officers have dreams of us becoming the Germany of the Orient."

"Oh?" was all I said. Disagreement over uniting with Germany destroyed the Yonai cabinet, and kicked Yamamoto from government. Butterfly did not need my opinion to continue.

"That alliance encouraged the army leaders, like giving candy to children."

In January of 1943, further educational reforms included a purge of English language study. Middle and high school courses were shortened by one year to hasten the students into the full-time work force, and the Board of Information issued a list of one thousand British and American songs that were prohibited.

On January 16 George Orwell took the BBC microphone again to speak on the German-Japanese rendezvous in the Persian Gulf: "The United Nations would then be separated from one another. Soviet Russia would be isolated and its armies would probably have to retreat behind the Ural Mountains, while China would be completely cut off and could be destroyed at leisure. After this, Britain could be attacked with the full weight of the German war machine, and if Britain were conquered, America could be dealt with at some time in the future."

The military logic was as sound as the discomfort it afforded. Bywater's prediction of American industrial might and technology overcoming Japan did not consider a German-Japanese alliance. Orwell was revising the script more fearful. Encouraging news came when the German army at Stalingrad under Field Marshal Friedrich Paulus surrendered on the last day of January, and against orders from Berlin to continue fighting. More than one hundred thousand men were already lost; they had neither food nor supply lines and it was winter in Stalingrad. *Only a fool does not know when to quit.*

In Japan, the battle for the mind continued. News reports announced the withdrawal from Guadalcanal as a "strategic shifting of position," and when I went to the Ginza one day, I was amused to see the government's latest way of mustering the populace's sentiments: the flags of Britain and the United States were drawn on the sidewalk so that people could walk on them. Then government propagandists adjusted professional baseball, and players took the field in army-type uniforms. Another government tactic brought a simultaneous scorn and laugh from Butterfly. "According to the Ministry of Health and Welfare, women are marrying too late."

"I remember a directive that put twenty-three as the age."

"Now they say it should be twenty, so I'm guiltier than ever."

"Then I'll give you a spanking." I embraced her, and gave her few taps on her buttocks. She tightened the muscles for me. But like a good teacher she could not break her mind away from the lecture of the moment. "Apparently the government sees the future of Japan in a swelling population, but what will happen to all the babies? They'll become soldiers and workers in war factories."

"It can't happen so quickly," I said. "Babies need time to grow up."

"But they're speeding up the process. They keep cutting down on the period of education. Now they're holding a big celebration in Hibiya Park for high school graduates drafted to work full-time in war factories. They're being sent off like industrial warriors. And primary schoolchildren are already working part of the school day. If the government can find a way to use babies, they'll do that next."

· 39 ·
The Race Starts:
Peace Versus Bio War

Suzuki Bunshiro and I met occasionally and exchanged thoughts on war, peace, and that complicated and ill-defined region that separates them. He was promoted to executive managing director of his newspaper, and this increased his contacts with the leading figures of government.

"I was talking with the newly appointed foreign minister, Shigemitsu Mamoru," he told me one day in the spring of 1943. "We had very confidential talks, and he wishes to speak with you. I personally request it, also. As a diplomat, there is nothing strange in your paying a courtesy call on him, and I wish you would do so."

"Nothing strange. . .?" Of course not, but putting it that way did make it sound, precisely, strange. I realized that he was preparing me for something more than a courtesy call.

I went to meet the newly appointed Japanese foreign minister.

"Excuse me for being slow to rise," Shigemitsu apologized, and advanced with his cane in his left hand, his left leg articulating in sharp movements.

"If you are more comfortable seated, please do not exert yourself," I said.

"Oh, I'm getting used to it," he smiled. "It happened in Shanghai, 1932. You know of the incident there?"

"Of course. The riots when the Japanese army withdrew."

"The real purpose of the pullback was to focus on the main goal of securing Manchuria. But the Chinese misinterpreted the move as a sign that the army was weakening and they rioted. A Korean threw a bomb and it caught me in the leg."

"I came to Tokyo five years after that," I said. "It was the year a Japanese naval officer was killed outside Shanghai and the Japanese response opened a full battle with Chinese troops."

"It opened one of the darkest pages for us in China," Shigemitsu went on. "Japanese forces pushed the Chinese back and moved on to take Nanking, where our soldiers went mad with rape and killing. Nanking caused the army to establish military brothels, to reduce disease among the troops."

"Chiang Kai-shek had to move his headquarters from Nanking and eventually inland to Chungking, and your bombers followed him. I saw then how the Shanghai incident brought Japan's navy into the war and turned the army's northern-advance ambition southward."

"That it did. Our naval base on Formosa became a point of operations for landings on southern China; the Pearl Harbor attack was a continuation of the southward expansion that started with Shanghai."

Shigemitsu had just returned from a post as special envoy to Japanese-controlled China to take up his new position in the cabinet. He smiled as we sat down. "I am not the first Japanese foreign minister to serve without a leg. Back in 1889—I was two years old—Japanese were objecting to the extraterritorial powers of Westerners. The foreign minister, Okuma, suggested compromises that some Japanese considered demeaning. Someone planted an explosive at the Foreign Ministry and Okuma lost his right leg. I lost the left one, so you might say that between us we have a pair."

"I'm glad to see that your humor has not suffered."

"Perhaps I learned that from Okuma. While he was recuperating, he joked that now there would be more blood to circulate to his head and improve his brain function. I hoped it would do the same for me."

Shigemitsu got to the war. "You probably know how I tried to avert this situation. It is no secret. In fact, some people are surprised that with my record, the army leaders even allowed me to return alive."

"Well, since you were appointed foreign minister by Prime Minister Tojo, it would seem that you are all in harmony."

"Not really. Every general and admiral knows that I advocated a policy of reality; Japan should accomplish that which is in our ability, and without military force."

"Yes, I have read your earlier statements."

"But the army became its own government in China, and Tokyo lost control there. Even Tojo objected to the break in the line of command. He was made premier in the hope he could repair that."

Shigemitsu was then fifty-six years of age. He had been in diplomatic service in Europe, the Soviet Union, and the United States, the last decade in spite of the hindrance of his lost leg.

"I know that you were friends with Admiral Yamamoto," he said, "and I know I can be open with you. I have discussed this with Suzuki Bunshiro. As a newspaper man under rigid censorship, he felt an obligation to help in this. There are steps that must be taken by Japan.... and your role could be vital."

"My role? As a mere representative of a neutral power?"

"As a person who can handle something of this weight. I have thought deeply about it and considered every possibility. When Germany turned against the Soviet Union, I imagine you would have liked to see both sides neutralize each other."

"I do not expect world events to happen that way."

"Do not fear offending Japan's ally. As you know, I was not happy with our Axis alliance. Your friend Admiral Yamamoto and I had similar thoughts on that. Germany has done us the favor of engaging the Soviet army, but with the defeat of our so-called ally at Stalingrad this past February, their future is not optimistic."

"That seems a reasonable forecast."

"The problem is that a victorious Soviet may bring a communist threat. And this is where I must be open with you and tell you—in confidence—that certain of us in the government are hoping for your cooperation in the future."

"My cooperation?"

Shigemitsu leaned forward, his hands clasped over the top of his cane, his artificial leg angled out. "I risk speaking with you because I feel you understand the delicate problem of the emperor. Also, we have a common stake in the results of this war." He shifted position to ease the pressure on his hip, and ease his communication with me. "There have been very secret.... Let us say, sentiments have been exchanged about the gloomy prospects for Japan. Some of us want to bring the war to an end, even with necessary sacrifices."

"And these are in the Tojo cabinet?"

"Yes and no. I would rather not go into detail. The secret police and the *kempeitai* are still fearsome. They watch everybody. No position is free from risk. If you help in this—you also."

I recalled the "cockroaches" on Yamamoto's train ride and nodded understanding.

"Some of us in the Japanese government see a negotiated settlement with the Allies as the only way to preserve Japan. We are a very small minority, and it is not possible yet to know the extent of these feelings in the government. But, when the time comes we will try. And we will need the cooperation of someone capable of communicating with the Western powers. You need not answer yet."

I again indicated that I understood, and waited.

"There is one great fear—a dread greater than American bombs. And that would be a takeover by the communists."

"I can see your concern about that."

"As a Scandinavian, I am sure you can. Now, in this war the Soviet Union presents a problem of a different sort."

"Their alliance with the United States, of course."

"Precisely. They are not merely allied against Germany; American foreign policy is so favorable to the Soviets, it is almost unfathomable. If we approach Washington to negotiate an end to the war, it would risk their including Stalin in any agreement, and that would mean terms with a Soviet vengeance. They want to crush the emperor and the emperor system, and this would destroy the very foundations of the Japanese nation. America would be kinder to bomb our islands into the sea. Japan cannot win this war and we must find a way out of it. As I said, we can do nothing yet, but I would appreciate your thinking of this—and, of course, your keeping this confidential."

"Of course," I answered, and we parted.

When I deduced the Pearl Harbor attack plan, I considered preventing it with a staged message. I chose not to because I wanted America in the war. But if the war Akira portrayed ever started, it could be doom on a scale never imagined. I considered thwarting the Pearl Harbor attack because of the chilling fear that Japan would launch the war with microorganisms. It had not happened yet. But when?

I did not know how much Shigemitsu knew about Japan's biological warfare plans. He had held a high position in China, but as a civilian with a pro-Western record, he could have been ignorant of Japan's work with anthrax and plague. If the war continued, it could enter the first stage of Akira's predicted eternal battle. On one hand, I wanted to start negotiating right away, but I was receiving insights into the risks, and even the futility, of the plan.

One incident was a continuation of what had started back in February 1942, when the Japanese police were intercepting messages to and from Georges Bagulesco. From the day he had sent the message on Hitler's attempt to split and share Europe with Stalin, strange things had happened to him. He was getting into his car one day when his chauffeur tried to stab him with a screwdriver. The chauffeur formerly worked for the American ambassador, Joseph Grew, and had a long and good working record. Bagulesco's message changed that.

Another day, Bagulesco returned home and his houseboy refused to unlock the door for him. A year of almost childish taunts culminated in a clubbing assault in the spring of 1943, and several days later he contacted me. "I must see you immediately, but my face and head are badly bruised and I am heavily bandaged. Might I come to your private entrance? I do not want to walk into the legation in this condition."

It was just when I was expecting Butterfly, so I asked Mrs. Saito to explain that I had a sudden visitor, and to please use my office in the legation until I was finished. Mrs. Saito had become an "aunt" to Butterfly when I wanted to contact her at school. And whenever Butterfly wanted to leave a message at the legation, she would ask for Mrs. Saito, whose functions overlapped regular staff duties and the role of my confidential secretary. I left a note for Butterfly at the garden door to go to the legation entrance, and while I spoke with the Romanian minister, Mrs. Saito and Butterfly sat in my office and sipped tea.

"On April eighth," Bagulesco recounted, "I went to the office of my military attaché, Colonel Nikolai Radulesco. As you know, the office is some distance from my legation. There were inconsistencies and omissions in messages, and I wanted to examine certain documents. I was seated in his office when the door behind me opened and two Japanese men rushed me.

I felt a heavy blow to my head, and that is all I remember. I woke up in my own legation, covered with blood."

"Do you have any idea who did it?"

"Japanese secret police or soldiers, but that does not matter. This was done on order or request from Berlin, of that I am sure."

"You reported it to the regular police, I assume."

"Yes, as routine, so they could not fault me later. And they handled it as expected. They did nothing."

"And who treated you?"

"Ironically, a German doctor in Tokyo. An anti-Nazi, though he cannot be too open about it."

"And what will you do now?" I asked.

"I am helpless. I have not been able to send or receive a message since I was assaulted. The culprits are the Japanese police with the collusion of our own military attaché, Radulesco. He set up the attack on me, and now all incoming messages go to him and my outgoing messages are blocked. I cannot communicate with Bucharest."

I knew what the next step would be. There were no options. I was forced to throw the card: "What can I do?"

"I hesitate to ask it of you, because it is a risk. But I must tell my government what is happening here in Tokyo. Would you send a message to Stockholm and ask your ministry to inform my government of the situation? I am asking the Spanish ambassador to do the same through Madrid, but with the high degree of Spanish-German cooperation, that could also be risky. I beg of you."

I promised him I would send a message by the time the working day started in Stockholm. After he left, I went to my office in the legation where Butterfly and Mrs. Saito were unusually quiet. Mrs. Saito was touching a handkerchief to her eyes; when I entered she got up, bowed to us both, then left the office.

"Is there something wrong?" I asked Butterfly.

"I'll tell you inside." We walked through to my residence.

"I got into trouble at school again," Butterfly said. "I was telling Mrs. Saito about it, and . . . it brought back unhappy thoughts."

"And what was the trouble this time?"

"Compositions again. I will not go running to the principal every time a student writes something that the secret police might jump on. I didn't do it again and got caught again."

"Will a sip of wine make it better?"

She nodded, and I brought it in—white, slightly sweet.

"It was one of the children who lost a father in the war. Naturally, there is a picture of the father in the Buddhist altar in their house. The boy wrote that sometimes he finds his mother sitting in front of the picture and crying. I said nothing about it to the school principal."

"You should have?"

"Japanese are not supposed to cry over losses in the war. It shows the wrong attitude. But the principal has other teachers read the compositions also—teachers he can trust. And because of that composition, the police went to the woman's house and scolded her."

"For crying?"

"Yes. They said that her husband died for the emperor and for the country, and that she should be proud, not sad."

I had no way to answer that.

"So, I didn't report the boy and the principal scolded me. Now the boy probably thinks I was the one who sent the police to his mother. The boy lost a father in the war, and his mother is punished for crying."

"And you told this to Mrs. Saito?"

"When I came to the legation, she asked how things were at school. She is concerned about her sons. Maybe I shouldn't have told her about this because she also lost a husband. That was my mistake. But I was upset, and when she asked me I told her. She said, 'I sometimes cry before the picture of my husband. Of course. My children lost a father. And perhaps one of my children may say or write something similar. I feel sorry for that mother, and for the boy. And when I cry for my husband, I fear that I may have to do the same for my children one day.'"

That encounter brought Mariko and Mrs. Saito closer together. Even though people talked with caution about things like the value of life and the emperor, there was understanding, and Mrs. Saito must have secretly wished that if one of her own children made a similar slip in school, it would be with a teacher like Mariko.

In the evening, I encoded a message to my ministry in Stockholm about the Bagulesco incident. A few days later, my foreign minister answered that a full reply would be sent through the Spanish representative. Why, I wondered, did he not take it upon himself? His reputed laziness? Fear of German reprisals? But the Spaniards finally did get word to Bucharest, and the Romanian government sent an official request to Tokyo that Bagulesco be allowed to return home. The Japanese refused, confiscated his funds in the Yokohama Specie Bank, pilfered his art collection, forced him to go to Japan-occupied Peking, and held him there under house arrest. I found out later that even before the assault on him, his death certificate had been made out, stating that he died after he lost consciousness and struck his head on a desk. His recovery was an unexpected complication.

During the early days while I waited to take my risk in negotiating a peace with the Allies, I received a message through the Danish underground that originated in Istanbul: "Anti-Hitler faction attempting negotiations with U.S. to end war. European protection from Soviets only condition. Outlook optimistic."

The message originated with a Scandinavian acquaintance of mine who was living in Istanbul, a shipping merchant by the name of Rasmussen. He held a Swedish passport—among others—which enabled him to mingle with the Germans in the city with minimal tension. Turkey was a neutral crossroads of friends and enemies, and Rasmussen's business, which included everything from wine to machinery, brought him into contact with different legations and groups in the country. He had another function: as a member of the admirable Danish underground network. A series of messages from Rasmussen put the story together for me.

In January 1943, just before the American president went to the conference in Casablanca, he appointed George Earle as naval attaché and special envoy in Istanbul. His assignment was to gather information on what was happening in the Balkans and in Germany. Background music for his task was provided by German officers filling Turkish restaurants with "Deutschland Uber Alles" in beer-laden syllables. Germany's big interest in the region was maintaining Turkey's supply of chromite for producing chrome steel and cutting tools for the German war machine.

Earle came to his assignment with a list of key persons in information and espionage activities. He had Rasmussen's name and contacted him for a possible exchange of information, and this is how Rasmussen learned of the scheme.

Earle was living in a hotel in Istanbul. One day, a broad-shouldered man in civilian clothes visited him and introduced himself as Admiral Wilhelm Canaris, head of the German Secret Service.

"I do not know if you realize this," Canaris told him, "but there are many of us Germans who feel that Hitler is leading the country and the world down the path of destruction."

The American knew of these sentiments in Germany, but he did not expect to hear it from the head of the Secret Service.

"As you know," Canaris went on, "the American president and British prime minister just concluded their meeting at Casablanca, and agreed upon unconditional surrender of Germany."

The American listened quietly.

"In a sense, that can be accomplished now," Canaris said. "The anti-Nazi group reaches deep, and we are prepared to make an offer immediately in order to stop the war and save what lives we can."

"And the offer might be. . . ?"

"The German armed forces will surrender to the Americans. Hitler will be delivered, alive if possible, or dead. The German army will stand by and if ordered by the United States, we will move to the eastern front to protect it against Soviet advancement."

The American envoy was shocked, then reviewed the terms. "There is a condition, then, of keeping the Soviets out of Europe?"

"Only that. Germany comes under orders of the United States and not the Soviets. Stalin is waiting to take over central Europe. His troops are armed with American weapons and equipment—your Lend Lease. We only ask that American assistance to the Soviets stop short of giving them Europe. We know that Soviet sympathizers are planted in the most sensitive places in your government; we have been following that for years. And that is why we could not make this offer until we had contact with someone who has direct communication lines to the president."

"And what would the next step be?" Earle asked.

"A meeting with the German ambassador, Fritz von Papen."

"He is part of the anti-Nazi faction?"

"Very much so. Would you meet with him?"

They met at a remote wooded area. Earle was convinced and radioed a coded message to the president and then sent another message through the diplomatic pouch. No reply came. Canaris kept checking with Earle and each time he was told "No reply from Washington." Another message by Earle, and again no response. The Germans increased the offer with a proposal that they surround Hitler's Eastern Military Headquarters, move the German army to the eastern front, and wait for orders from America.

Earle repeated the information, again through the usual diplomatic pouch, backed up with a duplicate sent through army-navy channels. Still, no response. By the time Canaris called on Earle again, the two had established enough of an understanding to discuss the matter more openly. There was also the immediacy of danger to the anti-Nazi faction and to Europe, but Earle was stymied. He told the story to Rasmussen, who advised me: "Danish underground contacted our agents in the United States and our plants in the Communist Party. Soviet-American alliance prevents acceptance of offer. Indications of influence from Morgenthau in Treasury. Also president's fear of massive unemployment if war ends. American economy just now recovering from effects of depression."

Months elapsed and leaks opened. "Anti-Nazi faction discovered by Hitler," Rasmussen advised. "Scheme over." The anti-Hitler faction members were executed; Canaris was hanged with an iron collar to a slow, agonizing death. Efforts to assassinate Hitler intensified, and shortly afterward Colonel Count Claus von Stauffenberg walked into the map room of Hitler's forest headquarters with a bomb in his briefcase. Hitler was only wounded. A purge that followed ended the anti-Hitler movement and the war continued.

This all came to the front of my mind when Shigemitsu told me of the plan to attempt a negotiation with an identical objective to keep the Soviets out. I was to assist the Japanese counterparts to Canaris and his associates. I had previews of how I would be treated if I were discovered: the botched assassination attempt on Georges Bagulesco, Melville Cox's "suicide leap" ... Yet, I was holding other frightful cards: I knew about Japan's microscopic weapons. I had Akira's prediction of where it could lead if the war did not end. And, I had the terrible feeling that I might be the only person who held that hand.

▪ 40 ▪
Yamamoto's Omen-Haunted Life and Death

Admiral Yamamoto was killed in action. When the announcer's voice came over Radio Tokyo I recalled what Yamamoto once said: *News is someone else's poker bet; one must assess what is bluff and what are the probabilities of the real cards.* It applied to his own death.

The broadcast came on May 21, 1943, one month after his death. It had been a secret among a few naval officers in the South Pacific and withheld even from top officials in Tokyo. According to reports, Yamamoto was killed when American P-38s shot down the twin-engine Type-1 light attack-bomber he was aboard. I knew that he was dead. I also knew there was a faked bet in that news. I had information others did not have, but even without it, I am confident that I would have seen through the deception: I knew him too well.

Yamamoto's death marked the end to a friendship that had started with his speech at Harvard twenty-four years earlier and had been nourished by cards. His reputation for gaming rose in rank as a conversation piece among naval men, paralleling his rise in rank in the navy. He practically ordered his subordinate officers to play cards and *shogi,* and gambling almost became his profession.

"I'm thinking of getting out of the navy," he once told me when we were at cards again.

"You? Leave the navy?"

"Bickering! Bureaucrats! The navy is run by people who have the minds of clerks in the ward office. Some of them have the same naval ability, too.

Always looking for a payoff for giving out contracts. That's how we got cursed with those giant battleships."

We made a few throws in silence.

"Ever been to Monaco?" he asked.

"Just once, on a short stopover."

"I may make it my home."

I recalled when a naval officer once told me, "I became pretty good at cards because I was serving under Yamamoto. When we went to the casinos it was uncanny. He even won at roulette. I never believed it possible for someone to know where a roulette wheel would stop, but watching him makes me wonder. He knew when he was going to win."

A feel for a winning number hiding just out of normal human awareness has a counterpart in sensing defeat. At some point, as Yamamoto said in his speech, *Only a fool does not know when to quit.* I am certain that this belief was part of the cause of his death.

Yamamoto said that similar stimuli will cause different reactions in different people—poker players or military commanders—and one must assess each person's likely reaction to a given stimulus. By this same reasoning, the omen value of a number varies with the person reading it. The more one believes in omens as message bearers, the greater will be the person's reaction to them. And reaction can lead to action.

Yamamoto was a gambler and mariner, a member of the two groups of people most sensitive to seeing messages in numbers. I found out at Harvard that the Japanese cultural bad luck number, *four,* became his personal number, with his birth on the fourth day of the fourth month. Japanese shun the fourth floor in buildings, and rooms with the number four. When sick, they avoid being admitted to or released from a hospital on a date with a four in it. Dishes in Japan never come in sets of four; five is customary. Since months in Japanese are called and written simply "first month, second month," every time he filled out a paper with his date of birth, those two fours sent him their bad luck message. A four also appeared in the last digit of his year of birth by the Western calendar, 1884, and the year he graduated from the Naval Academy, 1904.

During the war in the Pacific, Admiral Halsey ordered a change in his task force designation from the thirteenth to the sixteenth and changed a planned sortie that fell on a Friday the thirteenth. Japanese naval authorities were not moved similarly; the Imperial Japanese Navy's Fourth Fleet remained just that. And most of Yamamoto's shipboard career—plagued by disasters—was with the Fourth Fleet.

At Harvard, I learned how Yamamoto's given name, Isoroku—"Fifty-Six"—was taken from his father's age by the Japanese method of reckoning when the future admiral was born. Yamamoto pointed out to me how his name written in Arabic numerals and added like dice totaled eleven, which later became his number in the graduating class of the naval academy. After Harvard, the numbers *four* and *eleven* emerged in disasters and the events that led to them, events that either involved Yamamoto directly or followed in the war that started with his Pearl Harbor attack plan.

In 1929, when Yamamoto's fliers took off from the deck of his *Akagi* and were lost in fog, the two last digits of the Western year added up to his omen number, eleven. By the Japanese year designation, according to the reign of the emperor, it was the fourth month of the fourth year of the Showa era.

Yamamoto's number rose again in 1935, when *Yugiri* and *Hatsuyuki*, "Evening Mist" and "First Snowfall," lost their bows in a storm. The bow of "First Snowfall," bearing number 11, had to be shelled and sunk, possibly with men aboard, to seal the navy's codes on the ocean bottom, and Yamamoto would have imagined the cries of the men as they were sent to the bottom in a metal tomb bearing his number. As an added juxtaposition, in the naval investigation that followed, when Yamamoto saw his number "again and again, shelled by our own guns," the committee was headed by Admiral Nomura Kichisaburo, later the ambassador to America who negotiated for peace while the task force steamed toward Pearl Harbor.

Yamamoto was navy vice-minister and still trying to stop the army's push to join the Nazis until the summer of 1939, when an army squeeze forced him from government and into the nonpolitical position of commander-in-chief of the Combined Fleet. From there, he would plunge Japan into war against America. He was given that post on August 29: *2+9=11*.

The following day he called to say that he had just returned from the investment ceremony at the imperial palace for his new position. It was August 30: *8+3+0=11*. By Western methods of reckoning age, he was fifty-five years old; by the Japanese system, his new—his final—assignment, in which he would lead Japan to war, came when he was fifty-six, his own name and the origin of his personal omen number.

America's entry into the war, according to Americans critical of the administration and those of us looking for a sign of hope, was the Lend Lease bill of 1941. It was enacted on a date bearing Yamamoto's omen number: March 11. The Nazi slap-in-the-face to Japan when Germany signed her nonaggression pact with the Soviet Union—while Japan was fighting the Russians in Nomonhan—was announced in Berlin on August 21: *8+2+1=11*.

Yamamoto's omen rose again in his message to the strike force that signaled the final go-ahead date for the Pearl Harbor attack—"Climb Mount Niitaka 1208": *1+2+0+8=11*.

The attack planes lifted off. After those not flight-ready were withheld, the number that reached target was 353: *3+5+3=11*. Japan's officially announced loss in the attack was 29 aircraft: *2+9=11*.

About eight hours after the Pearl Harbor attack, an Imperial Rescript announced Japan's entry into war. It was issued at 11 A.M.

I am sure that each occurrence of Yamamoto's number stood out in relief to him like a roll of the dice of Heaven. Only someone absolutely ignorant of Yamamoto's thinking could question it.

When I likened the Pearl Harbor attack to the Kawanakajima battle of 1561, Yamamoto added his sardonic comment about the carriers: *This time, two snakes escaped.* Pearl Harbor came just 380 years after Kawanakajima: *3+8+0=11*. And the Western year designation of that battle that resembled the seed of Yamamoto's grander plan is his 56 inside an 11.

Some time after the Pearl Harbor attack—*four* months after—two Kawanishi flying boats were sent on another bombing mission to the harbor. "You know the Ten-Ten Dock in Pearl Harbor?" Yamamoto asked me.

"Yes, just across from Battleship Row. It's called that because it's one thousand and ten feet long."

"About ten days after the attack, and again in February, we sent submarine-launched seaplanes over Hawaii on reconnaissance flights. We saw that the damaged ships that were still afloat were towed over to the Ten-Ten Dock for repairs. That was our target."

"The news reported that; also that it was another successful raid."

Yamamoto frowned disgust: "Japanese news. It was a total failure. One plane bombed the woods, the other unloaded over the ocean. I wonder if the planes weren't jinxed."

"Jinxed. . .?"

"Those flying boats are superb machines; America has nothing to compare. But they were powered by four Kasei 11 engines."

"Kasei—the planet we call Mars, the Roman god of war."

"If they weren't designated "11" they might have made it."

Japan's initial major loss of the war came at the beginning of the Coral Sea battle and augured her defeat to come at Midway: the sinking of the carrier *Shoho* on May 5, 1942. Yamamoto's omen number rose in her displacement: eleven thousand tons. Another carrier was damaged, and the six carriers intended for the Midway assault were reduced to the bad-luck number four.

Even the record setting twenty-eight-inning baseball game in Tokyo that wedged between the battles of Coral Sea and Midway carried the double bad-luck number—Yamamoto's birthday—in its score: 4–4.

Japan's reversal at Midway was a bad omen dating from the Pearl Harbor attack. The *Lexington* and *Enterprise*, the "two snakes that escaped," were not in port because they departed from normal routine to deliver planes to Wake—and Midway. When the Japanese striking force steamed to its launching point two hundred thirty nautical miles from Midway, the first planes took off for air attacks against the island on the Tokyo reference time and date of 0145 on June 5: *6+5=11.*

The local time at Midway was 0445, fifteen minutes before sunrise of the previous day. The first wave lifted from the decks—dive bombers, level bombers, and fighters, thirty-six of each type: 108 aircraft. It would be consistent with Yamamoto's way of interpreting events for him to see the great religions of the world also throwing numbers at him: In Buddhism there are 108 human sins; on the new year, temple bells in Japan toll 108 times. There are also 108 beads in the Catholic rosary.

At the battle of Midway, Yamamoto commanded the Combined Fleet from the *Yamato* away from the battle area. The situation for Japan deteriorated and he received the message that the *Akagi*—the ship he was closest to during his naval career—was crippled. Yamamoto told me that he sent the order to scuttle the carrier and his subordinate officers pleaded to spare her. Later, I heard from naval officers that while the Japanese navy was being melted down and his subordinates were pleading to spare the *Akagi*, Yamamoto barked to them, "In 1935 the Fourth Fleet ran into a storm and we had to shell and sink the severed bow of a destroyer, probably with men aboard. We can't let the *Akagi* fall to the enemy. Scuttle her immediately!"

The officers were puzzled why Yamamoto took time then to reflect on a peacetime disaster of seven years earlier. I knew him and Japanese literature well enough to decipher his remarks.

Yamamoto, like many educated Japanese, occasionally quoted from the ancient anthology of Japanese poetry, the *Manyoshu*, to add a literary emphasis to a point. When he called to say goodbye on his way to take command of the Combined Fleet, he mentioned that he was taking a copy of the book with him. It was certainly on board the *Yamato* that day. Two of the poems in the anthology carry the same titles as the names of the destroyers that broke apart on maneuvers in 1935. "Evening Mist" recalls a scene of desolation:

> *In the evening mist*
> *The Saho highroad lies in ruins*
> *with only plovers*
> *singing in the solitude*

"First Snowfall" speaks of death:

> *The first snowfall*
> *lies in flakes a thousand deep*
> *while I desire the return of my love*
> *who lies deep in my heart*

When Yamamoto gave the order to scuttle the *Akagi*, "First Snowfall" rose in his memory with flashbacks of his number 11 into the ocean under phantasmic recitations of ancient court poetry. I have no idea how many times he opened his copy of that book of poetry to read those works headed by the names of the doomed destroyers—as I did many times after his death—but he surely knew their numbers in the anthology by heart: *Hatsuyuki*, 4475; *Yugiri*, 4477, both headed by a double number four, his birthday.

Three aircraft carriers were sunk or destroyed at Midway on June 4, local date. Then the fourth carrier was hit hard by dive bombers. Fires and explosions broke out and the crew fought through the night, but early the following morning the order was given to abandon ship. Within twenty-four hours Japan lost four fleet carriers and Yamamoto ordered retreat from the intended assault on Midway. By then it was June 5 locally; the omen number had crossed the international dateline to rise on the unmanned ghost ship carrier number four as it drifted and burned. It continued that way through the day, then settled to the bottom. The Imperial Japanese Navy's records listed the local time for the sinking as 1820 hours: *1+8+2+0=11*. The remnants of the Midway fleet headed for Hiroshima Bay still under the cloud of Yamamoto's omen number: the remaining ships limped into port on June 14: *6+1+4=11*.

Yamamoto's omen numbers appeared as if dealt by some deviant deity. I remember the day he invited me to his office to test the progress in my *shogi*. While we were playing, an orderly came in with a message that required him to leave for a few minutes. He invited me to browse among his bookshelves. As I did, I came across a copy of the Bible. It was in English, and I casually took it down, opened the cover, and saw that it bore the sticker of a London bookshop. I browsed among some of the other books, then came upon a volume of the short stories of Sherlock Holmes; it was the book that he wrote me about, and it bore the label of the same London bookshop as the Bible. Apparently, he bought them both on the same trip in 1934 that brought him and Hector Bywater together. I glanced at the words on the jacket: "This book contains all the fifty-six short stories concerning Sherlock Holmes. . . ." I pictured Yamamoto picking that book up and tried to imagine what was in his mind when he discovered his number delivered by the London sleuth. I noticed that the stories were not all in the original order in which they had appeared in the newspaper, and as I was paging through the book, Yamamoto returned to the room.

"Oh . . . that. You may have it if you wish. Perhaps you will be able to interest someone else in your father's favorite detective."

I thanked him, and added, "I see you're studying the Bible, also."

"More or less. I was sent to Sunday School when I was a child, so the interest continued. There's one with parallel translation also. You might find it an interesting text of sorts. Take that also if you wish."

We finished our *shogi* session—Yamamoto said I still had "too much chess in my blood"—and I brought his presents to my office. After his death, I took Holmes from the shelf and glanced through some of the stories I had read years earlier. I turned to the final story in the book, where Holmes had solved a case and the police requested that he turn the results over to them. Holmes agrees, as is his custom, and the newspapers credit "brilliant police investigation" for the success. In story number fifty-six, the "brilliant work" was not really performed by those who took the credit. Yamamoto's number was on a story that reflected—according to his own opinion—his role in the Pearl Harbor attack. The final line in story number fifty-six had been underlined in pencil: Holmes says to Watson, "Some day the true story may be told."

These can all be assigned to casual occurrences with a high rate of coincidence; for most people that is the least tiring interpretation. But Yamamoto did not read numbers with such frivolity. He responded to them to the point where they played a role in his death.

I always regretted that I never met Hector Bywater; he died in August of 1940 from alcohol-induced sickness, with Britain under German air raids and before his Great Pacific War was reenacted.

If Fate did not permit me to meet Bywater, the next best thing would be someone who knew him and who might have heard stories of that meeting with Yamamoto when Bywater was working for the *Daily Telegraph* One day after the war, I wired the newspaper from my ministry asking if any of the staff might have known him then, but more than a decade with a war in between had left no traces other than his articles. "Try the *News Chronicle*; it was his last place of employ," came the advice. The answer came back: "Last known residence was close to Richmond Park, a minute's walk from the Park Road Arms, a pub where he spent more time than he did writing in those days. You might contact the landlady, Margaret Savage. The pub has been in the family for years."

Richmond was a quick commute to Fleet Street, and it survived the war in quite good shape. I put in a call and the landlady's voice came through with the body of a good, strong ale. "Park Road Arms!"

"I'd like to ask about one of your former customers, a Mr. Hector Bywater."

"You were a friend of Mr. Bywater's, were you?"

"Not really, but an avid reader. I regret that I never met him, and as second best choice I'd like to contact anyone who knew him, especially his writer acquaintances. I'm starting by calling the last pub he frequented in hopes of turning up some of his former pub mates."

"Oh, there are enough of those around all right," she came back. "When Mr. Bywater was living here in Richmond, a lot of the Fleet Street reporters used to come here to talk with him. And to hear his jokes."

"I would like to throw a little party there one day for any of his associates you can round up. Can you fit us all in?"

"Oh, I think we can work it out. If we run out of space, some of them can crawl in behind the bar. They'd feel at home there anyway."

A few weeks later the drinks and food were on me in Richmond. "Mr. Bywater was a family topic," Mrs. Savage told me. "Of course, it's a pub, and people come here to drink, but I tried to get him to slow down. I knew it was doing him no good. I even told him if he kept it to one pint a day, it was on the house."

"There's not much profit in running a pub that way," I joked.

"Oh, there would be if it was Mr. Bywater," one of the gathered men said. "He had fantastic stories to tell, and we came to hear them."

"Right," added another. "We'd gladly keep the sales going to hear his tales. But he was drinking heavily, and I think it was whisky that finally got him. It's a shame nobody ever made a record of his stories."

Some of the old-timers had been lost as war correspondents or in air raids; some had died fighting in the armed forces. I had an uneasy feeling about being from a country that was Germany's ally in neutral war against the British. I also wondered about mentioning that I had been close with Yamamoto; but since I was planning this to be another Bywater-Yamamoto meeting with the principles in absentia, it could not be avoided. As it turned out, the men gathered there, all being writers, were interested in the human drama, and they were as eager to hear about Yamamoto as I was about "meeting" Bywater. I told them about our days at Harvard, about our interest in poker, and about my discovery of Yamamoto's omen numbers, and how I was convinced that official accounts of the way Yamamoto had died were wrong. Then we came back to Bywater.

"When Mrs. Savage here told me about your wanting to call this gathering," one of the journalists offered, "I looked through my collection of articles about Hector and came up with this: something I wrote that I never gave to the newspaper."

"How was that?" I asked.

"I was still pretty new to the game then, bright-eyed and looking for some kind of scoop. Hector's book was the talk of military men then, and one day I found myself drinking in the same pub with the man who wrote it. I felt like I'd been splashed by John the Baptist himself. I said something to the effect that probably no American publisher had given thought to a book about a war with a country on the other side of the world. He chuckled a bit and said something like 'Don't underestimate the whole nation; an American publisher was a big influence in my writing the book in the first place.' To me, young ambitious journalist, you know, that sounded like a possible article—why a story about America's war with Japan wasn't published over there. So I did a little research with his publisher, Constable and Company, and they were good enough to look up the records and all that. Well, it seems that Constable had made an arrangement to print and distribute the books here, and also supply the American market."

"That seems strange," I said. "The only Briton in *The Great Pacific War* was the author himself."

"Exactly. If an American publisher had encouraged the book in the first place, why was it not published in America also? Why in London to supply the American market? So back at my desk I wrote up a draft of the story with the question left unanswered, and ending with, 'According to Mr. Bywater.' I kept it with me until our next pub encounter."

"And did you find the answer?" I asked.

"I did. And that's where the thing ended. I thought he'd be sympathetic to a young reporter, and I told him what I was doing and gave him the article as far as I had gone. He looked at it and asked me not to go ahead with it, at least not just yet. He said the publisher in question was deeply concerned that in America it might be looked on as warmongering, or trying to provoke what Bywater was actually trying to prevent. That was his purpose in writing the book, to keep America and Japan from ever having a go at it. And he did not want to cause trouble across the seas for someone who steered him into his masterwork, as it were. In fact, he said the American publisher was relieved when Constable agreed to print the book for both markets."

I looked over the typewritten draft of the article and stopped at the line, "On March 8, 1925, the editor of Constable and Company signed a contract to publish the book in London for the British market, and to also supply the American market."

"This date," I asked the formerly young reporter, "is it correct?"

"The contract date? Oh, that's correct. No question. It's from Constable's records. Bywater later told me that the American publisher was relieved because it kept his role in the book hidden and took him out of a tricky spot."

"Add it up," I said.

"Add it up?"

"The contract date; the month and day."

"By God! It's the same jinx number; eight and three—eleven!"

"The contract date for Yamamoto's war script," I emphasized.

There were a few curious looks, a *Blimey* or two, and the stories continued. "Hector was an actor, he was," volunteered one of the men. "I knew him when we reporters used to meet at the Fleet Street pubs, right where most of the city's newspapers were. We called ourselves 'The Fleet Street Press Gang.' That was a gag, you know. I don't know who made it up, but it's a play on the eighteenth-century press gangs that used to capture blokes to be forced into service in the Royal Navy. We weren't quite so bad."

"No," added another. "We were just writers. But he's right about Bywater being a bloody good actor. He'd come in and start singing ditties, sometimes he'd recite limericks. Jokes and puns? He could supply the entire Royal Navy. He once interviewed Mussolini, you know. His first time back on Fleet Street he comes into the pub and before he even orders a drink—which is pretty fast for Hector, mind you—he comes out with a riddle: 'What's the shortest book ever written?' Answer: *Great Victories of the Italian Navy*."

"Some people said that he could have made it on the stage," offered another, "but then we'd have lost a pub performer."

"And a damn good espionage journalist," added another.

The ale flowed with stories of his drinking, his marriages, his disagreements with publishers and editors. Then we came to that December night in 1934. All of them had heard of the meeting and Bywater's request for an interview that had brought it about. Apparently his anticipation echoed off pub walls for days before it happened. Bywater's article appeared in the *Daily Telegraph,* and as we tried to re-create that evening of more than a decade ago, one member wiped the suds from his lips and said, "You know, that reminds me of something Hector mentioned that night. He said that Yamamoto told him how he believed that all naval strategists should gamble."

"Gambling strategy was part of Yamamoto's way of living," I added, thinking to myself that it was also his way of dying.

"Hector said that of all the Japanese he ever met, Yamamoto was the most poker-faced. Cordial and all, but cool and—protective, about what was in his mind. Except once. And it was . . . this seems strange now, but your mention of numbers and all that brings it to mind. He said it was a number—*that* number—that did it."

"Did what?"

"Broke him of the poker face." He downed the remainder of his ale and the landlady, as I had requested, did not let empty glasses sit too long. "Hector was a high-energy man. His subjects were, too, you know. Top speed, firepower, and things like that. Oh, he was a performer, all right, but when he spoke navies, he became a preacher. Early in 1939—he was with the *Daily Telegraph* then—he wrote an article that raked British leaders over the coals for not strengthing the Royal Navy when world tension was heating up. He tore into Chamberlain for not being able to see Germany's aims. We had the Anglo-German Naval Agreement at the time, from 1935. 'Scrap it' is what Hector pushed in his article. He said that Germany had already violated it—which they did, the buggers—so Britain should denounce it and build ships. That's the way he was writing till a few days before the war started. Then the paper kicked him out."

"But he was on the mark," I said. "Why did he get fired?"

"Bloody well on the mark he was—but with too much criticism of the government. Actually, it was a feud with the paper that had been brewing for a long time. You know, people were trying to avoid war, and when he kept saying that we were headed that way and we'd better gear up for it, something popped in the office. He was out of work for a couple of months and then got taken on by the *News-Chronicle*—an old employer of his when the paper went by another name. But during that in-between there, it looked like Hector was trying single-handedly to drain the United Kingdom dry."

"Drinking heavier than his usual heavy?"

"God, yes. Like a sailor fresh ashore from a cruise. And heavier in poundage, also. He was a great walker, you know. Used to go through the streets like a destroyer at flank speed. But about the time he had that run-in with his paper, he got sloppy a bit. Heavy drinking and heavy in the bilge, he was. And it was during that time that I ran into him in the Fleet Street pub that was our home then. He was nursing a hangover and was geared down to a slow drink to chase away yesterday's. The war had already started, and the two of us talked a bit about it, and what Japan might be up to and what she would do next. But he had no job, no place to write his opinions. So maybe that made him take a vacation from the whole thing and his mind sort of backed into reminiscence. We talked about the Japanese navy, and naturally Yamamoto's name came up. Hector gave one little smile—just a tiny light in the fog, you know; he must have had depth charges going off inside his head—and said something about the suit Yamamoto was wearing when they met. Said that when he went to Yamamoto's suite in the Grosvenor House, he didn't find an admiral but this man dressed in a three-piece pin-striped suit. And with his close-cut hair and sort of dark complexion, Hector said that Yamamoto looked like more of a New Orleans jazz musician than a Japanese. Then he gave a chuckle and said, 'I don't know what his instrument might be, but he'd have a rough time on clarinet with those missing fingers. He could handle slide trombone, though.' Even in a stupor, Bywater could squeeze out a funny something-or-other."

I recounted Yamamoto's single-glove fashion and the dummy fingers. "As time went on," I told them, "I don't think he bothered about it so much. Sometimes he just had the two fingers on the glove sewn up. Sometimes he just didn't bother wearing it."

The former Fleet Street Press Gang member continued. "Then, when he got talking about that meeting with Yamamoto, he did say something that had to do with numbers, as you mentioned. The way Hector told me, pretty much, was, 'Yamamoto and I had been discussing Japan in relation to the proposed naval disarmaments. I asked him what he thought about a naval arms race if disarmament failed, and he said Japan would do anything to avoid that happening. Then Yamamoto ordered drinks brought in—Scotch for me and soda water for him—and after the mood became more friendly, he brought up my book again, and in the end asked whether I thought the strategy I outlined in 1925 would still be valid. I said yes, except of course when I wrote the book, Hawaii was just a quiet navy yard and supply depot. I had the Japanese landing on the islands then, but two years after the book came out, Pearl Harbor was dredged to make it a naval base, changing its value as a target to top priority. But as far as America's ability to bounce back from an attack by another nation, I told him that no matter how America's naval power might be crippled by a surprise attack, as happened in *The Great Pacific War,* the industrial base was too great. And the inventiveness. I said that it wouldn't be a snap, but I told him that from what I know from living in the country and writing on such things, they would come through as they did in my book, even if it were in the eleventh hour.

'And when I said that, it seemed to break his composure. He started. He seemed shaken a bit. I remember, because then he asked me, "What do you mean by that?" I thought for a second, have I insulted the man or something? He asked me, "Why eleven?" Then I realized that it was a colloquialism that was strange to him. I told him that it meant at the final moment, in the end. And he asked again, "Why did it become *eleventh* hour?" Actually, he caught me for a second, and I had to think hard to remember the origin of the expression. I told him how it started with an episode in the Bible, and he asked me what part. I told him it's in Matthew somewhere. I was there as a journalist requesting an interview and he was questioning me on the Bible. Yamamoto said, "I went to Sunday School when I was a boy— and I even got into arguments for keeping a Bible on my desk when I was at the naval academy. I never saw that number appear." I joked a bit, told him that it was not my habit to carry a Bible when I interviewed distinguished naval officers, and assured him that if I'd had one, I could've steered a course to the eleventh-hour origin. He just nodded. I have no idea why, but for some reason that *eleventh hour* expression seemed to turn him strange.'"

I remembered the Bible on Yamamoto's bookshelf in Tokyo, purchased at a London shop, and I realized that he went out to buy it after that meeting, to search for the roots of the saying that carried his number in Bywater's predicted defeat of Japan.

The Park Road Arms gathering broke up, and when I returned to Stockholm, I discovered why Yamamoto's Christian education had failed to reveal his omen number. I still had the Japanese-English parallel-translation Bible among my belongings. I took it out, and in chapter twenty of Matthew, I came across the parable of the owner of a vineyard who goes to the marketplace seeking workers to pick grapes. The man hires workers "in the third hour," again "in the sixth hour," then "in the ninth hour," and finally "the eleventh hour." The Japanese translation, though, simplified it and rendered the ancient time periods into present-day equivalents of nine, twelve, three and five o'clock. In Yamamoto's Japanese Bible, his number was eliminated in translation—but waited for him in London, in a predicted defeat of Japan.

The year after that meeting in Grosvenor House the disaster of the two destroyers occurred, then a series of naval and national disasters with his omen numbers turning up like losing cards. He finally realized it was time to quit. And, to borrow his words again, I see the report of his death as somebody else's bet. Yamamoto was shot out of the sky by American pilots, but they did not kill him: he was already dead on board. The Americans shot down his corpse along with the others on the flight who were sacrificed in a plan to conceal the fact that Yamamoto died by his own hand. If the Japanese people learned of his suicide, half the country might follow him.

The Chinese communists saw a chance to gain strategic advantage and drive a bigger wedge between Japan's armed forces by issuing a statement that Yamamoto killed himself because of the split between Japan's army and navy. Their superficial propaganda gambit concealed a more complex truth.

▪ 41 ▪
Yamamoto's Vectors to Suicide

Why did Yamamoto decide to throw in the final hand? Someone who is cut by a saw cannot identify the tooth that cut, and human actions are not always monocausal; that is why they baffle those who look for monocausal origins. Multiple stimuli can build up a set of emotional vectors; each vector exerts its force and direction on the psyche. Vector forces that reach critical level resolve into an action.

Pearl Harbor was a heavy suicidal vector on Yamamoto. The last time we met, in that summer of 1942, I commented to him, "There's heavy criticism in America for allowing the ships at Pearl Harbor to get caught like sitting ducks."

A reply came from somewhere far beyond the Sakura clouds. "There's only one thing worse than a sitting duck."

"And what would that be?"

"A *kamo!*"

Kamo is the Japanese word for duck, but in the vernacular it means a patsy, a sucker, a person coaxed to a gaming table to be exploited by others. The image is a duck coming to dinner carrying scallions in its mouth to be cooked together with itself. It was a clumsy moment. Yamamoto remained silent and sullen for a long time, and I only offered an equally clumsy "Oh?"

He held onto the silence a while longer, then broke it with a comment that did not even cause a ripple in his sullenness. "A game with so many enigmas is phony somewhere."

The clumsy moment stretched. "Meaning. . . ?"

"Enigmas all around. For one, when the air and sea patrols north of Hawaii were removed, it looked like a lucky break for our task force. But it was incongruous. Negotiations in Washington were going bad. I can't believe the U.S. Navy would be so stupid."

"They *were* short of planes," I reminded him. He grunted silently.

"They had planes and they had ships," he said without changing mood. "We know what we destroyed on the ground and in the harbor. They were just kept out of the northern sector. And why were the carriers pulled out? Why the sudden departure from normal routine that left only old ships in the harbor? After the carriers and their escorts left Hawaii, our major targets were more than twenty-five years old—leftovers from the Great War. America should have been glad to get rid of them."

"They were old ships, that's true."

"And why was Admiral Zacharias pulled out of intelligence and sent to sea when America needed his ability most? I knew Zacharias from his Tokyo days, and he knew us. He was removed from intelligence, then Washington refused to let him meet with Kurusu. Why? Then after the attack, you saw how the president set up a special committee to investigate Admiral Kimmel, commander-in-chief of the Pacific Fleet, General Short, others."

"I was surprised at that. Kimmel wanted a court-martial. That would be the normal way of handling it, to determine whether or not he was guilty of dereliction of duty."

"That's what I mean," Yamamoto responded. "It wasn't normal. A court-martial would call up witnesses. Someone didn't want that." He took a long pause without seltzer or smoke, and broke it with another question. "And why was a Russian ship watching the task force?"

"It *is* a seldom traveled stretch of ocean," I had to agree. "A lone merchantman could always be pure coincidence."

Yamamoto frowned that he did not buy the theory. "Stalin knew where to look." He rotated his seltzer glass on the table as if trying to tune in to the wavelength of fact. "Remember, Russia was fighting Germany for five months before our task force set out. And the American president was so close with Stalin he was making enemies in America. The Russians were worried that we might join Germany in the two-front war that Hitler tried to set up. Stalin wanted us to go to war against America to drain our strength from China—and to give the president the opening he needed to get America in against Germany."

"So you think Stalin had advance knowledge of the attack?"

Yamamoto cocked his head in a gesture-expression combination that straddled *who knows?* and *maybe.* He stared into his seltzer. "We found out later from our people in California that a Russian ship due to sail home from San Francisco was ordered to another west coast port by the U.S. Navy—and held there until our fleet cleared the northern Pacific. Another Russian was ordered to a southern route."

"But the fleet did encounter a Russian, you said."

"It would have been risky to let the Russian merchant ships sight us. Crews talk too much. But Stalin could have sent a spy ship—manned by agents, not sailors."

"In cooperation with the American president?"

"With or without. Hell, Russians don't pay attention to protocol. Maybe Stalin wanted the information for his own war plans. The important thing is that Japan shouldn't have been part of the problem; we wouldn't have been if we weren't pushed into bed with Hitler."

"Of course, there were anti-Japanese movements in America well before then."

"Mostly to get us to end the war in China. The emperor wanted that, too. Many of us did. Our army was in quicksand there, but Japan was not a potential threat to America; Germany was. If Britain fell, America would be Germany's next target. And your iron would be shooting at Washington."

"That could have been one turn in the labyrinth of possibilities."

"Yonai, the emperor, most of the naval officers—we tried to prevent Japan's joining the Axis and failed. We all knew that if we allied with America's most hated country we'd be pulled into war against America also. The emperor always expressed his fear of that. He saw the trap our leaders were falling into. In August 1940 the Luftwaffe started bombing England; the next month, in America, the president almost caused civil war when he pressed for a conscription act and activated National Guard units. Then he swapped fifty destroyers to England for a lease on their bases in Bermuda, Jamaica, British Guiana. . . . It became a big issue in the election battles; the news was filled with it. Roosevelt's opponents said the destroyer swap was practically a declaration of war. It was obvious where he was trying to push America, but our soft-headed leaders couldn't see. So Japan signed with the Axis the end of September and about a month later Roosevelt won his third term. You remember what he did after that?"

"His Lend Lease bill." I recalled the encouragement it gave me.

"For countries fighting the Axis. By then, Axis included us. He fought until he pushed it through—March of 1941. Then American cruisers started intruding into Japanese territorial waters. I think you remember that fuss also."

"Three incursions—the last in July. I remember them."

"To antagonize us. Then about the time of that last one the American president closed the Panama Canal to Japanese ships and put an embargo on oil, aviation gasoline, iron, steel. . . . Once we were in a pact with the Axis, Washington kicked harder."

"But you never thought to abandon the Pearl Harbor plan for a southern advance?"

"Army and navy officers, they all tried to make me do that. The first big broadside I took was after Holland fell to the Germans in 1940. The oil wells of the Dutch East Indies shined like a pot of gold at the end of a rainbow. First our government tried to make a deal there."

"I remember when Japan started negotiations in Batavia to gain a contract for the oil."

"Idiots! What chance did they think they had? That was in September of 1940. Queen Wilhelmina and her people had escaped the Nazi occupation and set up the Dutch government in exile in England. Holland and England were both looking for America to get into the war and Roosevelt was doing his best. So if he tells the Dutch East Indies to refuse us, they would. A few days after negotiations started, Japan joined the Axis. With that, chances went from zero to less than zero."

"But Japanese officials kept negotiating until June of 1941."

"Because they're idiots. Then the government and military leaders wanted us to take the oil fields by force—and I knew we could have done it without American interference."

"You don't think America would have pulled her fleet from Hawaii to defend it?"

"You know how I always studied foreign magazines and newspapers. I knew that the president would never have been able to gain support to defend something foreign."

"Public support does seem to be a problem in America."

"Much later—October 1941—Roosevelt's Atlantic adventures finally got the Germans to return fire and they sank an American destroyer; one hundred fifteen men lost. But even that didn't get support for war. So I guessed right when I said we could have grabbed the oil of the Dutch East Indies without American interference—at least for a while. But I still held to the plan, even after I hit a bigger snag."

"The oil embargo, summer of 1941."

"Hmmm. Everyone screamed that the oil wells were a more necessary target than American ships located more than three thousand miles away. That's when I threatened to quit as commander-in-chief of the Combined Fleet and take my entire staff with me if they tried to cancel the Pearl Harbor attack." He took a long pull on his cigarette; the exhaled smoke was heavy with humiliation. "It would have been better—strategically—if I had agreed with them. But . . . there were other things."

"Other things?"

Yamamoto stood up and moved to another table with a *shogi* board. He maintained silence and started placing and moving pieces. As he journeyed on the board and through the world, I searched for the reason why he insisted so adamantly on Pearl Harbor. He even said that his critics were right, that he believed Japan could have grabbed the oil fields. Then why his stubborn tenacity to attack Pearl Harbor?

I recalled talks I had had with naval officers after the attack. Some confided to me that his dogged insistence started whispers that he was mentally unstable. Some saw him pushed by "yellow peril" rhetoric.

"We were insulted at the term," one officer confided, "and many of us feel that Yamamoto's short stature made him want to prove that he could take on America."

"Sure, this 'yellow peril' stuff hurts me," Yamamoto once said long before Pearl Harbor, "but it's fairly confined to a certain clique."

"And part of that clique is the press. That increases their punch."

"Japan is usually underrated. The experts don't expect much of us. The 'yellow peril' screamers at least recognize us as skilled enough to be a threat. It's a rare compliment, in a way."

I did not think Yamamoto insisted on Pearl Harbor to prove that Japan indeed had the power to cause peril. I first saw the reason behind his pig-headed adhesion to his attack plan—and the vectors it contributed to his suicide—that summer of 1942 after he moved a few more pieces in his solitaire *shogi* maneuvers.

"I always felt that if Japan had to go to war, I'd rather fight against Germany, like we did before." He seemed to be talking to the *shogi* pieces. "Army officers hated me for saying that. They were so infatuated with their idols; they were too blind to realize they were making Japan a lackey of the Nazis."

"Fighting Germany would also align you with your British naval heritage."

"And with the Dutch—and their oil. That makes more sense, doesn't it?" Yamamoto gave a minimal exhale of exasperation and continued. "When the Tokyo Olympics were cancelled, I thought it was good in a way. Hitler swung the IOC decision because he wanted to use us in a war against Russia. He had us lined up to fight his battles."

"Apparently it almost worked when Matsuoka tried to get Japan to violate the pact he himself signed, and attack Russia."

"Matsuoka should have been drowned long before then, but at least our emperor got him out of government. I can't believe the Russians took the pact any more seriously than Matsuoka did. They expected war with Germany. Japan was Germany's partner. Two major border clashes and the Russo-Japanese War were still giving them historical nightmares. It was childish to hope that the Russians believed Matsuoka's signature protected them."

When Yamamoto said that, I did not yet know about Pavlov and Operation Snow, but Yamamoto called the play right. The NKVD was laying plans to use America in an attempt to squeeze Japan away from Soviet borders and into a war against America herself, if necessary.

"Japan was only a pawn as far as the Nazis were concerned," Yamamoto continued. "Everything backs that up. Hell, they never advised us before they signed a pact with the Russians. Or before they broke it and attacked."

He came back to where I was sitting and lit a Sakura. "You've read *Mein Kampf,* I'm sure."

"Of course."

"In the original, I assume—you read German."

"The original and the Japanese translation. And I know what you're getting at: the Japanese version omitted . . . *embarrassing* parts."

"Hmmm. I don't read German but I know people who do. Scholars of German literature and the like. You saw what they left out: racial insults against the Japanese. We were just funny monkeys to Hitler—or whoever wrote that book for him. The dunces in Japanese government wouldn't tarnish their idols in the eyes of the Japanese. So they controlled the translation. National deception. To hold hands with their heroes."

I kept my appreciation for the dunces quiet.

"After Germany attacked the Soviet Union," he said, "Hitler pressured us to avoid war with America and Britain."

"For once Hitler and you agreed."

"Only because he wanted our undiluted strength to fight Stalin. The Nazis never changed their objective of using us for a second front against Russia. And there was always the danger that someone in Japan would take up after Matsuoka and push us into it."

"As Japan became closer to the Nazis," I agreed, "the chance would increase."

"The emperor tried to prevent our joining the Axis, but after Yonai and I were forced out of government, the emperor had no allies *in* government to help in opposing it. I always regretted that imperial prerogative didn't give him direct power to do it himself. And he regretted that I couldn't stop it. Every time the Nazis burped our leaders snapped to attention. Wide-eyed admiration. Obedient like brainless dogs. It was disgusting." Yamamoto stood and walked to the window; he seemed to stare at my punching bag as he spoke. "I was made commander-in-chief of the Combined Fleet by the Japanese pro-Nazis, to neutralize my political influence. But they were watching the board only, like we were when Doolittle made his raid. Somebody had to say 'No' to the Nazis, and Tokyo was filled with yes-men. I had one move left—from off the board."

The pieces fell with a strange enlightenment. I glanced inadvertently at the *shogi* board where Yamamoto had been a few moments before, as if I might read the chart of events. I must have sounded like an incredulous child when I asked, "Was Pearl Harbor your way of opposing the Nazis? And the Japanese pro-Nazis?"

He never answered that directly. "Pearl Harbor forced the Nazis to fight America before they wanted to. You should be glad to have America in there for you."

I was.

"The alliance with Germany was Japan's jump into hell," Yamamoto said as he stamped out his Sakura. "First we became patsy to Hitler and got tricked into the Alliance. Then Pearl Harbor made us patsy to the American president to get into the war *against* Germany that he wanted. It didn't come too soon for England; the Germans were on the verge of invading. And America was next on Hitler's list. Pearl Harbor forced Hitler's hand before Germany was ready." Yamamoto looked at me without expression. "The Nazis considered us a bad partner for doing that. But by playing universal patsy, Japan linked the wars in Asia and Europe into another world war. Not a very good character reference."

He stared out of the window at the world. "I felt . . . compelled to open war in the Pacific."

"Compelled. . . ?"

"Something like that. We can talk about it again some other time. But . . . I wanted Pearl Harbor to be *my* plan. Now, I'm not sure it was. Too many enigmas . . . transparent ones."

He went back to the *shogi* board and placed a piece on it with a loud snap. "A *kamo* is lower than a sitting duck."

When Yamamoto rated himself the patsy at Pearl Harbor, it added a heavy suicide vector. I was to blame for another, though it came by his request.

"You're getting information from overseas that we don't," he said after staring at the *shogi* board for a while. "I want to know what you heard about Pearl Harbor."

"Anything I heard can't change things now." He knew I was evading.

"I'm not talking about changing anything. I'm talking about facts." He looked into my eyes the way he had looked at the imaginary opponents in his speech at Harvard and whispered, "I want to know." It was a scream for truth. I had to comply.

"I did find out . . . America had a war plan — or a series of plans — called Rainbow." He watched me in silence. "I found out well after the attack. Channels in Washington. Scandinavians. Naturally, I have no information on anything current."

"What about the original plan?"

I continued against my wishes. "If hostilities broke out, America's first priority would be Europe. Germany."

"I believed that all along."

"America would temporarily abandon the Philippines and her other island outposts in the western Pacific." I paused. Yamamoto pressed: "And after that?"

"Six to nine months after war broke out, America would engage the Japanese fleet around the Marshalls or western Carolines. . . ."

"Engage. . . ?"

"In decisive battle."

Yamamoto was motionless for a moment, then muttered, "We couldn't have made a better plan ourselves."

The Imperial Japanese Navy was training for decisive battle before Yamamoto went to the Harvard class. It was their tactical specialty. "What else do you know about it?" he pressed again.

"Not much; only that the attack made America move to other war plans, but I won't hear anything else on it now that war has started."

The same thoughts were going through Yamamoto's and my mind. Japan was better equipped in ships and training for decisive battle — and underrated as usual. Their aerial torpedo skill had been demonstrated against the *Prince of Wales* and *Repulse*, and the Rainbow battle area was close enough to home to be to Japan's advantage. Decisive battle could have been America's own bait. I saw another suicidal vector form when Yamamoto realized that Pearl Harbor actually sabotaged the Imperial Japanese Navy. He seemed unusually drawn in. I had never seen him this way. He seemed to follow his line of thought down a dark tunnel to a darker pit at the end, where he repeated his earlier words: "So by playing universal patsy, Japan linked the wars in Asia and Europe into another world war."

What did Yamamoto mean when he said he was *compelled* to attack Pearl Harbor? I would never have the chance to ask him, but I believe the key is in his speech at Harvard twenty-three years earlier: ". . . we must assess the likely reaction of an opponent to various stimuli individually." By his own words, a stimulus acting on Yamamoto would produce results not expected in another. I believe this is what happened, and that *the stimulus acting on Yamamoto was Hector Bywater.*

Over the years Bywater's skill in reading cards at the world table first attracted Yamamoto's interest, then grew into something close to a fixation. Fate had both men born in the same year of 1884—Bywater on the anniversary of Trafalgar Day, an added naval allure. This concurrence of birthday numbers—just one element but an important one—intensified the effect. Then numbers struck again when Bywater died. He was fifty-five years old; by the Japanese system of reckoning age he was the same fifty-six of Yamamoto's given name. These all pressed Yamamoto to where he saw himself as Bywater's counterpart, or even alter-ego. Yamamoto became obsessed, possessed by an undertow of compulsion to follow Bywater and conduct his own Great Pacific War—and possession pulled harder than military logic. Military men of the world *discussed* Bywater, but he affected Yamamoto as he did not affect others. To Yamamoto—I am assessing *his* reaction to stimuli—*The Great Pacific War* evolved from military controversy into a tactical scripture, and under its spell, he set it in motion toward its preordained end. The Pearl Harbor attack showed the same Bywater compulsion as other Yamamoto war plans.

"The future of warfare in the Pacific," Yamamoto told Japanese leaders, "will be setting up a base on an island, and using that to move to the next one, and on and on progressively. The Pacific Ocean is a pond in a Japanese garden, each island a stepping-stone to the next. That is the future of Pacific warfare."

The Japanese-garden touch was Yamamoto's contribution, but the world's first island-hopping war was fought in Bywater's book, the second in the Pacific War—Bywater was also tactical advisor to America. Yamamoto told Japan's leaders that the country could fight America for a year and a half, after which there was no guarantee of success—which in the Japanese custom of understatement is an acknowledgement of defeat.

This was the theme of *The Great Pacific War,* and Bywater's "eleventh hour" prediction.

Why was Yamamoto's Philippine assault plan so close to Bywater's that it could be considered tactical plagiarism? It was the compulsion factor, the Bywater spell that obsessed him.

Then came Midway, thirty-seven years and a few days after Japan's victory over the Russian Baltic Fleet. The anniversary became a comparison of opposites, but Yamamoto was praised as a second Admiral Togo for a naval victory that happened only in Tokyo's propaganda chambers. The Bywater prediction of American technological superiority surfaced at Midway in shipboard radar; then as an added thrust to the heart of the gambler-tactician, Japan fell for a faked bet. Japanese coded messages kept referring to a location designated *AF.* American code breakers only suspected that it might mean Midway, so they threw out a phony card to find out; they sent an uncoded message that U.S. forces on Midway were running out of freshwater because of a breakdown in the distillation plant. The Japanese bit the bait and advised their units that there was a water shortage on *AF.* American intelligence got the face value of the joker they were looking for. Yamamoto had to bear the loss of the campaign and of a vital part of the fleet because the Imperial Japanese Navy fell patsy to a faked bet—the shame of a skilled gambler falling for a ruse that should have alerted novices. It told the Americans where to expect Yamamoto's next move, and was the first step in the destruction of the Combined Fleet.

The final vectors forcing Yamamoto's last throw of the cards came in the Solomon Islands, guardians of the southeasterly portion of Japan's defense perimeter. After Admiral Mikawa's force wiped out the Allied cruiser screen off Savo Island, the Americans landed on Guadalcanal with air cover but deprived of the cruisers. Yamamoto was en route to Truk where he arrived August 26, 1942. He commanded a series of attempts to retake Guadalcanal and ordered three air bases built on New Georgia for launching raids on it. His plan was to effect a siege from the air to prevent Guadalcanal from becoming a stage for further Bywater-type island hopping. Meanwhile, American bulldozers created Henderson Field, an air base on Guadalcanal named after a marine pilot who died at Midway.

In October Yamamoto organized a landing force of troop transports to take back Guadalcanal. He sent a fleet of ships to wait north of the Solomons and engage the American fleet if it came out, and he planned to fly planes from his carriers onto Guadalcanal after it came back into Japanese hands. But he lacked sufficient air cover. Carrier-based planes from the *Enterprise* and land-based planes from Henderson Field struck his fleet. Air power destroyed every one of the Japanese troop transports. Their total number: eleven.

The Japanese survivors on Guadalcanal began evacuating the first of February, and in a week thirteen thousand starving, emaciated remnants of men were removed. Guadalcanal remained in American hands as Yamamoto's command shifted from the *"Hotel Yamato,"* as Japanese came to call the giant battleship, to the sister ship, *Musashi.* Japan had sustained a heavy loss of carriers, and most naval carrier- and land-based aircraft in the area were transferred to Rabaul on New Britain, northwest of Guadalcanal and just east off New Guinea. On April 3 Yamamoto left the *Musashi* at Truk and boarded a flying boat to transfer his command for about one week to Rabaul—his first venture into the front lines of action. He landed early that afternoon and was installed in a cottage high on a hill that belonged to the German governor when Rabaul was under control of Germany: a reminder of the alliance that Yamamoto opposed.

Yamamoto wanted to reequip his air arm for an operation to destroy American air and sea forces in the Guadalcanal region. He personally took charge of the operation, reinforced his strength with one hundred sixty carrier-based planes and pulled five carriers from Truk Island to join one hundred ninety planes of the Eleventh Air Fleet—his number about to rise in disaster again. Most of Japan's finest pilots were gone, and few of the remainders could operate from carriers. This was going to be a serious drain on Japan's air power.

Yamamoto planned the assault for the day after his arrival, which would be April 4—his birthday. Severe storms prevented takeoffs, and the beginning of the operation was delayed until April 7: *4+7=11*. It continued on four separate days. Tactically, it was somewhat of a success, but merely a few good cards in a losing game. Guadalcanal remained in American hands to play a role in the last day of the life of Admiral Yamamoto.

Yamamoto spent the war years watching Bywater's predictions turn into reality. And, from the time the army gained control of the government in Tokyo, he was forced into playing someone else's game. He launched the war like Kusunoki Masashige, against his own judgment, yet with an overlapping compulsion to follow Bywater. Every unfolding of the Bywater prophecy intensified his addiction to it and reinforced his faith in final defeat, while he spent his life in the navy watching his omen numbers rise in disaster and debacle.

Poker player must then assess likely reaction of opponent to various stimuli. . . .

On April 14, 1943, Japanese officers at Rabaul sent a coded message to their bases that commander-in-chief of the Combined Forces Yamamoto was going to fly out to visit the advanced bases. The departure date would be the eighteenth—the first anniversary of Doolittle's raid on Tokyo. Takeoff time was given as 0600. The flight would be two Type 1 medium attack bombers, nicknamed "Betty" by the Americans, and powered by Yamamoto's omen number: a pair of Mitsubishi *Kasei* 11 engines—the same "Kasei 11" that powered the flying boats in their blundered attempt to hit the Ten-Ten Dock. Yamamoto would be on one of the bombers; six Zeros would fly escort.

The lax security in sending a message in such detail enraged the commanding officer of the Eleventh Air Flotilla—Yamamoto's omen in its nomenclature—on Shortland. He flew to Rabaul to express anger in person. "It's stupid to send that information by radio. You should cancel the flight." The administrative staff officer at Rabaul, Captain Kuroshima Kameto, argued that the code had recently been changed, and that America could not break it. The flight plans went ahead.

Thirteen men were scheduled to fly on Yamamoto's "Betty," including Kuroshima and a Combined Fleet staff officer, Watanabe Yasuji. At the final moment, Kuroshima and Watanabe decided to remain in Rabaul: the number of persons on board, alive and dead, totaled eleven.

I heard much later that only very few top officers saw Yamamoto up close as he boarded the plane. I believe there was a stand-in for him, and that the body of the real Yamamoto was placed aboard when those not in on the scheme were not present. Those on board were probably told that the commander's death could be kept secret by removing his body to a minor base. They did not realize that they themselves were patsies in a coffin flight.

The disagreement on America's ability to break codes was resolved when the details in the messages were so precise that they allowed a flight of sixteen fighters to take off from Guadalcanal—where Yamamoto's raids failed to dislodge the Americans and left them the airfield for the takeoff—cross more than six hundred miles of ocean, and intercept Yamamoto's flight. It was a Sunday, as it was seventy weeks earlier at Pearl Harbor. The first American pilot to sight their target broke radio silence: "Bogeys, eleven o'clock!" On the roulette wheel in the sky, Yamamoto's flight appeared in the attackers' relative position that fell on his omen number. If he had been alive as orthodox explanations claim, Yamamoto would have easily identified the unique twin-fuselage, twin-engine P-38 Lightnings as they came in for the attack, and he would have see his omen number for the last time: *3+8=11*. If he were already dead, as I believe he was, this would have been an early case of his number rising after his death to attend disasters as Japan was destroyed.

The Type 1 with Yamamoto aboard went down in flames and smoke into the jungles of Bougainville near Buin. Fate chose a location with his omen number for the plunge: information from Buin and from returning Zero pilots confirmed that the plane went down at a steep angle eleven nautical miles from Buin.

Officers at the Japanese army detachment at Buin organized a search party. Records showed they departed at eleven o'clock. After two days' search, they found nothing.

A Lieutenant Hamasuna was in charge of a road construction detail in the jungle west of the crash site. He and his men watched the dogfight over the trees and saw a column of smoke rise from the jungle. Regimental headquarters was only a short run away, and a messenger came with an order to organize a search party and look for the plane. The lieutenant picked ten men and led them into the jungle toward the smoke. The next day the eleven-man search party found the plane with its *Kasei* 11 engines and eleven bodies.

The Type 1 was first designed as an army plane and carried its fuel tanks in the wings, two-thirds the distance from the center line of the fuselage to the wingtip. American Grumman fighter pilots came in for the kill aiming for the tanks, knowing that a hit would cause an explosion. When the Type 1 was adapted by the navy, the tanks were relocated farther outboard, two-thirds the distance from the sides of the fuselage to the wingtip, so that enemy shots would be more likely to pass through empty wing.

But even empty wing posed threats. Japan was forced to produce aircraft with a minimum of metal, and the wings contained wood support members as metal substitutes. The Japanese *tokonoma,* a special alcove in the home, is set off with a cedar post. The trees are carefully attended during their life so that they will grow perfectly straight, and they are close-grained and strong. As metal became scarcer, trees intended for *tokonoma* posts were cut into support members for aircraft wings, interspersed with metal members. Some plane wings were even covered with cloth and sprayed to look like aluminum. Normally built planes can take bullets through the wings and keep flying, but bullets entering a wing with wooden members tended to ignite the wood, sending fire to the fuel tanks. Americans called Japanese planes "lighters," because when they were hit they burst into flame like a cigarette lighter. This is what happened to Yamamoto's "Betty."

Yamamoto's death was kept secret even from Japan's leaders in Tokyo. When the news was released a month afterward, Tokyo worked miracles: Yamamoto was the only unburned body among the plane's occupants. He was found thrown out of the plane still in his bucket seat, sitting erect and holding his officer's sword. Emerging in this condition from a crashed "lighter" would not make convincing fiction, but in Japan it was being offered as fact. Official fears ran deep over the potential results that knowledge of Yamamoto's suicide would cause, and Japanese authorities devised myth to ease shock. The greatest myth, I believe, was the report that Admiral Yamamoto "died in action."

Two weeks after Yamamoto's death was announced, a state funeral was held for him in Tokyo's Hibiya Park. His body had been cremated in Rabaul, and his ashes were brought aboard the *Musashi,* the giant battleship whose construction he had opposed, to the port of Kitarazu in Tokyo Bay on the shore opposite Yokohama. Thirteen days later, the urn—in a coffin covered with white cloth, according to Shinto ritual—was placed on a gun carriage and pulled forward slowly with two long white tapes held by sixteen navy men—a repetitious number: sixteen Billy Mitchell bombers had struck Tokyo. Sixteen P-38s had attacked his flight.

Admiral Suzuki invited me to pay my last respects at the funeral. Yamamoto's omen numbers were also in attendance in a juxtaposition that would have caused him pain: it was also the anniversary of Admiral Togo's funeral held nine years earlier, June 5: *6+5 =11*. It was the same date at Midway when the last of the four Japanese carriers sank. Written in the British system, his funeral date reads 5/6, the name with which he started life. The year designation reckoned from Japan's first emperor was 2603: *2+6+0+3=11*.

Yamamoto's omen numbers augured or rose in disasters in peace and war like channel markers that directed his life's course to a destination as predetermined as the war itself: the time to quit. After his death, his numbers evolved from omens to the eerie, as they continued rising through Japan's defeat and destruction in the war that started with his Pearl Harbor attack plan.

▪ 42 ▪

A 600-Year-Old Poem
Versus the Bio Threat

Shigemitsu was worried about the secret police and suggested that we not meet too often.

"Some of us were trying to avoid war while there was a chance," he told me that spring of 1943. "By autumn of 1941, many of us realized that the situation had to improve while Konoe was still premier—and that he would not be there much longer."

"That's back in the days of 'Mariko,'" I said.

"You know about Mariko?"

"I know it was a code word for the situation with America, but I'm curious why it was called that."

"Mariko was the little daughter of Terasaki Hidenari. He worked under me in our Shanghai embassy."

"Terasaki. He was married to an American."

"Yes, Gwen. Mariko was born in 1932, in the same Shanghai hospital where my leg was amputated. So I lost a limb there and gained a niece, in a sense. I suggested the name for her."

"And for the code name also?"

"No, but it was a good idea. Terasaki's brother was also in the government and the Mariko code name was decided before he left America to work here in Tokyo. We thought our embassy phones in Washington were tapped, and it would be reasonable for him to keep asking about Mariko's health."

"So Mariko was also in government—at an early age."

"You could say that. In the autumn of 1941, one of the phone messages from Tokyo was that Mariko must improve while the Terasakis' "elder" is still healthy. Hidenari did not catch it right away, so his brother clarified it. 'Our elder who lives in Ogikubo.'"

"Where Konoe's private residence is."

"Everyone knew that once Konoe stepped down, the army would gain more power and push us closer to war. But the Konoe cabinet fell apart and ... I regret that Mariko could not help us avoid it. It was obvious from the first day of the war that Japan had taken on too much of the world. Just three months after the Pearl Harbor attack, Kido, the Lord Privy Seal, advised the emperor that America had too powerful an industrial base for Japan to keep the upper hand."

Bywater, 1925, I commented silently to myself.

"Japan was making sweeping victories then, but Kido warned that America would eventually overpower us and we should find a way out of the war as soon as possible. This was back in February of 1942, mind you. I supported the reasoning and the proposal. There was disagreement among those close to the emperor, and fear of reprisals—assassinations, possibly even against the emperor himself. The army would undoubtedly make it look like the work of a communist or a traitor sympathetic to the Allies. They would then use that to stimulate further patriotic sacrifices."

"What came of the proposal?"

"While it was under secret discussion and we were sounding out others to know who might betray us, the battle of Midway occurred. Admiral Yamamoto knew that Japan could not win; he said that we could fight for perhaps a year and a half, but American industry and technology would eventually overpower us."

I could almost hear Hector Bywater telling Yamamoto the same thing in his book, and in the London hotel.

"Yamamoto," Shigemitsu continued, "lost the chance to use Midway as a bargaining point in negotiations to end the war. So, ironically, the Allied success cost them—and us—more sacrifices."

I could see the surface logic, but with the subsequent failure of America to act on the German offer, and with *Remember Pearl Harbor* ringing in America, I was silently skeptical about this historical "if."

"Our navy," Shigemitsu went on, "was utterly defeated at Midway, and anyone with the ability to think had to recognize it as the beginning of Yamamoto's predicted decline. A proposal was made that Prince Konoe go to Switzerland to open the negotiations."

"And when was that?" I asked

"Just four days after the Midway battle."

"Four days?"

"Yes," Shigemitsu clarified further, "June eleventh."

"You mean, it was secretly decided that Japan should give up *four* days after the Midway battle . . . on June *eleventh?*"

"Yes. Why?"

I shrugged off the question. "And, did he go?"

"It ended in talk. There was fear of the army."

"And was that the end of the proposal to negotiate a peace?"

"There were feeble attempts—those that could be made without alerting the military, which is to say, almost nothing. But the war grows worse. Only the inspirational content of the speeches made by our military men improves."

Yamamoto's words echoed: *The value of any probability varies with the temperament.*

Shigemitsu continued. "The German forces that Japanese army men put such faith in are being defeated in Russia. Germany's surrender at Stalingrad the beginning of this year has weakened them tremendously, and Russia is so much more confident because of it. We expect a complete German defeat. Then the Russians may be at our doorstep again, and you can expect them in Europe also."

"Yes," I agreed, "their other doorstep."

"As the war in the Pacific goes downhill, Japanese forces in China will be drained south, and the Soviets will storm in with little resistance. We should move to end things before that happens."

"And, you seem to think that I can do better than previous attempts, to negotiate a peace?"

"For one, we have a common reason. A weakened Japanese army in China would mean more power for the Russian war machine on your end of the Soviet Union. Japan's best hope—what little hope is left—is for a settlement with the United States, in spite of Washington's support for Stalin." Shigemitsu clasped his hands over the top of his cane and pulled himself up slightly. I suspect it was more the awkwardness of what he was about to say than any physical discomfort. "The Soviets are our common problem, and they are circling Japan like buzzards. Some of us are willing to make sacrifices to end the war, but our military leaders will not listen to reason. Japan needs the assistance of someone like you who understands our situation and who can explain it to the West."

My role was defined. Beyond this, I still wondered how much the foreign minister knew of Japan's work on biological weapons. He had already been this frank with me, and I could hear Akira's warning about Japan becoming the ghoul among nations. I asked, "Do you know, sir, about Japan's biological warfare program?"

"Japan's *what?*"

"In China. Biological weapons."

"I have just returned from China, and I saw nothing of that."

"It is only something that I heard. But I fear it."

"Since Japanese civilian government officials have been ejected by the military in China, it is quite possible that things happen there that only the military know of. If it is true, it is fearful. And even more reason to end the war. But I want you to fully understand the risk."

I understood. If I were discovered, the only options of fate would be a quick death or a slow, painful one. Bagulesco's smashed face was still in my memory, and he had done nothing against Japan itself. In the theater of the mind, I saw Melville Cox's needle-perforated body hurtling to the pavement again and again in a continuous-reel movie—only sometimes it was Melville's body, sometimes mine. Now I was being asked to join in betraying a military clique that saw blood as the only solvent to wash away problems. With a historical disadvantage behind me and threats lying ahead, there was little reason for me to agree to enter the plot, every reason to refuse.

I agreed. I blame my study of Japanese literature and history, and an inflow of Chinese poetry into Japan.

The four-line Chinese poem is a formidable device. It has a logical direction that Japanese poetry lacks. A Japanese *waka* cradles the reader in a sensation or mood. It can evoke understanding like sympathetic vibrations in an untouched violin string when another tuned to the same pitch is plucked. The four-line Chinese poem in terse, five- or seven-character lines has a forward direction to a rapid conclusion, and a structure that forces a recognition of similarity with the European symphony of centuries later. Educated Japanese borrowed China's poetry form.

A four-line Chinese poem starts with a statement, or a *lifting*. The second line supplements this thought with an *agreement*. The third line is a *turnover*, a new concept or direction change in thought. Then the *tie-up*, a conclusion that unites all the lines and carries the reader along in its direction. One poem, the work of a fourteenth-century shogun's official, compelled me to go beyond the last line, to continue the poem with my own involvement.

The first Ashikaga shogun started as a warlord in the service of the emperor, then turned against and eventually deposed him. Ashikaga set a puppet, child emperor on the throne in the capital who then followed the warlord's script and granted Ashikaga and his new shogunate imperial sanction. The legitimate emperor fled south and set up a Southern Court in exile.

Years later, when the grandson of the founding Ashikaga was a child shogun, a high-ranking retainer by the name of Hosokawa Yoriyuki was appointed to rectify the misfortunes of history and unite the two imperial courts. Hosokawa was a brilliant, faithful retainer, but his rise fueled jealousy among other officials. They whispered into young shogun ears that Hosokawa was planning a betrayal. The shogun believed it, and ordered Hosokawa out of the shogunate and back to his home island of Shikoku.

Disappointed in his attempt to bring peace and unity to the conflicting imperial courts, and disillusioned with the world of political intrigue, Hosokawa shaved his head, took a priest's name, and set out for his home island to enter a Zen temple and spend his days in meditation. By our method of calculating age, he was fifty years old; by the Japanese method he was fifty-one, the same number assignation as my age when I came to Tokyo. Just before embarking for his life as a priest, Hosokawa composed a Chinese poem.

Human life is fifty years,
  I feel shame for being deedless

Flowers and trees change with the seasons
  Spring has passed, and I am in midsummer

This roomful of pesty flies
  Though I sweep them away, they do not leave

So I depart to seek a meditation hall
  where I can rest in clean, cool breezes

In the midsummer of Yoriyuki's life, petty squabblers swarmed in like summer flies. Unable to sweep them away, his only recourse was to find a place where insects do not gather.

Hosokawa wrote that poem on the eve of his forced departure from the shogunate in 1379. I came to Tokyo in 1937, a rearrangement of the same digits. I was past the fifty-year limit of his poem and ready to start a new phase of my career that, by diplomatic definition, was one dedicated to non-deeds—an agreement with the poem. The political chaos of Hosokawa's time had magnified to the present war, claiming more lives than any other conflict in the history of the human race. I knew that each day's shortening of the conflict would save a large population of doomed innocents and hopefully disinfect the regiments of microscopic "weapons of ghouls." Now I had the chance of performing a deed.

Hosokawa's distress resurfaced in his poem: *Human life is fifty years, I feel shame for being deedless.* I felt an urge to make my life a sequel to that poem, to dedicate an act to Hosokawa back through six centuries for inspiring me to seek clean breezes with a sense of deed and not the weight of disappointment that he carried. I agreed to work against the military to bring an end to the war. I reminded Shigemitsu, "The threat of Japan's biological weapons increases the importance of this work."

"Of course," he responded. "But there are some important things to remember. One is that the emperor is inviolable. Calling for his downfall is tantamount to asking every man, woman, and child in Japan to commit suicide."

He waited a moment to verify that we were still in agreement. "Also, this plan is supported by Prince Konoe. As you know, when Konoe stepped down as prime minister, Tojo was put in office because the emperor, frankly, thought that he could control the army officers. You saw what happened. Konoe is out of politics, though as a member of the nobility and a former prime minister he is influential—but not bullet-proof. Most important is that we are going into this squeezed between certain defeat and destruction of Japan on one hand, and the danger of the Japanese military on the other. The former is not your concern; the latter would be."

Mentally, I added the threat of humanity's endless war against microorganisms. "I completely understand the situation," I told him.

"Let me emphasize again, diplomatic immunity . . ."

"Does not exist. I realize that."

Shigemitsu pulled himself to a standing position and walked me to the door. He stood in the doorway as I left, his back straight, his left hand clamping his cane to his hip, his body leaning against the cane, and his artificial leg in a port list.

▪ 43 ▪
Wartime Education Gains Weight

Butterfly drove her thighs through my garden with an expression as intense as her pace. It was spring of 1943 and cherry blossoms were in the fluttering-down stage.

"There's a blossom on your head," I told her. She felt around for it, retrieved it, and threw it to the ground as if to punish it for whatever was inside her. "I just saw some children playing soldiers . . . with toy guns."

"I did the same thing, only I was a sailor."

"No! It's different! When a boy is supposed to be shot, what does he do? He falls down laughing and screams 'Banzai for the emperor!' And he's in ecstasy! *In ecstasy!* That's a glorious end for him."

"I've seen the same sort of thing myself, but I don't know how seriously the children take it."

"Banzai for the emperor and die in ecstacy!" She went over to the heavy bag and gave it a few punches.

"You'll hurt your wrists doing that," I warned her. "And the pools are being filled. Save your energy for the water."

"And there's more stupidity from the government. This is what I'd like to do to those idiots." She kept punching.

"All right, what are the details?"

"The Ministry of Health and Welfare . . ." *Punch!* "They came up with a plan . . ." *Punch!* "To turn Japanese women into baby factories." *Punch! Punch! Punch!*

"You'll hurt your wrists. How are they doing this?" I massaged her shoulders and walked her to the house.

"They call it a 'Healthy Citizens Plan.' It's organized like a government within a government. Each area in Japan appoints an administration to push women into having babies. It operates through local chapters, so women are dealing with their neighbors. That makes it harder to evade it."

"Well, it's not your problem. So how about something to eat?"

"Speaking of food," she said with undisturbed exasperation, "did you hear about Suzuki Umetaro?"

"The scientist?"

"Right. He's being honored for developing potato bread. It's easier for Japan to grow potatoes than wheat, so Suzuki was reduced to finding a way to make bread from potatoes. Suzuki! He discovered vitamin B1! He's an internationally recognized scientist and Japan honors him for making potato bread! He should be doing more research into vitamins and things like that. This government makes even our scientists look foolish."

As the school year advanced, Butterfly found more to make her angry: elementary schools played records of the sounds of enemy planes in classrooms to teach children to identify them. "Are they expecting us to get bombed from the air again?" she asked more in anger than fear. But something raised her ire even more.

"No summer vacation for schools. This is idiotic!"

"I read about it."

"That's so the army officers can come and teach the children military drill. They want to train the children to be as stupid as the officers. The only good thing is that we can still swim in the Sumida. Maybe they consider that military training, too, but I don't. Swimming is swimming. I'd like to get some of those officers in the river with me."

"To race them?"

"To drown them."

That summer of 1943 Butterfly winged in with other news: "Guess what the government discovered?"

"Not that you have a blue-eyed companion?"

"They probably know that already. They just realized that there are many schoolteachers in Japan who cannot swim."

"And they think you're one of them."

"No," she laughed. "I'm being recruited to teach the teachers."

"And why does the government think it's time to start learning now?"

"Ask the government. It's part of this healthy nation plan. On one hand they teach us how to die for the emperor. On the other they tell us to get healthy. I'm much happier working with children or swimmers. Adults who can't swim are no fun to teach."

"You mean you wouldn't teach me?"

"Ha ha. I'd just push you in and let you learn by yourself."

"But you'd save me if I couldn't make it, I hope."

"Anybody can float."

"So you'd just leave me there?"

"No, I'd tell you to stay calm and kick your feet."

And as Butterfly started teaching the teachers, the German army dug its heels into Denmark and proclaimed martial law. One thing Germany could not stamp out was the Danish intelligence organization; its members were in all corners of the world, seeking and exchanging information.

In September 1943 I received an invitation from Shigemitsu to come over and sample some wine he just received.

"We must avoid any action for a while," he said as soon as I entered his office. "The Badoglio affair. After Mussolini was overthrown and arrested, and Marshal Pietro Badoglio capitulated and Italy surrendered, shock waves went through Tokyo."

"I would imagine so."

"Members of the military are on edge. Generals are looking at each other with suspicion. *No Badoglios in Japan* is voiced here with the fervor of *Remember Pearl Harbor* in America, and anyone who is not a complete idiotic militarist is liable to be interpreted as a Japanese Badoglio. Italy's surrender has put Japan's secret police on extra alert for any peace movements. Please think about this and wait."

While I waited, I joined Japan in listening to the narrated adventures of Miyamoto Musashi on Radio Tokyo, as the government drafted the ancient swordsman to stimulate fighting spirit. Then one day Butterfly brought another question: "What do you think is the latest order to teachers?"

"I fail the quiz."

"We have to drive the message into the children that Italy's surrender was disgraceful and that Japan will fight on with honor."

"And you tell them?"

"I tell them that Italy surrendered and that Japanese leaders are not thinking of surrender. I can't deform their minds more than that."

As winter approached, the Ministry of Health and Welfare designated 1,097 couples with ten children or more as "Excellent, many-children households," and days later ordered the demolition of homes in areas near important war material–producing shops and factories. Butterfly's interpretation was, "The Japanese are being encouraged to become baby factories while the government chases them from their homes. Where are people supposed to raise those babies?"

The war moved ahead close to Bywater's prediction with news that would have astounded even the great military seer. America announced a new giant bomber designed specifically to destroy Japan, a plane that would be bigger, faster, fly higher, and carry a heavier bomb load than anything in the skies. News of the plane reached Japan on Yamamoto's omen numbers: November 4. And when the designation of the new bomber was announced, B-29, it rose again: $2+9=11$.

Roosevelt, Churchill, and representatives of China met in Cairo, and on December first issued a declaration calling for unconditional surrender of the Axis nations and intent to punish aggressors responsible for the war. This could include the emperor, and with even the most antimilitary elements in Japanese government firm in their resolution to protect him, I saw the threat of a stalemate that could extend the war to total annihilation of the Japanese people.

"We're losing our schoolchildren to the factories," Butterfly said. There was a change in her this time as she spoke, closer to tears than to anger. "Elementary schoolchildren are being ordered to work in factories and on farms to compensate for the labor shortage. And the government leaders are not even ashamed of themselves. Did you see this?" She handed me a newspaper with a story eulogizing the children, with a photo of girls filing metal parts for weapons. "They shouldn't be making weapons; they should be in school. The children are having their childhood pulled from under them."

"I see that adults and children are being evacuated from Tokyo."

"Only those not working in war plants. Some schoolchildren are going to the country to move in with relatives or family friends. But many of the adults do not want to leave their homes, so what do you think is being done to convince them?" She did not give me time to guess. "The government shows them films of bombing scenes to scare them into moving. *Disgusting!*"

A few days later the news announced that twenty-eight circuses in Japan had to kill their animals for lack of feed to sustain them. The killings were followed by memorial services for the animals. Japan was pouring more energy into ceremonies of respect for the departed, even animals, than in valuing life, even—perhaps especially—human life.

▪ 44 ▪
1944—The Axis in Decline

The new year in Japan is a time of feasting. As 1943 ended, the Japanese were hoping to find enough food just to ease, not even eliminate, their constant hunger. Butterfly came to see me the end of December before she and her mother headed to Saitama to spend the new year with her father and the chickens.

"I tried to convince my mother to stay in Saitama afterwards," she told me, "but she is still a worrisome Japanese mother."

"Worried that you're spending too much time here, perhaps."

"No, mother is understanding that way. She knows her daughter. She accepted the fact long ago that I could never marry a typical Japanese man and live an ordinary life. But she still feels better if she can look after me. Even with her modern ideas, she is a Japanese mother."

The spartan Japanese new year of 1944 was followed by news that the Soviets began the battle of eastern Europe and Leningrad was freed from a three-year clamp in the jaws of the Nazis, with eight hundred thousand civilians lost to the Luftwaffe, starvation, disease, and cold. On February 17, Truk, the base of the Combined Fleet when Yamamoto commanded it, and Japan's "absolutely last ring of defense," was shelled and finally devastated. Days later, perhaps in the belief that it would help, Tojo took over as chief of the General Staff, the first time a prime minister held the two posts simultaneously.

This was a leap year. Fate provided the extra day to raise another eleven in Japan's road to defeat: on February 29, U.S. forces landed on Los Negros in the Philippines in an operation to recover the region that had been taken in Yamamoto's—and Bywater's—landing plan.

▪ ▪ ▪

"Did you hear our new song?" Butterfly asked with her usual sarcasm.

"The victory song? Of course; it's on the radio all the time."

" *'Til the Day of Victory*. How inspiring. Now children who graduate from elementary school are being enlisted in the workforce. They're sent from their hometowns to Tokyo and other industrial centers to work in war plants. They're called 'small industrial warriors.' Isn't that a pretty sound? The government uses trick words to declare war on a whole generation of its own people."

"It does place demands on the children."

"And the Women Volunteer Corps. It's not volunteer. They're forced to work. The government was taking them from ages fourteen to twenty-five. Now it's from twelve to forty—all for a war that shouldn't have happened."

"You can't change the war, so let's look at some of the things we *can* do. Relax in the bath, a sip of wine, something to eat, make love, a combination of any of them ... or all of them."

"I'd like to wash my hair."

"I'll help you."

Relaxing in the bath was a misnomer. Butterfly's world joined us.

"I heard a story from the girl students who work in the war plants," she said even before she settled all the way down in the water. "Sometimes machinery breaks down, and some of the girls have no work until the machines are fixed."

"I hope it gives them a much needed rest."

"The problem is that army officers always come to inspect the plants. So the girls who have no work are told to hide in the rest room. Then everybody the officers see is working. The girls are called 'the toilet gang.'"

"And the officers never suspect anything?"

"They're too stupid. Meanwhile, food is becoming scarcer, but on the emperor's birthday elementary schoolchildren will be called into the celebration. They'll be given two sweet rolls each, a present from the emperor to make them love him, I guess, and forget that they're hungry every day. And maybe with a wish that they grow up fast and give their lives for ..."

"That's right," I recalled. "There is an emperor's birthday coming up the end of April."

"April twenty-ninth. I'll probably help distribute the rolls." As she frowned cynically again, I added numbers. "It *is* the twenty-ninth."

"Yes. Why? Is that something special?"

"No, just thinking. Come out of the tub and I'll wash your back. It's a Japanese custom."

About three weeks before the emperor's birthday, the Soviet army invaded Romania. I thought of my friend General Bagulesco—according to information from overseas, he was still under house arrest by the Japanese army in Peking—and I saw in Romania's fate a precursor to the future of Europe, a change of oppressor from the Nazis to the Soviets. In Japan, there was a reach into the nebulous. In honor of the celebration of the ascension to the throne of Emperor Jimmu, the Justice Department announced the release of eighty-seven exemplary prisoners. Butterfly's comment was, "They probably didn't do very much wrong; it's just another way of publicizing the myth."

"Surely it's possible that there was such a man as Jimmu," I said.

"Probably. A powerful chieftain who subdued other tribes. But the dates cannot be believed. Or the story that the deities stirred up the ocean with a spear and a drop of water fell from the blade and became the Japanese islands . . . This has all been included in the new textbooks this year. One child came out of school crying to me the other day. A lot of the children confide in me because we become friendly during swimming lessons. We work hard, but I joke with them, too, so we become close. This boy's teacher was telling the class the story about Japan's creation and the boy said, 'That's just a made-up story, isn't it?' The teacher beat the boy over the head."

"My teachers also had to get tough with me sometimes. We boys are troublesome, you know."

"For not believing an unbelievable story! His crime was *thinking*."

"And the boy came to you?"

"I'm the only one the children can turn to at times like that."

"And the teacher who hit the boy? He didn't get angry again when the boy ran to you?"

"That's a secret between the boy and me."

▪ ▪ ▪

Tokyo's statues were rounded up, loaded onto trucks like criminals, and melted down for punishment. Then bizarre city planning officials marked fifty-five thousand homes in Tokyo for destruction to create firebreaks for expected air raids. Tokyoites were in an involuntary game of chance, their homes either smashed or saved on a huge board game laid out by the high command. People in the spared areas were helping their doomed neighbors pile belongings onto wagons. But the government had touches of consideration and extended the times of radio broadcasts of drama and music.

"I cannot understand where our leaders get their ideas," Butterfly almost screamed at me. "The people don't need radio entertainment, they need a normal life, and everything is going the opposite way."

"I saw people moving out of their homes, and there were very few tears. Most people seemed to accept it as their contribution to the war."

"Japanese are that way," she said in a softer tone. "That's true."

"And another thing that's true," I said. "I was invited to the sumo tournament, and it's the first time I saw one in a baseball stadium."

"Yes, the government requisitioned the sumo arena building for war goods. Personally, I don't miss sumo, but this whole trend that the country all belongs to the military . . . When will it end?"

Evacuation increased when electric trains were scheduled specifically for moving people out of Tokyo, and an additional several hundred thousand schoolchildren were sent to the countryside to take up life and studies far from homes and parents, and live in meeting halls, inns, and temples that were all turned into camps.

Japan "shifted position" off Guadalcanal, leaving Japanese and Allied objectives like unmeshed gears. Japan's high command was still looking for the "decisive battle," but the Allies were choosing islands for hopping. Leaders argued over the best route to Tokyo, but nobody questioned the Bywater basics and ignored even strongly fortified points to give precedence to location.

The first aerial attack on Japan since Doolittle's 1942 raid came as a harbinger of the coming season of explosives and fire from the skies: land-based B-29s flew from Sichuan province and bombed the Yawata Steel Works in Kyushu. This was maximum range from the China base; Saipan would put all of Japan within round-trip bombing distance, and in early July the island fell, along with forty thousand defenders. Ten thousand Japanese residents of the island also perished, half of them jumping from "Banzai Cliff," a geophysically convenient location for escape from life in obedience to their education. Americans felt a sense of revenge when Admiral Nagumo, commander of the task force in the Pearl Harbor attack, was killed at Saipan.

Tojo tried to reorganize his cabinet and even offered to call Yonai back as navy minister, as a bargaining chip. But, for the first time, the *Jushin*, an influential group of former premiers, opposed him and rejected a partial reorganization. There was even dissent within the cabinet itself, and it was forced to resign en masse. A few days later, on July 22, a new cabinet formed. I was surprised to see Yonai appointed again to navy minister; I did not hear the full story until later.

If a person's face really reflects the soul, or at least the mind, Japan's new prime minister reflected Japan's hopelessness. Retired General Koiso Kuniaki was even more humorless than the man he replaced, with a sculpted scowl that screamed unyielding adherence to ungainly principles. Koiso immediately went on the radio and promised Japan a glorious victory as her forces were being devastated.

Japan expelled the British from Burma, then tried to topple British-occupied India using Chandra Bose's Indian National Army. The gateway to India was Imphal, and early in 1944 Colonel Mutaguchi Ren'ya led an attempt to invest the area with the Fifteenth Army by first taking Kohima, to the north of Imphal and straddling British supply routes. The campaign failed and claimed sixty-five thousand Japanese troops in the retreat.

In the Pacific, American planes struck Iwo Jima and troops landed on Guam and Tinian. Hindsight later showed a particularly significant rising of Yamamoto's omen number when Tinian, later the takeoff base for the atom bomb flight, fell on August 3: $8+3=11$.

Shigemitsu was retained as foreign minister in the new cabinet, and in early September I met with him again.

"General Tojo is not only relieved of his premiership, he has been taken off the army's active list. He is now fully retired and spends his time working in his garden. It was not easy."

"He resisted the resignation, I understand."

"Very much so. As the war situation grew worse, Tojo increased secret-police activities. They asked people what they thought of the Tojo government, and anyone who fell into the trap and answered wrong was taken in for questioning, detention . . . who knows what."

"From the reports, he also criticized the *Jushin* for not allowing him to reshuffle his cabinet."

"He almost cursed them for turning against him. He is beyond reason, and he demands the same of the entire population. Many of us, even the *Jushin,* wanted to see Yonai take over as prime minister again, but there was one fear: that army men would listen only to army leaders. You've seen the pattern before."

"Yes, it brought Tojo to power in the first place."

"When the Tojo cabinet resigned, there was frantic confusion over who to select. The thought of an army on its own with no political control was frightening, and that is why Koiso became premier. But, there was a serious communication breakdown. It was intended that Koiso would share power with Yonai; that was considered a way to recover a balance in the government that had been lost under Tojo. Even the emperor wanted this. Koiso marched in and assumed that he would run things—with Yonai simply as navy minister. Nobody had the courage to tell him otherwise."

"Well, Koiso does not come with a record of cooperation."

"Indeed not. In 1932, he was part of a plot to create chaos in the Diet and fabricate a situation that would let the army oust the entire civilian government. As a commander in the Kwantung Army, he helped make the Japanese military in China its own government, ignoring Tokyo, ignoring the emperor. Then he was governor general of occupied Korea. And now . . . Have you heard the song, 'Dying for the Country on Saipan'?"

"It is impossible not to. It occupies much radio airtime."

"That was Koiso's order. That is how those people's minds work. They are unaware of military realities—with one exception."

"And that is. . . ?"

"Nobody expects Germany to hold out much longer."

"They realize, then, that Japan will be alone."

"They do. And army leaders blame the duplicity of Britain and France for it—for throwing the Czech Sudetenland to Germany to force her eastward into Poland and on a course for the Soviet Union."

"Of course, after Germany attacked Poland, England, and France both declared war on Germany."

"But according to the military men here, it was just to show Germany that she could not move into all of Europe. Remember, the Allies delayed any heavy attacks as long as possible and let the Russians do most of the fighting. But the problem we face is, how can we save Japan?" Shigemitsu leaned forward a bit and spoke in a lower voice. "Last June—it was just ten days after the B-29s bombed the steelworks in Kyushu—I met with Kido, the minister of the interior. It was highly secret. We agreed that only an imperial decision could end the war."

"And, do you see the possibility?"

"Unfortunately, no. Even if there were . . . Even if the emperor wanted to . . ." Shigemitsu hesitated, then gathered himself. "I will tell you honestly, the emperor would like to issue such an order. But it could be disastrous for him, and for Japan. The army would . . ."

"Disobey?"

"Worse than that. They would revolt against the imperial house."

I looked at Shigemitsu incredulously enough to bring his next reply.

"Yes, it is possible. We can discuss this further some day, but the pressing situation now is that Japan plans an assault on Saipan. That alone is no world secret because I am sure the Allies expect it, but I hear that it will be done with conventional—and unconventional—weapons. Developments from Manchuria. I can only assume from what you told me that killing with disease will be part of the plan. Even as foreign minister, I was not advised formally, but I did find out about it. General Ishii has promised Japan a decisive advantage in the assault."

"General Ishii?"

"He asked the military command for permission to include 'scientific weapons' on the attack. If what you tell me is true, that Japan may usher in the beginning of a world struggle against microscopic enemies, this is a crucial time for you to join us. Again I remind you, we are all at risk. The decision must be yours—as it is mine."

Akira's prediction was moving forward, and a six-hundred-year-old poem was telling me to take a step out of neutrality. That evening in my legation I encoded a message to Stockholm. . . .

▪ 45 ▪

My Messages Start

To Foreign Minister Christian Günther, Stockholm

19 September 1944

1. *I learned from a reliable source that there has been growing anxiety in civilian circles concerning the peace problem. It is believed here that a German collapse is imminent and that Japan cannot hold together. The civilian members of the Japanese government therefore believe it necessary to reach a peace as soon as possible before their land and cities are destroyed. It is also obvious that the British are weary of war.*

2. *A peace negotiation would be more possible with England than with the United States. Japan would be prepared to recognize all the areas taken from Great Britain during the war, and at the same time recognize all British interests and investments in East Asia. It is understood that even other areas occupied by Japan during the war must be returned.*

3. *Even the necessity of giving up Manchuria was considered. It was felt that peace feelers could be made through Swedish diplomatic channels in London, with the provision that there be no publicity in England. If there were response in London to the peace feelers, the Japanese would be ready for preliminary discussions to be held through Sweden.*

4. *My informant is backed up by one of the nation's foremost statesmen, and the above is to be understood without question as a serious peace feeler. If you find this peace feeler reasonable,*

it can be transmitted to the British Ministry. This should be kept confidential and revealed only to the most trusted persons. Your esteemed opinion is requested.

A few days after I sent the message, I received a call from Admiral Suzuki. He did not have time for his usual hand of cards. "If this war does not end," he said, "Japan has no hope for survival as a nation. Shigemitsu and I have discussed this for some time now, and your position in helping us. You may not know that on the fourth of this month Japan proposed to the Soviet Union that former premier Hirota visit Moscow to discuss continuation of our 1941 Neutrality Pact."

Was this another show of Tokyo's astounding capacity for misunderstanding? "Hirota," I reminded Suzuki, "was premier in 1936 when Japan signed the Anti-Comintern Pact with Germany. He hardly seems the one to beg a hand of camaraderie from the Soviets." Silently, I noticed that the date of the proposal to Yamamoto's enemy in the naval battle off Tsushima bore his omen number.

"To be honest with you," Suzuki went on, "the Soviets have been asking if it's true that we are attempting peace talks through Sweden. Naturally, we deny it."

"I would hope so."

"And now," Suzuki continued, "the army leaders are planning an offensive to retake Saipan. Militarily, this is impossible. The Allied naval forces are too great and most of our skilled pilots are gone. But as you were informed, we have assurances from a General Ishii that the attack will be accomplished with new weapons that will turn the tide of the war."

"Yes, I understand that."

"He had to go to the naval command to place his team on board the ships of the Saipan attack force. This is how word came to me."

"And how many men is he sending?"

"About twenty, all from his alma mater, Kyoto Imperial University."

"Twenty men? To retake an island air and naval base?"

"He claims that it is all he needs to eradicate the forces holding the island. From what I understand, you already know the weapons."

"I believe I can guess: plague, anthrax . . . And, did he receive permission to go ahead?"

"The leaders are desperate—except when they appear before the public or make dramatic statements. They are making the plan with one eye on Germany, for fear that it will collapse before the attack is launched. Germany must remain fighting at least until November for Japan to execute this tactic."

I debated with myself whether I should inform my ministry about Japan's intended use of biological warfare, but decided against it. The very image that caused Akira to take his life could derail any possible intentions to accept the negotiations; a "ghoul" nation would invite its own complete destruction. But a negotiated peace might present a chance to neutralize Japan's biological warfare program. I had heard nothing from my foreign minister, and encoded another message.

27 September 1944
The foreign minister is weighing the possibilities of my previous coded message. If Japan is successful in the battle for Saipan, the parties concerned will likely use the victory to advantage as a basis for putting forth a peace proposal. From reliable sources, I learned that Japan is preparing to launch an overwhelming onslaught with all available military forces to recapture Saipan, and achieve a major tactical advancement. After that, they will seek peace negotiations. The Japanese are hoping that Germany can hold out until November to leave Japan time to prepare this attack.

Stockholm answered:

30 September 1944
According to our previous experience, we know that the British are not responsive to these feelers that are not of an official nature. Therefore, we have not seen it appropriate to transmit this to the British.
With great interest in not breaking the contact.

My foreign minister did not understand subsurface politics, or did not want to know of them. "One of the nation's leading statesmen" lacked sufficient official position. My minister also failed to grasp the risks involved at my end.

I went into the garden and punched the heavy bag. I thought of Butterfly attacking the water as a replacement for beating army heads. Water and sand can serve similar functions.

In early October, an organization called the Soldiers' Protection Society commended and honored Japan's "Military-Nation Families," those who had lost two or more members in action since the Sino-Japanese War of 1895. Government reports advised that the total stood at 2,072 households. I added the figures automatically, involuntarily; Yamamoto's number eleven appeared again in the total number of families who had suffered multiple war deaths.

As Japan's maple leaves turned crimson, news reports advised that B-29s were arriving on Saipan. It was just about the time that Butterfly arrived with the latest story on Japan's way of handling the threat.

"Did you see that Hachiko is being melted down?"

"Of course. And pictures of the ceremony that accompanied its removal. Wrapping it in a white cloth for the sacrifice."

"You know why that statue was there, don't you?"

"As a meeting place? *Let's meet at Hachiko.* Everyone says it."

"And you know the story, right?"

"The dog used to go to Shibuya Station every day to meet its master. After the master died, Hachiko remained faithful and continued going to the station every day for the rest of its life."

"Where did you hear that?" she asked, again in her teacher's tone.

"Common knowledge. Hachiko was an Akita breed, very faithful. Helen Keller took one to America for the first time. . . ."

"The Hachiko story is phony," she said with a touch of smile, a touch of frown.

"You mean there was no such dog?"

"There was. Apparently some professor abandoned it and it roamed around Shibuya Station. A newspaper reporter saw the dog and dreamed up that waiting-for-its-master story. Then the government put up the statue to remind us that if a dog can be so faithful, we Japanese can do the same: faithful to the emperor, the government, the army . . . The government is full of tricks like that."

Another "trick" came when imperial headquarters announced "Eleven American aircraft carriers sunk in the air war off Formosa." This was not distortion; it was complete fabrication. But with all the numerical options available for their ruse, why did they decide on Yamamoto's omen?

▪ 46 ▪
Leyte—Birth of the Suicide Squads

In June 1944 the surviving Japanese ships struggled home from defeat in the Marianas to a scientific breakthrough: radar. Japan expected their new electronic eyes, developed two years behind America, to take them into battle to hold the Philippines by early spring of 1945, but the enemy moved faster. The prelude to the American recapture of the islands came in September 1944 when Marc Mitsher moved his Carrier Task Force 38 into position forty miles off the east coast of Luzon and launched the omen-number—four strikes—on the Manila area. Task Force 38—3+8=11—took the first step in reestablishing the American military presence that had "seriously perturbed" Yamamoto.

On October 17, 1944, American forces landed on Suluan Island at the mouth of Leyte Gulf. The same day, Admiral Onishi Takijiro took command of Japanese forces in the Philippines with only one hundred fifty planes in operating condition—Task Force 38 had destroyed more than two hundred aircraft—and a new organization called Special Attack Forces: men resigned to suicide strikes. Their main job would be to disable enemy carrier decks and clear the skies of air support to give Japan her chance for a decisive battle on the sea.

General MacArthur and his publicity cameramen returned to the Philippines on October 20, and American forces began landings on the Leyte coast. Japan's Combined Fleet headquarters drew up plans for a daylight surprise strike against Allied ships in Leyte Gulf, with a main and a secondary fleet approaching from different directions in a simultaneous attack.

The force of thirty-two ships, including the giants *Yamato* and *Musashi,* sortied northward out of Brunei on the morning of October 22.

The following dawn, American submarines torpedoed two cruisers in the force to the bottom, a bad start for an intended surprise attack on an enemy one thousand nautical miles distant, on a journey lengthened by half through zigzag and evasive courses.

In the pre-dawn two days later, the two fleets separated. The main fleet with the two giant battleships changed course easterly for the Sibuyan Sea at the approximate center of the Philippines; the secondary fleet headed for the Sulu Sea north of Borneo.

Yamato's radar picked up enemy aircraft: a wave of planes had lifted off the decks of the *Intrepid* and *Cabot* and came in hungry for the two "unsinkable" giants. The planes ran into a wall of anti-aircraft fire but their bombs reached target, though the heavy decks and plating of the battleships still upheld their claim to indestructibility. Each giant took one torpedo that did not affect its speed. *Musashi* took a second torpedo and more bomb hits near her bridge; her twenty-seven-knot speed held steady, but the attack broke up the fleet's formation and removed its curtain of anti-aircraft fire.

The fleet re-formed and a second wave of attackers flew in: twenty-four heavy torpedo planes, half assigned to the two giant battleships, the other half working on the rest of the fleet. Then a third wave of twenty-nine planes from the carriers *Essex* and *Lexington,* with one target: the wounded *Musashi.* Three torpedoes hit her starboard bow, tore away the heavy steel plating, and forged it into a water plow that shot an inverted cascade into the air. The ship's speed fell to twenty-two knots and she took on a port list. The fleet reduced speed to keep formation with the damaged monster until it had to be counterflooded with several tons of water to reduce the list. That buried her bow lower in the water, cut down her speed further, and forced the battleship to drop behind the formation. By then it was early afternoon, and the *Essex* and *Enterprise* spawned a fourth attack wave of fifty planes, more than half aiming for the *Musashi, now* running with bows awash and speed dropping. Her anti-aircraft batteries kept spitting into the attackers and took down two torpedo bombers, but others came in and drove more torpedoes into the hull. The ship's speed dropped to twelve knots and the fleet commander ordered her out of the battle area.

A fifth attack wave of more than a hundred fighters and bombers lifted off from five carriers. America was convinced that planes could sink battleships, and now the world's largest were special prey. *Musashi* took ten more torpedo strikes. Two of her four screws went dead; speed dropped to six knots. The captain could not turn for a grounding site because a change in heading with the bow submerged that low could capsize her. The bow continued sinking and the two forward main turrets looked like they were afloat on the sea. The list became heavier; every movable piece of equipment was shifted to the high side and three of the four engine rooms were added to the flooded compartments. The *Musashi* was an iron keg of seawater making meager headway under one remaining engine. The bow dipped deeper, as if the ship were attempting suicide by drowning, and the remaining engine stopped. The *Musashi* roared, belched smoke to the heavens, rolled over, and vanished with half of her twenty-two-hundred-man crew; the other half survived to carry the story back.

The *Yamato* was holding speed and the fleet continued eastward to the eastern approach of the Sibuyan Sea. The main fleet was now behind schedule, and the secondary fleet reduced speed to join for the planned simultaneous attack at the risk of being easier targets for submarines. The Japanese launched a plane to reconnoiter Leyte Gulf, and the pilot reported battleships, cruisers, some eighty transports—and about sixty kilometers from Leyte, twelve carriers with destroyer escorts. The information was of little use to the secondary fleet. Only one destroyer made it back to Brunei; the rest went to the bottom.

The main fleet was advancing with the *Yamato* at the center of the formation when American carriers came from sweeping conquests of Japanese-occupied lands and rose up on the horizon. The *Yamato*'s twenty-meter-barrel guns were finally invited to war. They roared two salvos of one-and-a-half-ton shells and the American carrier *Gambier Bay* was split in two. The *Yamato*'s crew cheered, but it was not their guns that did it: Another battleship had made the hit and scored the first American casualty of the campaign.

The *Yamato* closed to twenty-two kilometers of the American ships when her lookouts spotted six torpedo wakes heading toward them. The captain swung the ship away from the conflict into a course parallel to the torpedoes and ran together with them, three on either side, at twenty-six knots, until the torpedoes exhausted their run. Then the captain put about and regained the battle area where *Yamato's* secondary batteries sank one American destroyer. Another American air strike knocked two heavy cruisers out of the attack force.

The Japanese were trained to embrace death for their country—those children's war games that made Butterfly angry—and pilots sometimes slammed their plane into enemy aircraft on their own. But now, suicide was organized, and Admiral Onishi's first Special Attack pilots of the war took off in their Zeros from the airfield at Mabalacat on intentional one-way missions. One crash-dived onto the escort carrier *Santee*. The bomb penetrated to the innards of the ship, exploded and blew open a crater in the flight deck. Another Zero circled aft of the carrier *Suwanee*, lining her up for the attack. Anti-aircraft fire hit the plane; it spun, smoked, and veered off toward another carrier in the unit, but was brought down by a chance hit from the *Suwanee's* five-inch gun. Another Zero dived through the *Suwanee's* ack-ack and came down on the flight deck with a trail of smoke and a 250-kilogram bomb that pierced through to the hangar below and blasted holes in it and the flight deck above. While this new suicide squad was looking for targets, orthodox air action also attacked ships and held dogfights with Allied planes for control of the air.

The American escort carrier *St. Lo* took a strange, and a historic, suicide attack. The pilot brought his plane in low in a peculiarly cool attitude, almost a normal landing approach. Twenty- and forty-millimeter anti-aircraft fire filled the space between plane and ship, but the pilot went in with no attempt at evasive action. When he reached landing position, he released his single 250-kilogram bomb and rolled over into an inverted crash landing still close to the center line of the deck. Parts from the plane and the pilot's body spun and slid along the deck on a gasoline slick that burst into tongues of flame while the bomb penetrated the flight deck and set off a series of explosions and fires below deck. The captain ordered *abandon ship*, there was a final explosion, and the keel turned to the heavens. A lone pilot had taken down an escort carrier. It inspired the Japanese command to expand suicide attacks, and shocked Allied gunnery crews to accept the fearsome truth: there was no way to repel them.

The seas of Leyte ended the magnificent Combined Fleet. The remaining ships struggled back to Brunei after the omen-number four days of battle when the government in Tokyo ordered citizens to the hills with shovels to raise production of pine-root oil for military use. The number of ships in the attack force went from thirty-two to fifteen—digits that total eleven. Much of Yamamoto's former command was subsurface scrap, and ships still afloat were less of a fleet, more a random collection of vessels in various stages of damage.

The last surviving ship from Yamamoto's Pearl Harbor attack was among the losses at Leyte: the carrier *Zuikaku*. The official time of her sinking was 1415: *1+4+1+5=11*.

▪ 47 ▪
The Olympic Threat Reverses

Tokyo was a terrestrial game board waiting for American bombers to place their pieces. Families whose houses fell in the firebreak zones had been evicted, and old neighborhoods became clean swaths. Japanese knew the nomenclature B-29; news of the bomber came like air rushing out of a tunnel by a train approaching from the other end, and everyone realized that the gust of frightening information would be followed by a roaring sky and monsters of terror.

The first B-29 came over Tokyo on November first at one P.M. — was that Fate's way of throwing a double eleven? I was eating lunch when the sirens sang out. The legation staff and I ran into the basement, a palatial shelter compared with the shallow holes that government orders spawned in most neighborhoods. The all-clear sounded, and I finished lunch while Radio Tokyo announced that a single B-29 had flown over the city but dropped no bombs. It was a reconnaissance flight, and more flew over almost every day afterward, giving us at ground level a chance to see the size of the new plane, to hear the distinctive roar of its engines, and to expect the worst.

One day, weapons aimed at the psyche fluttered from the open bellies of the planes: leaflets printed in Japanese and addressed to the Japanese people. I picked one up from the streets:

To the Japanese People! Saipan and Leyte have fallen to American forces. These facts have long been hidden from you. Japan's military leaders do not want you to hear the voice of truth and will try to block our radio transmissions. Before they do, listen to the Voice of America from Saipan. Tune your radios to between 850 and 1,100 kilocycles every day at 6 P.M. The broadcast frequency will change. We also promise news of Japanese soldiers on different battlefronts of the world.

Life for the Japanese was practice in running for bomb shelters, fire-fighting drills with buckets and straw fire-beaters, and food shortages. "All our leaders can think of is building ridiculous watery holes for shelters with wood scraps for roofs," Butterfly commented.

"I hope you have something better than that near your home."

"A little better. But what good will any of it do? If a bomb hits close enough, it will be the end."

"And the schools I hope have decent bomb shelters."

"Decent by Japanese government standards. They don't seem to understand what is happening. They're not realistic."

"And how are the children taking this—the air raid warnings?"

"Some are frightened, but with many of them it's still a game, running in and out of the shelters. And did you hear about the girls' high school where all the students donated their hair as raw material for gunpowder? The girls probably think it will help. *I* think our government is as innocent as the girls. And *nobody* thinks about ending this war."

"Wars are easier started than ended."

"You saw it start. You could have even prevented it, at least the attack on Hawaii. Can't you think of some way this could be ended before we are all destroyed? Japan is being run by idiots."

Whenever Butterfly went into antigovernment tirades like that, I always had the escape of erotic departure, changing her course with affection. It still worked as 1944 drew to an end; it would not forever.

One week after the first B-29 came over the city, I listened to Prime Minister Koiso broadcast his favorite historical allusion to a medieval battle at a mountain called *Tennozan*, where a commander pulled off a swift, one-sided victory. Leyte, Koiso told the radio audience, was the glorious *Tennozan* he had promised, and more victories would follow if the Japanese kept sacrificing and fighting. Those of us who received reports from overseas knew that the former Combined Fleet was scrap on the ocean floor. Even Foreign Minister Shigemitsu did not know the real condition of the Imperial Navy. I did not have the heart to tell him.

After Koiso's broadcast ended, I received a telephone call from a Japanese army officer whose name was uncommon enough to recognize: Mutaguchi Ren'ya, commander at Japan's punishing defeat at Imphal. Mutaguchi had pushed the campaign for personal glory without preparing supplies. Instead, he gave orders to forage for edible vegetation and eat the horses. The army pushed into unexplored mountains between Burma and India with severely limited food and ammunition, and light mortars as their heaviest weapons. They took heavy losses from the tanks and air cover of a British Indian Army. The survivors started the crawl back to Burma falling from starvation, wounds, and malaria. Enemy units forcing the retreat found the Japanese spread on the landscape like a giant Buddhist mandala that invited interpretation: Each commanding officer had ordered his men to commit suicide, followed by a pistol shot to his own head. One hundred thousand men were reduced to fifty thousand, half of them suffering from disease and malnutrition. Those who made it back to Japan told of their ranks thinning by the minute from enemy guns, wounds, disease, hunger, thirst, and suicide, and of comrades neither dead nor sufficiently alive abandoned in the jungle—and of their commander, Mutaguchi, accompanied by ladies behind the lines in his visits to army hospitals to rouse the wounded back to the front.

Mutaguchi's telephone message was brief: an overture of his name and rank, an apology for calling me suddenly—as if there were a gradual way to call—then the body of his message, stating that he wished to take a few minutes of my valuable time to speak with me, and another apology for the request followed by another apology for the sudden call. I invited him to come over right away if he so desired. He did.

"I understand you've had a long military career," I said in a diplomatic avoidance of the debacle of two months earlier.

"Yes," he said dryly, "I fought against the Chinese in Manchuria in the early 1930s and at Nomonhan. But I'm off the front lines now."

He was probably working in intelligence, though he did not specify, or he might have been trying to compensate for his past fiasco by gaining information for Japan. He arrived encased in the same dour respect that came sewn into every Japanese army uniform.

"I'm sure you have heard," he began, "that yesterday Stalin came out openly and denounced Japan as an aggressor nation."

I had spent yesterday with a Japanese lady who told me tearfully in the French she had learned of her desire for the war to end one way or the other, and how she wanted to go to France to visit the museums and sit at sidewalk cafes and never see another Japanese military uniform, like the one that was then in the same chair she was in when she told me. I could not help her get her wish, but we had a much more interesting time than listening to messages from Moscow. I'm sure Marshal Stalin would have forgiven me. "I can understand your concern," I said. "But you do have a neutrality pact with the Soviets that is in effect until April of 1946, a year and a half from now." My comment was as meaningful as an apology for a "sudden" telephone call—or a pact between nations.

"Yes, but we must know more about Soviet intentions. And since you Scandinavians have had extensive experience with them . . ."

Japan was in a pact with the Soviets and Sweden was neutral, but once again, in understandings that lie closer to realities, a Japanese and a Swede were talking of the Soviets as our common enemy.

"Quite frankly," he went on, "we wondered whether you might have any insights into Soviet intentions."

"I surely would not know any more than anyone else, and probably a lot less than your own intelligence officers." That was an undeserved compliment. Japanese intelligence on Russia was almost primitive; that is what sent this man to me, trying to tap into our knowledge of them.

"We are concerned," he continued, "that the Soviets might make a move into Manchuria again, and we are looking for any indication, or even your opinion if you would care to offer one. You recall how the Soviets were once afraid of having to fight a two-front war."

"Tokyo almost had an Olympiad to help it along," I reminded him.

"But with Germany beaten in Russia and on the way to utter defeat, the threat is gone. You understand what that means."

"Now it is Japan who could be in a pincers, between the Pacific and the Soviet Union, if Stalin attacks Manchuria."

"This time it would not be another Nomonhan. They would aim for Tokyo. You recall that next year will be the forty-fifth anniversary of our victory over Russia."

"Yes, and they may want to celebrate with a vendetta."

"Exactly," he responded. "Oh, it's a different Russia now, a post-revolution communist state, but to them it will be essentially a continuation of that war. This is an especially dangerous time for Japan, and after Stalin's statement yesterday, our concern is how to read the Soviet intention."

Japan's initial victories in the Pacific War made her leaders act like casino patrons who turn a winning streak into profits for the house. Japan's forces in Manchuria were now a pool for her war to the south.

"I'm sure we all expect that the Soviets have to have ambitions for Manchuria," I said. "Natural resources, strategically located . . ."

"It is that, and more than that," Mutaguchi replied. "Japan's victory in 1905 changed the value of race in the world. At the time, a good part of Asian territory was colonized or under control of the Western powers: Britain, America, Holland, Spain, France . . . For years, Asians felt that the white races were born to rule. This was accepted like heaven's will; Asians never thought of confronting the white rulers, much less fighting them."

"But Japan did confront," I replied, "and I don't have to tell you how the world watched."

"Only because these strange people from Japan were trying to do the impossible. Then when Japan came out victorious, America and Britain were not happy. Japan was encroaching on white territory, and the Russians had the dishonor of being the first nation—and a huge one, of big people—to be beaten by a race of small, strange-looking people from a small country."

"Of course there is a strong class consciousness, especially in Britain," I cushioned politely, "but you know that the British press was overwhelmingly full of praise for the Japanese army and navy. The papers constantly wrote of the bravery and the high moral level of the Japanese soldier. I read every British account of that war."

"They were also afraid of the Russians," he countered. "Gluttons for earth. Until we went to war in 1904, Russia had taken over the central Asian tribes and wanted to absorb Persia, Afghanistan, and Tibet. The only thing that held her back was the counterinfluence of other white colonizers—the

British in India. So two white countries were holding each other in check on someone else's land. You know how the West watched Japan fight China over Manchuria in 1894 and said little. We were only two Oriental countries. Then Russia ousted us from Manchuria, the usual situation of a big, white country pushing around the Oriental. Next they started building a railway linking the Trans-Siberian Line with Vladivostok—ice-free two hundred ninety-three days a year, longer than any Russian Pacific port and less than a thousand kilometers from Moscow. That justified bringing in engineers— but you know what happened."

"Yes, the army moved in with them."

"Typical Russian sneak tactics. The railway was a threat to Japan, and every promise to stop building the line was followed by more building. Then Russia obtained a lease on Port Arthur, ice-free most the year and an easy sail around the Korean peninsula to our shores. Next she began extending the railway down to Port Arthur. That would have linked it with direct rail communication from the homeland for rapid troop movements. And it was all done under a series of promises that they would stop building. Russia has a two thousand-year history of lies, and of all the non-Oriental and non-Asian regions, Scandinavia knows the Russians best. It is one reason I feel that I can talk openly with you, even though this is a matter of racial war." Mutaguchi lowered his voice in a feeling of greater intimacy. "I will be honest with you," he went on. "Japan's expansion of the war in China was not the way the army or the government presented it." I registered interest, and let him go on.

"I was in charge of a detachment at the time of the Marco Polo Bridge Incident. The army was acting on its own; we wanted no interference from Tokyo. The official story is that the Japanese army was on maneuvers, we were fired on by the Chinese, then we returned the fire. Do you believe that?"

I was not sure if he was looking for my opinion or was testing my loyalty to Japan's cause. There was no way of knowing how many levels of information gathering he was operating on. In the guise of asking for friendly opinions in one area, he might be probing my thoughts in another direction.

"I only know the orthodox explanations," I replied in the usual diplomatic words of noncommitment. No sensible person doubted that it had been organized by the army leaders in advance. No sensible person would talk about it. Mutaguchi leaned forward from his military posture, resting his elbows on his knees with his hands clasped. "My job at the Marco Polo Bridge was firing the first shot," he said, looking at me directly. "I started the full-scale war in China."

I gave his message a moment for absorption. "That was a shot of historical significance indeed," I remarked.

"We wanted to eliminate Chiang Kai-shek and his armies. So we decided to open full-scale war. The Chinese did not have the weapons or leadership to match ours, and that's how Japan could hold the country with fewer numbers. I was in charge of the detachment by the Marco Polo Bridge at the time, and my shot started the battle. We said that it was in retaliation, but military logic should tell you that we couldn't strike so fast and hard without preparation. My shot was a false retaliation and a starting gun. Our men were waiting for the signal."

Why was Mutaguchi telling me this now? I saw it as a bid to trade sincerity for sincerity, a step in a hopeful trade of information built on the Japanese tendency to gain advantage through linking emotions.

"I can agree with you personally," I answered, "that a pact with the Soviets is uncomfortable protection. If I were to bet, it would be that they do have intentions to move into Manchuria again, but it is only a guess. If I hear of anything more concrete, I will call you."

"I don't have to remind you," he said as a finale, "that the more Russia suffers on this front, the better it will be for Scandinavia."

Ordinarily, we at the other head of the two-headed bear would welcome a drain of Moscow's military resources. But Ishii raised a new fear. Japan's biological warfare experiments were all in China. Japan was expecting the Soviets to storm into Manchuria, and with the Kwantung Army being skeletonized, there was more reason to expect Japan to resort to unorthodox weapons. That could trigger epidemics that might reach Europe, and spread like the ancient diseases that laid vast populations to waste. But, this would be greater. When bacteria and viruses are bred for war, science improves their virulence, their fighting power. Measures to stop disease can never keep pace with ways of creating it. Would a Soviet invasion be the first step to a pestilence of global scale? I felt at the time that Akira's prediction was balanced on the border between Manchuria and the Soviet Union.

· 48 ·

War Comes to Tokyo

On November 13, 1944, professional baseball was ordered off the field as the nation braced for a more serious contest. The same day, the Sumo Association announced that all wrestlers would donate their trophies for melting down into war materials. In the game of greater reality, the Japanese Southern Army moved its command from Manila to Saigon, and the army copied Admiral Onishi and organized its own suicide attacks against Allied ships around Leyte Gulf. The *Kamikaze*, the sacred wind that repelled Mongol invaders from Japan, was reborn with younger and younger pilots.

The sole B-29 was followed almost daily by flights of two, three, and more planes, as if America were giving us on the ground a chance to become accustomed to the weighty roar in increments. On November 21 we heard the news that Kyushu was bombed by eighty new B-29s, and three days later I watched as 111 of the giant planes flew over Tokyo. They came in as they always had, high and above the range of Japanese anti-aircraft guns that sent smoke blossoms of welcome far below their wings while the drone of the engines drove into the ground. The targets were outside of our city, in the industrial belt between Tokyo and Yokohama that contained the Nakajima aircraft factory and both small and large war production plants. As the bombs fell, Japan's biological warfare plans were delayed: the Japanese task force headed for Saipan was sunk by Allied air and naval action, and the Kyoto Imperial University graduates went down with their pathogenic freight. But the loss of twenty men would not stop Ishii. Somewhere, he was shuffling the cards for his next hand.

Shortly after the air raid, Butterfly brought other news.

"I'll have more free time now, but I don't appreciate it. Children will be ending their school days at eleven in the morning."

"Because of the air raids, of course."

"Yes, but will they be any safer at home? And in my neighborhood, the government issued orders to evacuate some of the homes and tear them down," she said with anger and disgust.

"Not yours, I hope."

"No, we were spared. You remember I told you about the house of the imperial prince, Teru-no-Miya?"

"I had my driver take me past it one day, and the place where the six trees used to be. Just out of curiosity."

"You did? Perhaps you came by my home also."

"I don't know; I might have. How close is it to the prince?"

"Fortunately, not too close. All buildings within three hundred meters of it were ordered destroyed—to protect the prince's home from fire in case of air raids. That's disgusting! If the emperor is descended from the gods, why can't he protect his own family?"

Again, an area of discussion I did not want to voice opinion on. "And you're more than three hundred meters away, I take it."

"We are. But some of the people we knew for years had to pack up and move. Some of the neighbors with fireproof warehouses took in valuables for them. It was sad to see all those people forced out and their homes smashed. And those of us who kept our homes now feel that we're just waiting for the air raids to come to us."

As the era of the B-29—the Superfortresses—came in, the Japanese government increased lumber production to meet the increasing use of wood in their own military planes. But shortly, a ship like no ocean of the world had ever seen emerged from five and a half years of secret construction and slid down the ways at Yokosuka: the third *Yamato*-class battleship redesigned as a carrier. The keel was laid well before the Pacific War started, but Pearl Harbor and the sinking of the *Prince of Wales* and *Repulse* convinced Japan's high command of Yamamoto's argument for carriers as the backbone of the fleet. In the spring of 1942 the ship's plans were altered to make it an aircraft carrier. The change lengthened her construction period to three years longer than her sister ships, and the *Shinano*, displacing sixty-eight thousand tons and two hundred sixty-six meters in length, finally eased into Tokyo Bay. Japan had lost most of her carriers and this was a badly needed replacement. The *Shinano* was "unsinkable," as were her sister ships and Britain's *Prince of Wales,* all now pressing into the ocean floor.

The *Shinano*'s maiden-voyage destination was the Combined Fleet training area on the island of Shikoku, with the first leg scheduled to take her to Osaka Bay. The ship was forced into commission before the crew was fully trained, before all equipment was installed. But, she was "unsinkable," and this gave the naval authorities confidence to send her at night through waters known to be infiltrated by Allied submarines. Japan's decision-making process had a greater ration of irony than reason: A ship that was altered to conform to expanded respect for air power was sent on its maiden voyage at night, eliminating the chance for air coverage from land-based planes. Only three destroyers ran escort.

Thirty minutes past midnight on the morning of the day after starting on her maiden voyage, lookouts spotted a dark object on the horizon. The *Shinano* and her escorts went into a zigzag course until binocular examinations convinced the ship's officers that the intruder was just a low cloud. The ships resumed their regular southward course.

Shortly after 0300, lookouts on the *Shinano* spotted a torpedo wake at one hundred meters, then three more: an American submarine had found it. There was no time for evasion. Four explosions caved in the carrier's side and overloaded the pumping system. The captain still had pride in his ship and maintained twenty knots with no thought of heading for the nearest port or a grounding location. The ship listed, and continued listing. When it was impossible to stand on deck, the captain ordered *abandon ship* and the *Shinano* went down about a hundred miles south of the Wakayama coast.

Wartime education maintained influence. With the abandon-ship order, a young officer ran to the captain's reception room, took down the photograph of the emperor, wrapped it—carefully—in canvas, ran back topside and handed it to a sailor who floated with it until rescued by an escorting destroyer. The officer remained on board with five hundred hands who also went down with the thirty-centimeter-thick, special-steel flight deck with an underlayer of concrete. It was designed to withstand the most punishing aerial bombs. It would never have to.

The *Shinano* was launched on November 11, a pair of Yamamoto's omen numbers. It was rushed through a final fitting-out, then set a record for the shortest life of a capital warship—seventeen hours from the start of maiden voyage to sinking—as if something compelled her to culminate her disgrace on another pair of Yamamoto's omens. The ship went down on November 29, still the same month and a date that adds up to 11. The date was also the designation of the bombers built to destroy Japan. The log of the attacking submarine recorded the time of the first *Fire* order as 03:17: *3+1+7=11*.

The last day of November, the B-29s came over Tokyo in their first precision-bombing, radar-operation night raid with another strike at the industrial belt. Less then two weeks later they flew over the industrial city of Nagoya in the first all-out raid on that target. Radio broadcasts and fire-fighting team leaders kept assuring the Japanese that wet mats and bucket brigades could handle any fires that the American bombers could start; Admiral Suzuki was realistic.

"I realize that this is a danger-laden imposition we place on you," he addressed me in formal Japanese. "But the situation is as you see it. And worse. The mainland is being bombed from land bases and our leaders have to resort to ordering suicide attacks. Our nation is being destroyed from outside and within."

Almost two months had passed since Stockholm's frigid, bureaucratic response to my peace proposal message left me facing a protocol wall, while bombing runs were adding a new immediacy to the plot. But diplomatic habits can pull the backbone from a man. I remained in a communication lethargy through despair of getting my foreign minister to act, though I admit it was against a sequence of nightmares of the Romanian minister's smashed face, the British correspondent's "suicide," and Tokyo's celebration of the anniversary of the Bolshevik revolution on November 7: Sorge and Ozaki were led out of their cells and hanged with dramatic public announcement. I tried to imagine what auspicious anniversary might provide an option for my own execution. "We can expect the B-29s to increase in accuracy," I agreed with Suzuki.

"I have opposed the use of the Special Attack Forces—a deceptive euphemism. I was one of the few who could criticize without being insulted.

It was not only my rank and age; I commanded a torpedo boat in the Sino-Japanese War. Ten years later I commanded a destroyer squadron in the war against Russia. These bring me respect among the military, and at least they listened to me. I always said that intentional human sacrifice is not proper military action."

"And your criticism had no effect?"

"In the end, none. Did you hear the radio broadcast on the Leyte battle?"

"Yes, quite a dramatic presentation, just as if it were an eyewitness report of the suicide attacks."

"Adults and children working in the factories . . . everyone was gathered around a radio somewhere. Many of them cried. It is the government's way of raising patriotism among the Japanese. But there are still suicide weapons that the people are not being told about."

"Besides the planes?"

"Planes are apparent suicide attacks, but one naval weapon was intended to confound the enemy. It was called *Kaiten.*"

"*Kaiten*—Turning the fate of heaven. A stirring name."

"A disgusting tactic: manned torpedoes. They are carried by submarine and released some distance from the target. They were first used in the Caroline Islands, against Allied ships in the harbor. Naval officers wanted to keep it a secret from the enemy, to keep them guessing what new torpedo we had developed. But we know they soon discovered what they were." Suzuki's face drew more sad. He repeated, "This is not military. It is ugly. And other attempts are almost childish."

"Meaning. . . ?"

"The military leaders are trying to attack the American mainland with balloon bombs."

"Balloon bombs? That float to America?"

"Exactly. Released from several locations in Japan to ride the ocean breezes. Some of them may arrive and even explode, but what manner of warfare is this against a country with the armaments of America? Childish!"

"I regret," I told Suzuki, "that my government's answer was not according to our wishes. I will try again to move them."

Back at my legation, I sent another message in an attempt to evoke some understanding.

19 December 1944
The person mentioned in point four in my previous message was
prime minister before the outbreak of the war. This person's position
in the matter is extremely delicate and risky.

The year 1944 was drawing to a close with four air raids in the Tokyo-Yokohama area demonstrating that American precision bombing still lacked precision: the raids did more damage to the surroundings than to the targets, while factories kept producing. But the possibility of improvement in bombing techniques was always present. I received no further response from Stockholm, and with the approach of Christmas I did not expect my foreign minister to waken from his yuletide joy. As a diplomat, I might already be considered too far out of line in trying to press my superior; the manual instructs us to serve, not educate, and the threat of human extermination should not alter protocol.

On the year's last visit from Butterfly, she told me that she would spend the new year with her mother, either in their home in Tokyo or once again in Saitama with her father if they could obtain passage on the train.

I wanted to spend at least part of the season with her, but I substituted a few brisk punching-bag workouts in the mornings, then joined the Swedish community in toasts to survival in the coming months.

The year 1945 began with the United States advancing its campaign in the Philippines. Troops landed on the main island of Luzon and warships entered the island's Lingayen Gulf under increasing attacks by *Kaiten* torpedoes. They proved as deadly for ships as for the suicide crews. This American focus on the Philippines brought relative peace to Tokyo. I strolled the ghost town of the Ginza. Trees lined the streets almost dutifully, their branches as bare of leaves as the streets were of people. Stores and theaters were closed, and only tram stops contained clusters of life, with people transferring from one line to another. The Ginza was just a place for passing through on the way to somewhere else.

On the twenty-first of January, Prime Minister Koiso came over the radio in an emotional from-the-gut speech on defense of the nation, and a few days later America found time for Japan.

January twenty-seventh was a Saturday covered by low clouds. Shortly after noon air raid sirens screamed, and the Japanese thought of American radar that could see through those clouds. Soon, seventy B-29s came and struck the same streets I had walked on a few days earlier. Ginza was covered with death as people were caught in their race from tram stops to bomb shelters. One bomb found a crowded subway station and killed and buried its victims simultaneously—efficiently.

Those who were not victims were curious, and with movie houses and theaters closed there was a hunger for spectacle. Two days after the raid, as soon as the bodies were cleared away and the police blockades were removed, large crowds came to see. I also decided on a return to the Ginza, and I walked to the restaurant where Yamamoto and I once had lunch. I found a plot of ground filled with burned timbers and broken dishes. A police man approached me and said that it would not be wise for a white person to walk around, especially during or after an air raid: "The Japanese may get excited and kill you." Was this concern or threat? I felt that he might be one of those potentially excitable persons in his own message. In the jumble of debris that used to be restaurants and fashionable shops selling pearls and silks, spectators mumbled that this proves Japan had lost the war.

It was not without price on the enemy's side; a few days later radio announcements told the Japanese to go to Hibiya Park to view a B-29 that had been brought down in a suicide attack. I also went. The Japanese who came to view it were more impressed by the size of the aircraft and the terror it represented than inspired to endure more. When I returned to the legation, Mrs. Saito had a message for me: "Miss Hiraoka called. The raid on the Ginza hit the Taimei Elementary school in the neighborhood. Four women schoolteachers were killed; one was her friend."

"That's too bad," was all I could offer.

"It was Saturday afternoon and fortunately there were no children in school. One bomb hit the school directly, and . . ."

The smashed B-29 remained posed in Hibiya Park through most of February, during which Roosevelt, Churchill, and Stalin met at Yalta on the Black Sea to decide the fate of the world after the war—a war that was still to feast on generous rations of Japan's civilians in its diet of flesh.

▪ 49 ▪
One Purpose of War is Preparation for the Next

Scientists have a compulsion to test. Sometimes only war conditions will provide a suitable laboratory.

From late night of March ninth and into the tenth of 1945, with the Japanese biological warfare researchers in China experimenting on captives, America used Tokyo to test their own new war product. Some 1.7 million people had evacuated the city, leaving five million of us in a metropolis about 30 percent burned or burning from air attacks. The wide paths that had been opened by eviction and demolition through the heavily congested parts of the city had contained the incendiary fires to a limited degree, but the men behind the huge bombers now sought to cancel out the firebreak effect altogether.

This March was unusually cold. Residents of surviving houses scampered for the wooden debris of their neighbors' demolished homes to warm themselves and cook any food they might have.

My part of the city was distant from the target site, but it was apparent from my residence that this cold night was bringing a different kind of attack. The sound was heavier, more immediate — a continuous growing thunderclap that drove into the skull like the throb of a headache whose pain was obliterated by dread. B-29s had never come in so low. They plunged into our midnight in different flying patterns that converged over Tokyo's densely populated, working-class neighborhood — wall-to-wall houses of wood and paper under tile roofs. The fears and freezing temperatures at ground level were chilled further by high velocity winds: nature's dreaded bellows would be working for *them*.

The new weapon was a bomb containing a viscous, fire-creating chemical called napalm, and when these and orthodox incendiaries licked the ice out of the air and added their fire to the parts of the city already burning, the light reflected on the bellies of the planes and made them look like swarms of red, monster dragonflies coming to claim their human sacrifices.

The target area turned into a solid blanket of fire. People tried escaping into the Sumida River—where Butterfly used to teach swimming in the summer—and were cooked to death. Napalm danced on tile roofs and clung to clothing and flesh. The cursed accomplice of wind turned the fires insane, picked up flaming wooden structures and slammed them into people as they struggled to breathe and stay alive in the narrow space between cremation and freezing. The mad roar continued from above like a profanity on the damned.

It required several days for the big fires to die out for lack of fuel. Police again warned foreigners to stay indoors to protect us from Japanese who might kill us in retribution. I took some old work clothes from the caretaker's storeroom and put them on, then wrapped my head and ears in a cloth the way workers and indeed many other people dressed against the cold. I put on the caretaker's broad-brimmed worker's hat, smeared my face with soot, then took his bicycle and headed toward the razed area. It was a long pedal from my neighborhood, but I was in good physical condition—until I neared the target site.

As I approached the outer edges of the area, people wandered dazed, some in a perpetual wail, others like zombies without strength for utterance. Some seemed too exhausted to question whether they were living or not, immobilized at the threshold of freezing after surviving the fire.

I pedaled on. A burned-flesh stench thickened the air and seemed to coat my nose, throat, lungs, and stomach like palpable sludge. People on foot and on bicycles weaved through smoking timbers and bodies, trying to find where a home had been, or searching for family members. I pushed on through the wall of smell. The fires had burned away the wooden understructures of the houses, leaving patches of ground-level roof tiles that looked like they had been flattened by a crazed deity who pounded them down from the heavens.

The population density of charred bodies increased until those of us on bicycles had to get off to keep lifting the wheels over corpses. Women with babies strapped to their backs were seared into exceptionally large obstacles. Sometimes I inadvertently hit a corpse with my wheel and the black char simply fell apart. Only size and remaining traces of flesh or clothing gave clues to their demographic status: old woman; old man; male child; female child; baby, sex undeterminable . . .

The banks of the Sumida River were piled with corpses that were carried up by ocean tides, then stranded when the tide receded. Army vehicles roamed the area. A hysterical woman screamed at an officer, "Are you satisfied now with your military dream?" The officer ignored her; she was beyond need for punishment.

On the way home, the air slowly improved, but the sludge adhered to my innards like foul mucilage. When I arrived, I discarded the clothes and tried to bathe the smell away. The odor penetrated my skin and clung, as napalm had clung to those caught in its adhesive jelly grip. The dead clutched me with their stench in a final grasp on this world.

I learned more about that raid after the war, when I was stationed in Cairo. I was at an affair at the United States embassy and by chance I overheard an American officer talking about his career as a pilot on bombing missions over Japan. I approached him and asked if he was flying missions through to the end of the war.

"Not quite," he answered. "My last run was in March of 1945."

"March ninth and tenth, you mean?" I inquired.

"That's right. I was about to be retired from flight duty, but the decision makers thought that this run needed veteran pilots."

"For testing a new weapon, I imagine."

"Not only that. To test the B-29s."

"Test the B-29s? I would think that by then they were beyond the testing stage."

"Yes and no. They were developed to defeat Japan with high-altitude bombing. I was on the first raid on Japan; July seventh, 1944. We flew out of bases in Kwanghan, China, but with a bomb load at high altitude, the farthest point in Japan we could reach and return from was Kyushu. That's not the location of the industrial centers the planes were designed to destroy."

"The Japanese all knew," I responded, "when they lost the Marianas that air raids on the mainland would follow."

"Yes, the capture of Saipan and Tinian put us in range of all Japan—a fifteen- to sixteen-hour round-trip. So we bombed Nagoya and Yokohama. Then in November—it was the twenty-fourth, the day after Thanksgiving; we had turkey sandwiches aboard—one hundred eleven B-29s flew the first raid over Tokyo since the Doolittle attack."

"Apparently, there were only some scattered fires, and the firefighters had them all out in two hours."

"Our photographic surveys showed that damage was nil. Three days later we tried again, with eighty-one planes. Our targets were still the aircraft factories, and we missed them all. That was always the story. We hit the Musashina Aircraft Factory with eight hundred thirty-five planes—twenty-three hundred tons of bombs—and caused only four percent damage. We pulled a new year's raid in 1945 with another try against the Mitsubishi aircraft factory in Nagoya, but still couldn't destroy it. Even in Manchuria B-29s hit the Mitsubishi aircraft works there six times, but they still kept producing, mainly in underground factories. Our high-altitude bombing just wasn't working, and the bombing command was on the carpet."

"The world heard about your bombsight technology, and was expecting accuracy from high altitude."

"It was so *in*accurate we got into trouble for letting a few drop inside the imperial palace grounds. No damage, though."

"I remember how the Japanese radio screamed at the audacity of the Americans when that happened."

"You remember. . . ? You mean, you were there then?"

"I was in Tokyo," I told him.

"Well, I'm glad you're all right. Tokyo was no place to be then."

"Unless one lived in the imperial palace, perhaps."

"We were ordered to avoid it, but there was just no way to improve accuracy from that height. Remember there are high winds aloft over Japan, and visibility is not always good. That imperial fumble was on February twenty-fifth. I can't forget that date either—the biggest B-29 raid yet for the Twenty-First Bomb Command: one hundred seventy-two planes. After that, the debate over the B-29s really heated up. The Joint Chiefs of Staff in Washington screamed every time our bomb-survey photos showed that the attacks were more of a disaster to us than the factories."

"The reports made it sound like the factories were the safest place to be. Japanese news was generally not to be believed, but I was getting fairly reliable reports of the damage."

"Embarrassing to the command is the only way to put it. We were flying sixty-five-ton aircraft and not doing any more damage than a few Piper Cubs might have caused."

"That's right, they *were* sixty-five tons," I commented, adding numbers again to another eleven in the destruction of Japan.

"Yes. Why, was there something. . . ?"

"No, I was just thinking about their size. So the results were disappointing?"

"Worse than that. Our accuracy was as good as dropping bombs with your eyes closed, and we were losing planes to suicide attacks."

"You probably know," I told the former pilot, "that Japanese newspapers carried a photo of a Japanese plane ramming one of your B-29s. Just the photo was chilling."

"The only way Japanese fighters could get up to our altitude was by stripping off their guns and ammunition. So, when they did get to us, they were no longer a fighting plane. They could only ram. But with our poor results they could have just ignored us. Headquarters in Washington rated the B-29s a failure, and responsibility fell on the head of General LeMay who was in charge of the raids. He tried to blame bad weather, relying on radar and inferior pilot training, but he couldn't excuse his way out. His back was to the wall and he had to change tactics or face replacement. So he moved the Twenty-First Bomb Command from China to Guam and he put in a request to Washington to change tactics."

"And Washington agreed, of course."

"They did, and fast, too. A look at the figures tells why: between November twenty-fourth of 1944 and March fourth of 1945, the Twentieth Air Force pulled twenty-two B-29 raids over Japan. We knocked out only one factory and it cost us one hundred and two B-29s. We were all looking for a change in tactics, but we were shocked when we heard what it was going to be."

"Low-level raids, of course."

"It scared the hell out of us. Our high-altitude industrial bombing campaign ended on March fourth and we were briefed on the new tactics: we would bomb from five thousand to eight thousand feet."

"Five thousand feet—fifteen hundred meters. That does not seem the altitude that planes of that size were designed for."

"That is correct, sir. We said it was suicide. We had always gone in at thirty thousand feet; that's five thousand feet higher than Japanese anti-aircraft range. Sometimes at a bare minimum of twenty-five thousand feet, never lower. But General LeMay was up against it, and low-level bombing was his way out, in spite of the risk and no background in low-level operations. That's why we veteran pilots were kept on flight duty."

"And did the Americans think that bombing civilians would cause an upward pressure on the Japanese government and force it to capitulate?"

"Truthfully, sir, we all doubted that. But the B-29 had to be justified, and LeMay had to save his career. As we said in irreverent moments, if he didn't show results he was headed for latrine duty."

"If you will allow *me* an irreverent question, were any of the plane crews bothered about using huge bombers to hit civilian targets?"

"Oh, there was some talk about it, and burning civilian populations would not sit well with the American public, either. But at the staff presentation we were told that Japanese production depended heavily on home industries around major factories; feeder industries that are extensions of the production lines. So by destroying the flow of vital parts we could choke off their capacity to produce war goods. We were going for people in their homes who were making parts for planes and guns, and pins and casings for grenades."

"And what about the factories that you couldn't hit before?"

"Oh, the command did not forget them altogether. We were told that a general conflagration in a big city could spread to primary targets. Of course, we were not convinced of everything we were told, but pilots don't make policy. We just fly the machines."

"In other words, burn enough homes and the fires would eventually reach some of the factories from ground level that your explosive bombs could not hit."

"That's about it. The first raid started the night of March ninth in Tokyo. We left from different bases, three hundred thirty-four planes in all. Some took off from Guam and Saipan. I took off from Tinian; that was the largest airfield in the world at the time. Some planes had to turn back because of mechanical trouble, and we lost fourteen. So two hundred eighty-five planes made the bombing run that night."

"And that's when you first used your new incendiary weapon, correct?"

"Yes, sir. That was our first attempt at carpet bombing with incendiaries."

Carpet bombing, I thought to myself; *sounds so . . . neat!*

"Japanese terminology is different, you know," I advised him. "They call it 'indiscriminate bombing.'"

"No, it wasn't indiscriminate. It was a well-planned tactic. Our intention was to cover the entire area and nullify the firebreaks. We encircled the target area with thirteen thousand M-47 bombs."

"Forty-seven. . . ?" Once again, I was adding numbers in the destruction of Japan.

"M-47; the designation for our one-hundred-pound napalm bombs. The pathfinder planes dropped those first to encircle the target area."

"And then, conventional incendiaries?"

"Once the M-47s created a wall of flame that trapped everyone inside, we filled the space with incendiaries—two hundred thousand of them, six-pounders in delayed-opening clusters to achieve saturation."

"And Tokyo was the first test of napalm, I understand."

"The first against an enemy, yes. But we had experimented with it in America at army test sites."

"Japanese homes are different from your test sites, I imagine."

"Oh, we had them, too."

"Japanese homes?"

"Yes, sir. We had them built especially to test fire bombing. Then we went in for the actual test on Tokyo."

"Americans tell me that they're famous for griping. Wasn't there any over the plans for low-level bombing?"

"Griping and fear. But, orders are orders. We knew that our purpose was to create a firestorm, but we couldn't imagine the enormity of it. When we were over the target, the thermal currents from the fires shot up and gave us some violent bouncing around. Some of our planes were boosted up two thousand feet in altitude by thermal shock waves. It felt like a vertical catapult launching. We were three hundred miles away from the city on our way home and we could still see the sky lit up. The planes in the later waves returned to base black with soot and smelling like burned buildings."

"So, you created your firestorm."

"Yes, sir. LeMay was very happy and the test convinced the command to pull similar raids over Nagoya, Osaka, and Kobe. But I was at the end of my combat flying career, and during that raid over Tokyo I was only too glad that I'd be leaving my seat to younger pilots. I assure you, we were eleven very shaken men up there."

"Eleven. . . ?"

"Yes, sir. We were flying eleven-man crews. That's reduced from full crew because all guns except tail cannons were stripped off."

The twenty-nine in the plane designation, sixty-five tons, forty-seven in the napalm bomb designation, eleven-man crews—Yamamoto's number would not stop.

A proper title can deceive. Calling this *war* gives carnage the illusion of orthodoxy and acceptance. The Tokyo firestorm death toll reached an estimated one hundred thousand people. Yamamoto's home district in Niigata prefecture was singled out for extra severe punishment: America was remembering Pearl Harbor. When Yamamoto the child was playing with his "bamboo dragonflies," he could not envision that he was preparing the air for real propellers that would deliver death to his playmates, their families, and neighbors who did not even know him at the time.

Where tram cars still operated in Tokyo, they were purposely left overnight at random places along their routes, like animals in open-air hibernation, so that a hit on the terminal would not destroy all of them.

Three days after the low-level raid on Tokyo it was Osaka, and less than a week after that, Nagoya, as the B-29s justified themselves. Then, a blockade of Japan started with the United States dropping sea mines in the Sekkan Strait. Japan was being burned down from the skies and choked at sea level.

Telephone communications were severely disrupted, and I had no contact with Mariko for some time. I wanted to know that she was all right, and to let her know that while I was not fighting at the front, I had finally left my neutrality and was trying to save what I could of Japan. I asked Mrs. Saito to accompany me and we drove to her house. The neighborhood was not in the target zones and except for slight damage from an occasional stray fire bomb, the locality was surviving. Mariko's home was closed. Mrs. Saito went around to the neighbors and asked, then came back with a look of deep worry. "She has been taken away . . ."

"Taken away?"

"The special police, apparently."

"Mariko? The police? Does anyone know why?"

"The neighbors only know it was 'for questioning.'" Mrs. Saito caught her breath and continued. "And for several days before they came for her, her mother did not return home. That is very unusual; everyone assumes that she was killed in the air raids."

"When? And how? This neighborhood is . . ."

"It seems that she went to visit a friend in another part of the city, someone who had lost family members in the raids. If she was killed, it was somewhere else in the city."

I thought that Mariko's mother could have been one of the black lumps that fell apart under my bicycle wheel, or one that scattered when the wind blew. Or among the piles of black forms that were floated up and deposited on the banks of the Sumida River. First Mariko's friend was killed, then her mother, and now she was being held for questioning. She was deviant by the standards of the day. The adherents of Japan's "strange religion" were about to become her inquisitors.

▪ 50 ▪

Operation PX—Bioattack Plan on America

"**P**rince Konoe has heard about a plan for a biological attack on an American city and he has no idea how to prevent it."

Prince Konoe, the rather fragile though large-bodied aristocrat with a Hitleresque mustache, resigned his last of three separated terms as prime minister in October 1941. His bloodline kept him close to the emperor and government officials, while he worked with the secret peace movement with me through an intermediary, a confidential secretary-assistant by the name of Hatano, who brought me this news a few weeks before the napalm raid of March 1945.

"The plan is named "Operation PX," and *PX* is their designation for plague-infected fleas. We expect they may also use cholera and anthrax. Ishii has used them all in China."

"And how will they carry this to America?"

"By aircraft-carrying submarine."

"I remember news reports back in 1942 of a submarine-launched plane that dropped two bombs on Oregon. And other submarines threw some shells at a California oil field and at a naval radio station on Vancouver Island."

"They were smaller submarines. On December thirtieth last year, Japan completed the I-400, more than one hundred twenty meters in length. It can carry three floatplanes, and of course, since it is new and the largest submarine in the world, the military men are eager to use it."

"And what do you know of the plan?"

"The submarine will surface within flight range of the city and the planes will spread their pathogens over the target. Three planes should be able to wipe out a city. As you surely know, plague usually kills within three days. When it starts taking effect, some people will flee—as happened in China—and will carry it outside of the target zone. The effect will continue and multiply."

"The pilot who bombed Oregon returned to Japan a hero and is still flying. Do the planners of this tactic think the same success will carry through this time?"

"Nobody expects to return. It is a suicide mission. The planes will crash after they release their loads and crew members will infect themselves and run ashore. I do not have to remind you that there are willing hands to carry this off."

"And does the military expect to gain tactical advantage from this, or is it simply a way to strike back at America?"

"It may be as ill planned as most of this war. No, such an attack cannot gain us any advantage. You have been doing your best to help us out of the war, but an attack with disease will incite America to the point where no negotiation will ever be possible. It will reverse whatever progress we might have made. Many of us who know about this attack plan do not want it to go through, but we are powerless to stop it. Any . . . injudicious action could cause the army to replay the antigovernment 2-26 revolt of 1937."

"It seems that it took an abominable scheme like this to bring cooperation between the army and navy."

"That," Hatano said heavily, "is correct. You will recall that when Admiral Yamamoto was killed, the Chinese communists announced that he committed suicide because of a feud between the army and navy. The Chinese tried to drive a finger into a wound that had always been there. But this biological attack plan forced them into a joint effort. The navy has the submarine and General Ishii and his doctors have the germs and the experience in handling them."

"And you think that I can help in preventing it?"

"We are desperate and have no other hope. We would like to stop the submarine before it leaves Japan. But in the absence of prevention, if the sub were sunk at sea as just another war casualty, its real nature need never be known. Biological weapons would not only remove all chance of any peace negotiation, it would open the way to our greatest fears—being overrun by the communists."

"About Japan's biological warfare activities," I asked. "How much else is known in Japan?"

"Imperial Household members tell of films and photographs viewed in company with the emperor—demonstrations of human experiments."

"Experiments?"

"Unit 731 sends photographs and movie films regularly. I can tell you that the emperor does not approve of these, but they are viewed in his presence. As you know, many members of the imperial family are in the army and navy. The finances for army activities in China are handled by Takeda-no-Miya, the emperor's cousin. That is a huge amount of money, but he is enormously wealthy and accustomed to large sums. He watches some of the experiments, perhaps to see how the money is being used, perhaps for his curiosity. People are exposed to poison gases. Others are infected with plague, anthrax, venereal disease. They are recorded until their deaths, then dissected. The films show everything. Prince Konoe has become sick several times viewing them."

"And what else do these films show?"

"Frostbite. People taken out into the cold, water poured over their limbs, then different methods of treatment. Special refrigeration machines freeze the limbs to minus seventy degrees centigrade. At that temperature, the skin and muscles fall off. Each person is shown on the films up until gangrene spreads through the body. I tell you all this in the strictest confidence because we who have no control over the military must find some way to stop this attack. Americans will tolerate what we do to the Chinese to some extent—they are a different country, a different race. But if this plan against an American city succeeds . . ."

"Do you know the time outline for this? The departure date?"

"It is still undecided, but we should know soon. I will inform you."

"One more question: Who is the ultimate authority in this plan?"

"General Umezu, Chief of Staff of the General Staff."

▪ ▪ ▪

In mid-March, Hatano brought me news that the I-400 was in a state of readiness for its mission. Aircraft-carrying submarines were considered a way to close the Panama Canal: a submerged approach, then a catapult launch of one or more light planes that could bomb a ship in the locks to block the canal, similar to Bywater's war.

I had to admire the engineering. The submarine's watertight hangar was at deck height below the conning tower and opened onto a catapult. The planes were specially designed; with the I-400, two planes were stowed in collapsed condition, the third had removable wings that stowed flat against the bulkhead. Each wing on Number 1 and 2 planes was locked in flight position with a single bolt; when the bolt is removed, the leading edge of the wing drops ninety degrees and the wings fold back against the fuse-lage like a bird asleep. The bolts were coated with luminous paint for night operations. The planes' engines were warmed up before surfacing by circu-lating heated oil through the engine blocks.

After the submarine surfaced and the hangar opened, two planes could be launched in four minutes; the third required another eleven minutes to fix the wing in place. In ordinary operation, when the planes returned to the submarine they were hoisted aboard with a crane. Part of the prepara-tion time for the planes was fixing the pontoons; on a suicide mission, these would not be necessary, shrinking the time from surfacing to launch. No conceivable American defense system could react with speed enough to prevent the sleeping birds from taking flight.

Convoys were still removing loads of charred bodies from the Sumida River when Hatano advised that the departure date for the submarine was decided: the twenty-sixth of that month. I tried reaching General Umezu, but downed telephone lines and the schedule of a general who held a top post made contact impossible. I finally reached him on the twenty-third.

"I know you're busy, but I was hoping you would have time for a quick sip of aquavit."

"It is tight now, but what about after the twenty-sixth?"

"I realize you have a tremendous responsibility, but I really would like to see you before. A very quick sip even."

I imagined and hoped that Umezu's work on the attack would be fin-ished before the sub's departure. From there, it would be in the hands of the submarine commander and crew. I waited for his answer. "Day after tomorrow?" he asked.

"Thank you. I'm looking forward to it."

We sat in the same room that Yamamoto and I had often used for poker. We discussed the war, the destruction of Tokyo, the threat of Soviet communism in the coming years. . . . Then I opened my hand.

"May I talk with you about Operation PX?"

"What is that?" he asked.

"Forgive me for overstepping my bounds, but these times press one into a direct course."

"I cannot say that such a thing exists," Umezu said, "but I would like to know where you heard that."

"I am a neutral and a guest in this country. The identity of that person is as secure with me as is any other knowledge of the operation. But would you permit me to offer you my personal view? You do not have to comment on it."

He agreed. I spoke two sentences. We sipped a final cup of aquavit and parted.

The next day, March twenty-sixth, General Umezu stepped into the secret tactical room where the plan was born. The officers present expected him to offer a *Banzai* shout as a sendoff. He did not: "If bacteriological warfare is conducted, it will grow from the dimension of war between Japan and America to an endless battle of humanity against bacteria. Japan will earn the derision of the world. *Cancel the attack!*"

Hatano brought me the news. Ishii and the others raged in protest. The submarine and pathogenic weapons were ready. The Special Attack crew was ready. Umezu's order held, but I knew that he was one against many, that the cancellation would hold only while he was alive and Umezu was as liable for assassination as anyone else. Or, he could have been struck by a sudden illness of human origin that could not be distinguished from one of natural origin. Operation PX—or its successor plan—was only one heartbeat away from activation. I asked myself where the next attempt would be. Hatano brought the answer.

▪ 51 ▪
The Police Close In

"Japan is expecting an Allied landing on Okinawa," Hatano told me, "and Ishii wants to launch a biological attack against them."

"How does he plan on doing this?"

"We can only assume from what facts we know, but the branch of the Ishii organization in Peking, Unit 1855, has been getting ready to move some of its men south to Okinawa. That unit was working heavily in bubonic plague, and they have large stocks of infected fleas—*PX*. We believe they may also use poison gas."

"Okinawa is made up of cities and villages. How can biological weapons be used without danger to the population?"

"But there are no Japanese living there."

"By that you mean . . ."

"There are only Okinawans."

I recalled the signs on schools, NO DOGS OR OKINAWANS ALLOWED! To Japanese nourished by an education of divine origins, Okinawa was spiritually far from Japan, yet army officers drilled Okinawans into loyalty to the Japanese emperor and sacrifice for the country of Japan. Now the plan was to make all Okinawa a defense line of pestilence insulated by sea from the main islands.

"We expected the Allies to land in May," Hatano told me, "and on April first, while I was still waiting for word on the southern movement of biological weapons from China, the Allies landed."

It was the most massive armada in naval history: more than forty aircraft carriers, eighteen battleships, two hundred destroyers, hundreds of support ships, and more than one hundred eighty thousand assault troops.

The incompatible conditions of preservation of the emperor and Allied insistence on unconditional surrender formed a backdrop to a war that de-
generated into mass civilian cremations. The bacteria in biological-warfare
laboratories needed execution, not the Japanese population, and the
Okinawa landing augured greater efficiency in turning the archipelago into
an open-air crematorium. Compromise was needed somewhere. I encoded
another message to Stockholm, hoping that I would not create added resistance in officialdom: sociological insight by their ministers is not always
appreciated by governments.

> *3 April 1945*
>
> 1. *Unconditional surrender according to Japanese comprehension
>   is unthinkable. The concept is tantamount to dishonor and
>   could lead to disastrous consequences on the part of the
>   Japanese people. On the other hand, acceptable conditions
>   could possibly be arrived at in the course of negotiations.
>   People realize that the war cannot be won, but consider it im-
>   possible for Japan to be defeated and occupied. The Japanese
>   soldier does not let himself be taken prisoner, nor would the
>   people submit to this. They would fight on to the last, as they did
>   on Attu and more recently on Iwo Jima.*
>
> 2. *A change in the Japanese constitution is beyond expectation.
>   The Japanese emperor is inviolable. But the democratization of
>   the emperor's position, similar to the situation in England,
>   could be considered. The Institute of Pacific Relations in
>   America recently demanded that the imperial family abdicate.
>   This has aroused anxieties in Japan and would surely be an ob-
>   stacle to every attempt for peace. Even in those circles in Japan
>   which are striving for peace, the abovementioned principles are
>   clear and definite.*

Koiso was on retired status, his army mind camouflaged in civilian
clothes while he served as prime minister. This kept him out of military affairs. With the landing on Okinawa, he put himself up for reinstatement in a
move to regain a seat on military councils. Both army and navy officers of

the supreme command were in rare agreement and refused his activation. The day after my message went out—April 4, Yamamoto's birthday; he would have been sixty-one years old—Koiso and his cabinet resigned in protest. General Tojo stomped from his garden to demand that any incoming prime minister must be dedicated to continuing the war, not giving up. He ran into opposition with Prince Konoe. "The people," Konoe stated, "are losing faith in the military and want a change in civilian government."

"Wrong!" Tojo shouted, while Okinawans died with bamboo spears in their hands or by suicide. "The situation now makes the military all the more important." Yamamoto's speech echoed again from the walls of Harvard: "Only a fool does not know when to quit. . . ."

The next day, the emperor requested my friend of many years, Admiral Suzuki, to become premier and to form a new cabinet. The admiral protested his age, his hearing disability, his lack of experience, then accepted under insistence by the emperor—just as American radar found a fleet of ten Japanese ships headed for Okinawa to reinforce the fighting. The repaired, seventy-two-thousand-ton *Yamato* was among them.

The fleet had set out from the Inland Sea on the afternoon of April 6. As the ships maneuvered into cruising formation, two B-29s spotted them and attempted high-altitude bombing. The main damage was the sighting itself. The fleet was in Osumi Channel at the southern end of Kyushu at 0200 next morning when the crews detected two enemy subs. The ships were being watched from above and below, but they continued southerly on a zigzag course. They were in the American-devised ring formation with the *Yamato* at the center, carrying more than one thousand shells that she could throw thirty-five nautical miles and that could penetrate sixteen inches of steel plate. A surfaced American submarine tracked the fleet from a distance of ten thousand meters through the dark, early morning hours. The sky brightened and was speckled with American planes, most of them going for the high-card *Yamato*. In three hours, fifteen or more torpedoes hit her below the water line and bombs struck from above. The ship was pushed to the limit of sustainability; she bellowed one massive explosion, her innards burst, and she settled below the surface, her nine 180-ton guns adding their mute weight to snuggle the ship deeper into the ocean floor. The rest of the ten-ship fleet sank with her in this final tragedy of the Imperial Japanese Navy, one day after the fleet left port. It was April 7: *4+7=11*.

The Japanese are fond of word plays, and a pun circulated in Japan that the pyramids of Egypt, the tomb of Emperor Nintoku in Osaka, and the battleship *Yamato* are the three *baka* of the world. This can be understood as both "three great tombs" and "three great follies." The pyramids are the world's tallest tombs, the tomb of Nintoku in Osaka is the largest in area, and the *Yamato* was the third great tomb/folly. The battleship, with its sister ship the *Musashi*, ended its life completing the dark pun, with the full-load displacement of seventy-two thousand tons setting a record for battleships that will last a long time — if not forever — as further proof of a folly nobody wants to repeat.

The Japanese army's poor assessment of the time of the expected Okinawa landing placed the world another step away from Akira's prediction. The microscopic warriors were still being readied in China when the Okinawa battle ended. Okinawans never knew how close they came to annihilation for the sake of the mainland; I can only guess where the microorganisms would have gone from there.

Okinawans were not the only recipients of less-than-equal consideration. American leaders arranged for the British Commonwealth's task force of fifty-seven vessels to attack a small archipelago between Formosa and Okinawa. They were open to sustained attack from Japanese air bases on Formosa and mainland China, but it was well away from the news cameras where they could not steal the stage from America.

I felt like a human version of the *Yamato* and *Musashi*: impressive credentials and a weighty title that accomplished nothing. I was prepared to accept risk, but I was not prepared for the barrier of inertia from my own foreign minister, or the obstacle to peace in the ostensible metaphysical properties of the ostensible head of the Japanese nation. I was also trying diplomatic and other channels at my disposal to find out where Butterfly was being held, but I was no more successful with this; I kept getting puffy answers and apologies.

All Tokyo knew the air raids would increase, and our legation was transferring records and equipment to our house in Karuizawa. I made several trips there during the move, where I again met William Vories, the missionary and architect of my legation. Now, he was a Japanese citizen.

"I became naturalized in January 1941," he told me, "and I moved here after the war with America started."

"It seems safer than anywhere else in Japan. But, with your country of birth now Japan's enemy . . ." I had thought that a neutral was a strange position. Mr. Vories's was in an astonishing cultural crossweave.

"Mister Minister," he said warmly, "I came to Japan in 1905, during the Russo-Japanese War. I first came as a Christian missionary, but I also began designing buildings and then established a company for selling Mentholatum. I'm sure you've seen my products."

"Your products and your advertisements, in magazines and newspapers. I've used it myself for little cuts and such."

"It's also in the first aid kits of Japanese soldiers and sailors."

"Well, it is not a weapon so I imagine you don't feel bad about that."

"Oh, I contributed something more; I donated a Shôki to the Japanese army."

"Shôki?" I remarked. "I have one at my legation. I bought it in Kyoto and had the caretaker mount it to the wall, to protect us of course, and your architectural creation."

"No," he laughed. "This is a military plane. It took its name from the Chinese protector, and its function is similar: It's an interceptor. It mounts a 1,450-horsepower Double-banked, fourteen-cylinder radial engine. It's designed to climb fast and meet intruders."

That was understandable—with an implausible tinge. "So the flying Shôki is designed to protect the homeland against attacking planes, correct?" I replied.

"Yes. It's a defensive plane."

"In which case, I imagine the authorities are not hostile toward you."

"There is no room for compassion in the secret police. The Japanese government uses my products for their soldiers and sailors, they thanked me for the Shôki, my wife is even a member of Japanese aristocracy—we've been married since 1919. But the police harass me here. I am still suspected of being a spy, though what I would glean in Karuizawa is an interesting question. But I will persevere."

■ ■ ■

There was only a skeleton staff remaining at the legation in Tokyo. When I returned there, one of the members told me that a messenger arrived, apparently in great haste, that he was waiting for me, and that he would speak only with me personally and only in private. I thought that it might be an assassination mission resulting from the discovery of my peace attempts. I greeted the man, and the two of us walked to my office—I gave him the courtesy of walking ahead of me. There was a small Buddhist statue on a shelf just inside the entrance of my office and as we walked through the door, instead of going behind my desk I remained near the entrance and close to the messenger. If he used a knife, distance would be to my advantage. If he used a gun, distance would be to his advantage. Without knowing, better to assume a gun and stay close. If he pulled out a weapon, and I was fast enough, I could smash his wrist or his head with the statue. I stayed aware of any movement in his hands. As soon as I closed the door, he bowed politely.

"I bring you a very urgent message from my superior, Mr. Shigemitsu. Do you know Mr. Yoshida Shigeru?"

"Yoshida? Yes. He retired from the diplomatic service—back in 1939, I believe."

"He had to, because the government hated him for opposing the alliance with Germany. He tried to stop us from going to war in 1941, and earlier this year he helped prepare a statement to the emperor that the war was lost for Japan and we should seek a way out."

"And what have I to do with Yoshida?"

"He is about to be arrested by the *kempeitai*."

"Yoshida?"

"And his associates also. For suspected peace movements. My superior thinks it would be wise for you to leave Tokyo. Leave Japan. This is a verbal message only. If I were caught with a written note . . ."

"I have been trying to locate a lady acquaintance who is being detained by the police. I want to find her before I leave."

"If you wait, you may never leave. You can do nothing for her; if you are arrested, surely not. As the war turns worse, the authorities become more severe. It is their only weapon. Japanese and foreigners are arrested on the slightest suspicion of opposing the war, and you may not have much time. You must have your government radio the foreign ministry immediately and recall you to Sweden. My superior strongly urges you."

"I understand."

"He also feels it will give you a chance to work on the peace plan from Sweden. He will explain when you pay your formal respects before leaving. A recall may be your only way to avoid arrest."

I encoded an emergency message to Stockholm that my life was in danger and requested my immediate recall. I knew that at least this message would draw an answer from my foreign minister if for no other reason than he could be held responsible if he did not respond and something happened to me.

He moved at admirable and unusual speed. The next day, April 10, Shigemitsu's office officially advised me that his ministry had received a request for me to be provided with transportation to return to Sweden by way of the Trans-Siberian Railway. I went to his office for the official farewell, and in confidence he asked me to continue working in Stockholm with the Japanese ambassador there.

I tried to convince myself that I could still put my one deed into motion before departing Tokyo. Again, I tried to crawl through the gelatinous backpressure in Stockholm, knowing that even under the mounting police pressure in Tokyo, I could not exceed the limits of my office without danger of negating the entire effort.

11 April 1945
I have maintained contact with my political associate and have repeatedly discussed the peace problem. He has influential friends in the government and has recently informed the foreign minister about our discussions. When I went to visit Shigemitsu to bid farewell, we had an hour-long talk along similar lines. When Shigemitsu asked me for my honest opinion, I did not hide the fact that I saw the war lost for Japan and that continuing it would result only in the devastation of land and people without altering the outcome. The foreign minister offered no objection to this. He stressed the emperor's love for peace, and mentioned his own wish to end the war, with the offers

which would be inevitable. The foreign minister asked me to make suggestions for an acceptable solution. He asked me to work with Ambassador Okamoto in Stockholm toward this purpose after I arrive home. A representative for Shigemitsu visited me today and stated that this was urgent and that Okamoto had been informed concerning the contents of our talks. On the basis of this, Okamoto will soon take up the subject with the Japanese emperor.

If only the Japanese could be made to realize that there is no metaphysical attribute to the occupant of their throne. Peace proponents were ready to give up the lands for which the country went to war: the oil, rubber, tin, rice . . . even the riches of Manchuria. The Japanese people might stand personal humiliation—apology occupies a generous portion of daily conversation—but the emperor, and that invisible thread of some semi-defined sacred value that was supposed to bind each Japanese individual to the emperor, this and only this must remain undefiled. The emperor was the only point on which the Japanese begged "understanding."

An incredulous attempt to gain this understanding came on April 12. The voice on Radio Tokyo, broadcasting under the eyes of army watchmen from a bomb-shelter studio deep in the ground, announced the death of the American president in somber, respectful tones. Then came solemn music, and Premier Suzuki's compliments to the enemy leader. The bombing of Japanese cities was a surrealistic backdrop to this childlike, unvoiced entreaty for reciprocal compassion: We'll respect your president; you respect our emperor. I could see the struggle to *wish* America into a peace offer that would originate—or appear to originate—from their side.

My recall came through, but no response to my peace attempts. The next day I tried again, wondering with each word I transmitted whether the Japanese police were outside the door.

13 April 1945

Following is my clarification of my previous coded message.

The Japanese persons concerned wish for peace, but a negotiated peace and without themselves taking the initiative, which could be interpreted as a sign of weakness. The Japanese need help in starting negotiations and they would like to see some suggestions made from the Swedish side, or at least have us draw some information out from the counterparties.

The Japanese persons concerned wish for understanding from Great Britain and from certain other nations.

There were criticisms within Japanese circles that Japan should never have gone to war against Great Britain, and that the decision to do so was unnecessary and unwise. The Japanese are counting on the war weariness of the British, and there is anxiety over the rapid advances in the Pacific by the United States, leaving England behind.

On the other hand, the Japanese are prepared to continue to the bitter end if acceptable conditions do not present themselves. My conclusions as stated in my coded message of April third were fully confirmed during my talks with Shigemitsu. The Japanese realize that the Americans must undoubtedly feel how important and precious a decisive victory could be, but that even the U.S. might prefer discussing conditions that would not humiliate the strong Japanese nationalistic feelings, rather than continue the bloodshed.

Would the flea that launches Akira's prediction be released because there was not yet enough "official nature" to the peace movement? Japan had been dealt another diplomatic blow. About a week earlier the Soviets announced that they would not renew the Neutrality Pact with Japan—the one signed with Matsuoka when he dreamed of a four-nation coalition against the United States and Britain. It would still be in effect, for those who place value on such agreements, but it was clear that with Germany about to collapse the Soviets were preparing to feast on the spoils of Japan. Seven hours later, I sent another message, commenting on the resignation of the Koiso Cabinet.

13 April 1945
The long-awaited government crisis occurred, arising out of the serious situation. The reason for the change is to create a stronger government, and the change probably means a step closer to peace. The navy, which had actually wished for peace, is represented by four

*admirals. The seventy-nine-year-old prime minister, who is very
close to the emperor, can be considered a proponent of peace.*

I followed this up with two more messages the same day.

*April 13
The breaking of the Russo-Japanese Neutrality Pact had been expected. The Japanese felt that scheduling the San Francisco
Conference for April 25 was timed to coincide with this breaking of
the treaty.*

    *There is some impatience toward Shigemitsu because nothing
has been done to alleviate the growing anxiety. The former foreign
minister, Togo, who was once ambassador to Moscow and is considered an expert on the Soviets, has been offered the position of foreign minister.*

My departure from Tokyo was less than one day away when I had a
sudden visit from a Japanese diplomat I had known for years, the former
minister to Finland.

"I wish to assure you that the new foreign minister, Mr. Togo, strongly
desires you to keep working from Sweden to negotiate a peace for Japan,"
he told me.

"Then you are involved in the peace plot also?"

"I am. But we are powerless. We need help from outside."

"I understand. I will contact Ambassador Okamoto as soon as I reach
Stockholm."

I tried clinging to whatever hypothetical progress I had made by advising my foreign minister of the latest developments.

*April 13
Togo has accepted the post of foreign minister, and just before my
departure a representative from the Ministry of Foreign Affairs advised me that Togo has been informed of my discussions with
Shigemitsu and that the change in cabinet does not include a change
in opinion of the subjects discussed by us.*

Togo had been ambassador to Moscow, and was appointed foreign minister in the Tojo cabinet in October 1941. The Ministry of Foreign Affairs wanted authority in ruling Japanese occupied territories. General Tojo and his associates had stripped the ministry's power, kept civilian authority out, and brought all control under the army. In 1942 Togo quit his post in protest. Now he became foreign minister again on the eve of my departure from Japan.

Togo came from an unusual background considering Japan's race-fueled attacks on Asians. He was descended from Korean potters brought to Japan in the sixteenth century, following Hideyoshi's attempt to conquer the peninsula. I wondered how he felt about Japan's annexation of Korea over the past thirty-five years, and the disdain that Koreans were subjected to in their own country under the Japanese boot. Did he still feel a thread of contact with his heritage? I believe I saw the answer emerge in the final days of World War II. But on my last wartime day in Tokyo, I tried to evaluate how his assumed Soviet expertise would affect our peace plans. As I did, a reply to my messages arrived. I decoded it. It was disheartening:

Stockholm, 14 April 1945
Sweden takes no initiative, either on the proposal or the information.

I collected all the messages on my peace attempts to destroy them. I could not help counting them: they totaled eleven. In my failure to end the war, I had been dealt Yamamoto's omen number.

▪ 52 ▪
Through a Needle's Eye:
A Solution to the Emperor Problem

I could feel the eyes of the secret police. I had several hours left in Tokyo, and my foreign minister had not taken the first step from his desk to push my efforts forward. Germany was about to collapse, so the danger of reprisal was watering down to zero; just the inertia of sloth kept him from moving. I participated in this war through silence on the Pearl Harbor attack. Later, I learned of Japan's biological war plans, and I was successful only in bringing about the cancellation of—or at least a delay in—an attack on the American mainland. I still wanted to save some from the fate of what Napoleon called "cannon fodder." And, bring an end to Japan's biological warfare potential. I fooled myself into thinking that if I had direct voice communication with Stockholm I would launch a tirade at my foreign minister to get him to move, but I know that the diplomat in me would have filtered out all communications except as outlined in official government instructions to me and my kind. It was not all self-protection: *The value of any probability varies with the temperament of the player*, and I knew the temperament of officialdom. Excessive departure from ministerial docility could cancel the entire effort and bring my reassignment as a diplomatic janitor.

I pictured poison gas victims foaming at the mouth, anthrax victims sprouting black pustules, Chinese fleeing from plague-blackened families and neighbors and carrying the disease to wherever they thought they were escaping, and the same thing happening in London, Paris, New York . . . all the fashion and financial centers of the world. During my last moments in

Tokyo, I tried a final gambit to solve the problem of one man standing between the terms of East and West.

Mariners in the days of wind-driven vessels said that a good captain could sail his ship through the eye of a needle. I saw a needle-eye's breadth of compromise between Western demands for unconditional surrender and Japan's one condition of protecting the emperor. I called on Shigemitsu again in an attempt to navigate the needle's eye.

"There can be no concealing Japan's hopeless situation in this war," Shigemitsu said bluntly. That statement could send him to jail if the wrong person heard it, yet the fact was long since apparent. Island bases for B-29s made flights to Japan airborne strolls for them as they razed and cremated the nation. The bombers came like swarms of monsters, each pregnant with more than eight thousand kilograms of packaged fire in its belly. Life for the Japanese was running from air attacks and gathering corpses. "The military clique dragged us into this war," Shigemitsu went on, "and now it is for us diplomats and civilian politicians to get us out. Most of the members of the diplomatic service were against the war from the beginning, and during my years as ambassador to London I never dreamed that my country would be at war with the British. It was unthinkable then; it is still unbelievable now. Please do what you can as soon as you reach Stockholm."

"Once there, I will be more free to press this forward."

"The only point," Shigemitsu said again, "that I feel the Westerners still do not understand is the position of the emperor. He is a peace-loving man who has always been against the war, but he is helpless in the hands of the military. He is a constitutional monarch; if he were a supreme ruler, there would have been no war."

That opened the way for me to take the first tack for the needle's eye. As a sailing mate, I chose the Japanese government's choice of a symbol to lead the nation in war, the fourteenth-century warrior Kusunoki Masashige. This paragon of pure loyalty to the emperor rode his horse into school textbooks and citizen-oriented publicity with no mention that Kusunoki's defeat resulted in an illegitimate Northern Court taking the imperial throne, which made the present emperor a descendant of that false imperial line. In 1336, just before taking his own life at the battle site, Kusunoki swore, "Man is born seven times; I shall avenge this traitor." But the false line of emperors started by the "traitor" has held the throne for six centuries—with intermingling of other bloodlines that are also not spoken of. Thus, when Japanese official-dom enlisted one of Kusunoki's rebirths to generate emperor loyalty, they assigned him to serve an emperor of the false line. This is where I saw a chance for floating—like Sweden between Axis and Allies—between de-throning the emperor and maintaining him.

"Any Japanese with even the slightest knowledge of history," I told Shigemitsu, "realizes that your emperors have been kicked about by the military for centuries."

"Yes," he agreed, "that is taught to some extent in schools."

"And I find it amazing how a single historical figure like Kusunoki Masashige can inspire loyalty, and even deeds."

"Yes, but don't all countries have their hero figures?"

"Of course. But few countries can claim that their people of the past serve as so strong a unifier and inspirer of action. Today, people can rally around living leaders. But one from ancient history . . ." I hauled in and sailed closer to the wind with a question—a way of broaching an opinion without stating it. "Hasn't anyone in the field of education—or in poli-tics—brought up the problem that Kusunoki died for the emperor of a dif-ferent line?"

"Problem? It is not a problem."

"But every Japanese knows that much of history. . . . they realize that this emperor is descended from the Northern Court. And that Kusunoki died defending the legitimate Southern Court."

"Nobody thinks that far into the matter."

"Then perhaps . . . just perhaps . . . we may have a solution. May I give you my thoughts in confidence?"

Shigemitsu shifted his weight and invited me to continue.

"I realize the spiritual meaning of the emperor, that he is more than a mere monarch. But I also feel that the person of the emperor and the em-peror system are two concepts that have been viewed as one." He strained his exhausted face into a quizzical look. I went on. "I will be as frank as you have been with me. You have been trying to save Japan from further de-struction, and you want to do it without jeopardizing the emperor. If you were offered the opportunity to end the war with the safety and position of the present emperor guaranteed, with the provision that there would be no successors, no emperor system after he dies or steps down of his own will— would you accept?"

It seemed that his remaining energy went into thinking about this future for Japan. "If the war continues," I went on, "you told me yourself that the worst, and highly probable end would come with the Soviets taking their hammer and sickle to the imperial throne."

"That is our fear, yes."

"And even if the Allies might strike a bargain for the emperor's safety—in exchange for Soviet occupation of part of Japan, for instance, the Soviets would fight for ending the imperial system. I think we all know them well enough to expect that."

He nodded agreement.

"Now, you and the others who want to end the war will have to sort out one thing: the difference between the present emperor and the emperor system." He watched silently; I continued like a salesman who does not give his potential customer time to think in another direction. "I see a possibility to save both. But it will take . . . cooperation, shall we say? . . . from the present emperor."

I felt a luff in the sail, but I kept going. "I think that if someone created . . . re-created the historical break in the imperial line, and tied it in with a solution, there is a way to satisfy both the Japanese desire and the Allies' demands."

"By this you mean . . ."

"The present emperor would request to step down from the throne. He could cite fatigue, health reasons . . . details can be worked out. He would retire to somewhere in Japan distant from Tokyo—just as other emperors have retired throughout history. Perhaps by the sea, where he could follow his interest in marine biology. You have a centuries-old custom of cloistered emperors in Japan, and an emperor in retirement sometimes gained more political leverage than when he was on the throne. The Japanese would be free to interpret the emperor's retirement this way." Shigemitsu was expressionless but still on board. I kept the helm. "The delicate part is that to the Japanese, it should appear a retirement to a detached villa; to the Allies, the emperor's retirement should be somewhere distant enough from Tokyo to make it seem—to the Allies only, of course—like semi-exile, and tantamount to dethronement."

"And the imperial throne. . . ?"

"The purpose of this plan is to protect it while ending the war. As you know, the family line of the Southern Court still exists. The descendants of Emperor Godaigo—the emperor for whom Kusunoki died—live in a rural area near Nagoya under the family name Kumazawa."

"You seem well versed in our history," Shigemitsu said with the closest approach to a smile that he managed so far.

"An advantage of being assigned to a post with little effort required, other than avoiding bombs, of course. I researched for this proposal, and from what I uncovered in newspapers and books the descendants of Kusunoki's Emperor Godaigo have come forth to make their claim to the throne."

"Yes, they gave us some trouble. One appeal was made toward the latter part of the shogunate era, in the eighteenth century. And again, the following century, after the Meiji Restoration, a member of the Kumazawa family requested an imperial audience."

"At first his request was granted," I continued. "But in the end it was decided that since he posed as a rival to Emperor Meiji, in the name of social tranquility it would be best if the audience were not granted."

"You have researched this well, I see," Shigemitsu commented.

"I did. For a reason. Then in 1910 the Imperial Household Ministry investigated Kumazawa's claim and judged it legitimate. And only a few years ago the grandson of the man who was refused an audience took up the cause again, but the secret police and military authorities convinced him to stop creating disturbances. I remember when it made a small noise in the news, then vanished."

"Yes," Shigemitsu said, "it was another occurrence of the claim."

"I believe the emperor system can be saved by using the Kumazawa claimant to the throne." Again, a forced surge of energy by Shigemitsu to react; this time he looked as if he were eating something not quite palatable. He accepted me because of my efforts in negotiating a peace; I had a captive audience—and license to sail closer to the imperial throne than ordinarily possible. I was in the eye of the needle.

"My idea is to protect the imperial throne by restoring the Southern Court. The present emperor and the Imperial Household Ministry would issue a statement that the emperor is retiring and a descendant of the emperor for whom Kusunoki Masashige gave his life was being placed on the throne. Japan would keep *an* emperor and—very important—the emperor system. For the Allies, the present emperor's retirement would create what I call a "tantamount dethronement"—that is only our term for it; it would not be publicized that way and there would be no image of punishment in Japan."

Shigemitsu remained silent. I continued.

"We would also be enlisting Kusunoki. The Japanese are accustomed to honoring him, so he can remain as a familiar symbol to bridge the gap between emperors as we repair a six-century break in the imperial family line. Also, remember there will be an occupation of Japan afterwards."

"We expect that. There is no doubt of it."

"And there will be action taken to punish those responsible for Japan's aggression—that was made clear in the Cairo Declaration at the end of 1943. Since the newly installed emperor would not be the one who was on the throne before or during the war, he will be free of charges of aggression. And he would also be free to work cooperatively with the Allies to restore Japan. Right now we can only hope that the Allied authorities may agree, but I would like to pursue it."

"Before I say whether I agree or not, do you think it could be presented with success to the authorities of the Western countries?"

"I cannot promise, and it will be difficult. I have spent almost a decade in Japan, and I've studied the language and history. I have interest in areas where others will not have patience. I can only try."

"And the present emperor would be protected?"

"We can only request that the "tantamount dethronement" satisfy the Allies. It will give Japan a bargaining point. From a historical view, with emperors forced to abdicate by one warlord after the other, this would be the kindest, most benevolent way the throne has ever been yielded. It would be announced as imperial will. And we could invoke the wisdom of the emperor's grandfather, Emperor Meiji, to help you and the emperor point the blame at the military—the military you told me was the cause of Japan's present situation."

"Emperor Meiji?" he asked.

"You remember around the turn of the century there was the attempt by an anti-imperial activist to assassinate Emperor Meiji. Or rather, an alleged attempt—but that's not the point. After it was announced, Emperor Meiji's reaction was somewhat unique."

"Yes," Shigemitsu recalled, "he issued a poem. Emperor Meiji was known for his poetry composition."

I recited the poem:

> *If there is transgression, punish me, oh heavenly deities*
> *for the people are children born of my body.*

Shigemitsu gave a fatigued twinkle at my recitation. I continued. "If we can get the Allies to agree to this plan, the emperor can recite that poem of his grandfather and the Japanese will cry with compassion—that was the intention of the poem in the first place, I believe. The Japanese people are becoming more disillusioned by the military and will gladly shift any blame for the war in that direction and away from the emperor. You know how the Japanese dislike rhetoric and accusations. The emperor could never indulge in this. Self-blame is the way to gain sympathy; I don't have to tell you that."

Shigemitsu was not against the idea, that was all I could be sure of as I went on. "Talks of international war crimes trials in Germany and Japan are gaining momentum. Neutrals like myself will probably be asked to testify, and I can say honestly that I saw the military takeover of the government—and the imperial throne—as the origin of Japan's aggression. Against this, I offer one way of handling the position of the emperor. It will be far better than what the Soviets have in mind."

Shigemitsu thought silently for a while. "There seems a chance," he said, "but I see no way that anyone here could bring it up to the emperor. And if the army found out about this, we could place the life of the emperor in peril. There is one change, though. From last month, we peace-seeking members in the cabinet have achieved a balance of power with the pro-war faction. In fact, the possibility of sending out peace feelers is now coming under open discussion in cabinet meetings. This has never happened before. There is only one point of agreement between our faction and the military fanatics, and that is protection of the emperor. Nobody will ever voice a different opinion. Nobody!"

"But nobody has considered something like I propose."

"It sounds feasible, but who could bring this to the emperor?"

The Japanese way of suggesting the next step is to throw the problem at the other person. "If you think it might work," I pressed gently, "how do you think we could go about it?"

"The only way would be for the suggestion to come from some neutral source—from your government for example. If it comes from an Allied country it will be seen as a demand or an ultimatum. I pray that you pursue this when you arrive home."

Shigemitsu rose against the leverage of his artificial leg and the burden of my proposal. He saw me off at the door. I turned for a final bow and farewell and left him standing at the doorway, cane in his left hand clamped against his hip and angled out from his artificial leg, his back straight, his slender body in its port list.

· 53 ·

Home Through Enemy Territory

The Siberian Railway gave me too much time to review my failures and to recall that bacteria were thriving in secret Japanese war laboratories. *Just this much can kill half a small city,* Akira had told me. Fifty times *this much* could be carried in a knapsack.

We pulled into a station. The locals were drunk and drinking, dancing, singing, and kissing: *Germany had surrendered.* It was an ominous joy with visions of Soviet entry into the German void. On the train and at the stopovers I was given all the courtesies of a neutral foreign representative, but I felt like a mouse dangled by the tail under Stalin's mustache. And I felt him—Stalin means *steel*—being pulled toward the magnetic iron ore of Kiruna. I feared that the defeat of Germany would prove worse for Sweden than the state of neutral war we had existed in under her.

I was imprisoned in motion on the train. I reviewed.

In 1943, Soviet economist Eugene Varga issued a plan for the postwar Soviet takeover of Germany. He wanted to reduce the country to a bare-subsistence, soup-kitchen society and remove all means of employment to channel the entire German working class into the Communist Party.

In September the following year at the Second Quebec Conference, Henry Morgenthau Jr. presented the basics of the plan under his own name. Churchill was "aghast," I believe the British press said, at the proposed cruelty toward the German people, but three billion dollars of Lend Lease bought his vote. Even the American president's associates opposed "the Carthaginian attitude of Treasury."

That was all I knew of the Morgenthau Plan when I was counting rail clicks across Siberia in 1945. In the postwar years—1953—evidence surfaced that Harry Dexter White had borrowed Varga's scheme and drafted the Morgenthau Plan. Back when I was crossing Siberia, I knew only enough of it to fear for all of Europe.

And the dread of Ishii's biological-warfare ambitions were on the rails with me. The Japanese army in China was being drained southward, leaving Manchuria open to a Soviet invasion. If the Soviets gained control of the microorganisms, they would be able to use them at the bear's other head to create enough sickness for an easy takeover. Or, the pathogens would escape human control and produce a grander reenactment of the great European plagues of the past.

The train was fueled by vodka; the Soviet crew and passengers were in a continuous victory toast. I hoped that the engineer was sober enough to keep us on the rails. The smell of napalmed flesh and the fourteenth-century poem followed me on the line:

> *Human life is fifty years*
> *I feel shame for being deedless*

In Stockholm, I approached my foreign minister with my plan for peace. I was trying to build a historical labyrinth with bifurcating paths that arrived at two interpretations of a single phenomenon. It was laborious trying to re-create the Japanese psyche for him by starting back in the dim light of history and mythology. He was impatient. His golf bag seemed impatient. He finally suggested that we have lunch with the American representative to Sweden, Herschel Johnson. We did, and I gave them a comprehensive view of conditions in Japan and the situation with the emperor. "The time is overripe for a peace offer," I said. "There are still stone-headed Japanese army fanatics who see the mass immolation of the race as the only honorable way out. But an offer from America would stir argument among leaders and might bring about a cease-fire and discussions."

Mr. Johnson listened politely. As far as I know, he never communicated anything to Washington. He did say that he would include a note about our "interesting meeting" in a letter to his mother. I believe he did that.

I contacted the Japanese ambassador, Okamoto Suemasa. I told him of the mission entrusted to me, and how the new foreign minister was informed of my efforts and expected me to continue. I told him of my imperial compromise plan. He listened, then became animated.

"Why hasn't it been thought of before?" he remarked. "Sometimes an outsider can look at our culture and see things from a different aspect. I think it might work, but I could never initiate such an idea. It would stop with the army leaders; I would probably be recalled, and . . ."

He sat quiet for a few moments, then dropped his voice much as Shigemitsu did when I spoke with him about it—and offered a similar comment. "No Japanese could attempt the first approach. And it could not look like a demand from the Allies; the initiation would have to appear to come from the emperor himself. Otherwise the Japanese government would not move. I will contact my foreign minister."

Okamoto dispatched a coded message to Togo—and we waited. Two weeks passed, and finally the answer came: "Since this was handled by the former foreign minister, it will require investigation. This will take some time, after which you will be informed."

It was a heavy blow to us. We understood. Togo was trying to use his expertise—alleged—in Soviet affairs to make a grandstand play with Moscow. Something blinded him to the reality that the Soviets were more likely looking for a slice of Japan than ready to offer a helping hand. It was only the previous month that Moscow advised she would not renew the Neutrality Pact with Japan. It was still in effect, just as the German-Soviet pact was when the Nazis launched their attack. There was still no way for Japan to know that at Yalta, Roosevelt had invited Stalin to join in the war and take Japan's northern territories, but there was sufficient evidence that the Soviets were placing themselves in an antagonistic position. The Japanese foreign minister's mind was either paralyzed while Tokyo burned, or something even stranger, yet more realistic could be in his mind. It was a chilling conjecture that would have to wait. For the moment, the wall had followed me to Sweden. I decided to take one more step than I probably should have, and looked up the American representative again. If America asked Sweden to make the proposal so that the origin was neutral and not Allied, my foreign minister might move. I would have to start with Japanese history—the emperor—about the contents of my messages from Tokyo.

There was too much ground to cover in one sitting. I met the American representative several times and tried laying out the same plan I gave Shigemitsu and Okamoto, as seen from the Allies' side. With the Japanese I stressed the apparent nondethronement of the emperor; with the American minister, I tried to convince him of the opposite.

"It would be tantamount to dethroning the emperor," I explained.

"You know how the Allies are calling for unconditional surrender," he reminded me.

"Yes, I know. But I feel that a narrow area of compromise—the breadth of a needle's eye—exists."

"If the emperor is removed and replaced by another one," the American argued, "it will still leave an emperor in place, and that will not satisfy those who want to see an end to the emperor and the system itself. Some people see the institution of the emperor as highly dangerous, and something that will have to be done away with."

The discussion was repeated and reworded, stirred, and turned day after day. Okamoto was still unable to pull any response from his foreign minister in Tokyo. Summer came and in July Togo officially crawled to the Soviets and asked them to mediate a peace. They stalled Togo the same way he stalled Okamoto and me to prevent our making progress with Britain or America. I questioned whether any man with his knowledge of foreign affairs could be so innocent of Russian history and Soviet intentions. I did not think so. I can only suspect that he had an emotional reversion to his Korean heritage and wanted to see the invader and occupier of his ancestors' land smashed, imperial throne and all. The Soviets were like buzzards circling over Japan; Foreign Minister Togo was either a duck with a mouthful of scallions flapping to Moscow or, in the end, a loyal Korean.

"I heard that you were back in Sweden. Come over for dinner one evening and I promise you an unusual dish." It was Gunnar Fredriksson, an old colleague.

"Not Japanese cooking?" I joked.

"No, and not Swedish, either. Nor Russian! But you can thank the Soviets for it."

His son, Bo, a strapping man of about thirty, was chef for the evening and he dished out a stew rich in beef, lamb, pork, and kidney.

"This is a dish for weddings and the like from northern Karjala in Finland," Bo said. "But do not fear that we're trying to end your bachelorhood. Consider it a welcome home party. You remember after Hitler and Stalin agreed to carve up Poland, Germany moved into the Balkan countries and the Soviets forced Estonia, Lithuania, and Latvia to accept Soviet garrisons on their land."

"Yes, and then the Soviets demanded the same of Finland and they refused. That was in 1939; I was in Tokyo then."

"Right. Finnish delegates went to Moscow the beginning of November 1939 to negotiate. The *suggestion* from the Russians—*they* called it that but they threatened like gangsters—was that the Finns would be wise to sign a pact peacefully. You know the rest: two hundred thousand Finns and volunteers from Sweden, Norway, and Denmark ran to the Finnish-Russian border and faced about a million Russians. I was one. The Russians invaded but they underestimated things like Finnish terrain—forests, lakes—and a unified Scandinavian determination to save us from the Russians. And, the best ski fighters in the world."

He took a moment to work the ladle in the pot and serve the stew, then he continued. "We knew that if the Soviets took Finland it would be the end of Scandinavia. We were camouflaged in white: white suits, white hoods, even our skis were white, and we beat the Russians back in guerrilla warfare on skis. We had light arms and we covered ground fast. We hid and attacked before the Russians knew what was happening. And I don't have to remind you how good we Scandinavians are in cross-country skiing."

"Yes," I agreed, "we had to ski in order to learn how to read and write. For many of us it was our transportation to school."

"Then in 1940," Bo continued, "on the first of February, fourteen Russian divisions hit a fifteen-kilometer stretch of our defensive line. Soviet airplanes broke up our counterattacks, and the first week of March the Finnish government realized it was hopeless and was forced to cede large tracts of land to the Soviets. The Karjala region was lost in the deal, and a lot of Finns evacuated the area. Most went to other parts of Finland, but some came here to Sweden—and they brought the recipe for Karjalan stew with them. Once in a while they'd have a party for us, to thank us again for saving most of the country. And they made their stew."

"And that's how you learned to make it?"

"As my father said, you can thank the Russians for tonight's recipe. And if they cause trouble again, we still have our skis and guns."

"I brought a few bottles of very good aquavit with me," I said. "I propose a toast to keeping the Soviets away from Scandinavia in the postwar era."

"I'll drink to that," Gunnar said. "But first I must tell you that in a sense, you're too late. The Soviets already moved into Denmark."

"The Soviets? In Denmark? I heard nothing of that."

"You were crossing Siberia when it happened, and the whole thing was minor and brief. The Russians moved into the island of Bornholm as soon as the Germans surrendered. You know that for all their evils, the German armed forces were extremely well disciplined."

"Yes," I commented, recalling how the German navy resisted getting pulled into President Roosevelt's *undeclared war in the Atlantic*. "We can credit them with that."

"Toward the end of the European war the Soviets shelled the major town on the island. They *said* it was to hasten the defeat of Germany, but the Soviets wanted Bornholm for obvious reasons."

"Obvious. It sits in an extremely strategic position in the Baltic Sea. Of course it was ours until about three hundred years ago"

"It was, but it's been Danish ever since, and the German army occupied it with the rest of Denmark. As soon as Germany surrendered, the Russians moved in to take its place. And knowing the Russians, they would use it as a foothold for further expansion."

"Of course. The island lies northeast of the German-Polish border, and with a land area of almost six hundred square kilometers it could be made into a formidable base; they could control ship movements in the Baltic Sea. And just thirty-five kilometers off the southern tip of Sweden. Not very comfortable. But what happened?"

"Well, the Soviet detachment landed on the main town on the island and the mayor called the commander of the Danish armed forces in Copenhagen to ask what to do. 'We'll welcome them,' the commander said. 'I'll send a group of my officers to throw them a party.' The mayor was puzzled, of course. Well, the commander rounded up the hardest drinking officers he could find. I cannot guarantee that they were all really officers, but they were dressed that way. So this contingent of Danes handpicked for alcohol tolerance arrived on Bornholm with smiles and cases of aquavit. They held a party, and they proposed a toast to welcome the Soviets to Danish territory. And after that, another toast . . . and another . . ."

"The tactic is clear."

"It worked as planned. The Danes kept filling glasses and one by one the Soviets began dropping. Their commander left the party hauled away by two of his subordinates."

"Don't tell me that ended the occupation."

"Except for the hangovers. The next day, a very pale and shaky commander had just enough energy to be embarrassed when he met the very spry Danes. After that, he led his hungover and shamed Soviet soldiers to the dock and they all sailed away from Bornholm. I would guess that they added vociferous decorations to the Baltic Sea on their way to the continent."

"In which case," I said, "I suggest that we also offer a toast to the Danish drinking team."

We did.

▪ 54 ▪
Return to Tokyo

I was a neutral, contributory aggressor to the war through silence. I had failed to prevent Pearl Harbor because I wanted America in the fight against the Axis. Later, I failed to negotiate an end to the war. The Japanese minister and I waited in Stockholm for Tokyo's permission to go ahead while I had lunch after lunch with the American minister, with the British representative. We talked of history and, now, of napalm and fire and people turned to charcoal in the streets and boiled in the Sumida River, while sandwiches toasted and coffee percolated. In August, Japan surrendered.

> *Human life is fifty years*
> *I feel shame for being deedless . . .*

I counted the months since Pearl Harbor: forty-four—the double-four of Yamamoto's birthday.

Where was Butterfly? *Was she alive?* I wanted to find her—or find out what happened to her. With the end of the war, the staff started moving from Karuizawa back to Tokyo, the city that had been my home for almost a decade. I had not spent that much of my adult life in any other single location. I was about to request that my ministry send me to Tokyo immediately to help reorganize the legation, when the foreign minister called me to his office for the same purpose. "Your experience will be valuable to the legation and to the Swedish business community in the postwar era," he told me, and I left Stockholm with images of a decade in Japan spinning and crashing in my mind: spies in kimono, Yamamoto, Akira, Shigemitsu,

Konoe, Tojo—and Mariko, laughing with her beautiful teeth, pulling her hair back after we made love, her sculpted shoulders, erotic back . . .

Tokyo was a black desert. Survivors lived in spaces defined by accumulated debris. Our legation car had been preserved in Karuizawa, and the driver wove us through the paper and scrap slums, an unnoticed fly buzzing through a human garbage heap. Most landmarks were gone, and I would have had trouble finding the legation on my own. It seemed that some gigantic hand had scraped the earth flat, burned it, then let a few fireproof storehouses and iron safes drop through its fingers as it carried the city away. Tokyo was at the vanguard of the Buddhist End of the Law.

Some sturdier buildings survived the incendiaries. My legation was one of them; the American architect proved himself in a hideous test of his skill. Shôki was still mounted on the outside wall, blackened like everything else around. Two Japanese-style homes on the same property as the legation had fueled the fires. The garden was burned level and was only part of the flat, charred surroundings, where mounds of black roof tiles rose from black cinders like a moribund, magnified version of a Zen garden. I found the metal remains of my punching bags; the frame of the heavy bag lay on a pile of the bag's sand innards, disgorged when its cover burned away.

The legation staff had cleaned the soot from the rooms and furniture, and boarded over broken windows; glass was scarce. Mrs. Saito was there with the staff. I wanted to I ask her what she knew about Butterfly, but I could not do so without first asking about her sons.

"Thank goodness, they survived," she said. "The younger was working in a war factory that was bombed. But fortunately B-29s had trouble hitting their targets—until the firebombing started. He is living in the country with his grandparents. The older, Shuichi . . ." She stopped and caught her breath. "He's here in Tokyo."

"He's all right, then?"

"Disillusioned on one hand, excited on the other, but healthy. He had been drafted and sent for . . . pilot training."

"Pilot . . . ?"

"He was in the Special Attack Forces. I almost lost him, too. The war ended . . ."

I could see Fate's other option pass through her mind. "And what is he doing now," I asked.

"He wants to stay in Tokyo. He's thrilled with the occupation. He wants to go to technical training school and become an engineer of some sort. He learned about machinery when he worked in the factories, and he has automobiles and motors in the mind. But about Mariko," Mrs. Saito volunteered, "I tried to inquire before we left Tokyo, but the police told me nothing. Telephone lines were down when we left, and I haven't had any better luck since we moved back."

Two weeks after the emperor's high-pitched voice announced the end of the war, the first planes bearing American troops landed at the Atsugi airfield. It was the evening of August 29, the same number totaling eleven as the designation of the Superfortresses that brought death fires to Japan—and carried the final bombs to Hiroshima and Nagasaki. My legation received information that the same August 29 marked another step in Japan's decline, with the initial postsurrender policy for Japan radioed from Washington to MacArthur. Yamamoto's omen number rose again the next day when the general himself flew into Atsugi and posed with his strange pipe as a prelude to taking charge of the nation. It was August 30: *8+3+0=11.*

The surrender ceremony for the war that began with Yamamoto's Pearl Harbor attack plan was scheduled for the next day on board the battleship *Missouri*. A typhoon blew into the islands and delayed Japan's official bowing down until a date with Yamamoto's omen number rising, September 2: *9+2=11.*

I boarded a small craft with other guests and correspondents, and we headed out to the battleship anchored near the southern extreme of the huge inlet known as Tokyo Bay. The *Missouri*'s mute sixteen-inch guns were angled up at forty-five degrees. We pulled alongside and climbed to the veranda deck, forward of the bridge on the starboard side. It was around seven in the morning, and crewmen were arranging the table for the signing. An officer approached me. "Sir, diplomatic guests are invited to witness the ceremony from over this way."

"Sweden did not fight the war," I said with self-disgust as I recalled how neutral Swedish iron in Nazi weapons punished Americans in the European fighting.

"But we do have relations with Sweden, sir."

Press-affiliated people were climbing aloft to the next higher deck for a bird's-eye view. Two men I had been in close contact with were the signatories for Japan: Shigemitsu was foreign minister again in the first cabinet formed right after the war and was going to sign for the government of Japan. General Umezu was given the job of signing away the Japanese armed forces. I did not want to watch them from a platform of officialdom. I thanked the officer and joined the correspondents on the deck above. I found a place on a forward gun turret, about seven meters above the veranda deck, and—as I was informed by an American correspondent who had done his homework and had his feet hanging over the edge of the gun turret—just above where one hundred or so high-ranking American officers would line up.

"They call this Tokyo Bay," I said to him, "but I always thought of it as a small ocean."

"It sure serves a huge area before it even gets to Tokyo," he agreed. "Yokosuka and Yokohama on the west, Chiba on the east ... according to the information I received, right now we're fifty-six kilometers from Tokyo—or what used to be Tokyo."

"How many?" I checked again.

"Fifty-six."

In Japan, striking a person on the head with a folded fan was considered the most demeaning form of insult. The revolt of Akechi Mitsuhide against his warlord in the sixteenth-century was partially triggered by this act. Of all choices in this monstrous bay, the *Missouri* chose a relatively microscopic spot that represented Yamamoto's name to drop anchor for the surrender ceremony.

The sun was shining over the bay, but Mount Fuji to the west was obscured as if it had pulled a cloud blanket over its head to hide from the scene below. We had a lot of time on the gun turret, and many of the observers had come through heavy action as war correspondents. They were discussing their experiences, and some of them were interested in hearing my stories of Tokyo from the belly side of B-29s. As we talked, I asked them, "Did any of you uncover anything about Japan's biological warfare?"

"Biological warfare? Did they use that?"

"Against Chinese armies, and on villages, probably in tests."

"We knew they used poison gas," the American offered, "but nothing else." He had come through the war with the United States forces and was setting up the first postwar Tokyo office for his news agency. "How big an operation was it?" he asked.

"I don't know for sure, but they had laboratories throughout China. It was organized by a General Ishii, who . . ."

"Ishii. . . ?"

"You've heard of him?"

"In a sense. The name only. I was in the first line of press corps to land in Japan. We were at Atsugi a few days ago when troops from the U.S. Eleventh Airborne Division landed. . . ."

"The . . . *Eleventh* Airborne Division?"

"That's right. And the next day when MacArthur flew in, just about the first thing he said—after he stopped for his publicity shots at the gangway—was, 'Where is General Ishii?'"

"And, was there an answer?"

"That's all there was to it as far as I know. From then, there were all sorts of handshakes and salutes, but none of us knew anything about this Ishii fellow. He's not on my list of Japanese officers."

Below us, the foreign delegations started coming on deck: Chinese, Australians, Canadians, French, Dutch, New Zealanders . . . and the Soviets. Their incursion into Japanese-occupied China on August 8, in violation of the pact still in effect with Japan, gave them the right to be part of the ceremony. The Japanese Kwantung Army had been drained south to the war zone and Soviet troops advanced fast as the Japanese used their energy fleeing, not fighting. What did the Soviets gain from Unit 731? What happened to the potential to turn human populations into black-rot, silent, repeating land mines? How much of Japan's biological warfare knowledge was in the hands of the Soviet officers then on board the *Missouri*? These questions still invaded my mind as high-ranking Allied officers took their places behind the cloth-covered desk at the after end of the veranda deck.

The books for the signing were on the table. At 0850 a destroyer with the Japanese party aboard came alongside. Shigemitsu disembarked first, and I could see him as he appeared on the ship's stairway just below the veranda deck. He had his cane in his right hand and grasped the chain with his left as he worked his way up one step at a time. On deck, he took his cane in his left hand again and walked aft with his articulated gait. An American officer directed the party members to their positions with Shigemitsu and Umezu at the head of the delegation, facing aft and the cloth-covered table. Shigemitsu was in formal morning coat with striped pants, a wing-tip collar, and tall silk hat, Umezu in his army uniform. The Japanese delegation consisted of seven generals and admirals in uniform, and four civilians. I counted them—and counted again: eleven members in the Japanese surrender delegation.

After the ceremony, a quiet grumble from the skies to the south grew stronger and nearer, and a formation of B-29s roared overhead leading a flight of about one thousand Allied fighting planes. Most of them carried names of power or purpose: Superfortresses, Flying Fortresses, Hellcats, Avengers, Corsairs, Helldivers, Liberators . . . One type carried the name of an aviation hero: the B-25 Billy Mitchell, the man who built Yamamoto's faith in the ability of airplanes to sink battleships.

We returned by launch to Yokohama, and from there on to Tokyo.

Representatives of the Allied Powers drew up a list of Japanese to be arrested and held for standing trial as war criminals. The date to report for incarceration was nine days after the surrender ceremony: September 11. If Yamamoto were living, his omen-number would have been his day also. The internees were scheduled to take their places in the dock before the judges of the tribunal, one from each of the Allied nations: Australia, Canada, China, France, India, The Netherlands, New Zealand, The Philippines, The Soviet Union, The United Kingdom, The United States. The war that started with Yamamoto's attack plan brought the total Allied nations to his omen number eleven.

In the days following the surrender ceremony, I kept asking among the foreign press corps what they might know of Japan's biological warfare. Amazingly, some could not believe that Japan had the scientific ability for such a venture; preconceptions live long. But an Australian journalist, Wilbur Dennis, filled in pieces of the puzzle.

"I was on two different ships that were hit by *kamikaze* attacks," Dennis told me. "When I came to Japan, I decided to look up anything I could about those suicide pilots. Now, my parents were immigrants from Germany. Luckily, we changed our family name, but I learned a sort of household German as a kid, though with the war I kept quiet about it. I was snooping out stories in Japan when I heard that medical students were enlisted to work with Japanese doctors. And sometimes *kamikaze* pilots were drugged before being sent off."

"You mean it was not all love for the emperor?" I asked.

"That was part of the story I was after. I located a young Japanese medical student who was assisting in this. I wondered if he wasn't the one who charged up the pilots who hit the ships I was on," he said, with a journalist's attraction to irony. "Well," he continued, "Japanese medicine is based on German medicine, and German is somewhat familiar to medical students here, so that's how we managed to communicate. I got a story and asked him if he would work as my assistant and messenger, and with the shortage of work in Japan he was only too glad. Then the other day an American ship pulled into Yokohama. The *Sturgess*. There were some Americans arriving that I wanted to interview, some relationship with Australia during the war. We were on the dock when my Japanese assistant told me he recognized a face in the crowd. 'That man is famous in Japanese medical circles,' he told me. 'He's a specialist in microbiology and in blood.' Well, there was enough blood spent in this war, I told him. 'He's got a lot to study.' My assistant then said that this guy caused a commotion when he tried to obtain yellow-fever viruses from the Rockefeller Institute in New York back in the 1930s."

"Yellow-fever viruses?"

"It seems he had an introduction from the Japanese ambassador in Washington and said he wanted the viruses to develop a vaccine."

"And did he get them?"

"Actually, there was a pact in force then that prohibited sending pathogenic substances to Asia. On top of that, it was right after the Nanking bombing filled the newspapers, so there was a lot of bad feeling toward Japan then. The Rockefeller Institute refused him, but the story got into medical circles."

"Did you get his name?" I asked Dennis.

"Naito. Doctor something-or-other Naito. I can't pronounce some of these names. 'Naito' rhymes with 'my toe' so I remember that. The reason my assistant recognized him is because during the war, he went into the Japanese army and was in charge of the Army Medical Research Laboratory in Tokyo. He got a lot of publicity from that."

"You didn't speak with this Naito fellow, I take it."

"No, I was waiting for my own assignment to disembark. But I was inquisitive, of course, why this well-known medical researcher was at the dock. Always looking for stories, you know. As the passengers started disembarking, this fellow kept glancing at a photograph he had in his hand. Then he approached an American officer—the officer was wearing Medical Corps insignia—and says, 'Colonel Murray Sanders?' And the officer says 'Yes,' and this fellow then tells him, 'I am your interpreter.' And they left the dock. Now, when you say you're looking for anyone connected with Japanese military medicine, maybe this has something for you, I don't know."

When I heard *Army Medical Research Laboratory,* I recalled Akira's accounts of the specimens in his glass preservation jars, of Ishii's lectures at the Army Medical College. If Naito was a top man in the laboratory, he must have been important to Ishii.

I decided to look up my acquaintance from the forward gun turret of the *Missouri.* I found him in his bureau office inside the smoke-stained walls of one of the standing buildings in the city.

"I heard that a Colonel Murray Sanders arrived on the *Sturgess* the other day. Would you be able to tell me anything about him?"

A few days later, the American let me know what he had found. "I checked with some people I know, and this Sanders fellow is a microbiologist attached to Camp Detrick."

"And what is Camp Detrick?" I asked.

"It's in Maryland, not far from Washington. It belongs to the Chemical Warfare Service. It was set up during the war as a center for biological warfare research."

The American Eighth Army carried the major part of the Occupation. I am sure Yamamoto would have read it as a double-four.

On September 17 the Occupation's General Headquarters moved from Yokohama to the Dai Ichi Building in downtown Tokyo. I contacted headquarters and requested an appointment with General MacArthur; in a few days I was ushered into his office. Workmen were putting the finishing touches on a renovation. MacArthur extended his hand and apologized for the disorder.

"Bomb damage?" I asked.

"Not really," he answered, "just an improvement. This Chinese carpet you're standing on is a favorite of mine. I brought it with me and it was too large for the room, so I had them move the walls."

We sat down in the lingering aroma of paint and exchanged a few words on Japan, my life in Tokyo under the bombs, and the future.

"Apparently the Japanese are proving very cooperative to your administration," I told him.

"The Japanese are no great problem as far as cooperation is concerned. The Russians are kicking up the sands."

"It's obvious they came into the war at the end to grab part of Japan the way they grabbed part of Finland."

"And the way they grabbed northern Korea."

"Their czars were trying to gain control in that country for a hundred years and couldn't do it. They just made headway."

"They did," MacArthur said from his position deep in his big, worn leather chair. "And it forced us to make a deal. Japan and our troops stopped fighting August fourteenth, but the Soviets kept fighting and moving into the Korean peninsula. We had the job of accepting the surrender of Japanese forces, so we called on an expediency; we offered to divide Korea at the thirty-eighth parallel and give the Soviets responsibility for the northern zone. They weren't happy with it, but they concurred, and finally stopped fighting August thirty-first—reluctantly."

"If I know the Russians," I said, "they'll try to keep influence in the northern part of the country."

"That thirty-eighth parallel is just an arbitrary line—a temporary measure for accepting the surrender of Japanese forces. It has no basis in law. But here in Japan, we knew before the war ended that we'd be wrestling the Russian bear. I already had to kick their representative in the butt—in a manner of speaking. He came to me and said his government wanted to put troops on Japan's northern islands."

"That would not be the most comforting situation. They'd try to make Japan another Finland."

"It won't happen. I told the Russian, 'If you place any troops there I'll throw seventeen divisions in, decimate every Soviet soldier, and throw you in jail.' He took a long pause and said 'General, I believe you would.' That ended it."

"Actually, General, I came to tell you about a problem that may just be starting. I have some important information you should know." And I told him about Akira, and anthrax, plague, cholera, frostbite, the human experiments, and Japan's biological war development and tests. "I believe you know of a General Ishii . . ." I ventured.

"I'm not sure. Some of these Japanese names are so similar."

Did the general forget his first words on alighting at Atsugi?

"There are dangerous microorganisms, built up and collected over the years," I told him. "I think they should be secured as soon as possible. If they fell into the wrong hands, or if an accident happened . . . I think the known and suspected researchers should be taken into custody and questioned. Crimes such as mistreating or killing prisoners should be investigated, of course, but these are crimes in the past only; I'm talking about consequences for the future."

"I understand your concern, Mister Minister. Thank you for the information. I am sure you will not be discussing this with anyone, especially the Soviets or their associates."

"General, you already know the Scandinavia–Soviet relationship. You have no worry about that. The real worry is microscopic—and big enough to threaten the world."

It was obvious that General MacArthur's reaction did not match the reality of what I had told him, or what I had expected.

Some days later I received news that a Lieutenant Colonel Thomas Morrow had arrived in Tokyo to gather information for war crimes prosecution. If the supreme commander did not see the potential consequences of what I had learned from Akira, perhaps a man directly connected with information for the coming tribunal would react differently.

My staff located Colonel Morrow and I soon found myself giving him the same information.

"This is interesting," he responded. "The young man you mentioned, the glass craftsman. Can we reach him?"

"He's dead. Suicide. He was not made for the work."

"That's too bad. If called upon, would you either testify or offer an affidavit on the information he gave you?"

"Most certainly."

"Thank you. I will stay in touch."

On October 4, Mrs. Saito came running into my office without knocking. The door was open as it often was, but even before entering an open door she always knocked. This news eroded even her inbred manners: "Mister Minister! MacArthur's headquarters just issued a directive ordering the release of all prisoners in Japanese police custody for political reasons and thought crimes."

"That means that Mariko . . ."

"I think so. I hope so."

"How did this happen?"

"I don't know whether you saw the newspapers yesterday. A famous Japanese communist leader by the name of Miki died in prison. MacArthur realized it was police violence and ordered all political prisoners released by October tenth. He also ordered the repeal of thought-crimes laws and the so-called Peace Preservation Law that made it easy to arrest dissidents. The Japanese government has to issue a detailed report by the fifteenth explaining all action taken to comply with the directive. It's all happening fast. So if she is still in custody somewhere, she should be released in a few days—unless she was arrested on false charges. The Occupation authorities know that some people were, and they will get a retrial; others will be released soon."

On October tenth I picked up the Yomiuri *Shimbun* and saw an announcement that more than twelve hundred prisoners were being released. Of them, twenty-one were listed as political prisoners. "Probably members of the Communist Party," Mrs. Saito said. "The rest must have been in for religious reasons and other thought crimes." Prison officials scurried to meet the directive deadline, names were published, and we located the jail where Mariko was being held. The next morning Mrs. Saito and I got into the old legation car and drove to the prison. People were outside waiting for relatives and friends to be released. American soldiers were on guard.

"Diplomat," I said and presented my identification to the guard. "I believe there is a relative of one of my employees imprisoned here and I would appreciate it if you would allow me to enter."

He gave me a courteous salute and waved me through to the officer in charge, who was in a roomful of other American officers and Japanese interpreters. I repeated my lines, adding that I speak Japanese, and I was given permission and another salute.

The cells were on the second floor. The cell doors were open and prisoners were sitting and standing around waiting to go downstairs for clearance. I went from one open cell to the next through sobs of pain and joy, until I found her. I held out my hand; she did not take it. "I'm all right," she said, looking down. She was thin. Her face was bruised, her clothes hung ragged and torn, and her back was no longer straight, but sagged under the burden of her experience. One of her teeth was chipped. Her vitality was replaced—not just covered—with grime and bruises visible through the rents in her clothes. Her expression matched the glum surroundings. I wanted to call her name. Should it be Mariko? *Butterfly?* I could only stand there with a mouth full of dumbness. "I'm all right," she said again. Just as it always was with us, she spoke more than I did.

A Japanese man came through the corridors advising all persons to proceed to the main office on the ground floor for clearance. She looked at me and nodded, then joined the rest of the people heading for the stairway. As her shabbiness melted in with the rest, I noticed other women also bearing signs of beatings.

"They mistreated you," I half questioned, half stated the obvious. There were nods of assent, but those with strength were eager to tell. As a foreigner I represented one of their saviors.

"Kurotani. He was the one. He enjoyed beating prisoners. Beating us and starving us." Another joined. "Kurotani. He cursed the Communists, the Christians. He enjoyed cursing us so he could beat us up. Some never survived. They were executed by beatings."

"Kurotani?"

"Kurotani. And he did more than beat us."

"Meaning. . . ?"

There was no answer.

"And were you all here on thought crimes?" I asked.

"Those of us who were let out of the cells. A few prisoners were taken for further checking."

"Do you know Hiraoka? Mariko?"

"The schoolteacher . . . yes."

"And was it this Kurotani who beat her?"

"Kurotani. It was Kurotani."

"You are sure?"

"Of course. We could always hear him screaming at the women when he beat them. Scream and beat. Scream and beat. He screamed at her for not teaching correctly—for talking against the emperor in front of the children."

"She got angry at the army officer assigned to her school," one of the women offered. "She said the army had no place in education. She was arrested right after that. We heard Kurotani scream at her when he beat her. 'Why do you hate the Japanese army? Why do you not respect our divine emperor?'"

"I heard it, too," another offered. "We all did. Many times. He was angry because she dared talk back to an army officer in the school."

The prisoners moved forward through the corridor, a tightly packed mass of rags and pain. I walked along with them. "And where is he now?" I asked.

"An interpreter came through earlier and told the prison staff to wait in the office at the back end of the corridor. He should be in there." The prisoners disappeared down the stairs, eager for the freedom of the razed city beyond the walls. A Japanese orderly came and called to the prison personnel to report downstairs. Mariko's face came to me again and the name Kurotani sounded like a ritual drum. "*Kurotani! Kurotani!*"

I walked back through the corridor and stepped into one of the empty cells; they started moving down the corridor toward the stairs. I waited until the last had filed past me, then I called out, "Kurotani!"

One man stopped and turned.

"Kurotani! Over here please," I called again. He started back to where I stood inside the open cell doorway.

"Are you Kurotani?"

"Yes!"

His name pounded like the rhythm of an overhead punching bag: "*Kuro-tani-Kuro-tani-Kuro-tani* . . ." Maybe it was my own heartbeat with the volume turned up by adrenaline. I grabbed him by his shirt, spun him around from the corridor into the cell and against the rear wall. He was well fed; there seemed no shortage of food for the police. His head whiplashed into the wall and he was stunned. He also metamorphosed—into a punching bag. "Heavy bag!" something said as he bounced off the wall. I plunged my right into his gut, two fast-succession blows: *Heavy bag! Heavy bag!* And a quick left to the same hole in his gut: *Heavy bag!* He wheezed. "The backbone" I heard myself say. "The bag starts at the backbone." Punch to the gut—*Deeper! Deeper!*

The air was out of him and his body wanted to fall. I could not be so kind. I heard Mariko punching the overhead bag and laughing, and saw him punching her, giving pain and bruises to the flesh I worshiped. He started to collapse; I stopped him with an uppercut. "Don't fall down," I shouted to him. I grabbed him by the shirt and pinned him to the same wall he had just bounced off. "You gave it, now take it." His head turned into a punching bag. "Don't try to kill the bag," I used to tell Mariko. *That lesson was over*. A right cross and backhand knuckles on the return. In rhythm: THUD-THUD-THUD-THUD-THUD-THUD . . . Blood ran down his shirt and into his throat. His head drooped but he sputtered enough to show that he was conscious. "This is for some of the prisoners you did this to. Not all of them, just some. Behave yourself and you may not get the rest of your punishment. Understand?" He sputtered his answer.

I plunged my fist into his gut again and a Zen teaching flashed through my mind: "Become one with your opponent." An ugly thought rose, that this man I turned into a lump was a replacement for me—we were partners in making Butterfly suffer. His method was stupid, physical. Mine was clever evasion, denying her the companionship of minds she wanted.

I pulled him away from the wall and plastered him into it again with both hands; his head whiplashed back again and he sputtered some more. "*Understand?*"

A groan and a nod told me that he understood. I released him and stepped back. He collapsed.

There were fire buckets in the hallway and I used one to wash the blood from my hands. My knuckles were skinned and the water made them sting. It felt good. I wet my handkerchief and tried cleaning the blood from my clothes. The upper floor was empty, all prisoners and prison personnel were downstairs. I thought that by the time someone found Kurotani, most of the prisoners would have been released and the case would probably end up unanswered, that retribution had apparently been sought by one or more of his prisoners. I did not think that Kurotani would say anything. He would not want the rest of the punishment I promised him, and he did not know who I was. For all he knew, I had the authority to find him again. The Americans knew how prisoners were tortured and killed, and they would undoubtedly have more important work to do than to look for the perpetrator or perpetrators of justifiable retribution. Surely nobody would suspect a neutral diplomat.

I went downstairs and slid past the crowd and into the street where Mrs. Saito was waiting in the car. "She's being cleared now," I told her. "She was let out of the cell so apparently she was not jailed on a phony charge."

"What happened? Your clothes are wet."

"The plumbing in there is a mess." I got behind the wheel. "I feel strange calling for Mariko in a car when many of these people don't even have a home. Would you please wait for her in front of the prison? I'll pull the car around to the side of the building."

After a while, she came out. Mrs. Saito had the foresight to bring some clothes along and helped Mariko change into them in the back of the car. We drove to her home in Roppongi, hoping to find something still standing. U.S. military trucks and jeeps rumbled over the debris of Tokyo with only an occasional nonmilitary automobile visible. Ours moved ahead filled with silence.

We approached the home and Mariko said her first words since getting in the car: "*It's still there.*" Several hundred meters away, the neighborhood was now rows of roof tiles that hugged the ground, remains of houses that were demolished to make a firebreak for the prince's villa. Mariko's neighborhood was far enough from it to be spared, and there were no targets in her area of the city, since better-class neighborhoods like hers had no workshops. There was some damage to the house, some broken windows and a few missing roof tiles, but structurally it seemed sound.

We went to the front door. The lock had been broken. We took our shoes off even though it seemed pointless; the soot and dust were heavy on the *tatami* mats and the passageways, and removing our shoes soiled our stockings, but this is the way things were done. Inside, the house was almost empty of furniture, filled only with the remaining breath of incendiaries, of napalm, sticking to straw and wood. Mariko walked through the house in a dream state. She probably saw her mother again, in this room, in that room.

"I can help you clean it up," Mrs. Saito offered. Mariko just nodded, then added a *thank you*. We went upstairs, and there was still bedding in the closets, though it, too, had the incendiary stench. A man's voice called from the entrance below: "Hiraoka-san . . ."

We went downstairs. "Ah, I'm glad to see you're safe," he said.

"I'm all right," Mariko answered, slightly more enthusiastic than when she told me the same thing earlier.

"I saw the car and I thought it might be someone from your father's days. The neighborhood group pulled the furniture from empty houses and put it in fireproof warehouses. We carried what we could."

"Everything is safe then?" Mrs. Saito asked.

"I think it is," the neighbor said. "It should be in the storehouse of the Sakamoto family. A lot of the other neighbors' belongings are there also, piled on top of each other, so it may take a little work to sort it out. I'm sorry we did not have time to separate things more carefully."

"The houses that were closer to the imperial prince's estate were destroyed, weren't they?" Mariko asked the neighbor.

"All destroyed. The authorities wanted to make a big firebreak."

"I feel sorry for those people," Mariko answered. "And our homes were spared." She said it almost with a sense of guilt, forgetting her own price in the war—her mother, her imprisonment, her beatings.

"We can only be thankful for what was spared," Mrs. Saito told her. "I lost my husband, but my two sons are alive."

The neighbor did not seem to notice that Mariko was not the same. Most of the survivors of the air raids were underweight and weak looking; many were in a constantly stunned state. "The neighborhood association is helping people get their houses in shape. My grandchildren came back from the country and they help, too. We'll look for your furniture and carry it back."

"I'm all right," Mariko answered.

"First," Mrs. Saito said, "we've got to air out the house and bedding and clean at least one room upstairs."

"I'll help," I offered, feeling helpless and stupid knowing that Mariko did not want me to.

"If it's all right," Mrs. Saito offered, "I'll stay here a while and help her."

Autumn in Tokyo is good for drying out houses. The summer humidity is past and the air is crisp. I wanted to hold Butterfly again, and lick her wounds and let her sleep in my arms and melt away her suffering, but I felt that my presence was only salt in her wounds. I left, and later asked Mrs. Saito to visit Mariko often. I gave her food and money to take along. I wanted Mariko to have someone to talk with, and Mrs. Saito was good for that. Thanks to her I started finding out things about Butterfly.

"You know that she was arrested because she refused to make spies of her students," Mrs. Saito said. "And she refused to teach the myths of the Japanese emperor as history. Her Christian upbringing prevented her from doing so."

"Mariko? A *Christian?*"

"You didn't know?"

"She never spoke of it, except when Christians were arrested in Japan . . . . *Wait!* Yes! The first time we met. Our first conversation. She asked why Europe had such a long history of war when the people are all largely the same religion, Christian. I assumed she was looking at it from a historical viewpoint. She never mentioned a thing about being Christian."

"Mister Minister, you know that you cannot tell a card from the design on the back. The only thing I know about poker is what I heard from you, but I do not think players tell others all about the cards they are holding. Remember, most Japanese Christians are usually not evangelistic about it. Her ancestors became Christians generations ago and it simply continued quietly in the family, as with many Japanese Christians."

"But, did she keep her religion?"

"She lost faith in Christianity as any kind of guiding principle or hope for the world. 'Christianity and war spent too much time in partnership,' was the way she expressed it. That was the source of her disappointment in the religion."

"A Japanese viewpoint would back that up," I answered. "The first Christian influence in this country came in the sixteenth century with Francis Xavier and Portuguese guns. The next was in the nineteenth century from America with Commodore Perry and his warships. And now this war ended with a new type of bomb . . ."

"And MacArthur's plan to Christianize Japan," she concluded for me. "I'm sure you have heard of that."

"But, what did Christianity have to do with Mariko's life?"

"She surely did not think it could save the world. But as Japanese education became stronger in promoting emperorism, her Christian background revolted against it. She told the principal, 'I'll teach mythology as mythology, but I cannot deceive my children by telling them that Japan was made by heavenly deities, that the emperor is superhuman or a deity, or any other fantasy.' School principals would surely report that."

"She also screamed at the army officer assigned to her school."

"Did she tell you that?"

"Not directly . . ."

"Army officers were stationed at schools to make sure the teachers followed the curriculum. There was an officer's desk in the principal's office. My sons' schools had them, too; Mariko was brought to the police station several times and they tried to get her to change her mind. She refused. Finally, they put her into detention and then imprisoned her for thought crimes. They knew that she was Christian and that Christian ideas are a barrier to believing in the divinity of the emperor. So even though she was disappointed in her own religion, it was part of her crime."

"But why did she never tell me about that part of her?"

"Mister Minister always told us about the value of gambling in learning to read people. Perhaps something prevented you from doing it with her."

Mrs. Saito was reading *me*. I was so concerned with someone who might be standing behind my Butterfly that I lost all chance to speak *with* her. She wanted someone to talk with about her bitterness and frustration; she needed a casement for her tears, and I only diverted the flow.

Mrs. Saito continued: "A lot of stories are coming out now. Interrogation officers used to stare down dissenters to get them to change their mind. Some people were in detention simply because they were antiwar. Some were communists. Some were religious objectors. The officers called people by their number—not even a name—and stared. 'Why are you against your country? Why do you abandon your friends and relatives?' Some people could not stand up to the staring and turned their eyes away. Some recanted. Mariko tells me she always stared back. She said, 'Sometimes a teacher has to be strict with children, so I stared back at the interrogator the way I used to do with a naughty child. That upset them and I knew that I had won. Then all they could do was send me back to my cell.'"

"But they also beat her."

"As you surely know, torture was always simply a part of police procedure in Japan. Mariko was a single woman, and that made her unpatriotic. The officer screamed at her, 'Why didn't you marry and have children the way the government ordered? Are you a virgin or a slut? I'll check . . .'"

Mrs. Saito turned away for a moment as she recalled what happened after that. Then she continued. "Toward the end, people in Japan knew that the emperor was an obstacle to ending the war. One day when the guard tried to force her to bow to the emperor, she screamed, 'The emperor should commit suicide. Because of him Japanese keep dying.' That brought her the most cruel beating."

"And she didn't think of obeying just to avoid beatings?"

"That was not Mariko."

▪ 55 ▪

Ishii Eludes

In early November 1945 I read in a Japanese newspaper that Lieutenant General Ishii had been shot to death and a large funeral held in his village. He did not deserve to live, but he deserved something worse than death, and the world deserved his testimony. The technology, the pathogenic weapons, the medical data of the research units must still exist. But where?

A month later a man with a record for prosecuting gangsters in the United States came to Tokyo as President Truman's appointee to be chief prosecutor at the forthcoming International Military Tribunal for the Far East. His name was Joseph Keenan; I made an appointment and called on him. When I did, his breath reached me before his outstretched hand. He was flushed and not quite steady. He offered me a drink. I took Yamamoto's favorite, plain seltzer water.

"There is something I think you should know about Japan's activities in China," I said. He showed interest diluted with alcohol as I told him about Akira, what I knew of Unit 731, of plague and cholera tests on Chinese villages, of people forced into sexual acts to transmit venereal disease, then vivisected to study its progress.

"Do you have evidence on this?" Keenan asked.

"I have spoken to someone who worked at the unit."

"And where is this person?"

"Unfortunately, he died. He took his own life because of this . . ."

"I cannot accept testimony from a dead person. Look, Mister Minister. My job here in Tokyo is to find the men responsible for the war and try them and fry them. But we need evidence. You did not see these things yourself."

"But I spoke with the person; I can testify to what he told me and I can tell you where to find the main unit in Manchuria."

He closed the matter with a brusqueness that superseded his stupor: "Mister Minister, my assistants and I are gathering all the necessary information. The Allied nations who fought the war are perfectly capable of handling this without the help of neutrals."

"This goes beyond such considerations, sir. If these men and their microorganisms are not located, the consequences will reach beyond any national borders." I managed the last line as he walked—unsteadily—toward the door to push my exit. I realized later that his alcohol content had nothing to do with my unwelcome.

A few days later, there were reports that Prince Konoe killed himself after he was ordered to report to Sugamo Prison. His suicide note spoke of the irony of being forced to stand trial with his life for a war that he saw as an error in Japanese guidance, and one that he had attempted to end. And, that he could not bear being tried by the Americans with whom he had tried to work for a peaceful solution. Konoe's attempts to avert war were recorded in the messages to my ministry, and I expected these might help him at the trial. But I did not believe the words in his death note.

Back before Japan joined the Axis, I was at cards with Grand Chamberlain Suzuki when he told me, "Konoe is going into secret Imperial Diet sessions singing songs about a German victory in Europe. He wants to borrow the German mantle of power by pushing Japan into an alliance with the Nazis." Following this, Japan's incursion into French Indochina gave Washington reason to freeze Japanese assets and cut off oil exports. Konoe offered to meet Roosevelt to avert war. But again, Suzuki told a different story: "Konoe's praise for Germany grows more fevered, while he spouts hatred for Anglo-Saxons."

If Konoe did take his own life, I feel that he was pressed by his failed prediction of a German victory and his role in forcing Japan into the Axis—these viewed from a destroyed Japan. His death-note statement could have been what he *wanted* to believe, and taking his own life was a way of convincing himself and others that his written word was true. But, Konoe was extremely close to the emperor, and his potential testimony content would make the Occupation authorities much more comfortable if he did not appear in court. I find it hard to believe that he took his own life.

The United States armed forces came into Japan with jeeps, trucks, and their own newspaper, *Pacific Stars and Stripes.* On January 6, 1946, it carried a United Press article stating that Japanese medical officers in Manchuria had injected Chinese and American prisoners with the pathogens of bubonic plague in medical experiments. *The New York Times* ran a shortened version of the report, and sentiments of Japan as a "ghoul among nations" seethed. A week later, strange news broke: Ishii was alive and well in his village and his funeral had been a staged sham. I expected the Occupation forces to arrest him, but he was handled with great delicacy and kept under house arrest at his Tokyo home. Small articles emerged in the press that he and his associates were under questioning by Occupation authorities, and in late February, *Stars and Stripes* reported that Ishii and several associates were being interrogated by specialists in bacteriology from Camp Detrick and the War Department. Colonel Morrow was the only person I spoke with who seemed interested in the case. I went to see him again.

"I saw that information, too," he said, "and I already sent a memo to Keenan requesting that arrangements be made to investigate Ishii. I also advised him it's apparent that prohibited methods of war—poison gas and biological warfare—were used on orders from Tokyo; it was not possible for field commanders to use them on their own. I'll soon meet the American investigators and I'll let you know how things go."

The second week of March, Morrow came to my legation. "I spoke with the investigators who took up after Sanders," he said, "but I did not get much from them. I'm leaving for China in a few days to search for evidence on Japanese war crimes."

"In which case," I said, "I can give you one suggestion."

"That would be appreciated."

"About twenty-four kilometers on the railroad line south from Harbin, at a place called Ping Fan." I wrote the ideographs for him. "The Japanese pronunciation is *Heibo.* There is a huge, walled-in complex, the home of Unit 731." I told him what I had heard of the place from Akira; he took notes and thanked me.

The latter part of April, Morrow returned to Tokyo and contacted me again. "I found some damning evidence, in Nanking and in villages where Ishii's units were using captives—men, women, and children—for strange medical experiments. And I found Unit 731—or what is left of it—just where you said it would be."

"In the village of Ping Fan?"

"In what used to be a village. The people were chased out years ago to build the unit."

"And was it as I described? As I heard from the glassmaker?"

"It was before I got there, but most of the buildings have been destroyed. From stories I collected among the locals, dynamite wasn't enough; the Japanese had to call in their own bombers to help finish the job. That was just as the Russians crossed over into Manchuria."

"And the Chinese saw this?"

"The Chinese knew early that Japan had lost the war. They had an information network developed as part of the resistance to Japanese occupation. Some of the Chinese ventured near the unit for a peek. They knew that prisoners who went in there never came out, that smoke from the furnaces had the stench of human flesh. Then they saw the Japanese destroy the buildings. There is little if any equipment left."

"What happened to it? They couldn't take everything with them."

"The local people watched Japanese army trucks shuttle all night between the unit and the Sungari River. They were dumping things in it. I spoke through interpreters with people who hid near the river to see what they were dumping."

"And . . . ?"

"Glass jars. All sizes; some as high as a man."

"Specimen jars. Akira's works. Those specimens could have been body parts of the relatives of those people who were watching. Or the complete bodies. It would help the investigation if salvage divers could pull up some of those jars."

"It may be possible, I don't know."

"And there is nothing left at the unit?"

"Two huge smokestacks are still standing at the edge of the complex; the frostbite laboratory is still standing. Here are some photos I took of the site."

It was a huge track of demolished buildings. The ponderous smoke-stacks rose from a fragment of wall like some ominous sculpture that represented souls in agony striving for heaven.

"Local people led me to corpses that were recently burned and buried," Morrow went on, "obviously in a hurry. All this could put Ishii and his cohorts on the gallows. I'll present these findings to Keenan."

"You are doing an admirable job on this," I told him.

"Nothing outside the line of duty; this *is* my duty."

"I'm sure you know that Japanese newspapers carried the names and pictures of twenty-eight men to be arraigned on war crimes charges. But I hear that preparations are far behind schedule."

"There's confusion and personal clashes," Morrow said, "but the trial will definitely convene next month. Incidentally, there are changes in the arraignments that may interest you."

"Meaning. . . ?"

"I know that you were in contact with Foreign Minister Shigemitsu and General Umezu from years back. They were not on the original list for standing trial, but they will be added."

"Why is that? And why at this late date?"

"The Soviets. Their prosecuting team came to Tokyo and demanded it. Shigemitsu was once ambassador to the Soviet Union, and Umezu of course was Japan's highest-ranking officer."

"So the list will get longer by two men then."

"No. When MacArthur's office had the hall redesigned into a court-room, they provided just twenty-eight seats for defendants. So two men originally on the list were excused: a former prime minister and an army scoundrel who was behind the scenes in the 2-26 revolt."

The number twenty-eight stood out in relief. Was it Fate's way of pointing to Yamamoto as the twenty-ninth defendant in absentia through death?

"In any event," Morrow continued, "I want my findings from China in the chief prosecutor's hands before the trial starts."

"Their testimony," I reminded Morrow, "could tell us where the biological weapons are. What types, how much, how they have to be handled. It's not simply putting someone in jail. It could involve a major portion of humanity—perhaps more than just a major portion."

"I will see this through," Morrow reassured me.

The emperor's birthday, the twenty-ninth day of the fourth month, contained two of Yamamoto's omen numbers. On the emperor's birthday in 1946, prosecutors for the International Military Tribunal for the Far East lodged indictments against twenty-eight Class-A suspects of war crimes. Other Class-A suspects were not indicted but remained in custody. The court proceedings were open even to the Japanese public, and I arranged to view them through diplomatic channels. On May third the tribunal convened in the former Japan War College, another survivor in central Tokyo surrounded by burned debris. For months, carpenters had worked to convert the auditorium into a courtroom of stands and enclosures for defendants, observers, and reporters. The judges sat on a high platform that symbolized their status of supreme beings with the judgment of life or death over those mortals on trial down below. A battery of floodlights burned continuously and created the mood of a theatrical stage removed from reality, which, in a sense it was; until Nuremberg and now Tokyo, there had never been a precedent for bringing people to trial personally for the conduct of war. In the real world, war was not a war crime.

The twenty-eight defendants were asked one at a time to stand and plead guilty or not guilty. Tribunal President Sir William Webb called each name with a distorting accent that was embarrassing. The names and charges were repeated by interpreters, and I felt that without this service the defendants might not recognize their own names. I tolerated the tastelessness as each defendant pleaded not guilty to the charges.

I attended some of the early sessions and realized that this would be a long process, with all emotions planed down to a standardized drone as utterances passed back and forth through translation. Many of the foreign journalists in the city were eager to speak with this foreigner who had lived here through the war, especially once the story of my peace attempts had circulated somewhat. This gave me reverse access to what was happening in the trial as it moved ahead. In mid-August—just days after the first anniversary of the surrender—as I was looking for signs of Morrow's "damning evidence," I received another call from him: "I just want to let you know that I've been ordered back to the United States."

"But the trial looks like it's just begun. What about your findings on the human experiments and biological warfare in China?"

"I've turned over my reports to the chief prosecutor. My job here is finished. I could stay in Tokyo and receive pay for doing nothing, but I won't do that. I want to thank you for your cooperation and I suggest—I request—that we leave Keenan to handle the information as he sees fit."

There was a different tone in his voice. The "damning-evidence" passion of a few months earlier was gone. Now it was simply *leave Keenan to handle the information as he sees fit*. And I already knew that Keenan did not want to handle this information—gears were not meshing.

I had not seen Mariko since the day she left prison. One day Mrs. Saito came to tell me that Mariko would be moving to her father's family home in Saitama. "She wanted to get away from Tokyo, and now that the Occupation authorities have removed emperorism and militarism from the education system, she wants to start teaching again. They can rent out the house in Tokyo, so that will provide some income."

"They have swimming pools in Saitama, I hope."

"Of course. She'll be back in the water. It will do her good."

"I'd like to see her again. Would you ask her. . . ?"

"I already thought about that. I don't think . . . I think she would rather be by herself, with her family. . . ."

I understood. "Then help her move. Use the legation car and driver."

"It would be easier, true. And we'll have a chance to talk."

"I'll prepare something for you to take along—food and some other things that might be useful. Some wine, too."

Mrs. Saito left one morning in the legation car, and I waited for her return that evening.

"Mariko looks a lot better," she said, "but there is still a dark remnant of suffering inside her. You know how children wave at cars on the road. Just waving back was good treatment for her. It made her smile. She'll probably start teaching when the school year starts in April. That will be an emotional lift, and help the family financially, also."

"And her father is well?"

"Well and busy in the garden, growing food. They have some fruit trees, and the chickens are multiplying. Compared with Tokyo, the country is like heaven. It's almost as if there had been no war. The only reminders are the American army trucks that come around."

"Army trucks?"

"Yes. To collect rats. For research."

"I did hear that people in Saitama raised rats for the Japanese army during the war. . . ."

"The farmers there made money with rats. Japanese army trucks used to call for them. Now American army trucks come and pay more. They're conducting some kind of medical research in Tokyo."

The year 1946 ended with no hint of when the Tokyo Trial would end. In January 1947, I received a letter from a British attorney in London, George A. Furness, defense counsel at the military tribunal for former Foreign Minister Shigemitsu. Furness asked for my written testimony on the peace attempt and for Shigemitsu's part in it. "It is of course a matter of life and death for Mr. Shigemitsu, and I therefore most respectfully request as prompt a reply as possible," he wrote, advising that he would soon move to the War Crimes Section of the United States War Department in the Pentagon and from there to Tokyo. I outlined Shigemitsu's efforts to negotiate a peace through me in secret from the military leaders, and silently wished him luck. I also wondered what discussions were taking place in the Pentagon about Ishii. A short while later, one of the correspondents I was in touch with came with some news that pointed to an answer.

"The Russians practically dropped a bomb in court," he told me. "This Ishii fellow who faked his own death—the one you wanted me to keep an eye out for? Soviet prosecutors put in a request that he be brought to trial together with some other Japanese officers, for alleged human experimentation and biological warfare."

"And. . . ?"

"After the waves quieted down, Keenan just swept it under the rug. He wouldn't listen to talk of biological warfare or human experimentation. It seems like something a prosecutor would salivate over, but . . . I don't understand."

Neither did I—*at first!* Keenan, Webb, MacArthur, Morrow—they all avoided a major issue that the tribunal was supposed to pursue: crimes against humanity. As Yamamoto had said in respect to something else, *A game with so many enigmas is phony somewhere.*

As the enigmas became illuminated, George Furness arrived in Tokyo. "I've been conferring with Mr. Shigemitsu to prepare his case," he said, "and he told me of your plan to have Kumazawa replace the present emperor. Have you heard that someone from the Kumazawa family has come forward again?"

"Yes, some of it was in the news. He has a small following here, and he also made an appeal to President Truman. Kumazawa said that he never declared war on anyone and he should take the throne in the name of peace and replace the spurious Northern Dynasty. I wondered if the president really understood that."

"Shigemitsu told me that Kumazawa's claim is exactly what your plan was based on. It's regrettable that you could not put it into effect."

"And do you think Kumazawa will get anywhere with this move?"

"I think that now it could be dangerous for him," Furness answered. "The Occupation forces and the Japanese have the emperor they want. It's a bad time to rock the boat."

It was at this point I had my first insight into the days leading up to Pearl Harbor from inside the White House: Henry Stimson's diary was published and I obtained a copy from America. I remember the chill I felt when my eyes fell on the entry for November 25. As the Japanese task force was just hours away from standing out to sea, the entire meeting in the White House was occupied with the president's question of "how we should maneuver the Japanese into the position of firing the first shot without allowing too much danger to ourselves."

Yamamoto's comment echoed again: *There is only one thing worse than being caught like a sitting duck. . . .*

▪ 56 ▪
A Visit to Sugamo Prison

I found myself adding numbers once more when the Tokyo War Crimes Trial ended in 1948. It was April 16: *4+1+6=11*. The judges retired and the world waited for the verdicts.

"Who planted the cosmos in the garden?" I asked Mrs. Saito.

"One of the new ladies on the staff. She is fond of them."

"Apparently a lot of Japanese are. You too?"

"I remember them from my childhood."

"And you can call them *cosmos* now."

She smiled slightly, as she always did, with a touch of lingering sorrow. "Ah, you remember when we could not?"

"I remember."

"The silly prohibition of foreign words was the least of our problems back then," she said.

"How are your sons doing?"

"The younger is still with his grandparents; the older, Shuichi, is working at the American base. He's saving money for his education. He wants to study mechanical engineering."

"He'd be about twenty-two years old now. I'd like to invite him for lunch one day. I'd be interested in talking with him."

Shuichi arrived in the Japanese manner: with a present. His was a box of dried persimmons, neatly packed, from his grandfather's home in the country. Also according to Japanese custom, he apologized for it being such a humble gift.

"Years ago," I told him, "a Portuguese missionary, Luis Frois, gave the warlord Oda Nobunaga a present of an alarm clock. This was the sixteenth century, remember. In appreciation, Nobunaga gave Frois a box of dried persimmons from his province. Frois did not consider it a gift of lower value than his clock. He wrote in his diary that apparently the Japanese place a high value on persimmons. I agree with Frois."

"I didn't know that," he responded.

"Perhaps because your education was cut short."

"It was. First I was sent to work in a factory, then I was drafted."

"And, you were being trained as a pilot?"

"If you could call that pilot training. We were taught how to take off and dive; they never taught us how to land. They taught us to put the plane into a fifteen-degree dive, but on the actual flight we were told to dive at forty-five degrees and go into the ship's stack. At forty-five degrees and carrying a bomb, the plane can't be pulled out of a dive that steep, so that was only for the last flight. In practice it was fifteen degrees. That's not pilot's training."

He reflected a moment, then went on. "I saw my friends go on one-way missions and I resisted. Secretly, of course. I pretended to be a slow learner; I faked determination."

"But I thought that the Special Attack Forces were volunteers."

"Schoolteachers kept telling us that the greatest fulfillment in life was to die for the country and emperor. I think it was like hypnosis because that really became the ambition for a lot of Japanese boys. They had this vision that we'll all meet again in Yasukuni Shrine. But not all of us. I never wanted to die a *kamikaze*."

"Then how did you end up in the corps?"

"One day the commanding officer lined us up with the roster in his hands and called for volunteers for the Special Attack Forces. Then after a second or two, he said, 'All men volunteers,' and marked all our names. There was no escape from it. A lot of us were scared. Later, I saw my buddies climb into their planes for their one-way mission and they were shaking from fear. The officers brought schoolgirls to wave goodbye to the fliers when they took off. It was all a scheme to stimulate the minds to crash into the enemy. And to help they were given a drink of sacred *sake* before leaving; a gift from the emperor, they were told."

"I wish the war could have ended sooner, to save your friends, too. But I'm glad that you never had to drink the sacred *sake*."

He smiled slightly at that. "I tried. When the war ended, some people broke down and cried—maybe some because Japan lost. With us, it was this tremendous pressure taken off our heads: *We wouldn't be sent out on a suicide mission.* So some of us asked if we could have a sip of *sake,* but the officer said it wasn't for us. He said we might get reckless. We said we've had alcohol before, and he said this was different; it contained a drug to make people lose their fear."

"And what other methods did they use?"

"I learned that for about three days before takeoff, the boys were forced to stay awake, to get the adrenaline flowing. And they were injected with drugs. Sometimes an officer warned the pilot, 'I'm going to follow you in another plane; if you turn back, I'll shoot you down.'"

"And how do you feel about Japan now?"

"At first we were all worried about what kind of devils the foreigners would be. Japanese officers were so strict they were scary, so we figured that Americans must be even worse. But when we saw them in Tokyo we were puzzled. We asked each other, 'Are these the people who beat our armed forces? They joke, they whistle, they laugh ...' I never saw a Japanese officer laugh. Oh, sometimes an American gets in a fight or a drunk soldier raises hell, but even a drunk American soldier or sailor is heaven compared to a sober Japanese officer. And did you see how well dressed the Americans are?"

"Well dressed. . . ?"

"Their trousers are pressed, their shoes are shined . . . And so many pockets! In their trousers, in their shirts. They carry wallets with pictures of their sweethearts or family, chewing gum in this pocket, cigarettes in that pocket, lighters . . . so many pockets."

"I see that chocolate and cigarettes are in big demand in Tokyo."

"Very big. The soldiers sell them and they end up on the black market. We were all puzzled by those Lucky Strikes. We couldn't understand why American cigarettes came packaged with a Japanese flag design. We asked the Americans and they laughed."

"How is your work at the base?"

"I learned to drive a truck when I was working at the factory, so now I drive American trucks. And I drove a jeep. They're fun. And someday I'd really like to learn to fly. And go to engineering school."

"Are you picking up English?"

"A few words at a time. I learn that by trading things."

"Trading things?"

"The Americans want Japanese kimono, scrolls, things like that. They either pay money or swap all sorts of food for them: canned goods, powdered milk, meat . . . And have you seen the American field rations?"

"No, I can't say that I have."

"Unbelievable! A whole bunch of things in one package—cheese, meat, biscuits, butter . . . even cigarettes. It's like food from the future."

"And you have no bad feelings about working for the conquerors?"

"It's like heaven compared with before. But I can't believe that these are the same Americans who dropped those huge bombs on our small wooden houses. Or the people I was supposed to crash a plane into. It's strange. They laugh, they whistle. . . ."

After the War Crimes Trial closed, the judges retired for seven months to process the testimonies and evidence—until another *eleven* rose in November. Seven men, Tojo one of them, were sentenced to death by hanging. Of the two men on trial I was closest with, Shigemitsu was given seven years in prison from the date of arraignment; Umezu received a life sentence. Shortly after the verdicts were handed down, George Furness called on me again.

"Mr. Shigemitsu implored me to thank you for your written testimony," he said. "It helped our case immeasurably."

"I only wrote things as they happened. Is he well?"

"As well as can be expected. As you know, he received the lightest sentence of anyone at the trials. He would like to meet with you, and he said that former General Umezu would also. You knew Umezu?"

"We met."

"You'll need clearance from SCAP—that should be no trouble for you—but Umezu is not in good health."

"I'll make the arrangements. And will you be going back home now that the trial is finished?"

"Actually, this looks like the beginning of things. My performance with Shigemitsu's case earned me friends here and I've been invited to practice law in Japan. I'm going to become a Tokyoite."

I contacted SCAP headquarters. It turned out that the executions of those sentenced to death were delayed because several of them, Tojo included, were trying to file petitions for habeas corpus with the U.S. Supreme Court. I was asked to wait until after the decision. When it came, it was predictable: the petitions were denied, and the executions were carried out in the dark, early morning of December twenty-third.

A few days later, my driver pulled up to Sugamo Prison. I was given a full course of salutes and courtesies from the American guards and officers and shown into the visiting room where I waited for Shigemitsu.

"I want to thank you for your attempts to negotiate a peace for us," he said.

"I regret that it came to nothing. I wanted to save more of Japan from destruction."

"The destruction was beyond comprehension. Even after living through it, I find it hard to believe that entire areas of a city along with its inhabitants could be reduced to such a field of ash."

"If only I could have resolved the emperor problem. It seemed the one obstacle to bringing an end to the destruction."

"The Japanese were educated to obey the emperor's wish. Japan turned into a burning holocaust with voices screaming from pain and hunger rising with the flames. And yet, if an order were given in the name of the emperor, they would leap into the flames. This is the mind of the Japanese. Sacrificing the emperor for the good of the country would be the ultimate debasement of the Japanese. The problem, as you know, is that the army leaders used the emperor's name when it suited them, and disregarded his will when *that* suited them."

"And you think it was wise for the Occupation to retain the emperor?"

"You see the order in Japan today. That is the answer."

Shigemitsu thanked me for my testimony at the trial, then slowly pulled himself up with his cane and left the room.

In a few minutes, Umezu half walked, half stumbled into the room and took his seat opposite me. He simply nodded—a bow from the neck.

"I hope I'm not disturbing you," I said.

"Not at all. I want to talk with you. It's good to see you again. You look well." I'm sure he did not mean it that way, but I felt guilty for my health—

and my freedom. "There are things I must talk about." This was the former commander-in-chief of Japan's mighty Kwantung Army, until 1944, when he was promoted to chief of staff of the General Staff. Yet his first comment was, "I feel that the greatest deed in my military career was when I cancelled the biological attack on America."

"From what I know of the trial, this was never brought up. And you never mentioned it."

"That is true. And there are other things, also. In November of 1945 I was interviewed by an American officer who was investigating Japanese biological warfare activities."

"That would have been Murray Sanders."

"That's right. I said that Japan had to be ready for biological attacks from other nations. He asked what I knew about Japan's program in China, and I said simply that I was kept informed of what was going on. Actually, as commander of the Kwantung Army I had given the order back in September 1941 to proceed with biological warfare. I share the guilt for the use of biological weapons."

"Is it not risky even to think of these things now? There's talk of paroles and commutation. . . ."

"I am beyond that. Someone has to halt the morbid progress that was initiated by scientists under my command of the Kwantung Army."

"You are talking about General Ishii?"

"I am. On Okinawa, a plague epidemic came close to reality. Specialists moved south from the units in China to cover the landing sites with disease. The Allies landed earlier than we expected and preparations were still going on. That spared the Allies and Okinawans from biological warfare."

I wondered if Umezu would have cancelled that attack also. I did not ask. He continued.

"At the end of the war, most of Ishii's subordinates went by train to the Korean border, then down through the peninsula to Pusan and by ship to Japan. Ishii rode the train as far as Dairen—there was a pharmaceutical unit there—then flew home by army plane. He and his scientists hid in Japan while Naito negotiated with the Americans for freedom from war-crimes prosecution in exchange for the data on biological warfare and human experiments."

"I heard that Naito met Sanders when the *Sturgess* docked; Naito was there to act as an interpreter and apparently seemed to have a photo of Sanders. I never understood how . . ."

Umezu gave a weak nod: "The Americans got that photo to him almost as soon at the war ended. Actually, it was a copy of Sanders' identification photo from Camp Detrick. Sanders also had a photo of Naito. They were looking for each other." Umezu rested for a few moments while I digested this photograph story. He continued:

"Naito was a blood specialist. He was working on drying blood for battlefield use. The technique is similar to drying bacteria; that would simplify handling biological weapons and reduce the risk to one's own personnel."

"Naito was apparently the key man in the deal."

"He was an information filter. He wedged himself between the American investigators and those being questioned, and he let just enough information through—enough bait—to entice the American mind and work the exchange. He got a promise from MacArthur's office that America would keep all information in intelligence. That prevented it from being opened as evidence in court. In other words, it kept the Russians from getting it."

"Your order for biological warfare never surfaced at the trial."

"We thought that it might. It would have been a problem for the Americans. It would have fueled Chinese and Russian demands to have all the evidence brought into court. But America wanted only data and silence. And they especially wanted to keep everything from the Soviets."

"Both Keenan and Webb prevented biological warfare and human experiments from surfacing in court. How far up America's chain of command did that action come from?"

"When Naito was negotiating with the Americans, the investigators said that the agreement had the approval of the president. But some were worried anyway. With Keenan's record of prosecuting gangsters, we thought he'd be hungry for a high score on convictions. But he had political ambitions in America, and if he went against the president and the U.S. military it could have ended his career."

"Webb also blocked biological warfare charges from coming into court, and he came to Japan after two years as war crimes commissioner—

in charge of investigating Japanese war crimes in the Pacific regions where Australia had fought. In fact, there were opinions that with his record as prosecutor, he should have disqualified himself as a judge. But he cooperated the same way Keenan did."

"Diplomatic swaps happen all the time—you know that. The Australians wanted to prosecute some Japanese, and they needed SCAP's cooperation." Umezu took a short pause again to regain his strength. "I think," he said, with the faintest hint of a cynical smile, "that Shigemitsu and I were a swap of sorts. SCAP agreed to throw us to the Russian wolves to satisfy some of their hunger, while America kept Ishii and the rest for themselves. It was the best option. Can you imagine the Soviets as partner to the knowledge?"

"It would," I admitted, "be a more uncomfortable option. Of course, relations between America and the Soviets were already strained over occupation policy—areas of authority and so forth. Then in May 1946, about two days before the trial convened, Winston Churchill made his 'iron curtain' speech about Soviet plans for world domination. So the Soviets went into the trial as one of the Allies but knowing just how the real Allies considered them. So in that atmosphere, we can expect that America's protecting Ishii and his men accelerated the chilling of relations between America and the Russians."

"That," Umezu said, "may be Ishii's and Naito's greatest contribution. America and Russia were too close—from long before the big war started. Soviet participation in the Occupation would be a horrible curse for Japan. That's what they were aiming for when they came into the war. And Japan rests easier—at least for now—with Ishii's information in American hands and hidden from the Russians."

"What did the Russians get when they crossed into Manchuria at the end of the war?"

"They captured a few of our researchers in biological warfare—probably not too much actual data. They were hoping to get some in Tokyo. The Soviet prosecutors tried for months to interrogate Ishii, but the Americans kept stalling and the Soviets were getting upset. The Americans saw that they'd have to grant permission and spoke with Ishii first; they rehearsed him."

"And the interrogation took place?"

"On two different days, at Ishii's Tokyo home. His wife and daughter were there, and they were also rehearsed by the Americans."

"And when did this take place?"

"In the summer of 1947, right in the middle of the trial. American officers were with the Russian investigators all the time, not just to monitor Ishii, but to listen to the Soviet line of questioning for clues as to what the Russians already knew about biological warfare."

"I was keeping up on events at the trial through journalists, and I know that the Russians tried to get Ishii into court."

"They tried. But Keenan washed away their request."

"Knowing the Soviets, I'm surprised they let it pass so quietly."

"Remember, they sat on the tribunal by reason of coming into the war for just a few days—and in violation of a nonaggression pact with Japan that would still be in effect until April 1946. On August 8, 1945, they declared war on Japan. That could be grounds to bring them to trial as defendants, not judges. But by whatever means, it's better that this knowledge is in American hands."

"And you are even willing to accept your role of a trade to the Soviets to be put on trial in order to keep Japan's biological warfare technology from them?"

"Of course. I fought for the preservation of Japan, and if this is what is needed, then I'm still fighting here in prison. But I know it is a holding battle. And also, remember that the Scandinavian end of the Soviet Union is a logical place for testing the viability of biological weapons in cold climates. Would you rather bring Ishii and his associates to trial and have all his research data opened to them?"

I could only look in silence at Umezu. After he read my face, he continued. "So I'm sure you understand that a cover-up is the best temporary tactic. The problem is, when does 'temporary' end? The ideal decision would have been to destroy and ban all biological weapons, but how can that be done? Things have progressed since then, and if something is not done to prevent the insane research, the consequences will be worse than I had imagined at the time."

"So you think that biological warfare will be used in the future?"

"In warfare as we have known it, perhaps. But also for another type of warfare. Not open, but closed."

"You mean a secretive, terrorist-type of warfare? Is that what Ishii was researching?"

"To some degree, but not completely. When I gave the order to proceed with biological weapons development in China, we were looking at disease as a military weapon. I did not yet realize what it would mean on a world-wide scale." He paused again to regain his strength. "When we air-dropped plague germs on villages, it was obvious. When we used poison gas against the Chinese army, it was obvious. In fact, the American president threatened Japan when he heard of it. So these methods are not for closed warfare."

"Meaning. . . ?"

Umezu straightened his back and took a laborious breath. "The principle was laid out by General Ishii long ago: 'Disasters of human origin cannot be distinguished from those of natural origin.'"

As I recalled those same words from Akira's suicide note, Umezu's next comment came almost as a telepathic response. "You remember the message I sent you about Akira's accidental death?"

"Of course."

"His death was not an accident," Umezu said. "It was suicide. And fear of this next evolution in war, using silent, unseen microorganisms, was part of the reason."

"Actually, I knew it was suicide. Someone informed me."

He gave a slight nod. "I had to send you that message. Secrecy and procedure; I am sure you understand. He was not the only one. There were even experienced doctors who could not stand it—cutting open men and women while they screamed—and took the same way out."

It was my turn to nod; I could think of no other response.

"This erasing the line between natural and created disaster," Umezu went on, "is what troubled Akira, and this is the most fearful prospect: undeclared, closed warfare of the future."

"And how do you see this being carried out?"

"What are the reasons for war? One is resources. Japan fought in China for its resources. France, England, Holland—they colonized lands for natural resources and it became part of the bigger problem and grew into war. Natural resources have been a curse to the native population, and they will become a bigger curse in the age of closed warfare. China had resources Japan wanted, so the army used opium to make the Chinese docile."

"Opium? How. . . ?"

"Mostly, we distributed cigarettes. Do you know Golden Bat?"

"Yes; in fact I remember that Colonel Sasaki smoked them."

"There was a special version of Golden Bat made in Japan and shipped to China. They were loaded with opium and they helped us control the country. To a degree, they replaced weapons. But biological warfare can replace opium, weapons, even armies. A well-planned epidemic could eliminate enough of a population to prevent an uprising. A handful of technicians could replace invading armies, tanks, guns. It will require better control of microorganisms than we have now; that was one of the aims of Ishii's research."

"The war ended with a terrible new weapon, a bomb with unprecedented destructive power. Do you not see fear in that also?"

"Of course, but it is an extension of conventional war. Its use is obvious. It may be called super war, but it will be open warfare continued. With closed warfare, the enemy does not define himself. 'It was a natural disaster and you are blaming us.' The script is written."

"Apparently, you do not think that the consequences of biological weapons running out of hand would deter their use, as you cancelled the submarine attack. Alfred Nobel thought his dynamite was fearful enough to eliminate war and he had to change his mind about it."

"Guns," Umezu answered, "did not grow bigger by worrying about backfire. But with living organisms, the equivalent of a backfire could cover huge areas and continue over many years. That is the fearful part."

"And you feel that America will continue developing biological weapons?"

"Of course. They are conducting part of their research here in Tokyo."

"Not on humans, I take it."

"Here, they use rats. The Americans buy them from farmers outside the city and continue the work of Unit 731."

"I heard that American army trucks go up to Saitama for them."

"Those are the same farmers that sold us rats for use in China. Unit 731 used them to cultivate plague germs."

"And the American army researchers. . . ?"

"I don't know the full extent of what they're doing, but I have an idea. Remember, America didn't want Ishii's experimentation data to *prevent* its use. They wanted it for military science—for further development. And if someone or something doesn't turn this around, it could bring a new age of plagues upon the world. I did what I could; I stopped one biological attack. Now others must do more. The long-range fears I had for the world when I cancelled that attack are moving toward reality."

He wiped his brow and took another few seconds to rest. "Did you ever make a slingshot when you were a child?" he asked.

"Of course. That must be a truly international toy."

"And what is the first thing you do after making one?"

"Why, see how it shoots. Try to hit something."

"How far you can send a pebble. Try to hit a target. You tested your new toy. Military weapons are only bigger slingshots whittled with higher-education tools. This is the threat: the human urge to experiment. And weapons improvements come out of experimentation. Perhaps a bigger caliber gun. Or a more viable and virulent bacteria." It was becoming more laborious for Umezu to continue talking. He took a few shallow breaths and continued. "Some testing can be realized only in war or in situations of military control. Unit 731 happened because our army gave the Japanese medical profession an opportunity they had always wanted but had never had."

"And you see the danger of that continuing?"

"Ishii's work thrilled American researchers. They had no opportunities for using human subjects and had to gather biological warfare data through animal experimentation. Occasionally an accident in a laboratory or in industry gave them some human data, but there could be no controlled experiments. Ishii and his men got passports to freedom because they gave American military scientists data for building weapons for future wars."

This man in front of me was once in the most powerful position in the Imperial Japanese Army. Now, I felt, he was cleansing himself of his career in preparation for leaving this world.

"Worship of testing," Umezu continued, "is part of the religion of scientists.

It will continue unless some drastic measure is taken, and I have no idea— even if I were free and healthy—how to stop this. I was able to stop one submarine. It will take a grand scheme to stop what I believe is going on now. Hiding our research from the Soviets is a temporary measure. I am sure they will continue on their own. They feel robbed of research data by America and they will try to catch up. The more momentum this gains . . . I beg you to do what you can. As an influential person from a country that was neutral during the war, you should be in a position that is not antagonistic to any party. Use any advantage you have. The world needs people like you."

Umezu's energy was expended. I took my leave and my freedom and walked out the gate, where my driver was waiting. These last days of December people were preparing for the new year's holiday in a Japan still short of food and with some people still living in scraps of cardboard and wood. But no bombs were falling, no napalm fires came to envelop people and burn them all to a uniform death char. There was peace, but Umezu did not make peace comfortable. He outlined the next evolution in warfare, which he termed *closed war*. I saw Ishii's dream of creating disasters that cannot be distinguished from those of natural origin as an evolution in neutral war. Science could enhance the ugliness of neutral war while elevating its innocence. And in that ugly innocence slept the threat of biological backfire.

I held a traditional three-day observance of the new year at the legation in the form of an open house, where staff members and their families could stop in for something to eat. My business acquaintances contributed food and drink, and it was as joyous as could be expected: Every Japanese who came had suffered the loss of some relative or friend to the war.

A few days later, on January 8, 1949, Umezu Yoshijiro completed his life sentence in Sugamo Prison.

In 1950, war broke out on the Korean peninsula. Announcements in Tokyo called for blood donors, and I soon found the link between the two. I received reports that a blood specialist by the name of Ryoichi Naito had set up a blood bank under the direction of SCAP. Lack of money and employment in Japan brought donors in to sell their blood and answer the need of the American forces in Korea. The marriage between Unit 731 and the United States was complete. What were they planning for their future together?

▪ 57 ▪

Japan Departure

The thought of leaving Tokyo, probably for the last time, made Butterfly seem all the more precious. I was sixty-two years old, and soon headed for my final assignment in Cairo. After that, I planned on retiring in Paris. Butterfly would find both those cities interesting, and from Paris we would have Europe for our playground. I felt like a teenager dreaming about repairing a broken romance. I decided to make an attempt to take her with me. I was not sure how to approach her, and like other men in history and in literature, I sought an intermediary. I felt like a miniature reflection of the Japanese peacemakers trying to find a way to maneuver an approach from the other side. I asked Mrs. Saito to take another trip by car to Mariko's home and tell her that I was scheduled to leave soon. "I would like to ask her to come with me," I confided, "but I admit that I don't know how to go about it."

"I'll do what I can," she answered, and in a few days Mrs. Saito prepared again to head for Saitama in the legation car. I filled the trunk with food and included a few bottles of wine—white, slightly sweet. And I waited.

I should not have been surprised at the answer. "Mariko is looking forward to the new school year and plans on staying where she is. She said she'll write before you leave. I'm sorry; that's the best I could do."

The letter came:

There were many times when I wished that we could leave Japan together and live somewhere else. It was not just to escape the war. As you know, I looked to you to take me away from the ugliness of Japan for moments at a time. Secretly, I wished those moments to grow into greater time. But it is too late now for that. I am back in the classroom with children, and it is refreshing. There are no army officers to watch us and tell us what to teach, no emperor mythology and no imperial portraits that the children have to bow to. Japanese children are once again children, not soldiers.

One of the teachers at the local school is a man with a high rank in judo. He told me that he once played with the great Kanno Jigoro, and the experience was 'like trying to throw an empty judo outfit. There was not enough resistance to pull against.' That is what I felt every time I tried to talk with you about the things that tortured me. You gave me an escape from Japan, but when I needed more of you, when I needed someone to hold onto in an emotional sense, you slipped away and left me with empty space to grapple with. You accepted my body, and I enjoyed that also. I wanted those momentary escapes from Japan—but you rejected my thoughts. You were simply an empty garment when I wanted a person to hold. I did not fight for your mind for fear of losing the escapes that you did offer me. I desperately needed them. In those days, when Japan was turning more grotesque by the day, I could not share your neutrality, and I was arrested and beaten because of it. I cannot say whether mine was the wiser decision, but the experience has made neutral noninvolvement an ally of those who punished me.

Times like this make people wish everything could start over from the beginning, but thinking like that belongs to myth, and I was beaten and raped because I refused to believe and teach myth.

My mother always worried that I was too strong-minded to marry, and I told her that perhaps I was not made for love. But she often told me that one day someone would appear. Someday. One day. You did, and when I felt love between us, I thought that my mother's promise was coming true. Then you made my mother a liar.

So please forgive me for not wanting to meet you. It would be impossible for me to visit the past and ignore the bridge of pain in between. If only you had known when to stop being so neutral.

And Yamamoto's speech rang from the Harvard classroom again: *Only a fool does not know when to quit.*

And so I was sentenced to depart Tokyo a modern-day Pinkerton, a cad leaving his Butterfly behind. I put in a request to travel by steamship—I wanted to revisit my younger naval days, and maybe, I thought, the ocean would wash away unpleasant thoughts and give me time to think—and forget.

The British philosopher Francis Bradley wrote of an inverse time, a state in which the scar precedes the wound. I thought that an ocean voyage would give me some self-deceptive moments to transport me back to a time where everything that happened was yet to start. But once on the ocean, I found that the only way I could forget Butterfly was to think of the greater question of the past war—and future ones.

In the past, Bradleyesque time inversions were used to enter war. The American president tried to come to Europe's aid when he ordered retaliatory fire to an attack that had not yet been made. The Japanese used a time inversion with success at the Marco Polo Bridge Incident to expand the war into all of China. But even the time inversion will become obsolete.

One purpose of war is preparation for the next one. Unit 731 was developing Japan's next-war weapons, but in reality, it was building a foundation for the new age of neutral war.

My countryman, Alfred Nobel, erred when he stated that his dynamite would end war because its destructive power would make commanders more rational. He later amended his thoughts by saying war would end when it became equally dangerous for the people at home as at the front. "War will stop if the weapon is bacteriology," he stated, but he was thinking of orthodox war, of bacteria as brazenly distributed as bullets. Neutral war is a faked bet, and different victims will play it differently, but a silent attack does not identify the attacker. A suspected offender can only be suspect and can wear a face of innocence. The attacked will have to decide whether to retaliate and draw Bradleyesque first blood.

World War II expanded the war ethic—if such is not a contradiction in terms—to acceptance of civilians as military targets. Neutral war will not have to pioneer that phase. Regions cursed with natural resources needed by industrial nations are at especially high risk from neutral war.

Invasion and control will be done with quieter means than by human troops and armaments. Commercial powers can gain control over global regions by decimating populations directly without delegating the function of killing to governments and armies. Then the suffering countries will go running for help, perhaps to the creators of their catastrophe.

Neutral war against one of the world's financial centers can shift the economy from one part of the globe to another. On more limited scale, it can be waged by one economic bloc against another. And the target is not limited to humans. The livestock of a region or nation can be infected to eliminate a competitor, with a side effect of raising the market price of the survivors' products. Killing entire flocks is not even necessary; enough of an outbreak to cause fear can be effective. Neutral war will require refining control over microorganisms, but this only parallels the history of the development of other weapons. The first rifle ammunition was a ball that was lobbed through the air with little accuracy. From there, it advanced to becoming a pointed, rotating device that could be aimed to finely defined targets.

Epidemiological studies show how certain races and ethnic groups are prone to specific diseases. New technology may be able to isolate the susceptibility factor and design pathogens to aim in on it. I am confident that this ethnic Achilles heel is enticing the developers of biological weapons to find pathogens that can be aimed at determined targets of race, sex, perhaps even age. Diseases outside of human control already make these distinctions. Finding why will be the first step to putting a specific group in the bio-sights of an aimed pathogen. It is a matter of a will to use science for killing, research, and testing. The history of this will is as old as human science. And every new creation ignites the childish urge that Umezu spoke of, to see how far the pebble will go.

In the Japanese language, it is said that technology "accumulates." This is accurate. Each new development starts from the wellspring of knowledge stored by earlier generations. Technology accumulation provides a continuously elevating base to begin the next tier of development, driven by human ambition. Every development in weapons is a foundation of technology for further development. And every new creation ignites the childish urge to "try the new slingshot."

The application of intelligence is an extension of the opposed thumb: There is a thrust for creating, but evaluation of consequences is a rare hindrance. Those who do hesitate will not be numerous enough to affect the general trend of striving for the next improvement. A Nobel fallacy–type of justification may sometimes be necessary, but human intelligence is driven by a lust to exercise itself.

Human intelligence, like the Japanese kimono, is to be admired for itself, by itself, like a wall hanging. When wrapped around human society, intelligence forces people to conform to its creations, and can be as destructive to human life as the kimono is to human form.

Intelligence is fueled by ambition, and human ambition cannot be reined in. This is why pacts between nations live according to the Buddhist principle of one day at a time—each day it is not broken. Pacts cannot neutralize ambition and are more often made as a mechanism in a greater ambition. Neutral war does not need this ruse. And no pact can deter neutral war.

Ambition cannot be clamped by governmental structure, either. Faith that a certain framework will deter ambition is as erroneous as believing that a weapon can be terrible enough to deter its mimicry. White, Sorge, Ozaki, and others serving Stalin were sincere in thinking that they were working for a better life for the world through the spreading of Soviet ideas. The search for the fountain of youth with waters that neutralize human aging was relegated to fantasy; the search for a system that will neutralize human ambition still goes on, and will probably continue until the End of the Law.

I was haunted by a poem of a fourteenth-century shogunate official: *Human life is fifty years; I feel shame for being deedless. . . .* The official resigned himself to the forces of bureaucracy and left the world of officialdom. After the war's end, I realized that my efforts at trying to negotiate a peace were not doomed by a lazy foreign minister. I was defeated by the human intelligence's unconquerable thirst for testing. Whether it was a single-vector force or one of several is as eternal an argument as whether Japan would have surrendered without the atomic bombs. But without doubt, America's atomic scientists should have bowed daily in the direction of Japan's imperial palace in gratitude for the emperor's cooperation in keeping Japanese cities on laboratory status. If the Japanese government had communicated its willingness to eliminate the imperial throne and abide by unconditional surrender, I am sure that American authorities would have handled the offer in a way that would have kept the war going until the new slingshot could be tested on a real, virgin location. A surrender offer to America might have been handled like the German offer: with simple, unexplained silence. Or it might have been claimed that the offer was "not sincere" or that it was never received . . . I believe this would have happened even if an unconditional surrender went out after Hiroshima and before Nagasaki to complete stage two of a comparison test between a uranium bomb and then a plutonium bomb.

Jonathan Swift called his floating island nation "Laputa" because it was inhabited by what he considered the whores of society, the blasphemers of science who spoke of the principles of the earth and the universe. The scientists of our world who advanced war to its present state have made this planet a grander version of Laputa. It has been shaped by the whores of science who advanced the art of destruction by selling indiscriminate technological embraces for the market price. In time, their microbiological creations will mutate into Frankensteins, and laboratory warriors in white coats will go mad looking for where they took wrong turns in the scientific maze.

I believe in the prophecy of the End of the Law, not with the belief of an adherent but with my final attempt to assess. If, as my Buddhist instructor taught me, it will be realized by humanity's departure from the teachings of the Buddha, so be it. I suspect the human race has remained fairly constant in morality; it is the advance of technology that has given constancy the appearance of disintegration. The wisdom of the prophecy of the End of the Law may simply be extremely long-range foresight in betting on the point in time where the vectors of human intelligence and human ambition will converge in total disaster. The doctrine of Unit 731 will add a surge of inertia to the prophecy to assure that the world will abide by it.

· 58 ·

A Way to Keep Living

Yamamoto knew while he planned the attack on Pearl Harbor that Japan would lose. I had to wait until after the war to realize that my failure was also written into the script. But losing Butterfly was by my own hand.

In 1951 I took retirement and came here to Paris. Surely this is not a symbol of the peace I hoped to effect. From 1600 to the end of World War II, France was involved in more major wars than any other European nation. But that has nothing to do with the present, and Paris is good for this. The cool social breezes repel the distressing flies of the past. The last time I was pulled back into that past was in 1953, when a letter arrived from Mrs. Saito with photos of Butterfly in her swimming suit at a pool. She was smiling—not for the camera—with the children. Her back was straight again, and I felt a teardrop swelling, for sadness and happiness. Mrs. Saito wrote:

A lot of the young swimmers here are practicing the butterfly since the controversy was resolved and it became an independent competitive stroke of its own. Naturally, Mariko has been practicing the stroke for a long time and is helping the children with it. She is glad that she does not have to swim it in anger now, the way she did years ago.

There is also talk of building heated swimming pools in Japan. The idea came when a group of Japanese toured Germany and saw them there. If there is one sensible idea Japan ever got from Germany, this is it. Mariko is excited over the idea of swimming almost all year long.

I was happy that Butterfly was flying on her own. In the days when past and future enslaved me, I thought of the options I could have had with my diplomatic position to take her from Japan during the war. But hindsight is useful only when there is a future to which it can be applied. I am no longer shackled to nonexistent time.

I had become a member of the diplomatic corps because I expected the challenges and options that the position would open for me. But when there were chances for actually influencing world affairs, I failed and became a representative of my own low esteem of those in my profession. People can lose wars and find a way to continue living; it is greater agony to see oneself as a failure for being an unsuspecting dupe in a prearranged scheme. This was one overwhelming vector among those that made Yamamoto take his life: The gambler and admiral in him revolted when he realized the cards were stacked in his favor.

Human life is fifty years. I tried to accomplish a deed and realized later that the cards were stacked, that I, too, was forced to play someone else's game. Enlightenment brought depression, and I thought of following Yamamoto. I can thank my Buddhist teachings for my ability to continue living, and I am grateful that they remained with me. *Live each day one day at a time, one moment at a time. When in the bath, the bath only, when sitting meditation, meditation only . . .*

I was sandwiched between a past of failure and human misery on one side, and a future of even greater misery on the other. I looked for something that would save me from following Yamamoto, and I found it in the teachings I learned in Tokyo.

At the moment of the first awakening of the Bodhi mind, a person already has achieved enlightenment. I see Kawaguchi in his Tibetan robes sitting cross-legged on the desk: *If the entire earth were covered with cowhide, we could go anywhere barefoot. Of course that is impossible. But we can wrap a length of cowhide to each foot, and then go where we want.* His voice rings, his robes flow with his gestures: *You cannot cover the earth with cowhide! So stop trying! Arouse the Bodhi mind! Wrap a length of cowhide to each foot and live your lives according to the goals you envision for the world!*

Like Francis Bradley's scar that precedes the wound, a providential turn in the Tokyo labyrinth gave me a way to keep living before I needed a *way*. It is here now, when I do need it.

It is the eternal ideal to have a world of no sickness, no dispute, no war. This is impossible! But the moment we arouse the Bodhi mind and aspire toward enlightenment, it will be the same as achieving the goals we envision for the world. A length of cowhide . . .

And so I came to Paris and *wrapped my mind in a length of cowhide.* Thoughts of past and future have been exorcised, and I am free where I used to be enslaved.

Six centuries ago, Hosokawa Yoriyuki wrote a poem of shame after he failed to accomplish his political goals. I shared his sentiments for my own failure. But now, in the deep autumn of life, I can finally absolve myself of that shame with one success: My family line ends with me. On this last page of my last message, I take comfort in that I never married, I have no children, no family to be part of the days of the End of the Law. This one success has helped me keep the length of cowhide on my mind.

I rarely wander out of the present. I live each day one day at a time, pouring my energy into each moment, one moment at a time. When I am assailed by transitory aberrations and I feel myself deviating into the past, I remember the lesson of the meditation hall and pour more energy into the present. And my wanderings into the future do not go beyond planning my next trip to the wine shop—to help me *stay* in the present.

▪ ▪ ▪

Fact and Fiction in *Neutral War*

The suggestion for this story came when I found about Widar Bagge, the factual Swedish minister and intermediary in the attempted peace offering. This is his fictionalized memoir. His term of service in Tokyo, his age, and his role in the attempted peace feelers are true as presented in the story. The eleven messages between him and Stockholm are real, translated from Swedish. His solution to the emperor problem, re-establishing the rightful lineage to negotiate a peace, is fiction; the historical basis for it is true. (The "true" emperor, Kumazawa, resurfaced after WWII, gained a small following, and was even recorded in secret reports by the Occupation Forces in Tokyo in 1946. The present "true-emperor" descendant is a businessman in Osaka.)

Bagge's comments and opinions concerning persons and countries are fictionalized, but I have used his actual messages and his correspondence to read his character into the fictionalized person. It was in fact Suzuki the journalist who acted as intermediary to initiate the negotiated peace attempts. Widar Bagge, according to the Swedish Foreign Ministry, never married and had no known family. He retired to Paris and died in 1970. Bagge's foreign minister, Christian Günther, did have a reputation among Swedes for laziness. His handling—non-handling—of Bagge's messages is representative of this.

Yamamoto in fact attended the English class for foreigners at Harvard as language officer; the protagonist's attendance is fictional, as is his naval background. Yamamoto was in America from 1919 to 1921, returning to Japan that year. He withdrew from the Harvard course in February 1920 but spent the balance of the time in America and in Mexico, where he went to inspect the oil fields. The account of Mitchell's fliers sinking the captured German battleship is fact, as is the "nitwit" title.

Yamamoto was in fact a feverish and skilled gambler and actually considered turning professional. Most of his comments on gambling and poker are fictionalized, taken from poker professionals, though his feverish attachment to the game and his insistence that officers under him also gamble would probably make the thoughts represented here parallel his own.

Admiral Togo's face on the Finnish beer is fact; the beer is on sale today. The battle between the Japanese ships under Admiral Kamimura and the Russian ships out of Vladivostok is true as presented in the story, as is the origin of the ships. Yamamoto's being on board during the battle is fiction. Yamamoto was on board the *Nisshin* in the Russo-Japanese War where, as gunnery officer, he lost his two fingers as described in the story. Early accounts blamed it on an enemy shell, possibly to upgrade the accident to battle wound.

The account of the golf game is borrowed from Kurosawa Akira's first post–WWII film, *Waga seishun ni kui nashi* (1946); the placing of the educational system under the military is fact. Using schoolteachers to search out dissenting parents through their students' compositions and the reading of the Imperial Rescript on Education are facts; Bagge's fictional meeting with a schoolteacher friend is based on these.

Aiko Fumio and his shallow-water torpedoes are factual; the protagonist's connection with him is fiction. Aiko was researching shallow-water torpedoes from 1939, but from January 1941 he was actually designing for conditions at Pearl Harbor, testing in Kagoshima Harbor, which does have similar depth characteristics. His breakthrough came in November 1941, when he kept plane-launched torpedoes to twelve-meter depth. Aiko made his living after the war by continuing his work with inventions; he died in a fire in his home in 1991 caused by an electric heater setting fire to his bedding.

Bagge was fictionalized into peace negotiations earlier than written documentary evidence. His conversation with Shigemitsu in 1943 is chronologically advanced, but in 1943, Kido and Konoe were discussing the gloomy prospects of the war in one of the known beginnings of considerations of peace negotiations. And, as in the story, in February 1942

Kido did echo Bywater and warned that America would eventually over-power Japan, and that Japan should find a way out of the war as soon as possible.

The attack on Romanian Minister Bagulesco is an almost unknown, but documented, fact, as is Bagge's involvement in helping him. Bagulesco also lived in France after the war and initiated legal action against the government of Japan. I have a copy of the eighty-page "Instrument of Claims and Demands Against the Japanese Government" which I received from Joseph Choate, the lawyer who represented him. The story of the attack on Bagulesco, information on Hitler's proposal to split Europe, the assassination attempt, the Romanian traitor colluding with the Japanese, etc., are taken from this document, which also contains Bagge's written testimony. The claims were presented several times to The Japanese Foreign Ministry, and they refused to take action.

Bagge left Tokyo on April 13. His being on the Trans Siberian Railway at that time of the German surrender is calculated from his schedule. He met with Herschel Johnson in Stockholm on May 12, 1945; this according to Mr. Johnson's comment in a letter home. The Truman Library yields no record of communications between Johnson and the president on Bagge's work with the peace negotiations; Mr. Johnson's private and official papers reveal only the two lines in a letter to his mother mentioned in the story. The meeting is also documented in a letter Bagge wrote in 1947 to the attorney for Shigemitsu at the Tokyo War Crimes Trial. Bagge's written testimony was in fact instrumental in Shigemitsu's receiving the lightest sentence of those pronounced guilty.

The hypothesis that Yamamoto died before his scheduled flight and that his body was placed on the plane, the accounts of the poems of the *Manyoshu,* the shelling of the bow of the crippled destroyer, and the occurrence of just several of the omen numbers I owe to Prof. Anzai Jiro, a specialist in World War II history and writer on the psychology of military design. The preflight death theory is not completely unknown; some suspect murder by rival navy officers, and news releases by the Chinese Communists and reported in American newspapers did place the blame for his death on dissention between the Japanese army and navy, though this could also have been a propaganda tool to weaken Japanese morale.

After hearing Prof. Anzai's explanations, I found other occurrences of 4 and 11 in Yamamoto's life that escaped the professor's eye, but that I assess had serious influence on the admiral. The first was Yamamoto's given name itself, which I suspect Anzai overlooked because, even though Anzai speaks and writes English, the name in Japanese is a three-character compound (5+10+6) and has no relation to the number 11. This occurs only when written in the Arabic numerals 56 and read like dice. I analyzed the war and pre-war years with "omen eyes," using various Japanese and English sources, and discovered Yamamoto's omen numbers rising as presented in the story, where all occurrences of 11 and 4 are historically correct.

Prof. Anzai also furnished information on sighting the Russian ship en route to Pearl Harbor. His brother was an officer in the task force and told him about the stare-off. Accounts of sightings or non-sightings differ according to the source. In *Yamamoto Isoroku* by Agawa Hiroyuki, the author identifies the ship as belonging to "a third country." I suspect because it is a delicate matter of who really knew and what many Japanese do not want to know. The English translation under *The Reluctant Admiral* correctly translates the original as above.

The German surrender offer, Canaris's approaching Earle, and the failure of FDR to respond are reported in *F.D.R.: My Exploited Father-in-Law* by Curtis B. Dall. Earle, in addition to several ambassadorial posts, was governor of Pennsylvania from 1935 to 1939. The reason for the refusal of Roosevelt to act is, as far as I know, not documented. I have fictionalized the Soviet influence through Harry Dexter White, which I believe is the most logical assessment, but it was clear that the president ignored the offer and did not want the war to end. The subsequent exchange of letters between Earle and FDR show the president treating Earle with antagonism, and transferring him to a neutralizing position. Rasmussen is fictional; the Danes did have a network throughout different countries, with Erling Foss in Stockholm.

Harry Dexter White's spy activities while in the employ of the Department of the Treasury, the Silvermaster ring, etc., are supported by FBI documents and news accounts following his discovery. His draft from Pavlov's instructions (the beginning of the "Hull Note") is excerpted verbatim in the story. In 1996, a Japanese newspaper located Pavlov and carried his account of his mission in "Operation Snow," of the meeting in the Capital Restaurant in Washington, and handing White the outline for a plan that later evolved into the "Hull Note." This was the first evidence of Soviet instructions coming into Harry White, where FBI investigations centered on the information he was sending out to Moscow. A video interview with Pavlov showed his hair no longer blond but white and still abundant. The question of who deleted "except Manchuria" in the days just prior to Hull's handing the note is still, as far as I know, unanswered.

Treasury's infringement on State's territory is well documented, as is FDR's disdain for State and his carrot-and-stick handling of Hull. Bernard Baruch's knowledge of the "Hull Note," still unknown to Congress then, was revealed in Kurusu Saburo's postwar writings, in which he expressed appreciation for Baruch's help. The spying of Richard Sorge is common knowledge; the antenna and code methods are true.

Kawaguchi was real, and acted as presented in the story. The parable of wrapping the feet in leather was written of by the late Zen priest Yamada Mumon, and Mumon, in a small book of his I translated, wrote that it was this parable that turned him onto the path of Buddhism.

In 1990, the December issue of a Japanese magazine, *Bungei Shunju,* released a transcript of comments made by the Showa emperor, Hirohito, right after WWII. The notes were taken by Terasaki Hidenari, who appears in this story and was in fact in Washington at the time of the Pearl Harbor attack. (His wife, Gwen Terasaki, wrote the book, *Bridge to the Sun,* which later became a movie of the same title.) Terasaki later served as secretary and interpreter to the emperor. His handwritten records of the emperor's statements were found by his daughter, Mariko, in her home in the U.S., buried among her father's belongings, and she made an agreement with the magazine to have them published.

In these notes, the emperor lamented the Japanese trait of lack of self confidence. He said also, "The war with America started with oil and ended with oil. If there had not been a Japanese-German alliance in the negotiation stages before the war, it is possible that America would have been more relaxed in attitude and released oil to Japan.

Colonel Sasaki is fictional; his account of the Japanese medical corps in the Russo-Japanese War is fact, based on the activities of Louis L. Seaman, a U.S. Army surgeon who in fact changed American military medicine from his observations in Manchuria and Japan.

Akira is also fictionalized, based on a testimony by a former Unit 731 Youth Corps member who appears in my book *Unit 731: Testimony*. He told of the specimen jars at the unit being made by someone who studied glassmaking in France, and who did make glass birds as a pastime. Maps of the Unit 731 complex show that the glass factory was actually quite large. Ishii did lecture in Tokyo using specimens flown in from the human experiment laboratories, and in 1989 while a construction site was being excavated at the former location of the army laboratory, a quantity of human bones was unearthed. Analysis showed that they were the remains of some one hundred persons, and they bore signs of preservation before burial. A former employee at the laboratory told of the specimen-rat air freight system, and was quoted as saying, "There are more bones at the site than they discovered; if they look further they will find more."

The first use of napalm, the attack on Tokyo from around midnight, May 9, through the early hours of May 10, is well documented; a temple in the neighborhood still conducts a memorial service every year for the victims. Descriptions of the scene fictionally witnessed by the protagonist were taken largely from a book by Robert Guillain, a Frenchman in Tokyo at the time, *La Guerre Au Japon* issued in English translation under the title *I Saw Tokyo Burning,* as well as from first-person accounts from the ground by survivors, compiled and edited mainly by volunteers in Tokyo.

Operation PX was real and reported in my book on Unit 731. It was planned as in the story and called off in the final moment by General Umezu, as in the story and for his reasons cited. His meeting with the protagonist is fictionalized; Umezu was sentenced and died with the secret, as in the story. The account was first revealed, by a former naval officer involved in the plan, in 1977. The I-400 was one of the ships confiscated by the U.S. Navy after the war and scuttled or destroyed. At the time, it was the largest submarine in the world, and it held the record until the first U.S. nuclear-powered Trident class submarine appeared in 1960.

The pilot of the Brookings attack died in Japan on September 30, 1997.

Hector Bywater and his book *The Great Pacific War* are, of course, real as presented in the story. All information on Hector Bywater—including my first awareness of the book—was gleaned from the writings of William H. Honan: first a newspaper article by him, then his biography of Bywater, *Visions of Infamy,* which he kindly sent me after I could not locate one in all of New York City.

The account of the signing of the surrender on board the battleship *Missouri* is taken from an article by Frank Tremaine, who was United Press's first postwar Tokyo bureau manager, and who viewed the ceremony—on September 2—from the forward gun turret, with his feet dangling over the heads of officers below. He also reported the ship's location as fifty-six kilometers from Tokyo, and there were in fact eleven members in the Japanese party.

Australian journalist William Dennis is fictional, suggested by real-life Australian war journalist Dennis Warner, co-author of *The Sacred Warriors,* an account of kamikaze action in WWII. Warner actually was hit on two ships by *kamikaze* planes. In saner times, he was helpful via telephone conversation when I was writing *Unit 731: Testimony.*

"Where is General Ishii?" question by MacArthur when he landed at Atsugi is taken from audiotaped testimony by Ishii's daughter, aired on several Japanese TV documentaries.

Naito Ryoichi and Col. Murray Sanders were real, as was their meeting on the dock, where Naito self-appointed himself as interpreter for Sanders, forcing himself as a filter between Sanders and subsequent American investigators on one hand, and former unit members seeking to avoid war crimes prosecution on the other. Naito and Sanders launched the beginning of the data for freedom deal.

The epidemic hemorrhagic fever report, using the term "monkey" as an open code to indicate human experimental subjects, was taken from the report published in *Nihon Byori Gakkaishi* (*Japan Journal of Pathology*) 34 (1944): 3–5. The information as given is true; it appears in the story chronologically earlier than the actual report was published. Similar experiments on humans, however, were happening even earlier. The report on EHF is of special interest because of occurrence of the disease in the Korean War, where, as in the story, former Unit 731 researchers were called in to cooperate with American military medical doctors.

Source material came from newspapers, magazines, books, and documents too numerous to list. Especially helpful was a historical magazine series by Kodansha, *Nichiroku Nijuseiki* (Twentieth Century Journal) with one issue of the magazine dedicated to each year in the century. Each issue contained a complete calendar, which listed at least one event for every day of that year, from a Japan point of view.

The account of the Soviet occupation of the Danish island was contributed by Søren M. Chr. Bisgaard, whose father was in the Danish underground and a close friend of the leader of the alcohol-resistant welcome party.

Ulrika Ellinge translated the secret messages from Swedish.

Shibata Yoshimatsu, former pilot in the Imperial Japanese Army, offered valuable information on aircraft design and insights into the times. In his army days, he was appointed instructor of young conscripts: "I had to teach them how to take off and dive, but never how to land."

About the Author

Hal Gold, a thirty-year resident of Japan, is the author of *Japan in a Sake Cup* and *Unit 731: Testimony,* as well as two books written in Japanese and dealing with modern Japanese culture. He translated *From Shanghai to Shanghai: the war diary of an Imperial Japanese Army medical officer, 1937–1939.* Gold has worked as a columnist, in advertising, in video script narrations, and as a freelance writer. He has also appeared in acting roles in some twenty-five Japanese films. He makes his home in Kyoto.